North Wind in Your Spokes

North Wind in Your Spokes

HANS BLICKENSDÖRFER

Translated by Marlis Cambon

BREAKAWAY BOOKS
HALCOTTSVILLE, NY
2000

North Wind in Your Spokes: A Novel of the Tour de France
By Hans Blickensdörfer

Translated by Marlis Cambon

ISBN: 1-891369-18-0
LIBRARY OF CONGRESS CATALOG CARD NUMBER: 99-85885

Originally published in Germany by Verlag Schneekluth, Munich, 1980.
Original title: *Salz im Kaffee* (Salt in the Coffee)
Translation published by permission of Engelhorns Verlag GmbH, Stuttgart

Published by:
Breakaway Books
P. O. Box 24
Halcottsville, NY 12438
(800) 548-4348
www.breakawaybooks.com

For a list of cycling and other sports literature from Breakaway Books, please visit our website.

TRANSLATOR'S NOTE: For help with specialized vocabulary and technical expressions, as well as the organization of a bicycle event as important as the Tour de France, I wish to thank Scott Erdman, an Iron Man in his own right.

FIRST EDITION

1

IT WAS CLOSE TO MIDNIGHT AND AROUND THE MEN STILL SITTING in the dining room of the small hotel, tables were being set for breakfast. A fresh breeze blew in through the open windows and brought some relief from the stale muggy air, the smell of red wine, and the cold smoke from strong black cigarettes. But it didn't drive the men out. They paid no attention to the yawning hostess, although the terrifying hole gaping between her double chin and nose usually drove even the most reluctant cronies into a hasty retreat. These gentlemen were neither regular customers nor in any particular hurry. They asked for a platter of cheese and said that she could close down, as long as she left them with enough wine. Because tomorrow was their day off. The Tour de France had a rest day in Pau, catching its breath before the Pyrénées. Without a word, she put cheese and wine on the table and left, slamming the door behind her. She surrendered to the stubborn troubadours of the migrant people.

The men were celebrating halftime. Ten stages were behind them, and with the festive mood of which only a group of shirt-sleeved men completely detached from their work is capable, they were talking their way into the wee hours of the only day when they didn't have to pack a suitcase. No innkeeper would change that. Besides, they were discussing very important and manly matters about the deeper meaning of life, because the combined effect of red wine and calvados is a great stimulant: It makes every Frenchman a Descartes and every German a Kant. And probably a Dante out of every Italian. However, if he's surrounded by transalpine folks, as poor Ferruccio was in this particular place, his case is hopeless. So they were talking about the deeper sense of the Tour de France—and when France, Belgium, Holland, and Germany attack Italy at the hour of midnight, sparks fly.

Ferruccio, who had been assuredly leaning on the pillars of Coppi and Bartali, wasn't so sure any longer. Of course they were all becoming irrational—typically irrational like all reporters once the papers have been fed their stuff and when the unprintable trivia is too strong to resist. As a result Ferruccio was the target of serious men who have had it with serious matters. "Do you know," asked Pierre, "why they stick their finger up a newborn Italian baby boy?"

Ferruccio didn't know. "If he howls," said Pierre, "he'll be a tenor. If he laughs, he'll be gay."

Ferruccio had enough. But before he could get up to give the only possible answer to the roaring laughter, the door opened. Doctor Philippe Troussellier, chief of the Tour de France's medical corps, entered with a gust of air that set the curtains fluttering. He had three other physicians working under him.

"Is Lesueur here?"

Lesueur was the deputy race organizer. Lightly bearing responsibilities that would have crushed even the savviest manager type, he was always to be found somewhere, late at night as well as early in the morning, radiating the fresh energy for which the heroes of soap ads are envied.

Heavy heads were shaking, but behind the facade nothing clicked. The workday was over, the day of rest had begun.

"Sit down and have a glass with us, doctor, it's not doping."

"I need Lesueur."

"At midnight?" It was Pierre Delfour who said it with the serenity of the tippler who is done with yesterday and hasn't any plans yet for the day to come. The meaning was right there, in the glass, full bodied and red.

"You won't have much more fun boozing, messieurs. Especially you." He pointed to Kollmann, the German.

"Who, me?" Kollmann turned his heavy head toward the intruder, and his touching bewilderment made the doctor bite his tongue.

"*Excusez, messieurs.* I shouldn't have said that. Forget it. I'm looking for Lesueur."

He backed toward the door but already two had jumped up and barred his way.

"You won't get away that easily, doctor! Tell us everything."

Delfour, his hand on the doorknob, ordered: "Pour him a glass of wine and grill him, friends. Unless I'm totally off, he has some big news. A real potboiler."

They pulled him to the table, and Hennie, the Dutchman, got a clean glass from one of the breakfast tables. "*Bois, docteur, et raconte.*" His French grated like a saw gone wild.

But that wasn't the reason Doctor Troussellier made a face. He gulped down the heavy Bordeaux in one swig, mumbled something about the seal of medical ethics and a damn mess, and after the second glass was ready to disburden himself, without Lesueur. "You might as well bag Bud. He's out."

The effect was astounding. They jumped, wine spilled from the glasses. The unforeseeable was part of the Tour de France like the air they breathed, but this was too much. It could only be doping, if the doctor dropped such a bombshell. Kollmann was the last to get up. You could read only total noncomprehension in his eyes. Slowly he advanced toward the physician, who was clutching a small leather briefcase with both hands.

"Folks, be reasonable! I can't tell you much more, but the case is clear. Bud's urine test after the second stage reads positive. Tomorrow he'll be disqualified."

"That's bullshit," Kollmann breathed heavily. "You miserable pill-monger. Bud isn't taking anything. I'd put my hand into the fire for him. This is a setup, if you ask me. He's simply too good, and if they can't beat him on the bike he has to be eliminated in some other way. It's that simple."

He reached for the doctor's briefcase, but Delfour intervened. "You're out of your mind, Max. Sit down and let's think this over calmly. Doctor, you said the second stage?"

Troussellier nodded. "Yes, Caen–Dieppe. Coming in second he was checked automatically. "

"And why," asked Hennie, "would he have doped on such a ridiculously short and harmless flat country stage?"

"Just what I wanted to ask myself." Kollmann looked at the doctor, shaking his head. "Do you really think he'd take something and sprint for a few ridiculous seconds toward an easy finish, knowing he'd to have to piss into your test tube? First of all, he doesn't take anything, and second, he's not that dumb."

Doctor Troussellier shrugged his shoulders. The tone didn't bother him; they all had known each other for more than ten years. The great event of July brought them together, and they had drunk many a glass together. Theirs was a friendship of men in shirt-sleeves, but this was a damn serious matter of the medical field, and not mere bar talk.

"You all know that mistakes are impossible. The facts speak for themselves, and it's the only thing we can go by. Bud's out of the race, and he'll get a few months of suspension on top of it. And for you there's going to be work on rest day."

"*Merde,*" said Delfour and looked at his watch. "Ten till one. Can someone make a last push for it? We're just about done with printing."

Kollmann's fist struck the table hard. "I still could, but the hell I will. I'll take the early train, if you want to know. Finished, the end! Bud and doping—it just can't be, even if these urine sniffers presented a thousand medical experts. I'm going home."

The doctor got up and went to the door. "Better sleep on it, Max. That's what the rest day is for. I have to find Lesueur. Good night, gentlemen."

They went out into the street with him and the cool wind coming from the mountains raised goose bumps under their thin sport shirts. In the night the little town at the foot of the Pyrénées seemed an icebox compared to the oppressive heat withering the grass in the monotonous plain from which they had come. They went through empty streets. Even the Tour de France cannot deprive a little town like Pau of its provincial sleepiness after midnight. Only in a bistro across the square there was there some light, but no sound was to be heard. Official Tour cars were parked helter skelter and everywhere in no-parking spots, but that had been waived for the rest day.

Rest day. Kollmann stopped and lit a cigarette. Should he wake Bud and tell him what sort of a dirty scheme was brewing? And why not? It would net an interview, and the youngster's sleep wasn't important anymore. At this very moment he had been expelled, he was finished. No longer a number but a zero. And yet he had been number one, at twenty-two years old, the great front-runner. Nobody would have beaten him.

Damn job. You discover a youngster who has everything others chase after unsuccessfully all of their careers—one who stomps everybody who wants to compete with him into the ground—and now they're destroying him in this way, because there's no other way. Yes, *kaput*. Of course. It dawned on him how much Bud would have to deal with. How some reporters would rub their hands gleefully before they sat down at the typewriter.

They'd call him Budzinski again, as in the days when they didn't know him. And they'd write about the scandal in which Budzinski, the false prodigy, was unveiled unwittingly by himself. Caught in the doping trap. See? None of his victories would be worth a damn thing. That's exactly how it would be. They'd raise a stink to high heaven and get the most out of it. And the kid wouldn't be able to handle it. He'd chuck in his bike and get out of it.

At this point in his reflections Max Kollmann threw away his cigarette and went without another look at the others across the big square to the hotel where Budzinski was staying with the Valetta team. The rest day of the Tour de France was barely an hour and twenty minutes old. He crossed the hall where two drunk mechanics were arguing with the night porter. He didn't wait at the elevator but took two steps at a time as if it were a matter of urgency. He was glad that they had given Bud a single room for the rest day. It wasn't the customary thing to do, but the kid knew how to go after privileges reserved for stars. After all, he was one.

Kollmann knocked. First softly, then harder, but an eternity passed before something stirred inside. The key turned and he looked into the large uncomprehending eyes of a child's face. One hand was clutching the doorknob as if to hold back the intruder; the other brushed some wisps of blond hair from his forehead. He was wearing only pajama shorts.

"Max, you? In the middle of the night? What's the matter? I thought it was rest day."

"Let me in and close the door," hissed Kollmann.

Bud dropped his arms and Kollmann closed the door himself, turning the key. How white his torso is, thought Kollmann. His arms were almost black up to the biceps where the jersey started.

Kollmann dropped into an armchair and pointed to the large bed. "If you like, lie down again, but I'm afraid you won't feel like it."

"What time is it, and what's all this nonsense? You know I need my sleep."

"It's half past one," said Kollmann, surprised at how calm his voice sounded, "and unfortunately it's not nonsense."

"Let's have it then."

"Better sit down first."

Shaking his head, the half-naked Bud reached for his bathrobe on the chair, pulled it over his shoulders, and sat down on the edge of the bed. The wind from the mountains blew through the open window, but it didn't drive away the smell of massage oil that Kollmann's nostrils were registering now.

"Now listen carefully, kid. Of course it takes some nerve to come bursting into your room in the middle of the night, and I was undecided at first. But the more I thought about it, the clearer it became that I had to wake you up. Doctor Troussellier has a positive reading of your doping test, and at this moment he's with Lesueur. You'll be thrown out of the race. Actually, you're out already."

The man whom they called Bud—because his family name Budzinski didn't fit his popularity any more than his silly name Ernst—didn't even cringe. There was no emotion in his large eyes, which still seemed to search for the real reason for Kollmann's presence. He hasn't understood a thing, Kollmann thought. "Listen, kid," he said fishing for a cigarette. "Either you're sleeping with open eyes like a bunny rabbit, or you're deaf. They're accusing you of doping, understand? Doping."

What happened next, Kollmann had not expected. Bud grinned. And the grin changed to a resounding laugh.

"Anyone else who woke me with such dumb jokes, I'd throw out, Max. There's only one excuse—you must be drunk."

"I've never been more sober than in this moment, idiot. If you did dope, I'll go straight to bed sorry for every second in which I worried about you. If you didn't, then we don't have any time to lose, because some real dirty business is going on, understand?"

"Are you serious? You're not joking?"

"I've never been more serious, Bud. They have a positive test, and I really want to know the whole damn truth. If you have doped, we'll have to find a way. I implore you, Bud, level with me."

The young man jumped up, threw the bathrobe on the bed, and for a moment Kollman thought that he was going to come at him. But he padded barefoot over to the table and a small suitcase. He took out a notebook and threw it across to Kollmann.

"Here, take a look for yourself. I've kept a diary. More than thirty urine tests all over Europe. It's often my turn because I win often. Always negative. The last two entries are from this Tour. Dieppe and Saint-Nazaire."

"The positive test is from Dieppe," said Kollmann.

"From Dieppe? That makes no sense at all."

Kollmann watched as a helpless rage rose into eyes that had just been laughing, and he saw Bud's knuckles turn white.

"Dieppe. A stupid little flat stage. Nobody attacked, and at the end, just for fun, I sprinted along and came in second. That's why I had the urine test. But I have the clearest conscience in the world; you know that I've never taken anything illegal."

"That's what I told the doctor, Bud. But that won't get us any farther, even if you swear a thousand oaths. The test is positive, and they insist that any mistake is out of the question. You have to think very hard now what you took that day."

But there was no answer. Moving mechanically, the young man pulled on a white jersey and paced the room. It's over with the yellow jersey, Kollmann thought, and he's beginning to get it. But I can't give him much time.

"Maybe you took some medication. Try to remember. There's supposed to be something against hay fever on the doping list."

"Oh, cut it out. I haven't taken anything, and that's that. Am I that stupid? You know what the Tour means to me. I want to win it, do you hear? Win."

"But you're no longer in it, Bud. In a few hours you'll have it in writing, and you'll be under public attack. I hope Mercier has at least prepared a protest."

Mercier was the technical manager of the Valetta team, and there was no doubt that he had been informed already. He just had not wanted to ruin Bud's sleep, since everything else had been ruined. This Tour and much more.

If some water carrier is caught doping, it's considered a minor infraction. A few lines in the press. No commentary. He's taken out of the race the same way he was entered—without a name. But there is no mercy for the leader. He stands there, naked and humiliated, and his fame collapses with a roar. Something like rage and pity rose in Kollmann and he felt like spitting it out. Bud's voice, sounding hollow all of a sudden, tore him from his thoughts.

"You're serious about this? You think they'll disqualify me?"

Kollmann shrugged. "What are they supposed to do? There's no double standard. They can't spare the big fish when they get the small fry."

"But I'm innocent, Max. You at least believe that, don't you?"

Kollmann let his fist come down on the shaky little table, and it jumped.

"Drop it, will you? What I believe isn't worth a damn. We only have a tiny chance because it's rest day. Whether there's enough time to get at the truth is another question. But we have to try."

"What are you thinking about? Is there something like deferred punishment?"

For the first time since entering this room, Kollmann laughed, but it didn't sound happy. "You're thinking of suspension with probation, is that it? Don't even think about it. Not a chance. You're not going to turn your pedals any more in this tour unless we manage at least to construct a case of uncertainty that they would have to decide in your favor."

"And how do you want to go about it?"

"That," Kollmann said, "I don't know myself at this point. At any rate, I'll have to talk to the doctor, before the tour organizers get together with the race officials. Tonight, I'm sure, no decision has been made yet. But I can't wake up Troussellier at this hour. We have a few difficult hours ahead of us, you and I, because we'll be neither arriving at a reasonable solution nor able to get any sleep."

"Still, it was right that you woke me, Max."

"I think so too, Bud. Maybe you'll think of something that might have happened on that blasted day between Caen and Dieppe."

"The only thing I know is that nothing happened at all. Boring stage with a group finish."

"I know that. I mean, how you felt."

"Great. I caught up with some sprinters and they gave up immediately when they saw how easy it was for me. If I had meant business, I could have won the entire stage."

"Did you take anything on the road? A drink from a spectator or something like that?"

"No, I'm sure of that. I just drank from my water bottle and emptied the goodie bag."

"Mmm," mused Kollmann, "that's not much to go on. If only your physician were here."

"He flew home after the third stage and wants to return before the Alps."

Kollmann struck his forehead with his flat hand and jumped up: "Why didn't I think of this earlier, Bud? We'll have to call him right away."

"Now?" Bud frowned looking at his watch. "It's almost three in the morning."

"So what? Do you think the time of night matters, considering what's at risk?" He went to the house telephone hanging on the wall with small-flower wallpaper.

"Do you have the number?"

Bud leafed through the notebook where he had registered all the doping tests and gave Kollmann a number in Cologne.

"It wouldn't be bad," said Kollmann, "if Doctor Lindner could come right away."

But he couldn't. After the night porter had made the connection with some effort, a sleepy woman's voice squawked that he was on business in Munich, absolutely unavailable, especially for a biker.

"She's always been against his sports hobby," said Bud when Kollmann had put down the receiver, "and of course also against me. I think she hates me. But there's no physician whom I trust as much as him."

"That doesn't help us much right now, Bud. We'll have to manage without him. I'm going to air out my head for a while, and then I'll wake up Troussellier. Try to get some sleep or think of something."

His steps resounded in the empty streets littered with newspapers, programs, and all the colored paper scraps produced by the publicity of the tour. Under a street light a crumpled color photograph of Bud was laughing at him. He hasn't realized yet what will be in store for him during the next hours, Kollmann thought. Still believes that I can help him. But where do I start? Where is the weak point? Is it a setup or an error—or did he take something after all?

He excluded the last possibility. He had to in order to continue thinking. He had known Bud for too long. He'd been almost a child when he caught Kollmann's attention during a youth race in Westphalia palace, and since then Kollman had known every pedal stroke the kid had made in his so-called fairy-tale career. At fifteen his father had taken him out of school. He had to earn a living, because there were smaller siblings, and old Budzinski didn't have that much going for him any longer. He had been laid off early, taking nothing but a black lung from the mines.

When Bud started making money the Budzinskis fared better, but not until he earned professional wages could he get the family out of the gray house in the miner's district of Gelsenkirchen. The house he built in Dortmund, at the edge of town, was large enough. It had been completed on his twenty-first birthday, and that was only the beginning. All experts were agreed that Eddy Merckx had found a successor.

Kollmann recalled his first interview with Bud, who had just turned sixteen. It took place during an break in the race, in a room inside the Westphalia Palace. He had asked the standard question about beginnings, and the answer had been elaborate.

How did Bud get started? Through the church and a fall. "Really, Mister Kollmann, believe it or not. Perhaps I would've headed for Schalke and become a halfway decent soccer player, but my confirmation day changed everything."

Their conversation had started more or less like this. The part about the priest cyclist who had been the first to recognize the enormous talent in the boy really began to interest Kollmann. But

this Don Camillo didn't actually exist. Bud's words made it clear
that a higher Being had been at work in all of this. That was also the
reason why Kollmann followed his journalistic instinct and published Bud's words in the unadulterated dialect of the Ruhr.

"It was all great, the food and stuff. The church was boring, and
afterward at home wasn't much better. So I snuck outside pretty
soon. And there were all the guys with the bikes they had gotten as
presents. Some really cool bikes, honest. Bent handlebars, gears,
and stuff like that. What that must have cost. Couldn't come close
in my situation.

"'Come on, Ernst,' they called, 'run a race with us!' With my
junky old bike?

"'Who's going to lend me his bike?' I asked. And someone
handed me a gorgeous bike, all chrome and shiny. I hop on it and
I'm off. I'm out in front right away, but in the second curve I crash.
Everything ruined, the bike and the confirmation suit. That was
something. I hid the suit in the stable and then snuck into the
house. At first all went well, but then Uwe's old man comes by
wanting a reimbursement for the bike. And then! I hadn't had a
hiding like that in a long time, and all for the damn bike and the
confirmation outfit! But it something good came out of it."

In fact a guest at the confirmation, his uncle Oskar, intervened;
he wanted no punishment on confirmation day. Luckily, he was
willing and able to pay for the damage. Koslowski was his name,
and together with the Budzinskis, and probably also the Szepans
and the Kuzorras, his grandfather had come in 1890 with the large
wave of immigrants from East Prussia into the industrial Ruhr district. But Uncle Oskar had not only used his hands to dig himself
out of misery. He had achieved moderate well-being by letting
other hands dig for him, but under special circumstances he still
had an East Prussian heart for his relatives. And on that day it was
beating loud and strong, moving Bud's mother to tears, and moving his father to reach out the hand that had just now given Ernst a
harsh beating. Because not only did the uncle pay for the bike and

the confirmation suit, he also gave Ernst a shiny new racing bike with ten gears.

That was the day Ernst Budzinski's life took a different turn. His confirmation, unlike those of his fellow adolescents, actually permitted him to enter into the life for which he had been predestined.

He rode his bike every day, and when it rested at night, it rested next to his bed. At age sixteen he beat most of the licensed amateurs, and at eighteen the first pros. He ended his apprenticeship as a toolmaker, according to his father's wishes, but he already knew that he would earn his money in the saddle. At nineteen he signed his first contract as a professional rider.

2

WHEN MAX KOLLMANN ENTERED HIS HOTEL ROOM, THE DAY WAS breaking on which he was determined to prove that Ernst Budzinski was the victim of mistaken identity or some plot against him. And this determination was so strong that it devoured his need for sleep. In his bulky leather bag full of notes, by now obsolete, he found an apple and a banana—his breakfast. He then inserted a piece of paper into his portable, just to do something useful.

But it remained empty. There was nothing useful to be done. Not at this hour, when the Tour was still asleep. Even the mechanics, who early in the morning let wheels whir and checked gears, slept into this rest day.

Without taking off his shoes, Kollmann lay down on his bed and lit a cigarette. So this was the end of Bud's dreams of the yellow jersey. Only now was it beginning to dawn on Kollmann that they had been his dreams as well. Never before had a German won the Tour de France; but there had also never been one who had entered the oldest and most famous of all races with so much going for him.

And Max had discovered him. Had believed in him from the beginning, counseled him, perhaps better than most coaches who had tried to mold him. Because he knew this racket, what it was like behind the scenes, and the schemes that were concocted there, as well as the mentality and the secrets of success of the great champions. That's why he knew from the beginning that Bud would be a great one.

Once you knew the environment of the bikers you knew how different it was from that of the soccer players. There's no silly lobbying for the interview and its lies, stinking to high heaven, because it also has to please the coach and the president. The biker who spends five times more in the saddle than the duration of a soccer game will let off steam in the evening after a stage without having to consider anybody else—because no one can help him. Nobody turns the pedals for him, nobody clears away the sharp pebble boring itself into his tire. The danger of a trivial breakdown or a fall always hovers over him, and how is anyone to describe his sufferings during the climbs of the Pyrénées or the Alps?

But what is the injustice of the road when compared to an unfair doping sentence? If Bud were in the hospital with broken bones, it would be a blessing next to this devious mess. And up to this point Bud had ridden this tour smooth as butter. Not a scratch on him, and he radiated a physical freshness that was depressing for his rivals. Except for the time trial at Bordeaux, he had never pushed himself; and even there he had energy left, had coasted instead of straining when the victory was certain. And he had advanced to fourth position in the overall standings, trailing the yellow jersey by barely three minutes. On this rest day before the major stage of the Pyrénées, he was placed better than anticipated. Kollmann got up, staring at the empty piece of paper in the typewriter. On this rest day he should have pounded only the most optimistic projections into it. "Bud on His Way to Tour Victory" as a working title.

Now the title would be "Bud Disqualified." But his fingers wouldn't obey and reached for another cigarette instead. Damn job. From a church nearby rang five thin tolls.

For another hour he had to leave Troussellier in peace. He threw himself back on the bed and pondered which convincing arguments could raise doubts about the doping test. But he didn't get much farther than the drunk driver claiming mistaken identity in his blood test.

Investigate. Sniff for clues. If Bud told the truth, they had to be found, and there was no reason to assume that he went with marked cards into the dirty game that was awaiting him. He had too much class, which for Kollmann was the same as the single-minded correctness that had marked his brief and brilliant career. He had always set and reached attainable goals. At first they had called him a braggart when he joined his first league at age fifteen. "If I don't win five out of ten races, I won't go on."

He won seven. And later, in the amateurs, he lost only when he was careless or a victim of the witch with the green teeth. He corrected the carelessness and fought the witch. All the money that he collected, together with the wreaths and ribbons, he put into the best and most expensive equipment, and even before becoming a pro he had, in the basement next to his mother's racks of jars, an unusual collection of old frames that were much stiffer than new ones. Bud had known—if not everything—a lot about the profession into which he was headed. And this spring he had won Paris–Roubaix and Milano–San Remo. One a race through the hellish north under the fickle Flemish sky and on tricky soot-covered cobblestones; and the other, in the blazing Riviera sun, just as unpredictable because at the end there were the mountains to destroy whoever had led across the plains.

Bud had won the most prestigious of the classics and passed his doping tests without trouble. Why would the man need illegal stimulants on one of the simplest of the twenty-one stages of the Tour de France?

Doctor Troussellier—known as an early bird among the followers of the Tour but nonetheless little inclined to start the day with the roosters—showered the caller with the earthiest curses of which someone who has been awoken at six-fifteen after relatively little sleep is capable.

But Kollmann didn't relent, and two minutes later he was sitting once again in the room of a man who, with understandable anger, was rubbing his sleepy eyes.

"You have some nerve," snapped the doctor. "It's scandalous. I'll give you five minutes and you're out the door. Don't you think I need my rest day too? Every evening when you guys are drinking, I'm on call. I have to take care of a hundred bikers and not just some damn German who's doped."

"Careful, there." Kollmann's eyes narrowed. "Is nationalism making a comeback?"

Troussellier ignored it. In his coffee-colored pajama pants pulled up high over his paunch, he stalked back to his bed and got under the covers.

"Okay, I let you in. Cough it up. You have five minutes, and that's it."

"You can kiss my ass with your five minutes," said Kollmann with calculated calm, sitting down on the only available chair among a pile of vials and bright-colored medication boxes. "It's a matter of injustice being done to one of your precious bikers. Glaring injustice, no more and no less, do you hear?"

"I'm not deaf. But Teutonic volume doesn't change a thing, understand?"

He turned his back on Kollmann, who only saw a messy bed and a tousled head emerging from it as if from a bag.

"Listen," said Kollmann and reached for his cigarettes. "If you're going to sleep, my five minutes don't count. I admit, this isn't the right time to invade a hotel room, but I wouldn't be able to sleep if as a physician I'd pinned a case of doping on someone like Budzinski."

Sullenly Troussellier's head turned away from the flowered wallpaper.

"So that's it. I should have thought of it. You scribblers, all emotions, as is your duty, attacking the doctor and accusing him because he doesn't lose a night's sleep over the disqualification of a star. Not bad, pal. You're all alike. Where, I ask you, would it get me if I started crying every time, as you do in your papers, when I'm doing my damn duty?"

Kollmann exhaled blue smoke that drifted away. The window here was open as well, and the wind from the mountains was blowing harder.

"Your professional honor, doctor, may be more robust than mine. But just because of this you have to be careful that the honor of a man like Bud isn't tarnished by . . . by . . ."

"Well, by what?"

"By fraud."

"Enough of this. It's Budzinski who's cheating. If you don't believe this, there's nothing more to say."

"Okay," said Kollmann, "I went too far. Maybe I'm too nervous, because I'm not certain that there's enough time to clear up a huge mistake. Let's say mistake instead of fraud."

Troussellier jumped out of bed and pulled on his bathrobe. Second act, same scene, Kollmann thought. Only the bathrobe was yellow and the legs white and hairy. Riders have tanned legs that they shave. One slipper he found under the bed, the other Kollmann fished from under the table.

"Mistakes are impossible," said the doctor, shaking his head and shuffling over to the window to pull back the curtain. "There can't be any mistakes. The Paris institute is one of the best in the world."

"And why shouldn't there be any mistakes? How do you know what happens to the stuff the minute it leaves you? The procedures would really interest me. Why, for example, doesn't the Tour have its own traveling lab, so it could do the tests on the spot?"

"Let me explain," said Troussellier, slouching into an armchair. "Technically, it would be possible, and the Italians have done it in the Giro. But in so doing they went against the regulations of the International Bicycle Racing Association, which state unequivocally that the tests can only be conducted by three labs: the institutes for toxicology in Paris, Rome, and Ghent."

"So Paris is responsible for the Tour de France."

"Correct."

"And how do you transport this precious urine? By courier, I imagine?"

"No, by train."

"Aha, without any escort?"

"Yes, and mix-ups are out of the question. The bottle is packaged in a refrigerated box, after being sealed and labeled with a number, which has no significance for the physicians in Paris. They don't know if they're examining the urine of rider X or Y. What's more, it travels as registered express mail, which they receive within twenty-four hours."

Kollmann drew on his cigarette, gazing after the smoke as if he could bring light into a matter that didn't seem any brighter than before. "You can say what you want, doctor, I don't feel easy about that little numbered bottle traveling alone, and one urine looks like another. There are other possibilities besides a mix-up."

"I'm all ears. You read too many detective stories, I'm afraid."

"If you're suggesting that I smell a rat in all of this, you're absolutely right. How can you be sure that someone hasn't put something into Bud's food or drink?"

Troussellier blew up his cheeks and puffed disdainfully. "The great evil Unknown as the last resort of the doping offenders. Alas! You're not the first who's tried to melt down the race officials with such fairy tales. It won't even make a dent."

"Mmm, you're probably right." Kollmann scratched his chin and its day-old beard. "In fact, you're definitely right, but I also know that I'm right. Bud didn't dope. Why? He entered this tour in top shape, and he wanted to win. Who could have beaten him, and why should he have defeated himself with such brainless stupidity? During a ridiculous little flatland stage. At least during a time trial or a stage in the mountains you could have found a motive."

The doctor looked at his watch. "And I have a motive to throw you out. It's seven o'clock, and in one hour I have to be at the tour management. I'd like to take my bath alone, if you don't mind."

"You're going to talk things over at Lesueur's hotel?"

"Exactly. And now get out. You won't be able to help your Bud, never mind how much you're straining my nerves. Later on, I'm sure, there's going to be a press conference. They don't do that for the small fry, but the farewell of Mister Budzinski is something else. Tears and ink will flow copiously."

"And Schadenfreude," Kollmann snarled. "You make me think of some petty D.A., enjoying his breakfast because he can pull a few years in the penitentiary out of his sleeve. Your self-righteousness makes me sick."

Outside, in the hallway, he mumbled worse.

At the same time Bud asked the porter at the desk not to transfer any more phone calls to his room. The Tour was waking up and extended its fine antennas for news of all sorts. Mercier had been among the first to call, but some reporters had also come to life. Mercier was more important, but—assessing the situation correctly —he had rushed off to the tour management, not to Bud. Slowly the sun was rising on the day that was supposed to be a day of rest, and just as slowly the man who, a few hours ago, had been determined to win the Tour and now was no longer part of it was putting his many confused thoughts in order.

Eliminated, thrown out. Extirpated like a tumor. A fraud who stuffed himself with drugs to gain an advantage. Those who had coddled him yesterday would crucify him today, and he would have to lock himself into his room or run the gauntlet. In the night, with Kollmann, things had not yet been all that clear. But now the fog tore open and he saw grimaces of Schadenfreude coming at him, crowding the room. Of course, he hadn't been disqualified yet. Maybe someone like Kollmann could produce evidence of a mistake in the system of these damn alchemists. But his chances were one in a thousand and only because it was rest day. Otherwise the pack would already be on the Tourmalet. Without him.

All of a sudden he felt the crazy desire to get on his bike, to get moving. Just what they were going to prohibit. What was it that Felix had said that spring when they were training on the Riviera, when he felt depressed because you don't always want to step on the pedals when the sun gives a silver shine to the sea and a golden hue to the rocks of the Corniche? Bud needed sunshine in his spokes, Felix had said. And he needed it now.

He put on his sweats, took two bananas from the plate they had brought him last night, and went to the hotel garage where Felix had set up his shop. Felix knew. He was testing the gears on a bike, and when he dropped his hands he stood there like someone who had just washed them and couldn't find a towel.

"*Merde,*" he said. "They've done you in, Bud. You, of all people. Do you understand it?"

Funny, Bud thought. All he wants to know is if I have doped. Even he. Not even Felix believes in me. But he said aloud: "Give me a bike. I want to ride."

"*Bien sûr,* Bud."

He was almost running and seemed relieved not to have to talk about it.

"Here, there she is. Worked on her halfway through the night. Not a speck of dust on her, and you need sunshine in your spokes. It'll be good for you."

"*Merci,* Felix. Tell the others I'll be back for lunch."

It was Saturday. Rest days of the Tour always fell on Saturday. It was a journalistic ploy, because the Tour had been invented and kept alive by journalists, and few papers are printed on Sunday.

And it was only half past seven. The little town was still sleepy, and there were no lines of cars at the few traffic lights. The sun was already strong, warming the wind that came from the mountains, promising a hot day. In front of the Hôtel du Commerce, Bud saw a group of journalists. Increasing his speed, he turned into one of the side streets. They're waiting for the meeting of the managers with the race officials, he thought, and if they see me, I'll be their target.

He rode without a destination, but if you don't ride in circles you are at the edge of Pau very quickly. He had never been here before and oriented himself by the mountains emerging on the southern horizon in a bluish haze.

The Pyrénées. He had never seen them except in photos picturing bald and rugged peaks, black with cars and people, riders threading themselves between them, straining uphill with fists that were tearing the handlebars apart and faces distorted by the effort, smeared with dust and perspiration. The Pyrénées, he had been told, were wilder and more treacherous than the Alps.

The road wasn't rising yet, but he knew he was riding toward the mountains. They were pulling him like giant magnets. He had imagined his first encounter with them very differently.

An open car passed him, young people laughing, colored scarves fluttering in the wind. The driver braked beside him, and then they recognized him.

"*Vas-y, Bud! Tape dedans,* they aren't far ahead!"

Roaring laughter followed the harmless taunting. They were simulating the race, thinking perhaps that he would draft off their car. But he didn't laugh with them and wouldn't play along. He only thought that they had no idea what was up. There couldn't be anything in the papers yet, and they obviously hadn't listened to the radio. There must have been something on the early news. The radio people with the Tour got up early. Impossible that they wouldn't know.

The confirmation wasn't far behind. Three, four cars passed him briskly, without paying attention to him, but the next shifted down and lowered his window.

"Ate roids, eh? *Tu l'as dans le cul, Bud!*"

That was a different kind of mockery. Nasty and cutting. He saw bulging eyes smirking in a fat red face and a clenched fist before it grabbed the steering wheel again. The guy had said that Bud was down on his ass, and now he knew that the early news was out.

All of a sudden he felt a pang in his stomach: Nobody had

informed him officially. Kollmann's visit during the night had been the gesture of a friend. A warning, no more. But now the race organizers would be looking for him. Logical. Maybe they needed a hearing with a report. He wasn't familiar with the procedures for doping offenders, and perhaps they interpreted his flight as an admission of guilt. And Mercier would rage just as much as Lesueur and the rest of them. At least Felix knew that he had left.

Where to? He had no idea. All he knew was that he was headed for the mountains from which the wind came, blowing into his face. And then the next driver would yell into his face that he was a cheat. Of course, Bud thought. They see it from my sweat suit that I'm riding for Valetta. Then they recognize me, and if they've listened to the radio they know what's up. I have to get off this main road.

A few kilometers later he turned into a passable little road. It meandered through an enormous field of flax the color of egg yolks, and for some strange reason it made him hungry. He had eaten his last meal at the table of the Valetta team last night, and it probably was his last meal paid for by the organizers of the Tour. They had had a lot of fun, and because it was rest day today, he had indulged himself in one of the aromatic goat cheeses of the Pyrénées for dessert.

His hunger wasn't strong and came from somewhere far away. Not the usual appetite of a rider who, first thing in the morning would consume a mountain of calories, enough for three days in the life of an accountant. The two bananas he had taken along would suffice.

He was in form, nevertheless. He felt it in the easy stroke playing with the steady rise in the little road. Bud knew his body and that he was in shape. He felt it in the tips of his toes, which weren't imprisoned by the cage but were playing the piano. Klirribim, klirribim, with the lightness of Mozart. And he felt it in the pearls of perspiration exuding from the roots of his hair, because the climb took strength and he was riding in high gear.

The experts and those who pretend to know reproach him again and again that he is using too high a gear. Bud grins. He grins for the first time since he got on the bike that is still carrying the number 51, although the rider number 51 doesn't exist anymore. Canceled, eliminated, hounded. And yet he can crank in as high a gear as he wants. Because he feels like it. Maybe they've pinned that doping business on him because they don't like his way of doing things. The higher the gear, the more strength you need to keep it going. And why don't they want to understand that you can have that strength without stuffing yourself with what the bikers call roids?

Can't you have dynamite in your legs without taking the stuff? Kollmann once wrote this, and he's probably convinced of it. Most people don't know the miserable feeling of heavy and weak legs, hollow from the kneecap up and down. Only he who has to give up before some insignificant climb knows. And if you are out of shape, it comes and sucks you dry like the witch with the pointed green teeth. But now the form is right here, and you don't even notice that you are turning your wheels at a speed of forty kilometers an hour, where cars have long ago shifted down from fourth gear. You have sunshine in your spokes.

Bud is thinking of poor Felix now, whom they are probably berating because he gave Bud the bike. The guilty one has taken flight, and who knows if they're going to involve the police to find him? After all, the press needs its ration of sensation so that the people will gobble it up. Once you are an outlawed favorite of the Tour de France, you can no longer do as you please.

A road sign indicated a spa: EAUX-BONNES, ALTITUDE 750M. There are many hot springs in the Pyrénées, and Eaux-Bonnes is one of the best known. Bud doesn't know this, but he knows that here the climb begins to the Col d'Aubisque, 5,130 feet high. Only twelve kilometers to the peak.

Eaux-Bonnes consists only of a long square with many trees and a dusty old spa building, living off old people who put more faith in hot sulfur springs than in Sainte Bernadette in nearby Lourdes. It smells of them, too. And the lonely biker whizzes past them before they even notice him. After the spa a lot of forest, coming to an end where the ascent is 100 percent. The peak of the Aubisque, which the tour will take tomorrow, isn't yet in sight, but it's little farther than the Spanish border.

Bud is deliberating whether he should make the ascent. At least conquer the Aubisque, if they deny him this royal stage of the Pyrénées with the other mountains: the Tourmalet, the Aspin, the Peyresourde. The mountain provokes him; he is feeling its challenge. And he sees the sun sparkle in the spokes, hears the running of the brooks, which are called *gaves*. Why does he do it? Why does an outcast seek the terrain where the others will compete tomorrow?

He doesn't know the answer when he cranks out of the woods into the switchbacks drilling themselves like a corkscrew into the bleak sides of the mountain. He doesn't ride at racing speed, and his hands aren't gripping the handlebars at the wrapped ends but above, where it's bare; he has shifted to a small gear. The sun, which earlier was hanging in the pine tree tops, is attacking him head-on; the pearls of perspiration are getting larger and tickle as they run from his temples to his neck.

But he hadn't reckoned with the cars, and here there were no side roads to break away on. They recognize him and halfway up the mountain he has half a dozen on his trail. They slow down to a snail's pace, because the switchbacks push a biker down to fifteen kilometers per hour. The one in front wants to talk to him. Again and again he comes up level with Bud, pushing him either toward the abyss or against the mountain, because he wants to know what all this doping story is about. Bud is seized by anger and fear because there is traffic from the other direction and the drop-offs are steep and vertiginous. They may have the power to disqualify him, but he won't be killed by some sensation-mongering idiots.

And all of a sudden a feeling of hunger. He feels it in the back of his knees; it's what Felix calls *la fringale*. You don't conquer the Aubisque with two bananas in your stomach. He hadn't thought of this. What, if anything, had he thought at all? He won't manage the peak. He has to eat and get rid of these pests, and he knows how. On two wheels you are able to descend much faster than on four, and you can make quicker turns as well. Bud loosens his straps, gets off the bike, and before the puzzled line of cars understands what's happening they're sitting there, pointed uphill, while he is shooting downhill with a speed that would throw any car off the road.

When he cuts the curves, the knee toward the valley is straight, the other one sharply bent toward the mountain, although he can't shoot into them as during a race because there is oncoming traffic. He ranks among the powerful downhill racers who, calculating the risk, can make up another minute or two after having taken the peak.

But now the hunger is reaching from his knees into his fists on the handlebars, trembling with the vibrations of the road. He is becoming more careful in the curves until they lose their aggressiveness at the treeline and swing out in soft, long, drawn-out turns, no longer controlled by his hands and the cantilever brakes, but by his entire body leaning into the road. And the sun spins glittering silver in his whirring spokes.

3

BUD HADN'T TAKEN ALONG ANY MONEY BUT HE KNEW THAT EVERY innkeeper in Eaux-Bonnes would invite him in. Budzinski on the premises: It would spread like wildfire and fill even the largest dining room. He would rather not eat than be gaped at. On the other hand, how would he get back to Pau on an empty stomach?

By a fountain a few men with berets were arguing hotly, and they stared at the biker as if he were a ghost. "Hey, Bud, stop! We were just talking about you! Did they fire you already?"

He turned off the main street and fled the town of good waters on a narrow road. On the left he saw grazing sheep and on the right a brook, still rushing vigorously downhill, feeling the push of the mountain. There were yellow plum trees growing along its bank, and he was sorely tempted to get off his bike and pick the fruit. But he continued in the shadow of the poplars, and when they came to an end he saw a small church steeple, a cluster of a few low houses in gray natural stone around it. The village was quiet and merciful to someone like him; he sensed that it would help him in some way.

He felt the weakness in his legs when they had to support him as he propped his bike against the shady side of the wall. The heavy oak door was ajar and it creaked as he pushed it open. He blinked in the sluggish semidarkness and almost stumbled over a large wooden vat. Then he realized that the entrance led into a kitchen, and he looked into the large surprised eyes of a young woman standing at the hearth.

"*Vous désirez, monsieur?*"

During his three years as a pro, Bud had learned French. Not that he spoke it perfectly. But he understood the language of the peloton, which you had to master if you were earning your money on a French team and if you cranked most of your kilometers on French roads. And he knew some more because from the very beginning Kollmann had insisted that it was just as important to have your say as to ride along with them. The woman was irritated by the man in his blue sweats and the tousled blond hair over his flushed and perspiring forehead. Reluctantly she stepped from behind the stove and its smoke, which smelled of resin and burned the eyes. "If you're headed for Eaux-Bonnes, just follow the road."

"That's where I'm coming from," said Bud. "I'd like something to eat."

She raised her brows and frowned; his hard accent made her even more suspicious. "Then you have to go back. There's no restaurant in the village."

"But I can't eat there, madame. People are . . . bothering me."

The severe face, framed by dark black hair, became even more distant. "We don't serve any food, monsieur. Go to the youth hostel in Eaux-Bonnes if you're short of money."

The young man who had already earned his first million in the saddle grinned and turned the two pockets of his sweatpants inside out; earlier they had contained the two bananas. "I'm not short of money, madame, I have absolutely nothing on me."

A little boy, not even ten, burst through the door, cutting off her reply.

"Whose racing bike is outside, Mama?" The next minute he stared at its owner and shouted, "But this is Bud, how did he get here?"

The young woman took a step backward and her large dark eyes went from the boy to Bud, whose own eyes were red from the strain and beginning to tear in the smoke of the stove.

"It's really you?'

Bud nodded. "Yes, I made a little training run to the Aubisque. Before breakfast, it was a little rash, I guess?"

"But wasn't there something in the news this morning? My husband says that you'll be disqualified. Is this true?"

Bud, still standing in the entranceway between the door and the kitchen, replied, "I'm afraid he's right. But I know nothing more because I just ran off."

"Ran off?"

"Yes, I took my bike and rode to the Aubisque. Almost to the top. I turned around four kilometers short of it."

"And now?"

"Now, madame, I'm so hungry that I won't make it back to Pau."

"Would you like to eat with us?"

"That's why I came in. I know I have quite a nerve, but I didn't know what else to do. I haven't eaten anything for breakfast either. I got on my bike on an empty stomach, sort of in shock."

He took off the leather racing gloves and walked stiffly to the chair the woman was offering him.

"My husband will understand, and so will Grandfather. They'll be back with the tractor in a few minutes, and then we'll eat. Do you like lamb?"

Bud grinned. "I'd even eat raw potatoes."

She went back to the stove. "I make it Basque style. Most people in the village are Basques."

"It smells really good," said Bud, putting his gloves on the well scrubbed table. "I'm very grateful, madame. In every inn they'd swarm around me like wasps."

"Are you going to be thrown out of the race?" asked the boy.

Bud nodded. "Doping is serious business, you know. The crazy thing is that I haven't taken anything. They must have made a mistake, but I don't know how to prove it."

"You haven't doped at all?"

The young woman took painted plates from the old cupboard and began setting the table. "Leave Mister Budzinski alone, André. He came to us to avoid being pestered with questions." She turned to Bud. "Don't mind him. He adores you."

"Will you give me an autograph?"

"Of course," said Bud, "but first get my bike in from the street, before it gets the attention of all your friends. Can he put it into the entranceway, madame?"

"Of course."

The boy lifted it over the threshold like something rare and precious. "It's so light," he said.

Shortly after, the two men entered, the younger one with his shirt open, showing half his chest and strong arms, the old man in a worn linen smock over corduroy pants and an old beret on his shaggy white hair.

Both recognized Bud immediately, and their surprise made the boy clap his hands. "He's going to eat with us, and I'll get an autograph."

The mother nodded at their surprised glances. "Yes, he's been on the Aubisque and is hungry. I invited him."

"*Pour une surprise, c'est une surprise,*" said the old man shaking his head, holding out his hand to Bud. And in a solemn tone he added: "*Atehan psatzen dubena bere etchean da.*"

With a question in his eyes Bud looked from the weather-beaten face of the old mountain farmer to the smiling black eyes of the young woman. "That's the Basque welcome, Mister Budzinski. But only for friends. You should be proud of it."

"What does it mean?"

"He who enters through this door should feel he's at home."

"*Merci,*" said Bud. "I'm so glad I knocked at the right door."

The young farmer let himself drop on the bench behind the long side of the table, took a piece of white bread from the basket, and tore it into pieces. "We heard the news. Are you here as a tourist, so to speak, because you've been disqualified?"

"I don't know," said Bud and took off his jacket. Under it he was wearing the sleeveless white jersey he had pulled on in the night when Kollmann had woken him. And he remembered that he hadn't washed up or shaved.

"I don't know what's up. I just ran off."

"Leave him alone now," the old man said. "He should eat first and if he feels like it, he can talk about it afterward." And to Bud: "You were on the Aubisque?"

"Not quite. A whole line of cars cornered me. So I turned around. Fame has its two sides."

The old man grinned. "Maybe so. I've never been famous."

"I'm so glad I can hide out here, with you."

The young woman put the lamb roast on the table and an earthenware jar with dry country wine. "Do what you said earlier, Grand-père, and let him eat now."

"You're right, Pascale."

During the meal they exchanged only a few Basque words, which Bud didn't understand. He didn't hold back his ravenous appetite and poured a lot of cold well water into the red wine, which they called Juraçon. For dessert there was a soft, moist goat cheese, to which he helped himself with the same appetite as before. Little André gaped and the old man smiled.

"Isn't it surprising what athletes can put away? I had the same appetite when I did my sport."

"What did you do?"

The old man grinned and scratched the back of his head where his white hair protruded from under the beret. "That was another kind of sport where you could get suspended. I used to practice the sport of the Basques, if you want to know. The border doesn't mean anything to us Basques, and yet a great deal—but that's hard to understand. Three of our provinces are on French, four on Spanish soil, but we're neither French nor Spanish. That's a long story. To make it short: If there are people on both sides who really belong together and speak the same language, they must have an activity in common, right?"

Bud nodded. "And what do you do, if the border runs through harsh and inaccessible mountains? Believe me, smuggling in the Pyrénées was the cleanest sport in the whole wide world. The customs officials knew that a real man had to smuggle out of self-respect. There wasn't much money in it, to be sure. Compared to the effort, the gain was downright miserable. We lugged everything on our backs, especially tobacco and alcohol, because in the game with the customs people we had to be mobile. A mule is of no use. Across the steepest slopes and the most dangerous ravines, and when you got over there, it was kind of like winning a stage, see?"

"The only difference is that nobody knew about it."

"You got it. The smuggler can't boast of his successes any more than the poacher. But the feeling of outwitting the border guards and, on top of it, putting some francs or pesetas into your pocket was wonderful. It was the drug of my youth, you understand?"

"I think so," replied Bud.

But little André didn't like the conversation. He had pulled the bike into the kitchen and, lifting up the rear wheel, was playing with the gears.

"Why don't you let him talk about the Tour, Grandfather? I know your stories."

"Will you shut your mouth, you brat?" The old man shouted and let his fist come down on the table that the glasses were jumping. "Mr. Budzinski wants to know—or don't you?"

Bud nodded. "Of course I do. It must have been damn dangerous."

"It was, my friend, it was indeed. But, to be honest, the scree and the precipices were more dangerous than the border guards. You know, there has never been any shooting in the Pyrénées. The smuggler was respected because his sport was more important to him than his gain. The customs officials put him in the hole, because that was their job, but they never treated him badly. And they always had a warm blanket for him, because he preferred doing his work in the snow and the rain rather than on clear starry nights."

"Sounds quite romantic," said Bud.

"Something for real men, that's for sure. Where are they nowadays? You see, Monsieur Bud, I just remembered a story from your line of business, and its hero for me is bigger than all the others getting on a bike after him."

"In that case, I ought to know him."

"Possible. His name is Eugène Christophe. Ever heard of him?"

Bud shook his head. "Never heard of him. Must have been quite some time ago."

"That's true. Nineteen-thirteen, and I was as old as this one." He pointed at André, who leaned the bike against the wall and returned to the table.

"You know, already in those days the Tour went across the Aubisque and the Tourmalet, and I grew up at the foot of the Tourmalet. In Sainte-Marie-de-Campan. A small village like this one. But the Tourmalet is something very different from the Aubisque. You'll find out tomorrow. That is . . ."

His lively eyes looked embarrassed. "Pardon, Bud, I didn't want to offend you. But sometime, you will be the winner on the Tourmalet. I know it."

"I'm not yet disqualified," growled Bud. "At least nobody has told me so."

"*Tant mieux pour vous,* so much the better. Maybe you can conquer it tomorrow." He reached for the jar to pour more wine, and Bud did not draw back his glass.

"In those days only logging trails went up to the Tourmalet, and when the snow was melting bears came over from Spain to kill our sheep. The Tourmalet is six thousand feet high, and at the time it was the darkest wilderness imaginable."

"Bears?"

"Yes, real brown bears. I saw them myself, because I often enough minded sheep on the pastures below the summit. Nobody in Sainte-Marie-de-Campan and in all of France thought it possible that bikers would be able to conquer the dreadful wilderness of that mountain. Even mules went on strike on those scree-covered trails. Remember, that was 1913, and nobody dreamed of boulevards leading across the mountains, or of the ugly cement blocks for skiing tourists. Our winter sport was smuggling, but I've told you that already. But, and it has to be said, the Tour de France has become what it is today because of the Pyrénées. I wanted to tell you about the year 1913. It was the last before the First World War, and before you Germans wanted to do your own Tour de France, but after a few stages you got stuck at the Marne, right?"

"Mmm," said Bud. "You ought to talk to my grandfather about that."

The old man moved closer and put his hand on Bud's shoulder. "Just kidding." He chuckled. "Don't get excited. For smugglers those were rich years, and that's when I learned it." He toasted Bud. "Okay, listen. The Tour passed through our village. It had to, because there was no other way across the Tourmalet. I was ten, and the men coming down from the Tourmalet were all supermen to me. There's snow up there even in the summer, and it was inconceivable that bikers would make the summit without getting off their bikes. In fact, quite a few got off, but the tough ones remained in the saddle, and I want to tell you about the toughest."

"You're really making me curious."

"You have every reason to be curious. None of you will ever go through what he went through."

"Aren't you mystifying it a little?" Bud looked skeptical.

"Wait, young man, just wait. I know, the Tourmalet hasn't become any smaller, not even by a meter, and the paved roads don't reduce its nasty inclines. But I know whereof I speak, because I was there. Today they call it the heroic era, and you can bet your bottom dollar there was a reason for it. The smallest breakdown could become a disaster, because there was no sag wagon and the riders had to take care of it themselves. Without any outside help, understand?"

"I'm trying to understand," said Bud, "but don't tell me that a broken bike wasn't replaced."

"That's precisely how it went, dear friend. Nowadays, at the slightest sign of a defect, you get a new bike from the sag wagon, and I want to tell you about the man who was the unfortunate pioneer for all these improvements. His name was Eugène Christophe, and we all called him Cricri. And he would've won the Tour of 1913 on one leg if the rules had been only half as humane as they are today."

That was too much for Bud. "You're telling *me* these things? Do you consider it humane if those medical assholes construe a doping case for which there isn't the slightest motive?"

"I admit, in those days there were no doping tests, although the guys were taking all kinds of stuff to double their energy. Especially, to stay awake at night."

"Why at night?"

"Because quite often they were riding through the night or starting by the light of torches. The stages were much longer than today, but damn it, I really want to tell you about Christophe and his bad luck, which you guys can't even imagine."

"He probably took a spill."

"No, he didn't. What happened to him would nowadays have been fixed by the sag wagon within a few seconds. If you listen carefully, maybe your small bundle of woes will become a little lighter. Okay, Christophe on the summit—I remember it like yesterday—had a lead of eighteen minutes over the Belgian favorite, Philippe Thys. Think of it: eighteen minutes! Nobody achieves that today, not even with all their gears and on paved roads. So Christophe rode downhill and was happy. Perhaps he was singing. You sing sometimes during a downhill race, right?"

Bud nodded. "It's a fantastic feeling."

"Only it didn't last with Christophe. His fork broke. Those logging trails had more holes in them than Swiss cheese. That Cricri could repair about everything because he was a trained locksmith and fitter. But how can you repair a broken fork?"

"If there was no replacement bike, he was finished," said Bud.

"That's what you think. Do you know what he did? He took off his front wheel, took it in his left hand, and carried the frame with his right on his back. That's how I saw him run into Sainte-Marie-de-Campan, after he had slid down some steep slopes on his behind, to cut off the switchbacks."

"But in the meantime everybody else must have passed him."

"Of course. Even the stragglers. He had a twelve-kilometer walk behind him. But there was a forge in the village. It's still there, by the way. We boys showed him the way, and he looked as if he had come from hell, not down a mountain. His pants and jersey were in shreds, and his eyes glowed wild in his dirty face."

"Do you mean to tell me that he repaired his fork in the forge?"

"Exactly, my friend, just that. Listen to what happened. He had barely entered the forge when the race officials took it over. You should also know that Henri Desgrange was not only the creator and the boss of the Tour but also a journalist who knew what people wanted to read. Together with three race officials he had waited for Christophe, because he smelled a good story. So he blocked the forge so that the whole village wouldn't crowd into it; three or four kids, I among them, slipped in nevertheless. One worked the bellows, and our Cricri pounded on the anvil and the fork until the red-hot thing was fixed."

"And how long did that take?"

"Let's say, an hour. But the best is yet to come. When he mounted his front wheel, one of the commissioners said: 'Good work, Christophe, but you know, we have to give you a penalty. One of the boys worked the bellows. Therefore you've accepted outside help. But we'll take into account extenuating circumstances and give you only a one-minute penalty.'

"I would've put him across the anvil," said Bud.

The old man chuckled. "He was close to that, very close. Cricri spit into the fire and told everyone there that they could kiss his ass. And then he was back in the saddle. He had lost four hours with his walk and the repair, but he ended the tour in seventh place in the overall standings, and all of France called him "Le vieux Gaulois." He never won the tour, but this adventure made him more popular than all the winners of the tour."

"Four hours' delay," said Bud. "Today that's unthinkable."

"Of course, my friend. But you mustn't forget that Christophe's misfortune broke the rigid rules. From then on the race managers permitted that riders on a team could exchange bikes, and even outside help was accepted to some degree. Consequently a rider who had placed well in the overall standings did not lose all his points just because of a breakdown."

"You know a lot about the Tour," said Bud.

"I told you where I'm from and that the Tour always came through our village. It has to, because it cannot do without the Tourmalet."

"Mmm. I'll probably have to do without it." He looked on his watch. "Almost two o'clock. I have to get back to Pau."

"A few minutes more or less for someone they want to disqualify shouldn't matter that much," said the old man with a thin smile and put his hand on Bud's arm. "Think of the four hours of Christophe. Besides, listen to the news so you know where you stand." He got up and switched on an old radio sitting on a shelf on the wall.

The young woman cleared the table and asked Bud if he would like a coffee. He nodded, and then the news came on. He got prime coverage because the Tour had national priority, and if the radio could grab a story before the newspapers, it went for it.

"No decision has been made in the doping case of Budzinski," the speaker said. "While the German, who left Pau on his bike early this morning, is still at large, race managers and race officials are convening for the second time. We have it from reliable sources that instead of a disqualification, a time penalty of fifteen to twenty minutes might be taken into consideration, since Budzinski has no previous convictions. Of course we will keep our listeners informed of all further developments."

The old man switched off the radio. "There you go, Bud, things are never as bad as they seem. They don't want to lose an ace like you. I told you, I know their game. The Tour needs you, and if they slap twenty minutes on you, that's when it gets interesting. Someone like you can catch up."

But Bud clenched his fists, and his eyes narrowed. "Twenty minutes. Do you know what that means? Today that's just as much as four hours for your Christophe. I know what they're up to: They want to give me a handicap, as if I were a racehorse. Lead in your shoes, do you understand? But not me. Every day running the gauntlet. Here comes the doped one. Go on, kid, take another swig from your spiked bottle, then you'll beat all of them. No. I'd prefer being thrown out."

He hit the table, and the knuckles of his clenched fist turned white. Little André stared at him, his mouth open, and his father, who to this point had uttered barely a word, reached for his cigarettes; he was clearly embarrassed. Only the grandfather was unmoved by this outburst.

"You think about it, Bud. The Tour is something you don't throw away just like that."

"But it's the Tour that's throwing me out. Don't you understand? I haven't taken any dope, and I won't let them spit into my face. It's as simple as that."

But the old man with the weather-beaten face, born a few years before the Tour de France, who had seen many generations of bikers struggle with the Tourmalet, wouldn't give up.

"You don't throw away the Tour, Bud. There's nothing greater for the biker. You know that as well as I do. You were expected already last year, but you were well advised not to come. You weren't ready; twenty-one is too young. I was happy about your decision then, but now I'm against your feeling offended and wanting to give up, provided they build you a bridge with the penalty minutes."

"You call that a bridge!" Bud yelled so loudly that little André drew back in fear. "It's a trapdoor into the dirt, if you want my opinion. I'm supposed to play the black sheep who has to be grateful to the race management and those medical assholes for allowing me to pedal on. Do you realize that by doing that, I'd admit to having doped?"

"I know only one thing," said the old man without blinking an eye. "The Tour needs men like you. I couldn't give a damn if you've taken something or not. Do you really think that someone like Anquetil through his five victories of the tour ate like a friar?"

"That's the snow of yesteryear. Only one thing counts for me: I know what I ate and drank before and during the stage in question, and I can swear every oath there was nothing illegal in it."

"Mmm." The old man again scratched his shaggy white hair under the beret. "Every one of you takes something. Energy boosters, let's say, vitamins, minerals. You don't get through the Tour with the menu of an office worker. Wouldn't it be possible that something might slip in that looks bad in the test tube?"

"Say what you want," said Bud and reached for his gloves. "I've ridden the first four stages under the supervision of my personal physician, a doctor from Cologne who's been my friend for the past two years. He wants to return between the Pyrénées and the Alps. That is, he had intended to. But now I'll be back at home. I'm not playing this crazy game."

"And how do you know that he hasn't given you anything illegal?"

"Because we know each other. Whatever he gives me he can justify, and he was there to check me out every evening after a stage. And do you know what he said before he left? He said that all results were optimal, that I was in top shape. So who needs roids? What they're trying to pin on me is some dirty trick, and that's why I won't accept an act of mercy, which means admitting to an offence I haven't committed."

"To ride with the team is better than going home," said the old man. "Your team leader will convince you of that. Provided, of course, that you won't be disqualified."

Bud walked over to his bike. André, standing on a stool, had lifted it up to let the front wheel spin. "I thank you for your hospitality. You've helped me lot. But it's high time to return to Pau, to tell some people that I'm my own boss."

"I'm afraid these people won't share your opinion. Someone like you is his own boss at the finish line. But after having passed it, things look a lot different."

4

AROUND NOON MAX KOLLMANN WAS SITTING IN THE PRESSROOM, but the page he had threaded into his typewriter remained empty. Most of the other people had already written half a dozen of them, and the telephone booths, which really weren't much more than half shells into which you stuck your head, were as busy as during a stage arrival. And this was supposed to have been a rest day. Bud had thrown the press a big chunk to chew on.

Kollman was tired and he knew it wasn't just because of the sleepless night. Sure, at fifty you don't shake off such nights as you used to, when you went without sleep around the clock during the Tour. That was part of it and there was a good way to cope with it: a cold shower in the morning and then two hours' sleep in the car during the first part of the stage, when not much was happening. And there were enough colleagues taking notes of the exceptions. Once the notepad was on your knees, things moved swiftly.

That's the way it used to be. But now Kollmann sensed the fatigue not only in his bones. His hand rested on the keyboard like some lost glove, and he couldn't think of anything to do with it. Perhaps, he thought, the Tour is no longer something for a man my age. Not that the frenzy of the pressroom was irritating to him. The hammering of the typewriters and the shouting into the tele-phone—it was part of this kind of work and indispensable in the hours of high tension after the finish of a stage. But during the stages in the mountains he also loved driving ahead of the pack by an hour to sit with his notepad on a rock, high above the surging fog from which the bikers would emerge cranking into the switchbacks carved into the bleak mountainside.

He loved it. Once he had even written a poem. Just like that. All of a sudden, without any effort, it had been there. It was imaginative journalism of the highest order, what he did, and only the person who was able to depict the murmur of a brook in a gorge as vividly as the panting of a biker before the summit or his suppressed cry in the downhill race before a blind curve was doing it right. And he also had to feel what was going on in the man who had exhausted himself on the road and was getting into the mop-up wagon, demoralized.

All this Kollmann had done, because he knew how it was done. Bud, however, blocked him. Bud wasn't just another rider. Max had discovered him, and Bud was his friend, and now they were throwing him out of the race because of something that didn't exist, couldn't exist. Maybe they'd only take off time. That much had been leaked from the meeting of the race managers. They must have been aware that a star of this caliber was good for the race, that you didn't throw him away like a water carrier. But Bud wouldn't go along. That much Kollmann knew. He wouldn't run the gauntlet and start in the back of the field; instead, he'd pack his suitcases. Kollman knew the kid too well. Because he hadn't taken any dope, and everything that was being written right then in the pressroom was premature speculation.

Who knew where he went. They'd hold this escape against him. Those idiots would think he was ashamed of himself. Kollmann lit a cigarette and got up. Of course he shouldn't have run off. It was the wrong move. Smacked of a bad conscience—at least to those who didn't know him.

Mercier had been cursing as well. And he had suspicions that Kollmann was in cahoots with Bud. The race management had made it clear to the team manager that they held him responsible for the disappearance of the guilty rider. That made his bulldog face even grimmer, and the storm that was brewing for Bud's return was not very promising.

But did it really matter at this point? He'd quit in any case. If they didn't disqualify him, he'd refuse to drag along an alleged infraction like a trail of scorn and crank like crazy to make up the time penalty. And even if he succeeded, he would still remain the shady guy who had cheated. Bud was lost to this Tour, which he would have won. Unless Kollman could track down that mysterious test, which Troussellier had insisted was indisputable.

The tour couldn't wait and Kollmann felt like a detective who was trying to revoke a sentence of life without parole. It would be no use if the truth were discovered only a day late. Here and now it had to be found. Mercier, instead of acting wild, should cooperate.

Kollmann met the team manager in the hotel of the Valetta team, and the greeting was frosty. Mercier had had lunch with his men and stuck a cigar into his bullish face. The men were helping themselves to a dessert of fruit salad from a giant bowl.

"You can clear out right now," hissed Mercier, "unless you brought along your friend."

"I thought I'd find him here." Kollmann made a point of being calm and remained standing, since Mercier didn't offer him a seat.

"This is where you want to find him? Look for him, look. If you can find him at two o'clock in the morning, you ought to be able to find him during the day as well. It's about time he returned to where he belongs."

"Can I see you alone for a minute?" Kollmann asked.

Mercier at one time had been a good rider himself but over the years had put on so many pounds that a malfunctioning elevator could worry him more than the Tourmalet had in the past. He frowned.

"What's the big mystery? You want to confess where you've hidden Bud?"

"There's little time for jokes right now," said Kollmann, still standing in the door. "But I can't imagine that yours is too precious, if it has to do with Bud."

That worked. Mercier heaved his massive frame so abruptly that his blue Valetta sweats creaked in the seams.

"Let's go to my room. Too many press people in the hall. This is the lousiest rest day I ever saw on the Tour."

And then Kollmann sat, for the third time since the beginning of this rest day, in someone else's hotel room. The windows were open but the wind blowing in from the mountains was no longer refreshing. "At least eighty-five degrees," grumbled Mercier and pulled the curtains. "Or would you like the view of Henry IV's castle?"

"I'd rather have a clearer view of this doping business."

"You think I wouldn't?" With a groan Mercier dropped into the one armchair, and it didn't bother him that Kollmann first had to remove socks and underwear from a chair before he could sit down as well.

"Let's have it, then. We don't have much time. I imagine the gentlemen on high will come to a decision soon and order me into their presence. If Bud hasn't returned by then, to hell with him. I have no use for riders who get themselves into trouble and then leave me high and dry."

"What do you mean: get into trouble?" Kollmann's eyes narrowed. "You're not jumping on the same bandwagon as the others, I hope?"

"That's no bandwagon, my good man. Now, listen to me: There's a positive test result, and they say there's no possibility of error. I don't know anything, and the devil knows how it happened. After all, our fine Mister Budzinski, who's gotten me into all this mess, had his personal German physician by his side. Already acts more noble than Coppi and Merckx together. How should I know what cocktail this miracle doctor mixed for him? Did you ever think of that and why our hero does a disappearing act, not making himself available for questions? Don't you see how ridiculous I must look to race management?"

"Listening to you, one might get strange ideas."

"What do you mean?"

"Well, it sounds as if you weren't exactly fond of your number one, and also that the team spirit isn't the best."

"Team spirit. Listen, they're all pros who have their own interests at heart. The roads are not littered with tons of money. You have to pedal and bend to pick it up."

"Tell me something I don't know, Mercier. You're avoiding me and you know exactly what I'm hinting at."

The heavy man shook his head and concentrated on his cigar. "Not a clue, Kollmann. You'll have to be more explicit."

"I want to know if Bud has enemies on the team. He's never talked about it, that much you have to believe me."

"What does that mean: enemies? Among pros there's jealousy here and there, but they know they're all going to make good money if one of them wins the tour."

"Why don't you say Bud?"

"That's what I said yesterday. In the meantime, things have changed."

The telephone rang and Mercier went over to his bed. But there was no conversation. He slammed down the receiver, cursing, then picked it up again. "I do not want to be disturbed," he growled at the hall porter. "Only if the race management calls about Budzinski."

He reached for a new cigar, bit off the tip, and spat. "These damn moles from the press. As if it wasn't enough that I have one right here, talking nonsense."

Kollmann took a cigarette and gave Mercier a light. "You've already canned Bud and are betting on Merlin now, right?"

The bulldog face flushed bright red. "Don't talk nonsense. Like you, I'm still waiting for a decision in this bloody doping business. But since you're talking about Merlin, please take the trouble to look at the overall standings. He trails Bud by two and a half minutes and is in ninth place. And the mountains are still ahead. You know he's a good climber."

"Talking straight, that means he's the new captain."

"I didn't say that." Kollmann could not ignore the threatening undertone in Mercier's reply. "What I'm saying is that you'll have little satisfaction in saving Bud. Besides, the kid doesn't seem to give a damn. Unless you know where he's hiding out."

Kollmann angrily blew smoke into the bulldog face. "Get over your fixation that I'm hiding something. You know he has his own ways to come to terms with this. But he's not going to be able to take such a low blow, I'm afraid."

"Do you suggest he's going to go home if they slap penalty minutes on him?"

"Precisely."

"As a pro, he has no right to do that."

"You can spout your manager philosophy to me, but it won't carry any clout with him. Don't you know that? Do you know him so little?"

"If he gets a time penalty, he'll pedal on. I'll see to that."

"He's not your slave, Mercier. He'd rather lose half a million than take a penalty for something he hasn't done."

"And how does he want to prove it?"

"Obviously not with your help. You don't give the impression that you want to fight for him."

"Fight. How can I fight for someone who acts like an idiot—disappears without leaving a trace just when he should stand up for himself in this stinking mess?"

"We can argue about this till the cows come home. But instead of blowing hot air, we should find out if and how Bud unknowingly could have ingested a banned stimulant."

"Ah! So you want to play Detective Maigret," hissed Mercier. "I don't go in for interrogations of this kind. I do my job as best I can and, unlike yourself, I've acquired my expertise on the bike. Nobody on my team gets poisoned, and nothing is left to chance either."

"I'd like to hear more precisely about that."

"What do you mean?"

"Let's presume that in the hotel nothing could have been mixed into the food. I would also exclude the possibility that Bud got something spiked from a spectator along the road. Even on the hottest days, he'll only drink from his own bottle. He's never accepted anything else."

"There you go." The bulldog face almost turned friendly. "On hot days Bud's smart enough not to take part in chasing the bottles, this damn *chasse à la canette*. You know this, and you also know that he's well looked after by his personal slave Benotti. I put the Italian on the team because of Bud. He's the classic gregario who'll walk through fire for his master. I would've liked to get him a German but couldn't find one. Either they're not much good as bikers or they want to race for themselves."

"And your Frenchmen?" There was irony in his question, and Mercier's fist came down hard on the table.

"My Frenchmen? Spare me the sarcasm. You know very well that in this job I'm not representing France but the Valetta firm, and that there are no national privileges on my team."

"Nevertheless," said Kollmann, letting his eyes follow the smoke rings from his cigarette, "apart from the German and the Italian, your battle team consists of eight Frenchmen, and Didier Merlin isn't the only outstanding rider. That could lead to tensions, and maybe Bud doesn't fit as well into your team as you think. But I'd like to get back to Gianni Benotti. You said that on the road he alone takes care of Bud's beverages?"

"Exactly. According to what's permissible. For example, during the official periods when beverages can be withdrawn, he rides to the Valetta car while Bud stays in the pack. Every biker has his initials on his own bottles."

"As far as I know, in the morning Bud prepares his beverages himself," said Kollmann.

"Generally that's true. Occasionally I do it for him or for the others, and it wouldn't surprise me if you suddenly hit upon the idea that I've put something illegal into it."

"Nonsense, Mercier. I'm much more interested in Benotti."

"Why him?"

Kollmann scratched his chin. "You see, a lonely Italian among Frenchmen who don't really like him and a German for whom he does the dirty work gets to think his own thoughts during a particularly long stage. At least, that's what I'm thinking, and don't tell me he's popular with the team. His friends ride on other teams, and if my memory doesn't fail me, he used to be one of Antonelli's domestiques, right?"

Mercier nodded. "But that was five or six years ago. Benotti is thirty-two."

"And Antonelli wears the yellow jersey. I doubt that it was a good idea to choose Benotti as Bud's personal servant."

Mercier's paws drummed the table ill-humoredly. "And I'm telling you that he's the ideal domestique. He doesn't avoid any work and I've never heard him complain. I'd feel a lot better with some more like him around, if you want to know the truth."

"He doesn't have much of a career ahead of him. An old nag, perhaps changing his stable one more time. And I have a gut feeling that you're not going to put him out to pasture."

"You might be right."

"Perhaps he'd like to go back to Antonelli? Something could be cooking there, don't you agree?"

"There are always changes," Mercier grumbled. "They're pros looking after their own interests."

"Water carriers like Benotti have very little ahead of them. You know that as well as I do. And you also know that a wealthy man like Antonelli would have some leverage there. I can't help it, Mercier, but when I think of Benotti playing the wet nurse for Bud on the road, not being the happiest man on your team, I have to think of Antonelli as well."

Mercier waved it aside. "Scribblers think too much. Are you suggesting that he put something into the bottles before taking them to Bud? You have too rich an imagination, Kollmann. You ought to write mysteries and forget about the Tour."

"And do you know what you ought to do?"

The telephone cut off Mercier's reply. It was the race management, and the conversation was brief. Before hanging up, Mercier said that he would be over right away.

"They've been merciful, Kollmann. Only fifteen minutes' penalty for your darling, who still hasn't returned. I have to go."

"May I come along?"

"No," Mercier replied coldly. "Your kind will be informed at 5 P.M. at a press conference."

5

COMING DOWN FROM THE MOUNTAINS, BUD HAD SUNSHINE IN his spokes as he returned to Pau. Crickets were chirping in the park of Henry IV's castle. Again he had taken secondary roads, but even these had more traffic now. Still, a strange, almost serene, calm had come over him. Many drivers and people along the road had recognized him, and he had smiled at their insults. Some young people had also consoled him. "Courage, Bud!" they had called. "They can't throw out someone like you."

In the hotel he only found Felix, shaking his head, giving him a shy reproachful look as he took the bike from him. "Mercier is at the race management, Bud. He was raging because you had taken off."

"And the others?"

"Gone on a little training ride. You know, not to get rusty."

Bud grinned. "And what do you think I did, Felix?"

"Okay, Bud, but after what happened, you should have . . ."

Bud interrupted him. "Nothing happened, Felix. I didn't take drugs, understand? But they shook me up, and I had to find my balance. Now I have it, and even the most senseless verdict can't take it from me. Any news?"

Felix shrugged. "It's possible. But they don't send a messenger for that into my shop. Things are busy at the race management."

"Did Kollmann stop by?"

"Yeah. He spent an eternity in Mercier's room."

"Anything else?"

"There were three calls for you from Germany."

"Who from?"

"No idea. Maybe the hall porter knows."

"It doesn't matter, Felix. Tomorrow I'll be going home. You won't have to work on my bike any more. Whenever you have time, take my big suitcase out of the luggage car."

The mechanic stared at him, aghast. "You really mean it? You don't even know the verdict yet."

"And I couldn't give a damn. I came to race and not to get duped by the dirty maneuvers of some alchemists. This is the end, and it doesn't even bother me."

"At least wait for Mercier," said Felix, but Bud had already slammed the side door leading from the garage into the hotel.

He was barely in his room when the phone rang. "*On vous demande de l'Allemagne, monsieur.*"

It was Doctor Lindner. "What's up, Bud? I've tried you three times already. Have you been disqualified?"

The voice crackled and came from far away. Bud pressed the receiver to his ear, plugging the left ear with his finger. "I can barely hear you, doctor."

"I'm asking if you've been disqualified."

"Not yet, they're still deliberating."

"Our radio news is talking about a time penalty."

"Maybe, but I don't care. I didn't dope, and I'm going home, *basta.*"

All of a sudden the voice came in loud and clear. "If it's a question of a time penalty, you'll stay in the Tour, idiot. I'll find out about flights, and tomorrow I'll be in Luchon. If I don't see you there, we're through, do you hear?"

Bud wanted to reply, but the line was dead. He dropped down onto the bed, put his hands behind his head, and stared at the flowered curtain billowing in the breeze. The wind from the mountains blew cooler air into the sullen heat of the room. His thoughts started spinning again, but it wasn't the hum of the spinning wheels and the sunshine in his spokes. Luchon was tomorrow's goal of the big stage through the Pyrénées, and he couldn't go home if Doctor Lindner expected him in Luchon.

Ride in a car to Luchon? The idea was absurd and made him furious. Ernst Budzinski, the great favorite of the Tour de France, has himself chauffeured across the Tourmalet so that he can cry on his doctor's shoulder. He didn't have time to keep turning that wheel because, without knocking, Kollmann burst into the room.

"This can't be true—do I see right? First the disappearing act, then lying around sulking. Mercier's on his way. He'll get after you, and he has a damn right to do it. Because you're staying in the race. Fifteen minutes' penalty. Do you hear, only fifteen minutes."

When Bud didn't move and just turned his head from the window to the flowered wallpaper, Max grabbed him by the shoulders. "Get yourself together before Mercier puts you into handcuffs. They went out of their way to give you a chance. You'll be able to make up fifteen minutes."

Firmly, Bud pushed away Kollmann's hand and got up. "Now, listen to me, Kollmann. First of all I don't have that information, and second, I want no part of it. I won't pedal another inch, and I've thought it over very well. I'm not playing the part of the repentant sinner, because I've got nothing to repent. If you have room in your car, you can take me as far as Luchon. Doctor Lindner arrives tomorrow night, and I want to talk to him at least."

Kollmann whistled through his teeth. "Lo and behold, Doctor Lindner is coming. Does he know you're about to throw in the towel?"

Bud nodded. "I told him so."

"And does he agree?"

"Not exactly. But I make my own decisions. He doesn't give me orders any more than you do."

"What about Mercier?"

There was no need for an answer, because the team manager burst into the room. He was struggling for air and his bulldog face had the color of a ripe tomato.

"I guess I don't have to tell you that you have permission to go on," he gasped. "All day long this pest Kollmann is one step ahead of me. Now get going—the TV is waiting in the lounge and you're going to announce that you will continue."

"I'll go downstairs. But what I announce is my own business."

Bud headed for the door, but the bulldog blocked his way. "Stop. No way. We'll discuss what you're going to say—right now."

Another minute, thought Kollmann, and he'll put his teeth into Bud's shoulder. But Kollman only said: "I have things to do. I'm not needed here."

"Glad you finally noticed." Mercier bared his teeth.

There were almost two dozen journalists in the lounge, and between them cameramen set up their equipment. Kollmann avoided the crowd and went down to Felix.

"Has the team returned?"

"Sure. Ten minutes ago. Must be in their rooms. What does Bud say about the penalty?"

"In a minute you can hear that in front of the TV people. My name is Felix if he doesn't tell them that he's going to go home."

"But he can't do that."

"That and much more. If that's going to be sent live, there'll be some commotion."

He held out his cigarette pack to the mechanic. "By the way, Felix, what's Benotti's room number?"

"Seventeen. He has a single."

"I thought so. Four doubles for the French, it figures. Bud prefers a single, and Benotti gets one too, because nobody wants him. I'll pay him a visit."

"Why? Nobody's ever managed to get an interview from him. He opens his mouth only to put food into it."

"Maybe he'll make an exception," Kollmann said with a thin smile, "and I have a gut feeling that we'll get Bud back into the saddle."

Felix shook his head and looked after him, a cigarette in the corner of his mouth. Then he returned to his sprockets, because alpine stages required careful preparations in the shop.

Kollmann had decided to confront Benotti point blank. He wanted to catch him unawares and the moment seemed right. The riders could have been informed about Bud's penalty at the earliest upon their return from the training session. It hadn't been ingested yet completely, let alone digested, and if Benotti had something to do with it the moment seemed right to take him by surprise. Kollman knocked and heard the shower being turned off. "Just a minute," said a deep voice with a hard Italian accent. "I'll put on some clothes."

Gianni Benotti's dark eyes under the wet curls stared at him in surprise, questioning and frightened. I mustn't leave him any time, Kollmann thought.

"I wouldn't like to be in your shoes, Benotti."

He said it sitting down on the only available chair. His room was much smaller than Bud's and didn't look out on the quiet garden but on the street.

The result was remarkable. Benotti retreated until he bumped into the wardrobe and there he remained as if nailed to it, his hands spread wide, trembling.

Kollmann came in with his second blow. "It's known," he said coldly and sharply, "who put the stuff into Bud's bottle. The game is over, *signore*. There are witnesses who have talked."

Benotti's coarse face, with a nose distorted from a fall during winter training, changed color despite his deep tan from ten hot days on French roads. He pressed against the wardrobe as if he could hide in it. Sweat appeared on his forehead above his wide-open eyes.

I mustn't leave him any time, Kollmann thought again. He also noted that for the fourth time that day he had invaded someone's hotel room. This time it was the right one, and one word from Benotti was enough to acquit Bud. All means to this end were legitimate.

"No excuses, Benotti. You did it during the stage to Dieppe."

Pinpointing the location broke the last reserve. Benotti lifted his hands up from the wardrobe and covered his face. He was trembling all over now, and the words he tried to utter were inarticulate.

"Talk clearly." Kollmann barked into a face he couldn't see, and then Benotti staggered away from the wardrobe and threw himself across the bed.

"I knew it," he whined. "I tried to refuse, believe me, but then he offered me a contract for next year, one like I've never had before. I'm thirty-two and have three kids."

"Antonelli?"

"I thought you knew that?" Benotti lifted his head from the pillow and his eyes had the look of a beaten dog.

"I just wanted to have it confirmed, Benotti. And now you'll also confirm that you went to get Bud's water bottle from the Valetta car and that you poured something into it. Tablets or powder?"

"Tablets. They dissolve immediately."

"Good. I don't care who supplied them. You can tell that to the race management. Put on your sweat suit, and we'll go downstairs right away."

Benotti got up from the bed and like a sleepwalker staggered to the wardrobe. "Will they disqualify me?"

"What a strange bird you are. That's the least to be expected. And Antonelli won't fare any better."

"Jesus Maria," he moaned, making the cross over his dark hairy chest. "He's going to kill me."

Kollmann scratched his day-old beard; the only thing that had gotten a rest on this rest day had been the razor. "I don't think so. You may even have a chance to have him make up for your lack of earnings and do something for your kids."

"What do you mean?" Benotti straightened up from tying his shoes.

"Now, listen to me carefully, Benotti. You've disgraced yourself and we can take it for granted that you'll be fired. But you're at an advantage, because the general public doesn't even know your name. Also, you're at the end of your career. The molehill of a scandal will become a mountain only if you involve Antonelli as well. In this case the career of a star will be ruined. Do you understand that he has every interest in rewarding you if you protect his name?"

"You think . . ."

"Precisely, Benotti. Of course it's up to you how you'll talk your way out of it with the race management. But wouldn't it all sound very plausible if you took all the responsibility and told them that hostility or revenge toward Bud had been the motivating factor and that you're only the doormat of the Valetta team? Antonelli will appreciate that and I'll keep quiet. That's a promise."

Something close to gratitude shone in the frightened eyes of the biker. "If it remains between us, I'll go ahead with it," he said.

"Immediately. You must call race management and tell them that you have an important statement to make in the case of Budzinski. Here's their number." He pulled a piece of paper from his pocket. "Of course we won't appear together. But I'll take you to the hotel."

Benotti called the front desk and Lesueur came to the phone right away. Obviously the meeting was still going on. He's holding the receiver like an activated hand grenade, Kollmann thought, and he felt Lesueur's surprise like an electric tingling when Benotti stuttered in a pain-stricken voice that he couldn't say anything over the phone.

"Pull yourself together, man," Kollmann hissed when the Italian had hung up. "As far as I'm concerned, you can appear like the picture of misery that you are, but if you get yourself into a muddle you'll pull Antonelli into it as well, and then you'll really be in deep shit."

"He'd kill me," Benotti said in a flat voice.

"He probably would, Benotti. So you know what you have to do. Let's go."

They avoided the entrance where Bud, who had been sanctioned with a fifteen-minute time penalty, declared in front of the TV cameras and a crowd of journalists that he considered the penalty scandalous and that he would return home.

"It's a live broadcast," Kollmann said as they were creeping through Felix's shop. "Their broadcast van is outside the hotel."

Outside the hotel where the race management was meeting, he turned around, but only after insisting with Benotti another time and assuring him that he would keep his mouth shut.

They always catch the small fry, he thought as he walked through the streets of Pau, taking in with deep breaths the wind blowing from the mountains, driving away the heat. Antonelli is much worse than this poor devil who never made it to a winner's platform and only took care of the menial labor for the stars. And this was not the usual kind of degrading labor. Not just sacrificing his own chances in a race, as was common for the domestiques. It also wasn't deliberate pushing during a mass sprint, or whatever else happens when pros are out for profit. This was deceit in its most vicious form, and if Antonelli had chosen a smarter man, his surprise tactics would never have worked. He felt rage toward Antonelli, pity for Benotti, but also pride in his own instinct. He also thought of his work, because the afternoon was wearing on and, unlike the other reporters, he hadn't written a single line so far.

But hadn't they all written for the wastepaper basket? The thought cheered him in a peculiar way. He was the one holding out the large wastepaper basket to all those pencil sharpeners and spiteful types who had considered themselves endowed with a sixth sense. He quickened his step and his legs no longer felt tired.

He found Bud in his room. And a raging Mercier, blowing himself up like a bullfrog, screaming so hard that twenty journalists could take notes outside in the corridor.

Mercier wanted to throw Kollmann out with his own hands, and across the railing of the balcony seemed as suitable as out the door. But Bud stepped between them before Mercier could lay hands on Kollmann.

"This is still my room, Monsieur Mercier. And I decide who may come in."

"And I've decided that you will continue," gasped Mercier. "I will not accept a breach of contract—and if this damn reporter who's been underfoot the whole day doesn't get out immediately, I'll call the police. Who knows, maybe all that crap you pronounced on TV comes from him, but I'm telling you, that's the end of that."

Mercier was standing in the center of the room like a fighter gone mad, not knowing whether to attack the opponent or the referee, or both.

But first he had to catch his breath. The purple of his face was turning blue. Kollmann took advantage of the moment. "Bud's not going to give up; he will continue and what's more, without a time penalty. If you'd be kind enough to listen to me for a moment, you could stop jumping around like crazy." He said it in a calm, businesslike voice and was surprised at himself. The effect was remarkable. Bud looked at him with narrow eyes while Mercier gaped, his mouth wide open, his bulldog face shrunk to two big white bulbs over a large hole.

"What . . . what are you saying?"

"I'm saying that race management will cancel the penalty, if they haven't done so already. Just call them. Most likely they themselves will call in the next few minutes."

"What's all this about? Talk."

"That's what I'm doing already. One of your bikers is telling the management this very minute how during the second stage he poured some forbidden stimulants into Bud's bottle. And you won't believe who: It's precisely the one who, upon your orders, gets the bottles from your car."

"Benotti?"

"Yes. All of a sudden you're thinking fast. But it should've clicked earlier. Do you remember our conversation at noon?"

"And who's your source?" Mercier's wide open eyes narrowed.

"Benotti himself. I bluffed him. Why don't we sit down?"

Before Mercier could reply the phone rang, and before Bud could move Mercier was at the telephone with two jumps. What Lesueur told him made him sink down on Bud's bed. The voice squeaked so loud that Kollmann and Bud could understand almost every word. They had found the guilty one. Everything had been resolved, Bud was reinstated. Completely, without a shadow of a doubt. But he, Lesueur, had more important things to do than carry on over the phone. Would he kindly come to the race management and bring along Budzinski, whose presence would be appreciated.

Groaning, but with an elasticity that used to be famous among riders, Mercier jumped to his feet. And the friendliness he displayed all of a sudden was also uncommon for his character. "I must apologize, Kollmann, and thank you as well. You had more of a nose than I did."

He reached out his large hand and Kollmann shook it.

"Hurry up," Kollmann said, "you have to meet with the race management and I have to think of my paper. Most likely they'll have given up on me and don't have the faintest idea what kind of a morsel I'm going to prepare for them."

"I still don't understand," Bud said.

"They're going to tell you and apologize. I'm afraid you'll soon have every reporter on your heels and won't get any rest, if you don't hide. And before the Tourmalet you should get some rest."

"I'll vouch for that," Mercier said solemnly. "Even if I have to ask for police protection."

It was close to seven o'clock when Lesueur arrived for the press

conference in the overcrowded press room. He confirmed everything that Kollmann alone already knew, and there wasn't even the
slightest allusion to Antonelli. Benotti has listened to me, Kollmann
thought, and taken the full responsibility.

They cursed and wrote and wrote and cursed. The work of an
entire rest day, which turned out not to have been one, had been for
nothing. However, it was Saturday night and only the handful of
reporters from Sunday papers were under desperate time pressure.
All the others had a whole night to write up the story of the won-
drous salvation of a Tour favorite, whom they had already written
off. Many of them had done it with malicious joy and Kollmann
grinned as he watched them run to their typewriters the minute
Lesueur had left the room. On the TV screens suspended from the
ceiling Ernst Budzinski was making his statement that the whole
issue had been resolved to his satisfaction and that he would of
course start the eleventh stage. By his side, arms around his shoulders, the team manager, smiling contentedly, was sucking on a cigar.

Kollmann wondered if he should go see Bud again, but decided
to head for his hotel and have the first real meal of this day. Bud
had to wrest some quiet time from this tumultuous day, and
Mercier would see to it, like a menacing bulldog. He walked
through streets that, after the sports newscast, were crowded with
people arguing wildly. A smile came to his tired, unshaven face.
Like the sunshine in Bud's spokes.

But he also thought of Benotti. In the press center they were
busy tearing him apart and clearing Bud of all the dirt they had
thrown at him during the afternoon. And what about Antonelli?
Had he made contact with Benotti and implored him to take it all
upon himself? At a good price, of course. Not having his yellow
jersey splattered with dirt should be worth something. But
Kollmann doubted that Benotti was capable of seeking his advantage in this most critical hour for the star. He felt nothing for the
star, but pity for Benotti. He should really write much more about
someone like Benotti than Bud, he thought. Perhaps with the

headline "Fall of a Water Carrier." But these were details people really didn't want to know. Besides, he had promised Benotti to keep his mouth shut. All of a sudden an unknown person would have a name, and a dirty one. He had pedaled for twelve years or so to arrive at this point.

The blame for it went to what was being practiced in professional life every day, over and over again. But never was a shadow of reproof cast upon those who set the traps and who lay in ambush. The lower the means with which you battle against your opponent, the better your chances of throwing him out of the race. But sports is supposed to be noble fair play in a polluted world. That's what people think. They really do. What do they know of the pains of a nameless water carrier who has to labor in the service of stars?—and who is checked by them with an arrogant whistle when all of a sudden the energy propelling his rear wheel no longer seems the chain of a slave but the weapon against the slave driver?

Benotti, Kollmann thought, was too domesticated to seek his own advantage in a race. Not a spot in the sun, but the underground was his realm. And Antonelli had recognized this. For a moment he wondered if he should tell Bud, but only for a moment. He decided to stick to the pact he had made with the fallen water carrier.

6

ON THIS SATURDAY NIGHT. DOCTOR LINDNER IN HIS MUNICH hotel room had a surprise for which he didn't care too much. His wife, whom he believed to be in Cologne, stormed into his room; her luggage wasn't for just a day trip.

"Do you want to come along to France?"

Pent-up rage flashed in Kaj Lindner's beautiful brown eyes, a little too large for her small turned-up nose, and he knew that for the moment he could relax. Suitcase and travel bag were dropped at his feet, and she refused the armchair he offered her. After pacing the room twice on her long tanned legs, she positioned herself in front of him, hands on her hips. It wasn't a position he particularly appreciated, because even without the high heels she was wearing today she was an inch taller than him.

"Is this how you keep appointments? Yesterday you called to say that you had reserved a room at Tegernsee for a week, and today you call it all off because you want to fly to France to this ridiculous Tour. But don't count me out, darling. I took the first available flight to prove it to you."

"Sit down and listen to me, Kaj." It was the only possible answer. Martin Lindner knew that in her current frame of mind, she had a lot of ammunition left. He had imagined the trip to the Pyrénées much less complicated, and once again he had underestimated Kaj.

And she went on shooting from the hip, so much so that he had to close the window. Angrily she went on about unreliability, and worse, and of course about this silly hobby of his that was ruining the entire summer. The Tour de France? He really couldn't have found something more absurd. And on top of it, the personal care of a biker. She could have accepted a racehorse, but of all things, this Budzinski. And it was all Kollmann's fault. He had praised him a few times in his newspaper, and now Doctor Lindner was stuck with a neurosis about his own image, and this Budzinski had the nerve to call from France, and in the middle of the night. But there was an end to all of this, and that's why she was here.

Doctor Lindner, when he finally could get in a word, told her that her coming had been for nothing, and that he had the ticket for Marseilles in his wallet. He said it so calmly that she cried with rage, and he also added that she could recover from the shock by spending a week at Tegernsee.

Later, over dinner, when her resistance had weakened, he talked about Bud. He talked about an intrigue that had hurt him so much that he wanted to give up. But everything seemed to have been straightened out; he had heard it over the radio.

"So in that case," said his practically minded wife, "we can go to Tegernsee after all."

"No, we can't, Kaj. He does need me in this moment, and besides I have to find out what happened. And he may take the yellow jersey tomorrow."

"So what? As far as I'm concerned he can take the blue or the red also. Don't I count for anything? I was looking forward to a few days' vacation with you, and some biker ruins them. I can't believe it."

Martin Lindner put down his fork and poured more wine. "Look Kaj, you can't always look at it that rationally. Women do and they don't, as it suits them. I could tell you, for example, that for a mountain climber the Matterhorn is different from the soft peaks of the Black Forest, but then you'd probably question the sense of mountain climbing. If I tell you that the Tour de France is one of the last great adventures that has an entire country for both a stage and an audience, you'll tell me that I should leave you alone with the French and their foibles."

"That's pretty close."

"And you are wrong. You consider the Tour a collective French tic. They need it, you think, the way they need an aperitif before and a cheese after their meal."

"I'm sorry, Martin. I find your Tour terribly boring. I don't understand why a whole country is turned upside down because a herd of bikers covers its roads for three weeks."

"Okay. You can't relate to wheels that don't rotate on their own. But maybe you can imagine the following: A hundred runners, or walkers for that matter, start on a run or walk through France. It is quite possible that after three months some will reach their goal, but you can be sure that their most loyal follower is a total lack of national interest. Let's try the same for automobiles. It would rouse a few people, but most would probably complain about the imposition of closed roads. Strangely enough, the Tour de France attracts millions to these closed roads, and the high mountains are black with people when the Tour comes through."

"Save yourself the trouble." There was the faintest smile in the corners of her mouth, but her large eyes remained serious. "Listen, Martin, every time you have a bad conscience you become very loquacious. But you know perfectly well that I couldn't care less about your Tour. And you also know that I'll give in. But not the way you think. I'll go to Tegernsee, and I can't promise I'll be there by myself for a whole week."

The threat was not new and made him smile. Kaj never went beyond a harmless flirtation. He knew that for a fact. The tempest had passed and he looked forward to the unexpected night with her.

And he looked forward to seeing Bud. Of course he didn't say so; it would have been an unacceptable insult and would have spoiled everything. She had imagination and wit, but such combinations were beyond her understanding.

"Shall we have coffee?" he asked. "It'll be a lot better than the one being drunk in France these days."

"Why's that?"

"Well, they say that it tastes salty because madame cries salty tears into it. She cries when her favorite falls or breaks down at the wrong moment. When Poulidor was still riding, there was only salty coffee in July. On the days when he didn't take a spill his tires invariably found the one thumbtack on a stretch of two hundred kilometers. Women were waiting for his bad luck so they could cry over it. Mother hen instinct, if you like. As a result the man who never won became a ladies' man, and a winner nevertheless."

This time her eyes went along as she laughed. "That's quite amusing, your salty coffee story, but I guarantee you that it won't happen to you. Certainly not because of your Tour de France. What about this Bud? Does he make for salty coffee?"

"I would think he caused some today," he said pensively, looking after the blue smoke rings of his cigarette. "He's very popular in France, and today was the hardest day of his career, without a single stroke being taken on a bike. But in the evening, as I said, everything cleared up."

"So you could actually stay here."

"You should really stop this now," he said and put three cubes of sugar into his coffee. "We have talked things over, and I promise you that tonight not another word will be said about the Tour de France."

After his first meal on this rest day that hadn't been one, Max Kollmann had to struggle against the inertia rising within him with a big yawn, luring him to his large and comfortable bed.

He had to write. It had been satisfying and wonderful to have pulled Bud out of the mud, but it had not been his duty to do so. That was waiting for him in his room, and if he couldn't put together a long commentary about this turbulent rest day before the big stage in the Pyrénées he might as well give up. Then he would have missed his calling, although he had achieved more than anyone else. Before he sat down at his typewriter he needed a comment from Bud. Most likely he was still at dinner with the team, and after all that had happened this day good old fat Mercier, with all respect for his protective techniques, could not deny him a short interview with Bud.

But when Kollmann arrived at the hotel of the Valetta team he realized that he had underestimated the situation. The lounge was more like an army camp of journalists, and it was impossible to get through to the small room where the Valetta bikers were eating. Delfour and Ferruccio, the drinking buddies of the previous night, were there as well, and before Kollmann had a chance to nod a greeting, they fired the first broadside.

"Lo and behold, he's still around. There have been bets that you had gone home. It looked as if Bud put you out of a job. But he's put you back into the saddle. Good for you. You remain one of us."

It was harmless teasing among reporters without any deeper meaning, but Kollmann didn't have the nerves for it, and it showed. After all, he had been the one to put Bud back into the saddle, and what's more he needed him alone, not in this crowd.

"Have you talked to Bud?" he asked Delfour. The Paris reporter remained calm even in situations like this, because he could whip up a 150-line interview within fifteen minutes and, if need be, without an interview partner. He had a cold cigarette in one corner of his mouth, and Kollmann knew that Delfour only smoked cold when he was mad.

"Talked to Bud? Where have you been? On the moon? Since he's turned up again, Mercier keeps him under lock and key. He doesn't even eat with the others, but up in his room, with two bodyguards outside. But I trust you know more about all this. With this useless statement from the race management, nobody can write up a story."

"I don't know anything more than you do." He was sorry to disappoint a colleague like Delfour. If you only knew how I cornered Benotti, he thought. He hoped that Mercier had pulled not only Bud out of traffic but also Benotti.

Ever since Benotti had been disqualified and Bud reinstated, the fat team manager once again functioned like a precision clock, but he also showed his gratitude. He liberated Kollmann from the crowd of reporters and to the surprise of the two gorillas posted on the second floor, took him into Bud's room.

"Only ten minutes, Kollmann. If I let him go to face the hordes he won't sleep for a minute, and we have big plans for tomorrow."

Bud, in his sweat suit and slippers, came to greet Kollmann. There were bowls, plates, and bottles on the table that could have fed half a team.

"Are you trying to fatten up before the Tourmalet?"

"You're welcome to join. Guaranteed no steroids. What do you think about Benotti?"

"Poor guy, Bud. But at least he has a conscience. I know others who would've left you stewing."

"Maybe you're right, Max."

"He's finished as a rider; it takes some nerve to give himself up on his own." He poured himself a large glass of mineral water and drank it down in two gulps. "Do you know that you're at the peak of your popularity, Bud?"

"I haven't thought about it yet, Max. I'm thinking about the Tourmalet."

"It comes at the right time. If you win tomorrow, you'll have conquered all peaks. How do you feel?"

"Relaxed, Max."

"But a little too awake, I fear. Let me feel your pulse."

Kollmann reached for Bud's large wrist and looked on his watch. "Too fast, Bud. Almost seventy. That's the excitement. Normally you should be at about fifty. You'll have a hard time falling asleep."

"Maybe. But I don't want to go to bed yet."

"Why's that?"

"Do you have some time, Max?"

"No, Bud, I have to work. Just wanted to know how you are. Besides, Mercier gave me just ten minutes. Why do ask?"

"You could take me to Eaux-Bonnes."

"To Eaux-Bonnes? Are you out of your mind? That's at the foot of the Aubisque."

"I know, Max. I ate lunch there."

"In a restaurant?"

"No, with farmers. Basque farmers. Wonderful people. I had fled and they gave me back my equilibrium."

"And now you want to go back?"

Bud nodded. "If you give me your car, I can be there at nine-thirty."

"And when you get back, it'll be midnight. Mercier will have a stroke."

Bud grinned. "He should have had one three times today already. He'll get over it. I can't explain it in so many words, Max, but it's drawing me back to the old man; I have to talk to him before the Tourmalet. That's more important right now than anything else."

Kollmann shook his head. "You're crazy, Bud. And if Mercier finds out that you've taken my car, he's going to take me apart in midair."

"I can't go to sleep now, Max, but I know that I'll feel fine after having been with the old man. And you have to feel fine if you want to go after the yellow jersey, right?"

"You want to put everything on one card tomorrow?"

"Everything, Max. But I have to find out what the old man thinks about it."

"Must have made quite an impression on you. But it doesn't make sense to go on talking about it. In ten minutes my car will be outside Felix's shop. The key is in the ignition and you do what you like. It's your business how you settle things with Mercier. But come back before midnight. You need sleep if you have the

Tourmalet ahead of you."

"I'll sleep enough, Max. More than Gino Bartali, who they say smoked a pack of Gauloises between two high mountain stages."

"He was one of the greatest, and the greater they are, the stranger the stories about them."

"I'll think of him tomorrow on the Tourmalet. But I have to go. Will you get your car?"

Kollmann got up and held out his hand.

"In ten minutes in front of the garage."

"Thank you, Max," said Bud.

The night was cool and clear from the wind blowing from the mountains, sweeping across the dusky purple sky, so that the stars sparkled like diamonds. From the cafés came accordion music, and on a street corner he saw young girls in white skirts dancing. Felix had smuggled him through the garage without attracting the attention of Mercier's gorillas, and Bud didn't waste another thought on them as he steered the convertible sports car on to the road to Eaux-Bonnes. There was little traffic and he enjoyed cranking up the engine. It was also necessary: If the old man, who must be close to eighty, went to sleep with the chickens, he'd come too late as it was.

But Bud was lucky. It was twenty minutes to ten when he arrived and they were still sitting in front of the TV. Only little André was missing. The surprise was perfect. Their eyes and mouths wide open, they stared at the entranceway as if a ghost had descended from the Tourmalet and entered the house. And the old man, his voice croaking with surprise, said something incomprehensible in Basque.

Bud, in the same blue sweat suit as at noon, approached, a little awkwardly. "May I? I apologize, it's late, but I wanted to come by to say thank you."

"*Pour une surprise, c'est une surprise.*" The old man's fist first hit the oak table then opened to offer a bewildered greeting. And the young woman offered him a chair.

Bud shook hands with them and took the same chair as at noon. She poured him a glass of wine from the half-empty bottle on the table, and the young farmer switched off the TV. Bud felt that he should provide an explanation, which he really wasn't able to give. But the old man helped him.

"You're either crazy, Bud, or you've given up the race for sure. There's no other explanation, because if you haven't given up, you ought to be in bed, and ten minutes ago your team manager announced over the TV that you were in bed and that tomorrow you intend to bring off a big coup. One of those statements must be wrong. So what's the matter with you?"

The faint smile flitting across Bud's face remained in the corners of his mouth. Determination flashed in his eyes.

"I'll tell you what's the matter with me. This afternoon you helped me more than you can imagine, and when those stupid accusations finally came to an end, some powerful force for which I have no explanation pulled me back here. I think I want to thank you and again ask for your help."

He took a sip of wine, more out of courtesy than desire, and the young farmer joined him. But the glass of the old man remained on the table. His hand reached up to the tousled hair protruding from his beret, and his eyes met those of the rider who had come to see him.

The young woman asked if he wanted something to eat, but Bud shook his head. He was glad for the diversion that let him avoid the small, piercing, and not even slightly tired eyes of the old man.

"This time I haven't come to eat, madame. I also have to go back in a minute if I don't want to provoke a major fight with my team manager. This is the second time today that I got away from him."

The woman was about to reply but the old man put his massive, blue-veined hand first on her, then on Bud's arm. "Leave him to me, Pascale. I know better what he wants."

"What does he want?"

"He wants to win the stage tomorrow, right?"

This time Bud could not avoid his eyes. He felt them penetrate like X rays, and he was glad.

"You don't have to give me any answer," said the old man. "Not only do you want to win tomorrow, you also want to win the yellow jersey at the Tourmalet. That had also been your intention when you came at noon, but this doping business has shaken you thoroughly. Am I right?"

"Right," said Bud. "But you helped me and I need your help again."

The old man's watery small eyes looked at him thoughtfully. "I think I'm beginning to understand you, Bud, but I'm afraid I can't help you a second time. You think I can, because I know the Tourmalet like the inside of my pocket. But everybody has to face the Tourmalet on his own. Hiring a mountain guide won't do anything."

"What I want to know from you," said Bud looking at him with his large gray eyes as if he were the creator and the owner of the mountain, "is, if tomorrow I should attack. Attack unconditionally, with all my strength, do you understand me?"

"Is this why you came here?"

"Exactly. You know the mountain and you know the Tour. So does Mercier, but I'm not sure how straightforward he is with me. In Merlin he has another iron in the fire, and it's a French iron, if you know what I mean."

"But he can't possibly ask you to sacrifice your chances to Merlin. The man is a good rider, but he doesn't have your class."

"He knows the Pyrénées, and I don't. I've never been on a six-thousand-foot mountain. How high is the Tourmalet?"

"Six thousand three hundred and fourteen feet. If you've never been at that altitude, you could indeed encounter difficulties. Merckx and Anquetil had them when they went beyond fifty-four hundred feet. You have to find out for yourself. But I'll tell you something, Bud. It all depends how you feel. If you're in top form, attack. Ruthlessly and everybody. In the mountains team tactics don't count; everybody rides for himself. Don't listen to Mercier if he wants to hold you back, because then you know that he wants to favor Merlin. Do you think he climbs better than you?"

"Not exactly, but I know he has big plans and that there's little open talk about it within the team."

"In that case, go for it." His fist hit the oak table, making his point. But he opened it immediately, as if he had to consider something. "However, don't attack blindly, Bud. The challenge is not only the Tourmalet but also the Aubisque, Aspin, and Peyresourde. It's the most difficult stage of the Tour. The Alps, afterwards, will seem like a vacation, believe me."

"But not one in a rocking chair." Bud laughed.

"If you weigh your chances correctly in the Pyrénées, you can be invincible in the Alps. And nobody on the team will give you any trouble. If I understand you correctly, you don't quite trust the environment. Go for the yellow jersey tomorrow, and Merlin will eat out of your hand."

"Will it get hot?"

The old man nodded. "Did you see how the stars sparkle? The wind is coming from the east and you'll see the Tourmalet without clouds or fog. But be economical with your energy. You'll see how dangerous the sun will be when you leave behind the woods after Eaux-Bonnes."

"I've noticed that today."

"It will get even hotter," the old man said, "and this time it's not just training. Many have spent all their energy at the Aubisque only to fall off their bikes at the Tourmalet."

"But there's a large stretch of flat land between them."

"Right. It rolls smoothly until Argelès-Gazost, and don't forget to feed yourself on that stretch. Eat as much as you can hold; the Tourmalet requires it. He'll welcome you already between Luz-Saint Sauveur and Barèges, and then the Bastan will accompany for a while. Like a wild man he'll rage around you and torment you."

"One might think you're talking about a dog."

"The Bastan," said the old man and laughed, "is a raging torrent, running from the Tourmalet to Barèges, and seeing its foam will make you more thirsty. And when you lift your head you'll see the summit, several rows of switchbacks above. But it's harsh and forbidding, and you'd do better to keep your eyes on the road. The tar will be soft and the air will shimmer, but if you're in luck, it will be somewhat cooler in the next curves. You'll slow down to a spectator's pace, and maybe one or the other will push you a few meters, although it's not permitted."

"And if I'm out in front," Bud grinned, "I'll be penalized, because it will be noticed in the race management car."

"Ah, well, the yellow jersey is worth a small fine, isn't it? There are stragglers who get handed on from one spectator to another, like buckets of water during a fire."

"If I lag behind on the Tourmalet, I'm finished."

"That's right," said the old man, "but I think you'll take it; provided you get to bed. What time is it?"

"Ten-thirty," said Bud. "You're right. Maybe Mercier has already alerted the police." He emptied his glass and got up. "I owe you a great deal, ‚monsieur."

They all got up and the old man put his hand on Bud's shoulder. "My name is Iribar, Bud. A Basque name. All of us are called Iribar. And tomorrow we're going to be in Sainte-Marie-de-Campan."

"But the Tour also passes through Eaux-Bonnes."

Old Iribar laughed. "Of course it does. But there isn't much happening, if you know what I mean."

"Of course. Nothing very dramatic at that point."

"That's right. Someone like me who's from Sainte-Marie-de-Campan doesn't want to see a little brook but a foaming Bastan. We're all going to Sainte-Marie tomorrow, and by the old church I'll wave my beret at you. And I want it to greet the winner of the Tourmalet, do you understand?"

"I'll do my best," said Bud. As he took the curve into the road to Pau, he saw the old man wave his beret in the hazy moonlight.

Two minutes before midnight Bud was in bed, and he fell asleep immediately. The calm and confidence he had brought back from the little village were like a bulwark against the high-pitched emotions of fat old Mercier.

"You're foaming like the Bastan," he had said to him with a smile when the raging team manager burst into his room. The remark caused a lot of consternation. Anyone who doesn't know the Tourmalet doesn't know the Bastan either. Even Mercier in his rage could think that far.

But nobody solved the puzzle for him and he had to withdraw, grinding his teeth, because Bud pointed out the importance of his sleep. "We'll talk tomorrow," he had hissed, and Bud, shrugging, had replied that for tomorrow he had already an appointment with a certain Tourmalet.

7

OVER BREAKFAST WITH THE VALETTA TEAM HE FELT MERCIER'S searching eyes, but he knew that he wouldn't start an argument in front of the others. He ate well and then went to prepare his own bottles for the difficult stage in the Pyrénées. He headed for the start at the last minute in order not to be crushed by reporters, but he was cornered nevertheless and had ten mikes in front of him. Only when the stage began was he free again. It was already hot, and there was no wind from the mountains.

The bright colors of the jerseys were shining in the sun and the field, rolling slowly and compactly through Pau, was crisp and colorful as if newly laundered. From the tanned and muscular legs the sharp scent of massage oil rose into the air, which was already heavy and beginning to shimmer. It would soon eat away at the freshness emanating from the group, a freshness enhanced by the flashing spokes and whirring hubs. The bluish mountaintops on the horizon were in a haze, the large peaks invisible.

Black lines of people were everywhere. All of Pau was in the streets and Bud sensed that this was not the usual farewell from a town where the stage had its start. People knew that the mountains would tear up and reduce this smoothly rolling pack in which everyone seemed to have the same chance. It had always been like this. Here, at the foot of the Pyrénées, the Tour, riding counterclockwise, had a new beginning.

I haven't even talked to Mercier about tactics, Bud thought when they left the town behind and were out on the country road. My fault. But maybe Mercier was relieved about it. Perhaps he has given the green light to Merlin. If he arrives in Luchon before me I'm out of the game in any case. I have to keep an eye on him as well as on Antonelli.

A biker wearing the blue Valetta jersey caught up with him. "Long time no see, Bud." It was Marceau Lemaire, one of those tough Bretons from whom you'd have to amputate a leg before you could get him off the bike. In Bordeaux, after a heavy fall that had torn open his right hip, Mercier wanted to pull him out of the race. But he had pushed on until the rest day in Pau, and now he was astride in his saddle as if nothing had happened.

"Are you going to attack today, Bud?"

Surprised, Bud turned toward him. "Did Mercier send you?"

Lemaire grinned. "Nonsense, Bud. It's just that no one knows what you're up to, and my guess is that Merlin is dying to know."

Bud didn't reply. They were going along at an average of thirty kilometers an hour—called among bikers the pace of the rural mail delivery—and it looked as if they would keep at this speed until Eaux-Bonnes. They could talk as if they were sitting in slippers in front of the fire. No one wanted to sprint into the Pyrénées only to gasp for air at the first mountain. Although Bud was trying to hide in the center of the field, many spectators recognized him, because they were riding slowly. "Bravo, Bud!" they were shouting. "Courage! Show them!"

"Benotti has made you even more popular," grinned Lemaire. "I'd like to help you if I could."

"How do you mean?"

"It's obvious, Bud. They're all talking about you and if you pull the big coup today you'll be the greatest. They want you to take revenge."

"Did Mercier say that?"

"I don't need a Mercier for that," Lemaire said without taking his eyes off the road as it took a sharp turn. "But I mean it, honest, Bud. You're the only one on the team who can win the Tour, and who brings in money. Merlin won't make it, even if he attacks today. So I'd rather pedal for you than for him. That's logical, isn't it?"

"Do you think you'll make it today?" Bud looked at Lemaire's thigh just below the tight racing pants; it displayed all the colors of the spectrum. You didn't need much imagination to visualize what it must look like above that line.

"I'll make it, Bud, but I can only look after myself. But if I could, I'd rather help you than Merlin."

"Merlin can kiss my ass," said Bud also keeping his eyes on the road surface, by now soft under the scorching sun. "If I understand correctly, he wants to race against me today, and you're all supposed to rally around him, right?"

"Well, as much as you can talk about tactics in the mountains."

"In any case, some will stick with him if he falls behind."

"You can count on it, Bud. He's collected votes against you, which wasn't difficult to do. After all, you disappeared for an entire day."

Bud nodded, but Lemaire didn't notice, because they were shaken by a cobbled village pavement. "I was hiding out in a village nearby."

"Why?"

"I'll tell you tonight, if you like. Save your breath. I think our work is starting."

The pace turned brisker although the road was rising. The field was still holding together, but as they passed through Eaux-Bonnes it covered the whole length of the main road. The battle for the Aubisque had begun.

In the woods, where the gradient was still gentle like the turns, Bud worked himself to the front, Lemaire sticking to his rear wheel. It was shady and almost cool, and he enjoyed the ease with which he was still stroking in high gear. Many had already shifted down.

As they came out of the woods, they pedaled through a shim-mering wall of heat into the barren roughness of the mountain side; it seemed a glowing staircase without steps. The field tore apart in many spots, and Lemaire disappeared from Bud's rear wheel. Two Spaniards pushed past him, thin-legged mountain fleas who had less than 130 pounds to force uphill and who were still riding at an easy cadence, as if the road were level.

Bud too shifted back, but he was still in a high gear. It cost ener-gy but covered more distance, and after every switchback, his team lost three or four riders. He was in the group out front, and halfway up the mountain there were twenty men left. In the front positions gleamed Antonelli's yellow jersey, and he had three teammates with him.

He has strong helpers, Bud thought. Merlin was riding close behind Antonelli, but no other blue Valetta team jersey accompa-nied him. The second blue jersey in the top group was Bud's. Four kilometers below the summit he recognized the spot where yester-day he had turned around to get rid of the tiresome cars. But he also remembered how hunger had seized him, and he took a few cubes of sugar and a rice cake from his jersey pocket. Only ten men were left in the front group.

The tempo was set by the two Spaniards; again and again they tried to detach themselves with short sprints. But this was the meeting of the strong. Only in the rear groups did such explosive spurts still have an effect. Before the last kilometer below the sum-mit they lost a Belgian and one of Antonelli's domestiques. The others stayed together but didn't speed up as the two mountain fleas started their sprint to win the mountain points. They were ahead by 150 feet, and on the downhill stretch allowed the others to catch up.

Bud had a good feeling on the Aubisque, but wasn't euphoric. He had taken the fifty-four-hundred-foot altitude relatively easily, and the only thing that did surprise him was how quickly the field split up at the first challenge. Was it the heat, or were many more affected by the ten prior stages than it appeared? As he crossed the summit line he looked back and saw far down on the switchbacks small and larger groups between the pack of accompanying cars. And he was also surprised at the large crowds of spectators. The mountain was black with people and on the summit, the corridor was so narrow that he grazed them with his bent elbows.

He pulled the carefully folded newspaper from his back pocket and put it between his chest and the jersey, because the first part of the descent was steep and the cool airstream in the mountains was dangerous for anyone who has struggled uphill in a sweat. They raced downhill at almost a hundred kilometers an hour, and no accompanying car stood a chance of keeping up with them. Calculating the risk, they skimmed along the edge of terrifying gorges and past steep mountainsides and this rapture of speed, controlled with artistic precision, was the reward for the heavy labor on the opposite side of the mountain.

By Arrens they had covered a difference of more than three thousand feet in altitude; a few gulps of tea helped relieve the thirst, and also the pressure in the ears. From the black lines of people he heard his name called as if through a wall of cotton. And then his head was free again; he shifted to the large gear on the soft descent to Argelès-Gazost and, remembering the advice of the old man, ate everything in his pockets. They were going at a brisk but by no means frenzied speed, and before Bud had finished his second breakfast, others joined the group. Five riders had made up their delay in a breakneck downhill race, and once again Antonelli had two helpers by his side.

"His domestiques are tearing themselves apart for him," Bud said to Merlin as they were rolling through Argelès-Gazost, taking on fresh supply bags. Those were the first words he spoke to Merlin, but he only got a shrug by way of a reply.

All the better, Bud thought. I want to get even with you in a different way anyhow.

The wide road from Argelès to Peyrefitte. A boulevard, where you speed along easily; it lulls you into believing that you're going to finish the Tourmalet like the rice cake and the prunes from your goodie bag. Watch out, Bud. You're thinking too much about Merlin. Don't forget Antonelli and enemies of a different sort who are not riding a bike. Don't you feel the hot wind blowing into your face as if it came from the Sahara and not from the mountains? It doesn't happen often in these valleys, which usually produce a good upcurrent around noon, when the sun is high. But you've caught the day of hot downcurrents boiling from the gorges around Luz-Saint-Sauveur and stalling cars, their radiators boiling. Don't overdo it, kid. You wouldn't be the first one whom the Tourmalet brings to his knees.

Subconsciously Bud understands the language of the hot wind, which cuts off the breath of the men who are bending low over their handlebars as if to slip away under its guard. For the first time he accepts a water bottle from a spectator. He doesn't drink it but empties it over his head. Cool water drips down his neck, but after a few seconds it's once again sticky with sweat.

The gorges before Luz. The road winds under pylons that support protective roofs against avalanches, and the cascading torrents attract you like drugs for the addicted. Your tormented body craves water, lots of it, but you mustn't look, keep your eyes on the soft asphalt, which weighs down your strokes even before the Tourmalet mounts its steep ramps before you.

And there they are. It must be them. Luz is at an elevation of 2100 feet, the Tourmalet at 6312 feet. And the distance from the Luz church steeple to the peak of the giant amounts to only nineteen kilometers. Nineteen kilometers on the plain are nothing. Nineteen kilometers with an elevation change of more than forty-two hundred feet are endless.

The alpine landscape is turning wilder, the gradient more vicious. At the timberline there is another village: Barèges. Above it the Tourmalet towers like Mount Everest for the men moving forward assisted only by sprockets and a chain.

In Barèges there are only five men in the lead pack, and the two Spanish climbers start the major attack. Bud is biding his time and notes that Antonelli catches up to their rear wheels more easily than Merlin. His teammate has been taking "butt breaks," as riders call standing on the pedals, more often than sitting in the saddle. But he manages to close the gap, throwing his torso wildly from one side to the other.

As Bud is about to step up his speed, his front tire bursts. He had put on light tires because in the mountains every ounce counts. They have all put on light tires, but the small jagged stones of the mountain roads are their enemy, and the unlucky one gets impaled. It's not the same as a broken fork in the times of Eugène Christophe, but it may cost a lot of time if the sag wagon is far behind.

Bud is in luck. Since Mercier has two riders in the breakaway group, he is driving with the chief mechanic right behind Bud. On the roof they carry replacement bikes, their spokes sparkling in the shimmering air.

But a flat front tire does not warrant changing the bike that has your proportions. Felix jumps out of the car, opens the quick-release levers, and within ten seconds the new wheel spins in the fork. While Bud is still fastening the cage strap, Felix is pushing him ahead by the saddle.

Nevertheless, the others are gone. There is a gap, one of those gaps of three hundred feet that are crucial on a mountain. Some of the greatest racers never managed to close that gap.

Just when you've acquired a name, you may fall into such a hole. Because up front they're standing on their pedals to take advantage of your momentary vulnerability. They put all their energy into it, and you need even more strength than they in order to catch up.

It's a dirty game they're playing, and Bud knows it. Only when a switchback bores a wide loop into the bare flank of the mountain does Bud catch sight of them. There are four of them. Merlin stuck with them. He would have waited for Bud on the plain, and between the two of them they would have closed the gap more easily. But on the mountain every man is for himself. Still, Antonelli's domestiques would have waited, that much is certain.

Bud has regained his rhythm in a smaller gear and now shifts to a higher one. It hurts his legs and he feels that he is closing in very slowly on the men who want to shake him off. Of course that's what they want. Even Merlin. Rage seizes him. But not a helpless rage—more like the throttled fury of the athlete who takes on the challenge.

The Bastan. Old Iribar had warned him about the lures of the water, but the boiling foam spurs him on, and it feels as if it brings down the heavy heat. A hundred and fifty feet. Sixty feet. They no longer turn around—they know he is coming back. What they don't know is how aggressive this little crisis has made him. They don't know that now he is determined to play the big stakes. It's a cruel game: You tried to take advantage of my weakness. It was your right. But mine is worth just as much as yours. He sticks to their rear wheels, hears their heavy breathing, and waits for their reaction.

It comes from the two Spaniards. Both pull away at the same moment with a short spurt. Thin sinewy legs whirl on the low gear, but they are no longer sitting in the saddle with motionless shoulders: They are throwing their torsos in a seesaw rhythm from one side to the other. It looks like a last desperate attempt to save the honor of the kings of the mountains.

Bud feels in control of the situation and isn't very concerned. They're not great mountain kings like Bahamontes or Jimenez. Otherwise they would have broken away already. He pays more attention to what's happening behind them. Antonelli is standing on his pedals as well, his yellow jersey swaying behind the mountain fleas, without losing any ground.

But Merlin is losing it. Bud comes up alongside him and sees streams of sweat running over a distorted face. The eyes, avoiding any contact, are without expression, and only for a moment does Bud give his teammate the illusion of staying by his side. At the end of the curve he accelerates and it looks as if Merlin is pedaling in place.

Bud feels satisfaction but he also knows there's no time for that. Only after the heavier work is behind them can they talk about this duel. Merlin—that was a private matter. Now it's Antonelli's turn, and there are still six kilometers to the summit. That's a great deal when the road starts into a steep climb and slows you down to ten kilometers per hour, even as your hands are tearing at the handlebars and your feet pound the pedals. And a gap of sixty feet is a lot as well. Bud tries to close it with an energetic short spurt, but before he has covered half, his lungs are bursting. He straightens up and shifts to a lower gear.

Antonelli's yellow jersey. It weaves from one side of the road to the other, and the Spaniards can't shake it off. All Bud sees is yellow. The red-pink jerseys of the mountain fleas don't count. Both are many points behind in the overall standings and are only interested in the mountain prize. Antonelli is the one who counts. He never turns around, but he sees Bud approaching anyway as he bends low over his handlebars, squinting backward between his bent arms.

In the next serpentine Bud catches up to the trio; still five kilometers to the summit. A race official passes them slowly to show them an interim result, of which they can be proud. The *ardoisier*, as the race official holding the board is called, is an important ally of those who break away. He sits in the seat behind the driver of a heavy motorcycle, holding a slate board. With heavy chalk he has marked the advantage of the pack in the lead. They are more than four minutes ahead of the next group, not counting Merlin, who is floundering between groups like a drowning man. And Bud knows that in this moment the yellow jersey would be his if Antonelli weren't by his side. He can't write him off like Merlin. But if his energy lasts, he can defeat him on the last five kilometers of the Tourmalet.

Sport? It is combat in its most primitive form and it can't be any harsher. What would happen if Bud knew that the man in the yellow jersey had bought Benotti to get Bud out of the race? In one of those curves that bore into the mountain so steeply you want to scream, they are so close to each other that their elbows touch. The Spaniards, no real competition, are ahead by just a few yards.

Has the air turned thinner? Have they passed the critical fifty-four-hundred-foot elevation the old man talked about? Bud doesn't notice any difference but he senses that he can crank more, although this is the second mountain of the day. Once again they have cranked beyond the timberline, again the rows of spectators are turning thicker, and the second seat of the heavy BMW is occupied not by a race official but by a cameraman. Thirty feet ahead the red car of the race organizers, directly behind it the three sag wagons, which have priority. None of the four men struggling toward the summit can fall behind because of a breakdown. Now and then a press vehicle manages to squeeze by, but they are not allowed to linger. They gape and want to take in the drama before the driver once again has to step on the accelerator.

Bud, who doesn't know the mountain, is about to test Antonelli's resistance. At the outset of every bend he accelerates. That's when it hurts most. Antonelli keeps pace three times, but his step is choppy, not smooth, and at the third bend his torso, throwing itself uncontrollably from one side to the other, has to take over from the legs. The fourth bend swallows him. He zigzags through it as if he had lost control, and the gap opens faster than earlier with Merlin. The two Spaniards are taken by surprise as well. One of them keeps up for three hundred feet, then his spinning dance on the small gear comes to an end. His strokes become heavy; he straightens to wait for his teammate.

Felix brings the sag wagon up alongside Bud. "If you can, keep going," Mercier yells, forming his hands into a loudspeaker. "Antonelli is finished, completely. But don't overdo it, there are more than three kilometers left."

"And Merlin?" Bud pants.

Mercier waves his hand. "He'll be happy to finish. You've wrought havoc, but be careful and don't forget to eat something."

The car returns to its proper position directly behind Bud, and in its wake press cars are gathering. Soon some of them pass to be ahead on the summit. Kollmann is among them and for a second Bud sees the triumph in his laughing eyes and, until the next bend, his waving hands. He takes a few cubes of sugar from his pocket and a few swallows of tea.

In some rock crevices he sees the first signs of snow; he is forcing his speed on a road that's getting narrower because of the crowds of people. Now the corridor is so narrow that no car is able to pass. The small dirty snow patches expand into the large snowfields of the summit. The Tourmalet. A few more strokes to the old stone inn, nestling like an eagle's nest at the height of the pass, and a shout of jubilation goes up as no stadium packed with people can produce. It feels as if an entire city had climbed to the top of the Tourmalet.

Coasting now, his right leg straight, his left at a sharp angle, Bud puts the newspaper once more between jersey and chest as the air is beginning to whistle. It no longer shimmers and it is thinner. For the first time since Argelès the wheels are turning by themselves, and the sun of the Tourmalet is flashing in the whirring spokes.

La Mongie. A few huts below the summit, and the road drops downhill between them at what seems a much more dramatic gradient than the ramps of the ascent. It takes his breath away, but his thoughts are as clear as the wind whistling on the mountain, and it's not his hands that are doing the steering. They are holding the cantilever brakes lightly, ready at any moment to tighten their grip, but just like the alpine skier his body swings through the curves, which are gentler on this side of the mountain than on the other where hairpin switchbacks would have chopped up the descent.

Bud is a strong downhill racer. Not one to hesitate in the curves wasting the hard-earned advantage of the ascent with red-hot brakepads. That means taking risks, but they are the calculated risks of a man in top form sensing the harmony of all his energy, and all his reflexes intact. And never since he started competing on a bike has he savored the feeling of triumph with such intensity.

It is not just the Tourmalet. The mountain is certainly part of this euphoria tingling from his fingertips to the roots of his hair. Because he dreaded it, and because the old Basque was able to soothe that fear only in part. There is more to it. He had left behind everybody on the most famous mountain of the Tour. Even the yellow jersey. According to the rules, no tricks. Not even with one of those sprints where only luck and skill count.

There are stages where a hundred bikers flit across the finish line almost at the same time, and the last man doesn't show any more strain than the first. But now there is a great void behind him. He shook them off, one by one, on the mercilessly climbing road. For the simple reason that his stroke was more powerful and remained so where the air became thin and the mountain steep. Combat in its simplest form, without escapes or tactics; there is no substitute for the feeling of invincibility and the triumph that fills a man who has conquered the top.

The spokes are gleaming in the sun and the centrifugal force is putting tremendous pressure on the thin frail tires when, in the curves, the wheels, inches away from the drop-off, lean toward the mountain. The landscape is gradually losing its wild aspect. The first trees appear in the rich green of the meadows, but also hideous cement blocks serving winter sports. These meadows used to belong to the bears and the sheep. The steel structures of the ski lifts crisscross the landscape like power lines. Bud has no eyes for them. He sees the sun in the spokes of his front wheel bending and rubbing on the road with a good grip. At one time it was a wood-cutter's trail.

Anything but a breakdown now. The sag wagon is far behind. Its four wheels can't keep up this speed, and he is alone with the Tourmalet as it becomes increasingly more green and gentle. The airstream has dried the sweat on his face and now and then he strokes in a high gear in order to maintain the speed. Hardly any people by the roadside. A few mountain farmers or shepherds coming across their meadows.

The valley of Sainte-Marie-de-Campan. The incline diminishes like the outrun of a ski jump. The Tourmalet has shown its respect for its conqueror: no burst tire, no broken fork as happened to old Christophe here. The cars are catching up, and Mercier appears by his side. From the sunroof emerges a beaming and sunburned bulldog face.

"You've gained four minutes on the two Spaniards and more than eight on the next group. About fifteen men joined on the descent, including Antonelli and Merlin. Eight minutes, Bud. If you manage to keep only half, you've got the yellow jersey. You went downhill like the devil, boy!"

He didn't count on this much. Eight minutes are a huge asset. But there are still sixty kilometers till Luchon, and Aspin and Peyresourde come first. Not giants, but two mountains each forty-five hundred feet high, of which he has been warned. Sainte-Marie-de-Campan is only a midway station, but important, because he is expected.

From afar he sees the entire village gathered in front of the little gray church. He decreases his speed, and in the red car of the race officials, once again ahead of him, they already imagine a breakdown. Bud laughs and when he sees old Iribar waving his beret in the front row, he is tempted to get off his bike. But he remembers the pack behind him and also the Aspin and the Peyresourde ahead. Slowly, waving, he rides past them; it seems to be the honor round for the victory on the Tourmalet.

Old Iribar. Would Bud have confronted the Tourmalet with the same courage and assurance without him? He sees pride and joy flashing in the watery eyes of the craggy face, and the summer wind ruffles the white hair, free of the beret. Beside him the farmer and his wife and little André, and all of them shout and wave as if he has already torn the yellow jersey off Antonelli's back.

Before the curve Bud turns around one more time, and then he is alone again with himself and the road. Soon it begins to rise, because the Col d'Aspin is thirteen kilometers ahead. He knows that behind him the hunt has begun. That could offset the rhythm of the hunted, who has no point of reference and no help. Calories are important. At the exit of Sainte-Marie-de-Campan he has taken the new goodie bag, and for a few minutes he grants himself a moderate speed and eats. He ditches the empty water bottle by the roadside. The second is still full and will be enough.

This valley is more shaded and cooler than the approach to the Tourmalet. Old trees with enormous tops line the road; behind the meadows rise blue hills with thick conifer standings, reminding him of the Black Forest. The ascent to the Col d'Aspin has begun.

MAX KOLLMANN HAD A LEISURELY START OF THIS STAGE. HE HAD finished his article toward three in the morning, because the editors couldn't get enough of the commotion around Budzinski. They had reserved an entire page for him and he had some exciting first-hand news to offer. But he had played down his own role and not said anything about Antonelli. This much he owed to Benotti who started a humiliating trip home at the time the peloton rolled toward the Aubisque. It wasn't a bad idea to have the trump card Antonelli up his sleeve. He fell asleep with these thoughts, a long-overdue sleep that made him miss the start.

This was nothing unusual. Very often journalists race behind the pack after their nocturnal activity, and gasoline-driven horsepower permits a fairly rapid catching up to the men moving ahead with a single manpower. And the stragglers lose nothing because there is Radio Tour de France. The short-wave transmitter of the race management provides them with all the details of the race. This way Kollmann knew, when he had caught up at the ascent to the Aubisque, that Bud was in the lead and controlling the race.

He slept next to his driver, his seat reclined, until Eaux-Bonnes. First because he was tired, second because traditionally nothing would happen until the Aubisque challenged the riders.

He had telephoned in his report from an inn at Peyrefitte, and also had managed to eat something. At the speed of 160 kilometers per hour his driver—tested in many Tours and with only a few minor dents—had raced ahead of the field. That was four times the speed of the riders, and on closed roads where there was no oncoming traffic this meant quite an advantage. Later they had to catch up from the rear, and while Bud started his attack on the yellow jersey they were witness to the little dramas in the rear positions of which the general public received little information.

The Tourmalet hadn't even begun to unleash the battle that would last until Luchon, the goal of this stage, but Doctor Troussellier's white medical car staffed with three aids was already surrounded. They buzzed around him like bees around a promising flower, as if he could remove the poison from the steep gradient of the snow-topped mountain.

"Doctor, my knee hurts again, can you give me an injection?"

Troussellier beckoned him closer; he could hold onto the car. If in medical distress, you were allowed to hang on for a minute, like the construction worker who puts his pick down to see the company physician.

The man with the aching knee held out his thigh toward the physician and pulled his tight racing pants as high as possible. It is remarkable how the physician aimed as if he were holding a dart and not a syringe. A careful thumb pushed the painkiller into the muscle, and the leg once again began to stroke.

Many had knee problems. It is the overburdened joint of cyclists, and often gets damaged during spills. Another one put little faith in injections and wanted only an ointment for his knee. The doctor had barely handed him the tube when he pushed off the car, bent down low, and took off. The doctor cursed the thief but couldn't take after him, because right and left of the car others were being medicated. The Tourmalet was like a difficult exam; before taking it, all those who don't feel sure of themselves pass by the pharmacy.

Kollmann, at this moment directly behind the medical car, saw the thief take off, medicating himself, holding his hand to the outside of his knee, which kept coming up by itself. When the Tourmalet started in earnest, Kollmann no longer saw a trace of him. There is no ointment that mollifies the mountain.

They passed hopelessly isolated single riders and small groups reducing their numbers on those steep ramps, but also other groups that were holding together solidly, men who weren't mountain specialists but who knew how to economize their energy. They took the delays on the mountain for granted but they also counted on the long downhill stretches when they would make up some of the loss. And they counted on the collapse of those who had taken on the mountain too energetically and exhausted their strength.

The stage was a long one—there were four mountains in it. With the whizzing downhill race from the Tourmalet behind them, Kollmann put his notepad on his knees and began to scribble. Bud had made such a strong impression on the Tourmalet that he was expected to be the winner of this stage—and perhaps even the new wearer of the yellow jersey.

As long as he hadn't overdone it. Kollmann knew the Aspin and the Peyresourde from either side. They were not intimidating giants, but they'd proven disastrous to many a confident rider because he had the Aubisque and the Tourmalet in his legs. Had it been imperative to shake off the two Spanish climbers on the Tourmalet? Had it been a prestige move or had Bud indeed been strong enough for this extra effort and the rest of the stage?

Kollmann urged on his driver between Sainte-Marie and the Aspin. They had to close the sunroof because the wind, blowing from the mountains, became colder and stronger. The valley was still sunny, but in the east gray-black clouds were mounting. On the first ramps of the Aspin, climbing through pine forests that hid the peak, they passed the mop-up wagon. It was the red lantern— the rear light, so to speak—of the colorful dragon creeping up the mountainside. No car is allowed to stay behind it, and the wagon was going slowly because ahead of it someone was making his last desperate attempts to stay in the saddle.

It was a question of minutes. Jersey and pants were shredded on his right side, and the blood, already crusting over his thigh, had soaked into his white socks. It was the Belgian Dewaele, not a big name but a reliable domestique. Now he was of no use to anybody and nobody could help him. A case for the mop-up wagon and not for the white medical vehicle. Not even the photographers, who crowd each other like vultures when they discover a well-known rider in distress, bothered about this lonely man in front of the mop-up wagon. The driver, however hardened he may have been, granted him his dignity. He could have picked him up long ago because every attempt of this tortured bundle of a man to climb the Aspin had become senseless. Another kilometer—then, together with his co-driver, he lifted the rider into the semidark interior of the wagon. Six others worn down by the mountains were already sitting on the hard benches.

Slowly the mop-up wagon and its sad freight, invisible to the public, hobbled up the curves of the Aspin, while Zander and Kollmann in risky passing spurts worked their way from the tail to the head of the torn-up field. The name of this head was Bud, and they caught him as he cranked the final turns of his wheels before the height of the pass. The news gleaned from Radio Tour was encouraging. The group with Antonelli and Merlin was seven minutes twenty seconds behind; despite their grim chase they had made up only forty seconds. Between them and Bud there was only Perez, one of the two Spaniards, three minutes behind the man pedaling toward winning the stage and the yellow jersey. But the weather was not very encouraging. In the southeast, exactly in the direction of Luchon, a storm was brewing; and the wind was blowing from that direction right into the face of the solitary rider who could not hide behind someone else's back to get some respite, like those in the chase group.

If you are riding in a group with a sense of solidarity, you are able to brave the wind; at regular intervals one of the riders will lead the paceline, take on the role of the locomotive. This strategy saves

energy that the single breakaway cyclist has to expend in relentless-
ly taking on the wind. How well Bud is aware of the solidarity in
the group behind him. That's also why the descent to Arreau does
not bring back the euphoria of the Tourmalet. There is one mountain too many in this tricky stage, although he is less afraid of the
Peyresourde than of the flat stretch between Arreau and Anéran.
There they will pool their strength to cut down on his lead. And if
he rides against the wind in too high a gear, he won't have the
strength for the Peyresourde.

That's why it's a descent into the unknown. If the race organizers weren't such sadists, they would have been content with three
mountain passes in one stage—and the race would be over now.
Bud curses the organizers, as generations of riders have done before
him. But he remembers to cut the curves leading down to Arreau
with the precision required of someone who is being chased. Here,
on the downhill race from the Aspin they are not going to take a
single second away from him. That much he knows. The pack
becomes dangerous only on the plain. There it will eat slowly into
his lead, second by second, because only one at a time will brave
the wind.

Between Arreau and Anéran he rides into the storm. It bursts
over him with all the terrible force of a tropical rain. He is only
guessing the vicinity of the Col de Peyresourde, because the road is
beginning to climb once more. Its peak is hidden behind purplish
black clouds; the wind, which has become a tempest, is driving
large drifts of them down into the valley.

Halfway up the mountain visibility is reduced to 150 feet. The
downpour has ceased because the clouds are chafing the mountain,
and Bud has the miserable feeling of working himself into an endless pea soup. Head- and taillights of the Tour cars give him a
ghostly positioning, but he fears being rammed by one of them,
because they'll see him only at the last minute. In the past a rider
was run over and killed this way. It was in the Pyrénées, but it must
have been during a descent. During the ascent you are a snail, and

everybody can keep track of you.

But where is his strength? Where is the harmonious stroke of the Tourmalet that demoralized even the two Spanish mountain fleas? Should this be the end, in the fog that only lets you see small spurts of water from your front wheel after the battle under a burning sun?

Bud shifts to a lower gear. He feels that the high gear is consuming too much of his strength on a mountain he cannot see. In Anéran—where out of the fog thousands of people cheered him— he was still confident; now in this ghostly silent wilderness leading up the mountain he fears for the first time that all could have been for nothing. Mercier's car comes up beside him, and, protected by the fog that blocks the vision of the race officials in the cars ahead, he hands him a bottle.

"Drink this, Bud. Hot tea with glucose; it'll pull you up the mountain. You're still six minutes ahead!"

Actually it is only four minutes. The hunters are coming closer, but this kind of doping is permitted. Not permitted, on the other hand, is the passing of beverages from official cars. That doesn't bother Mercier one bit. Haven't dozens of riders been pushed up the Tourmalet without a word of protest from the race officials? Bud reaches for the tea with numb fingers. He thinks of blue sky and shimmering noon heat—how long ago was that? Hail pelts his face and bare thighs and covers this wretched road that has no end to it.

"Only three more kilometers!" Mercier yells. "We're going ahead now so we'll be close to you during the descent!"

Red taillights disappear into the fog, and the Col de Peyresourde, which is said to be a midget next to the Tourmalet, doesn't end. Instead of the long rows of cheering people on the Tourmalet, there is, cold and hostile, a dark wall of pines. It's been a long time since he could orient himself by the white marker stones with the red caps. Bud feels hot tea running down his chest, because his hand is trembling. He is weaving little serpentines in the hail and the desire to send the bike and the Tour to the devil meets with diminishing resistance. Subconsciously it registers on him that at least there won't be curious gawkers here if he gives up. A car pulls up close and presses him against the side of the mountain; it makes him scream with rage.

"Hold on, Bud. We'll pull you for a bit, nobody sees us."

It is Kollmann's voice; already he has taken his left hand off the handlebars and holds on to the door frame. The driver is pulling to the left to make room for him. But it doesn't last long. Maybe three hundred feet. New headlights emerge from the fog, because now the final sprint has started for the accompanying cars. From the summit of the Peyresourde it is barely fifteen kilometers to Luchon, goal of this stage.

"Let go, Bud. They see us."

Kollmann doesn't know if anybody has seen the biker hang on to his car, but he knows the man is finished. He has seen enough. He won't manage two more kilometers of elevation under the hail. He stays beside him, although behind them the other cars are beginning to sound their horns furiously.

What is he to do? He blames himself for not holding him back earlier, for sitting back, when Bud was wasting energy where he could easily have spared himself. The supermen who get away with using up all their energy during a stage like this one do not exist. And now the storm is about to finish him off. Only doping could raise the level of his performance.

All of a sudden Kollmann knows what to do. He leans out of the car, grabs Bud's arm, and he couldn't care less if they see him pull him up the mountain for a stretch. "Listen, Bud. You can't give up. And it's because of this bastard Antonelli. He was the one who bought Benotti. He's the one who doped your water bottle. Punish him! Take the yellow jersey!"

The unfathomable happens. The rider Ernst Budzinski, only seconds ago a worn-out tortured bundle with legs that seemed to falter in the smallest gear, takes in what he has heard and straightens up.

So it had been Antonelli. Benotti, whom they chased away like a mangy cur, was only his tool.

Kollmann can't take his eyes off the man whose legs all of a sudden start cranking again under the hail changing into a drizzle. He sees eyes turning clear in a head that begins to work again, transmitting its will to the legs. It's a fortunate coincidence that the hail has stopped, rendering the Peyresourde somewhat more merciful during the last two kilometers, but Kollmann hopes that the wind blowing down from the summit drives the hail toward Anéran into the pack of pursuers. Let them struggle with the same miserable circumstances as the man who broke away.

He puts himself in front of Bud to make room for the vehicles pushing from behind, but a few hundred feet before the summit he falls back once more alongside the man who by now is drawing from rationally unjustifiable power reserves.

Kollmann has an idea. In the fog of the Peyresourde he remembers how Jacques Anquetil once, during a foggy stage in the Pyrénées, was saved by the taillights of a car. He had seemed hopelessly isolated on a summit, but his reflexes were intact and he could descend faster than the others who were afraid of the precipice, because he attached himself to the taillights of a car, racing downhill at breakneck speed, helped by the car's fog lamps. Kollmann's car has fog lamps as well.

"When you're at the top," he yells to Bud, "stick to my taillights. Just keep your eyes open and don't worry about a thing. We'll be faster than all the others."

But the mountain hasn't been conquered yet. Only the thought of Antonelli keeps Bud on his bike, zigzagging across the entire width of the road like a drunk. Another curve, and still another. It feels like cranking in place, but he knows he is going forward as long as one leg brings up the other. He crawls on at a very slow pace, and he feels the imminent strike his muscles are threatening, hardened in the cold.

But he forces them to work because of Antonelli. He makes

them work, throwing his torso across the frame, from one side to the other, yard by yard climbing this mountain that for him is so much harder than the Tourmalet, although any amateur who never rode in a race could manage it.

He senses the summit, because there are a few spectators and his strokes become easier. Visibility hasn't improved, but he sees red taillights ahead of him and he knows: This is Kollmann. With those fog lamps he can be much more daring than a biker who cannot take his hands off the brakes and cannot reach the valley any faster than he climbed the mountain.

Bud, his eyes on the two red dots, lets himself fall into the gray bank of fog. He brakes instinctively when they become larger; he is probably riding a breezy speed of forty kilometers an hour on the upper mountain. His legs are heavy; his lungs, which wanted to burst on the other side, hurt; but his reflexes are there, and when the fog tears open and the road becomes more even he knows he has accomplished the hardest day of his career. He doesn't just coast, but in the valley of Luchon he changes to the high gear, and there is the finish line; and before he can reach for the pedal straps, he is surrounded by a cluster of reporters.

His legs, touching the ground, are like wooden stilts and he staggers, but there is no room to fall down. And there are no interviews, which they want to squeeze out of the man who has gone beyond the limits of his capacity and doesn't yet realize that he has earned the yellow jersey.

Mercier elbows through, bulldog style, and takes his bike. And suddenly there is also Kollmann.

"Not a word about Antonelli," he whispers. "We'll talk about it tonight!"

Bud nods and lets himself be taken to the winner's podium. "Never in my life have I worked so hard," he says into the microphones. And to Mercier: "How much do I lead by?"

The loudspeaker answers instead of Mercier: "Mesdames et messieurs, three minutes have passed since Bud Budzinski has won this stage. He therefore wears the yellow jersey!"

The shrill voice is drowned by a tempestuous cheer, but once again it commands attention: "On the summit of the Peyresourde Antonelli had recaptured the yellow jersey, because his group had reduced the gap to two and a half minutes, but the winner of the stage, in a fantastic final spurt, has repelled the attack. Ladies and gentlemen, witness now the final sprint of the pursuing group!"

Antonelli wins it before the Belgian Vissers, and he can't understand why the chase has been for nothing. This fortress was ripe for attack. They came closer and closer to the German, and all the information was promising. Bud caved in hopelessly on the Peyresourde, and now he's won the stage by more than four minutes. Shaking his head, Antonelli walks over to the podium, wearing the yellow jersey that is no longer his.

9

HALF AN HOUR LATER, AFTER THE EXCHANGE OF THE YELLOW JERSEY and the doping test, Bud lay in a Luchon hotel room, and with a new sense of relief he felt his tired and hard muscles loosen up under the kneading hands of the masseur. The curtains were drawn. Without any clear thoughts he was lying in the half dark, his face pressed into a pillow; it was burning from the sun of the Tourmalet and the hail of the Peyresourde. The blue Valetta jersey, crumpled and dirty, lay on the floor. The yellow one, shining and fresh, was draped over the back of a chair.

Mercier personally brought mineral water and hot tea; heaving a sigh, he dropped on the edge of the bed, as if he had climbed all four mountains that day.

"Boy, what a day, Bud. You were a dead man on the Peyresourde and then you went on to win the yellow jersey. By a lead of a minute and five seconds. The devil knows how you managed that!"

Without lifting his head from the pillow, Bud said, "The devil's name is Kollmann. Did you notice how his taillights guided me down from the Peyresourde?"

"You mean to say that wasn't a coincidence?"

"Exactly, boss. We agreed on it."

He didn't mention the business with Antonelli. But before Mercier could answer, he added: "I know you've put out guards against the journalists, and I'm grateful, because I really need to rest now. But when the masseur is finished you should admit Kollmann at least for a few minutes."

The bulldog face flushed bright red. "Kollmann! All I hear is Kollmann! Sometimes I ask myself if he hasn't already become your team manager."

"Without him I would probably have arrived in Luchon in the mop-up wagon, Monsieur Mercier. The yellow jersey definitely wouldn't be hanging there on that chair."

Groaning, chubby Mercier got up. "Okay, let's not argue. I have work to do." He looked at his watch. "It's almost half past five. We eat at seven. I trust you'll be there?"

Bud grinned. "Of course. And in ten minutes send Kollmann up, okay? I'm sure he's waiting already."

"You fry my nerves," grumbled Mercier. But noblesse oblige, he contributed a bottle of champagne; a waiter was about to open it in Bud's room when Kollmann came in, accompanied by Doctor Lindner.

The physician went to Bud and embraced him. "Congratulations. Max has already filled me in. The Peyresourde must have been terrible. Let me look at you, kid."

He took a step back. "You don't exactly look as if you had fun in the mountains. You want to bet it's cost you four to six pounds?"

The cork popped and the waiter asked if he should bring two more glasses. Bud nodded and then they drank to the yellow jersey.

"Let me feel your pulse," said Doctor Lindner. "Later, when Max goes to work, I'll examine you head to toe." And after a while he added, "You're already down to seventy. If by six o'clock you're down to fifty, I can go home; you won't need a doctor."

"I'm glad you're here, doc."

"Be glad Kollmann was there. If I'm not mistaken, he saved you yesterday and today."

"Don't exaggerate, Martin. Let's have another glass to the yellow jersey. It's better for us than for its conqueror." Kollmann took the bottle of champagne from the silver cooler, where the ice cubes were melting. Bud did not join their toast but reached for the bottle of mineral water.

He drank for a long time, wiped his mouth with the back of his hand, and said: "And now I want to know what's going on with Antonelli."

Kollmann lit a cigarette and pulled on it three times before he answered. "Listen, Bud. What I'm going to say must not leave this room, understand? It's a bloody mess, this business with Antonelli, to put it bluntly."

He talked in a low voice, looking toward the open window and the open curtains, as if his words could escape like the smoke of his cigarette, carried off by the wind.

"Yes, he paid Benotti to put the stuff into your bottle. I squeezed it out of Benotti, but no one knows except me and Martin."

Doctor Lindner nodded. "Max has told me everything. He also told me that he would not have told you the truth if you hadn't had the crisis on the Peyresourde."

"It was the only way," said Kollmann. "There was nothing else to pull you over the mountain. You needed a shock to find the strength for the rest of the mountain. Another kind of stimulant, if you will. Nothing else would've worked."

"Maybe, Max." Bud's eyes, still reddened by the exertion, narrowed. "But why didn't you just tell me earlier?"

"That's very simple," Kollmann said in a deliberately low voice, giving the door a meaningful glance. "You might have made a scene and caused a massive scandal. At the very least, you would've slept badly, and in that case the yellow jersey wouldn't be hanging here."

Bud insisted defiantly: "Maybe so; but you weren't straightforward with me."

With a thin smile Kollmann put out his cigarette. "Now you're talking like an ill-tempered child, Bud. Just think: As long as a water carrier like Benotti assumes the entire responsibility, it won't make big waves. The man gets banned and will probably lose his license. They make short shrift with the small fry. At least he's already at the end of his career. But Antonelli is a star, and it would not just have been a scandal, but a proper trial."

"In court?"

"Most likely," Doctor Lindner interjected. "We have a clear case of misdemeanor in a legal sense. You could and would have sued Antonelli for damages and compensation. But let the little guy off. Or do you want to sue him?"

Bud shrugged. "Listen, I've just finished the hardest stage in my life and really don't feel like sticking my head into some law book. The poor guy's been punished enough."

"And today you punished Antonelli in your way," said Kollmann. "Besides, the thought of Benotti must be haunting him."

"You think he might blackmail him?"

"I wouldn't put it that drastically. But he will make his demands, and you can be sure of one thing: When he returns to Italy, reporters will zoom in on him."

"And Antonelli will tremble," added Lindner, "every day."

For the first time since having assumed ownership of the yellow jersey, a thin smile flitted across Bud's face. "Listening to the two of you I might think that nothing better could've happened to me than being poisoned by Antonelli."

"The best thing that happened to you today was most likely Kollmann's taillights," said Lindner. "In the lead with the red lantern."

"Not a bad headline," Kollmann laughed and got up. "Almost half past six. About time I get to my typewriter."

"Shall we have dinner together later?"

"With pleasure, Martin, but not before nine-thirty. It would be best to come to my hotel."

"Fine, Max, I'll see you later. I'll have to take a good look at our Tour favorite, if he's good for some more rides in yellow. Take off your shirt, Bud." He got up to fetch his big bag from the bed where he had left it.

Bud was somewhat late for dinner with the Valetta team, because the doctor kept him for more than half an hour. But Mercier, chewing with his mouth full, didn't protest. Instead, he pushed a pile of telegrams toward his plate.

"There's your hors d'oeuvre, kid, and that's only the beginning. It'll go on through the night, and tomorrow morning you'll have a laundry basket full of it."

Bud was surprised to find congratulations from Germany already, but Mercier laughed: "Do you think Luchon is on the moon? Eurovision had live coverage."

"What a blessing that it was foggy on the Peyresourde."

"Right. Not everything happening up there was meant to be seen. Let's hope nobody saw you hang on to the car. But I don't think so. There would've been a protest from Italy by now."

"Antonelli must have worries of a different kind," said Bud as he began eating his vegetable soup.

"What do you mean?"

"Nothing in particular. Just imagining."

"He recovered on the Aspin in a remarkable way and did good work in leading the pack. He fought for the jersey like a lion. You can't write him off yet, Bud."

"I didn't say that. But things look good, right?"

"Of course," said Mercier stuffing into his mouth a piece of steak that reached from one cheek to the other. "Of course it looks good, if you ignore the fact that the mop-up wagon pushed three of our team across the finish line. A few more kilometers and he would've had to pick them up. Your assault on the Tourmalet finished off a lot of riders. You could've held back a little, but you found that out yourself later on."

"And how. But Doctor Lindner's satisfied. He gave me a thorough checkup and says that my legs will be all right by tomorrow. He also thinks that nobody will try to show off tomorrow."

"We'll be in control of the race, Bud, and the whole team will be at your disposal, Didier included."

Didier Merlin nodded from the other side of the long table. His face still showed signs of stress, but the disappointment was gone. "I lost more than ten minutes, Bud. From tomorrow on we'll all race for you."

And little Lemaire with the mangled thigh, who had made it across the finish line just ahead of the mop-up wagon, beamed: "You see, Bud, it all turned out the way I predicted this morning."

When Doctor Lindner looked in to say hello, he said to Mercier: "Don't let Bud out of your sight, please. The place is teeming with journalists, and he has to be in bed early."

"You can bet on it." Mercier bared his teeth. "Even if it means keeping watch with a shotgun."

And this time he was true to his word. At nine-thirty the new leader of the Tour de France was in bed, looking across at the yellow jersey gleaming in a diffused moonlight, and he soon fell asleep. To the reporters crowding in the hall, Mercier announced with the gentlest smile his bulldog face was capable of: "*Le Tour se gagne dans le lit*—the Tour is won in bed." That wasn't of much use to them, but there was also little to be said against it. It seemed a logical conclusion that someone intent on winning the Tour needed his rest after a stage like this one.

Martin Lindner walked through the streets of Luchon, where people were celebrating the Tour and the new yellow jersey; he was in a good mood and knew that his protégé had no need for sleeping pills. In a remarkably short time his heart, double the size of a normal person's, had reduced its pulse to fifty, infallible proof of his theory: Bud was part of a privileged group of athletes whose bodies recovered in the shortest scientifically imaginable period of time, even after the most excruciating physical effort.

It had become more than a hobby for him to observe this phenomenon. Three years ago Max Kollmann, during a fairly harmless race in the Westfalenhalle, had alerted him to Budzinski. This Budzinski, he had said, is a new Merckx. Only nobody knows it yet. He has all the marks of the great road rider, and if trained correctly he'll win the Tour de France, and not just once.

This had intrigued the hobby cyclist Lindner. He had admired the young man's smooth, extremely harmonious stroke on the wooden oval of the racetrack without drawing any other conclusion than the surprising fact that the man who wasn't a real man yet seemed to be playing where others had already begun pushing themselves to the limit, grinding their teeth. He was a talent with extraordinary reserves, and the scientist felt challenged to plumb these reserves; on the other hand, this could only be achieved in competition with the best. In the beginning it had been professional medical interest, and Martin Lindner remembered it well as he walked through the streets of Luchon where people were arguing vehemently about the Tour and his friend, who had conquered the yellow jersey in a way that electrified the crowds.

Lindner had to wait for almost half an hour before Kollmann arrived. In the meantime he had already allowed himself a crawfish and half a bottle of chablis.

Kollmann didn't talk much. He was hungry, but as he was savoring the first warm meal of the day the pressure and tension went away; it had been a demanding day for him as well. All around them the hangers-on of the Tour were eating and making a great deal of noise, but they were able to talk undisturbed at their little table for two. When the cheese platter and a bottle of old burgundy arrived, Kollmann said: "The evenings make up for a lot, but it's still damn hard work before you can tune it out."

Lindner grinned. "And then you settle back and forget that the Tour won't stand still. There should be more rest days."

"But not one like yesterday," grumbled Kollmann. Like a French peasant he pierced a piece of Pyrénée goat cheese with his knife and put it into his mouth. "What a strain on my nerves."

"If you hadn't put yourself out, Bud wouldn't be here. Not to mention the yellow jersey."

"That's true. And I'm a little proud of it, too. But I've lost sleep and energy, and since I feel it very acutely, I know that Bud won't be fresh as a rose tomorrow either. What's your opinion? You checked him out."

Lindner raised his glass and let the light sparkle in the burgundy. "Let's drink to his health, Max, he can use it; but as far as his physical and moral condition is concerned, you can rest easy. He's weathered his Peyresourde."

"And if tomorrow they start a massive attack against him?"

"What kind of prodigy are you talking about?" Lindner shook his head. "Antonelli and his ilk? They have enough problems of their own."

"Maybe, but there are others. People with reserves, people who spared themselves in the mountains."

"You can't mean that seriously, Max. Naturally one or the other will have ridden a so-called smart race, because he didn't push himself to his limits. But considering Bud's tempo, it's cost them so much time that they no longer matter in the total standings. Bud knows full well that he has to watch out for only a handful of serious competitors, and he's capable of doing so. Besides, all the difficulties of the Pyrénées were packed into today's stage. Tomorrow's stage is such a harmless one that you can't even call it a high mountain stage."

"This is all very true," said Kollmann and fished for a cigarette. "But let's not forget: We're sitting here, forging strategies like pub regulars. But in the end, every stage is decided on the road. Besides, you know better than I do that at this moment medicine chests are being opened everywhere to make strong men out of tired ones. And doping is just about the last thing Bud can risk."

"I couldn't agree more."

"And you also know that he does need something now. After a stage like this one, they're charging the batteries with a vengeance, and you want to tell me the fairy tale of the good superman who only sucks on his thumb, sleeps like a baby, and wakes up like Hercules, ready to pull up every tree in the Pyrénées."

"Well put. The wine makes you eloquent, Max. But rest assured. Do you really think I took this surprise trip only to give him a hug and fondle the yellow jersey?"

"You did give him something?"

"Of course I did."

Kollmann sought refuge in the vintage burgundy, pouring it down like a glass of tap water. "I think you're out of your mind, Martin. Would you repeat what you just said?"

"Gladly. But first allow me to order another bottle, so it won't throw you."

"Suit yourself. But I'm telling you now: If Bud has a positive doping test, I'm going to kill you."

"Mmm, if you go on like this, I'll have to put a sedative into your wine," said Lindner and blew smoke across the table.

He held up the bottle and with the amazing speed of which only a French waiter is capable, he had a new one. And yet, close to midnight, almost all tables were still busy. After stages like this one, which had to be thrashed out in detail, a night could be long for the Tour people.

"Now listen to me closely," said Lindner when the glasses had been filled. "In one breath you're telling me that Bud needs something and that I'm not allowed to give him anything, right?"

Kollmann cupped his empty hands toward Lindner, like someone in need of something. "So what? You're basically right, Martin. They all take something, and Bud knows it as well as we do. And in the meantime the entire press corps knows that his personal physician has flown in. You can't imagine how many of them wrote him off yesterday, and with glee. Yesterday you could have found hair-raising stories in the wastepaper baskets of the pressroom in Pau."

"But he has friends as well, doesn't he?"

"Yesterday in Pau you had to look for them like a needle in a haystack."

"Okay, Max. But now he's broken out way beyond a popularity test. If he had maintained his eight-minute lead from the Tourmalet, he would've received high praise, and the competitors profound sympathy. People would've taken off their hats respectfully and put them on again right away. But now they've thrown him up into the air without waiting for him to fall down back into their arms. And do you know why? Because on the Peyresourde he was no longer superman but one like them. Because they suffered with him, not with the others, and because they know that he's great but not untouchable. And that the Tour hasn't been decided yet. The thrill is only about to start. The masses tire quickly of the untouchables."

"So what?" Kollmann remained stubborn. "You can read all that in my newspaper tomorrow morning. I thought we were talking about something else."

"That others at this moment are charging up with pharmaceuticals, which your darling Bud mustn't even sniff. That's what you want to say, right?"

"Of course. You're avoiding me."

"Your voice is getting heavy," said Lindner and filled their glasses. "Do you know what impression I get of you and all those idolizing Bud's yellow jersey? You want to wash your hands without getting them wet, am I right?"

"Don't talk in metaphors," growled Kollmann. "Level with me."

"Your images come from the same drawer," Lindner grinned. "Do you scribblers consider metaphor your exclusive territory?"

"Tell me what you mean or fuck off."

"Literally?"

"Suit yourself." There was aggressiveness in Kollmann's eyes, and Lindner didn't underestimate its burgundy source. He put his hand on Kollmann's arm, which was reaching once more for his cigarettes. "Don't be silly now, Max. We both know that right now they're rummaging in their medicine chests, and I told you that I've done it as well. But I did it with great care, if you know what I mean."

"If you want to imply that you've doped him more subtly than some lowly trainer could, I believe you. But I'll stop pestering you only if you tell me that the stuff won't show up in a doping test."

He emptied his glass and Lindner lit his new cigarette for him.

"Okay, listen Max. I proceeded as carefully as possible, with a safety net, so to speak. Liver buildups in combination with vitamin A, and I've also given him B_1, B_6, and B_{12}. The purpose being to head off the drain on his energy and to maximize the burning of carbohydrates. And all this is completely legitimate; I could have given the injections in front of the Tour doctors."

"No cortisone? No Dianabol?"

Lindner was amused. "You talk like the dark alchemists of the winter racetracks."

"What do you want to bet that today the stuff is being swallowed by the pound?"

"No doubt. It's the old tune: They're all thinking of equal opportunities and scream for the stuff like young birds for worms. And if you ask me, you can also take a pinch of cortisone without risk, provided you have a competent physician. It all depends on the proper dosage for any given physique. The doctor must know it as well as I know Bud's body. The bad thing is that most riders get it from their masseurs and go by the rule: If you take two, I'll take three."

"Still, they have to reckon with the random tests."

"Do they really? You know as well as I do, Max, that the risk for the large pack is minimal. Only the winners of a stage and the second and third places are routinely tested; and there's one more, drawn by lot. The chance of being caught is one in a hundred. Show me the water carrier who wouldn't go in for this kind of a risk. And if any of the stars doesn't have a lily white conscience, he wouldn't be so stupid as to try for one of the three first places."

"As Bud did in Caen."

"Sure, because he didn't know about Benotti's little present. By the way, it's supposed to have been cortisone."

"Maybe that's why he was so wired that evening."

Lindner chuckled. "Possibly. It makes you cheerful like cocaine and a little horny. I've tried it."

"You take that stuff yourself?"

"Of course I do. As you know, Bud turned me on to cycling, so what's more logical than experimenting with some medications? I did it for his sake; now I'm able to combine my theoretical knowledge with a practical one."

Kollmann looked at him with a mixture of surprise and admiration. "Not bad. You know what's what."

"So you finally agree to that," Lindner mocked. "Yes, I do know something about it, so you can rest assured that tomorrow Bud won't pedal into another scandal. I haven't used any foul medical tricks, but I used a psychological one."

"Again. No end to your surprises."

"Can you keep your mouth shut?"

"I think I've proven that much."

"Okay, listen, Max." The doctor stubbed his cigarette into the brimming ashtray and rubbed his hands. "I told Bud that he shouldn't try for one of the three lead places tomorrow. And since he isn't dumb, he now thinks he's been doped."

"But you can't do that."

"Why not? Did you ever hear of the athlete who, taking a harmless glucose pill, thought he had taken a wonder drug and increased his performance considerably? They've achieved baffling results with entire groups."

"But I'm sure he wanted to know what you gave him."

"Yes and no. He tried. But you must keep in mind two things: first of all, he trusts me. Second, today he added a new experience to all the others. His energy failed him, and he was afraid— something he hasn't experienced before."

"You're right, Martin. I was by his side in the hail and the fog on the Peyresourde, and I was afraid for him."

"I don't think he would've arrived at the finish line without you."

"Perhaps. He certainly wouldn't have been a winner. I had promised myself to never mention Antonelli, but it was the last resort."

Lindner raised his glass. "Let's drink to that. It's almost one o'clock, and they're going to throw us out shortly."

As a matter of fact, only a handful of people were still around, and a yawning waiter opened the windows to the fresh air coming in from the six-thousand-foot summit of the Superbagnères.

Kollmann was yawning as well and looked at his watch. "So he thinks he's been doped."

"At least he doesn't exclude it," said Lindner. "And you can be sure of one thing: It will give him support. In situations like this, they need it, and I'm glad I came. Who knows what kind of stuff he would have been offered."

"But you're always saying that he won't take anything from someone else."

"On principle, no. But this attack of weakness wasn't only a physical phenomenon. It was also a severe shock to his self-confidence. He would've been easy prey to the people with the wonder drugs."

"Not bad at all," said Kollmann. "So he actually got two psychological dopings today."

"If mine works as well as yours, he's going to win the Tour."

"Don't forget, we're only at halftime."

Lindner asked for the bill, and the waiter offered a yawn of relief. "Of course we're only at halftime, but he has the yellow jersey and a clear situation within the team. They're all at his disposal to defend the yellow jersey—even Merlin. Only Bud can bring in the big money, and that's what counts. He's the strongest. The Tour can't be won by the opposition, it can only be lost by him. To put it differently: He would have to break down dramatically in order to lose. If all goes as predicted, he will win."

"In the Tour very little ever goes as predicted," Kollmann growled and got up with some difficulty. "You know that as well as I do."

"You just have to believe in Bud, as I do," said Lindner as they walked through the dark empty streets of Luchon, weaving the entire breadth of it like tired riders approaching a summit.

10

THE TOUR, AVOIDING MAJOR PEAKS, ROLLED OUT OF THE PYRÉNÉES into the plain. In Toulouse Bud was wearing the yellow jersey with the same lead, because Antonelli and his helpers realized quickly that any vigorous assault against the leader, who was protected by the entire Valetta team, was a useless waste of energy. At least for the time being.

Some kind of truce had been declared; it's as much part of the big races as the bitter and all-consuming battles in the mountains. There were instead the tactical skirmishes during which the big names caught their breath while the domestiques had their tongues hanging out, because the brooding heat forced them into a large-scale operation.

Bud was king of the headlines, and his daily mail by now outweighed the proverbial laundry basket. He no longer read all of it, because it would have taken away from his sleeping time; but in Béziers he fished out a letter from old Iribar. It had been postmarked in Eaux-Bonnes.

"Dear Bud," wrote the old man who as a boy had tended sheep on the Tourmalet, "you have surpassed all our expectations. He who has conquered the Tourmalet as you have done brings the yellow jersey to Paris. We're with you in every hour of the day, because you're part of us. You found our house when you felt worse than on the Peyresourde, because you trusted us, and now our trust in you rides along with you. You have no right to disap-point it, hear? In the meantime you will also have noticed that nationality has no part in the Tour de France. It demands the same efforts from all of them, and to those in the lead it grants the same triumphs. But there is only one yellow jersey. That is why you have to put the dry gentian flower, which I put into this letter, into your pocket. I picked it, many years ago, just below the summit of the Tourmalet. It will bring you good luck. Don't forget to take it out, because every evening you'll be given a new yellow jersey. And if you think of the gentian, it will remain this way until Paris. All of us embrace you. Your Iribars."

Bud read the letter three times before putting it into his jersey pocket, together with the gentian flower. He slipped it into the front pocket so he could touch it while on the road, because it was so different from all the other letters, and because he had the same faith in old Iribar as in Doctor Lindner.

Naturally he also read the papers. They were full of compli-ments, but although this was his first Tour he was able to read between the lines. Again and again there were hints of his crisis on the Peyresourde, and they weren't just meant to needle Antonelli. Journalists all over lay in wait for another such breakdown in the man whose lead had been small enough to maintain a constant level of suspense.

One minute. It was equivalent to a few hundredths of a second in an alpine skiing race. Bud knew it very well, and he also knew that the truce would not last beyond Marseilles. There was Mont Ventoux to be taken, and he had no answer to the question of whether on that bare giant of the Provence he would be able to muster the same vigor as on the Tourmalet. Only the truce had its logic: All of them were saving their energy for Mont Ventoux.

For this reason the stage from Béziers to Marseilles turned out to be one of those transit stretches when the leaders maintained a moderate speed and kept a watchful eye on each other, leaving to the domestiques not just the usual work but also the initiative, as long as they were harmless stragglers in the total point count.

But the rule of thumb did not fit this July day on which simmering heat drifted from the coast into the oven of the Provence. They allowed themselves to be hosed down with water, and got off their bikes at gurgling fountains to stick their hot heads into cool well water. The solidarity of galley slaves held them together. Nobody made an attempt to break away from the large pack, which adjusted its tempo to the scorching heat and moved along only because the pact between the organizers and the riders required reaching a goal.

People also dozed in the accompanying cars. Radio Tour permitted itself unusual silences in its coverage and recommended to the drivers not to get lulled by the thirty-kilometer snail's pace, which lay far below the prescribed speed. Max Kollmann was one of those who caught up on their sleep in their reclining seats. An uneventful stage was being run, approaching the inevitable mass sprint in the Stade-Vélodrome of Marseilles like a dried up tired little brook. Kollmann's car was one of the last in the long line of press vehicles. It seemed *une étape pour rien*—a stage for nothing.

All of a sudden a squeak on the radio, and a voice like a whip after all the empty routine bulletins: "Attention. Your attention, please! At kilometer 124 the number 51, Budzinski, had a fall. Make room for the medical cars and the sag wagons. We'll be back with details about the fall in a few minutes."

The fall of the yellow jersey hit the sleepy caravan like an electric shock. Water carriers fall without a noise, and men with ringing names arouse some interest. But the man in yellow makes the alarm go off. Backs straighten and legs begin to turn that until then were only doing only the bare minimum. That is part of the unwritten laws, because only one man can wear yellow, and because yellow is hated by all who don't wear it.

Except for the team that has to protect the yellow: There the alarm triggers different reactions. Whoever is ahead slows down;

whoever is behind stands up on the pedals. And the Valetta sag wagon, its siren howling, races to the spot of the incident. They have dragged Bud into the ditch by the roadside. From the right thigh blood is oozing from a wound, and the yellow jersey is a dirty rag. The front wheel is destroyed, one pedal broken off. Riders keep passing, casting curious glances at the man who up to this moment was their uncontested king. Now he's fair game. Wounded fair game, and if he doesn't get up on a replacement bike this very minute and turn his legs, he'll be surprised how quickly his jersey will change color. Provided he still needs one.

Antonelli has already sounded the attack when Mercier arrives with the sag wagon. Five Valetta riders are around the man on the ground; two are freewheeling out front to wait for Bud and his escort, and only one of them has attached himself to large break-away group led by Antonelli. The Valetta man will try to break their rhythm, but never go into the lead.

It all happens very quickly. One minute and forty-five seconds exactly. Then the man in the yellow jersey is back on a replacement bike. Mercier has bent the knee twice and declared it in working order. And the wound is much less dangerous than the delay of almost two minutes. For all practical purposes, the yellow jersey belongs again to Antonelli.

They push Bud ahead, pour water down his neck, and he's told to draft off the other riders. Out front they take short turns at leading, and very quickly they have caught up to the two waiting Valetta riders. But they are the tail end. Only the mop-up wagon is behind them, and out front Antonelli forces the tempo, and not only with the support of his own team.

Bud sticks to the rear wheel offered to him as if it's the rope that holds together mountain climbers. It is a meticulous technique that you learn on the ovals of the winter indoor tracks. Millimeter precision that allows no distraction. The torso is bent low over the handlebars and the eyes hypnotize the thin rubber of skipping tires. The ears play along as well. They register the click of the gear shift when the chain is moved to a larger or a smaller sprocket, and cause intuitive reactions, to avoid colliding with the rear wheel of the rider ahead, but without losing contact. A few millimeters of air are always between them. A few men in the lead are the locomotive of the team of eight that, halfway between Béziers and Marseille, is taking the yellow jersey in tow.

There are eight of them, and Bud is the only one who doesn't have to expose himself to the burning airstream that makes the tongue dry and the legs heavy. But since there are so many of them, they can effect seven lead changes in one kilometer and bring up the tempo on the level stretch; the speedometers in the car hover between fifty and sixty.

After twenty kilometers they are behind by only one minute and twenty seconds, and Mercier leans far out of the sag wagon to hand Bud an ointment for the injured thigh. He has ordered the medical car, which had tried to fall back to their group, to go ahead. No time for time-consuming treatments, gentlemen. The stuff burns like hell on the untreated wound, but sheltered by the group the pain is not a demoralizing factor. Bud knows that he would be lost by himself, but when they ask him if he can accelerate, he nods. Now and then his glove wipes across his nose when it itches from the sweat that's trickling on his handlebars.

After another twenty kilometers the gap hovers at about one minute, and they pass entire groups because under the furious attack by Antonelli, the field has broken apart. And people along the road are cheering this blue Valetta Express, a yellow jersey in its midst, with imploring enthusiasm.

Sixty kilometers before Marseilles they are behind by forty seconds, and if they can maintain this speed the yellow jersey is safe. But this time-consuming chase in the big gear eats into the infernal rhythm they have imposed on themselves. Little Lemaire, his face beet red, is the first to straighten with a groan and to fall back. Three others follow him, but Merlin, doing most of the lead work, doesn't reduce his speed. He increases it, pushes the other four riders to the limit of their reserves, and when Marseilles announces itself through its suburbs, three blue and one yellow Valetta rider close up to the breakaway group. Ten thousand fans are cheering deliriously. From the loudspeaker car they have been kept informed about every phase of this breathtaking chase, and they celebrate the man in the yellow jersey not only as one of theirs, but as the winner of the Tour de France.

Past the finish line Bud embraces his three teammates. None of them has sprinted to win the stage. They crossed the white line coasting, and they know they have won more than a stage. And Bud knows how close he was to losing the tour.

Marseilles, the sea of stone, gave off the heat like an oven. In the old port the sails were drooping, not a sign of a breeze, and in the crowded bistros of the Canebière the innkeepers declared a state of emergency for cold beverages. Ambulances carried away two reporters from the pressroom; they had suffered a collapse. In the hotels where the bikers were lodged masseurs groaned under the workload, owing less to the heat than to Bud's fall.

On his bed a brand-new yellow jersey lay next to the torn and dirty one. He had not lost a single second of his minute-and-five-second lead. Together with the impressive team performance, they had given him back his strength and morale, although at times he had been close to howling like a wounded animal during the hellish speed they imposed on themselves and on him. Only three of them had stuck it out, because such a forced tempo over a hundred kilometers, and the heat that singed the grass along the road and made the cows low with thirst, weighed down your legs. But cows don't have to run. No animal would be forced to do what we're doing, Bud thought.

That evening the masseur stayed longer than usual. The wounds on his thigh and elbow had been taken care of when Doctor Lindner paid his visit. The time between his personal care and supper with the team was Bud's favorite hour, and Doctor Lindner knew it. He was like a farmer who, after a long day's work, pauses between the stable and the kitchen door. It was a moment of relaxation and reflection after intense pressure when there hadn't even seemed to have been the time for food and drink. But they had to eat, even during the hundred-kilometer chase after Antonelli, because the human combustion engine needs its fuel like any other motor. And it was done in the most uncivilized ways imaginable. They burped and vomited, because a stomach under stress rebels; they pissed while turning their wheels, and there was the chance that for even greater needs there wasn't time to get off the bike. Those are circumstances that provoke the dreaded boil on your buttocks—worse than tearing open an elbow or a thigh.

Doctor Lindner was thinking about this as he examined Bud more carefully than ever. The wounds and the pain they were causing he dismissed as insignificant. Tomorrow Bud would have some difficulty during warm-up but he would find his rhythm; others in that field were tormented by worse symptoms and, from a medical point of view, should be in bed rather than on a bike. Of course Bud was hurting, but the extreme effort of catching up had left no trace. After the exam Doctor Lindner was convinced that Mont Ventoux would not bring about a change in the lead and the total points, and he told Bud this.

Bud was preoccupied with something altogether different. He was aware of how much he had impressed Antonelli once again but he also knew that the real hero of the day was Merlin. His performance as a leader during the chase had the mark of a first-class athlete at his best.

He thought of the Tourmalet and felt uncomfortable about it. There he had abandoned the man who today had rescued him; he had done so in open and unmistakable combat, not wasting another look at him, although Merlin might have been in need of support. Maybe he had a rebellious stomach or some other trouble on the day of the most important stage of the Pyrénées. Between Béziers and Marseilles Merlin had proven that he hadn't been in top shape on the Tourmalet.

"I have a bad conscience about Merlin," Bud said, as he was lying on his bed, wearing only a pair of shorts because of the stifling heat. The white skin of his chest contrasted grotesquely with his deeply tanned arms and legs, as if he had the extremities of a black man.

The physician, packing his bag on the table, looked up in surprise.

"What's all this, Bud? He did normal team work to defend the yellow jersey. You in his place would've done the same. Yellow brings in money, and you're the only one on the Valetta team capable of filling the coffers. They worked in their own interest, not just yours. Neat professional job as it should be, if you ask me."

"That's all very well, doctor. But I know what's on his mind. If he had been in the same shape yesterday as today, I wouldn't have left him behind, and now he's saved me."

"You should have another massage, this time a psychological one," growled Lindner. "For heaven's sake, wear your yellow jersey in the same spirit in which you won it, not like an old woman. Okay, you owe thanks to Merlin. Show him, but don't kiss his feet. He helped you because he was able to and because it was necessary. Tomorrow on the Ventoux he won't be able to, and, as far as I'm concerned, it won't be necessary either."

"I'm hurt," said Bud.

"Don't cry over a few scratches. Once you've warmed up tomorrow, and you'll get warm soon enough, you won't feel a thing; all you have to do is watch out for Antonelli. Vissers, Karstens, and Gosselin lost almost five minutes today, and you know full well that this Tour is only between the Italian and yourself. If you think that he's at an advantage because his leg isn't bandaged, I can't help you."

"And if he dopes himself?"

"Now, listen to me, Bud. You're like a child sulking because he's been smacked. Antonelli knows the mountain is where Tom Simpson died, and tomorrow it will be just as hot as on that day. Doping means taking a considerable risk, and I bet Antonelli wants to win. And so do you. What I'm preparing now and will give you after dinner will help you, but it will pass any doping test. I'll also give you a harmless but effective sleeping pill, because you can't lie on your right side. I'd like to see you in bed by nine-thirty. Is that possible?"

"Of course it is," said Bud and fumbled in the pocket of the dirty yellow jersey for the letter from old Iribar with the dried gentian flower from the Tourmalet. "Is it true, doc, that there's no shade on the Ventoux?"

Lindner nodded. "It's true. It's the mountain of the devil. But you'll manage it just as well as you managed the Tourmalet."

Around midnight the leaden heat of the afternoon was still brooding over the old port of Marseilles; the warm wind was barely perceptible and smelled of brackish water. The fish restaurants served their fare on the sidewalks. People lingered and ordered more wine and water after their meal, because the thought of a stifling-hot hotel room was enough to take your breath away.

Max Kollmann had tried to take a cold bath but gave up because all he got was a lukewarm trickle. Instead, he refreshed his tongue and palate with white wine watered down with cold mineral water, which instantly turned into perspiration on his forehead and chest. They were sitting outside and watched as fishing boats and sailboats rocked on the black water. But it felt as if they were locked up in a ship's bowels, like stokers.

"It's even hotter than the other time," said Kollmann.

"What other time?" Doctor Lindner wiped his forehead with a damp handkerchief.

"When Tom Simpson died. Two kilometers below the summit of the Ventoux. Marseilles–Carpentras. The same route as tomorrow —it should be changed."

"You're crazy, Max. In such a complicated organization you can't change the finish."

"You wouldn't have to." He took a pen from his shirt pocket and scribbled on the paper tablecloth. "Have a look. This is Carpentras, there's the Ventoux. We go through Carpentras, the climb to the Ventoux begins right outside town. We descend on the other side and make the loop back to Carpentras. In consideration of the heat, the organizers ought to eliminate the Ventoux and settle for the arrival in Carpentras. That would be a humane solution, but I'll tell you why it won't be done. TV broadcasts thrive off the Ventoux, and people want to see those shots at home because they can't be had in the Pyrénées or the Alps. You've never seen the mountain, have you?"

Lindner shook his head.

"Well, in this case, be prepared. I know you think that Bud will leave Antonelli behind on the Ventoux, but I'm not so sure. The Italian knows the mountain, and Bud is a novice. I've even advised him to give up the yellow jersey rather than defend it stubbornly on the Ventoux, of all places. So what if he loses a minute? He can easily make it up in the Alps, and the big time trial in the last stage is his strongest event, which Antonelli won't be able to match."

"I still think he should defend the yellow jersey by all means. His injuries are harmless, and his physique is in top shape. Antonelli doesn't know this. Maybe he'll consider the injuries more serious and, being aggressive, he'll overdo it."

"Let him," Kollmann muttered and poured fresh water into his wine. "All you guys see is yellow. You don't have a clue about tactics. Of course all of Germany will be glued to the screen to celebrate Bud's big victory on the Ventoux. But nobody imagines that the man will have to resort to energy reserves that could fail him tomorrow, after the spill, which I don't consider quite as harmless as you do. And who's taking the heat into account? It doesn't bother anyone in front of a TV screen, but what a thrill in all the living rooms, when the riders are going to fall off their bikes on the Ventoux like tired flies. Contented potbellies sit in comfortable armchairs to get their kicks from the humanly impossible. I'm telling you the Ventoux is inhuman and should be canceled in this heat. It could be done without any difficulty, but they won't do it.

Since the Pyrénées the show has lacked drama—not counting Bud's big chase, which was due only to a stupid coincidence. The Ventoux is a staged scenario. It guarantees high drama."

"Aren't you saying all this because you're afraid for Bud?" The doctor's eyes were skeptical under a wrinkled forehead.

"Nonsense," Kollmann grumbled. "Just take a good look at the Ventoux. I'm covering it for the fifth time, and I know what I'm talking about. Tomorrow they'll be chased through hell six thousand feet above where we're sitting right now. Maybe the breeze we thought we'd get by the sea will blow on the summit, but the price for that cool breeze is too high. They should have taken out the edge of this stage. Tomorrow night you'll agree with me."

11

AT TEN O'CLOCK IN THE MORNING THEY LEAVE MARSEILLES; ITS stones haven't cooled down overnight and once again reflect blazing heat. Theoretically they all could have had a good rest; twelve hours' sleep was possible. But in stifling hotel rooms they have tossed and turned, and many, if they got only half the sleep they had wanted, could consider it a good night. And doping kept them up as well. Hot nights are a pest to those who take pills regularly. And also to those with injuries. One of the two legs that have to propel the yellow jersey has trouble during the first kilometers.

Kollmann, who is keeping close to the pack, sees it; he's surprised that Antonelli doesn't attack right away. Bud will warm up, but he's vulnerable in this first phase of the stage, and if he should have to fend off an attack, he'll have to sacrifice energy he'll need at the Ventoux. But nothing happens; the explanation is simple. The Ventoux slows them down. They roll toward it as if it were a sinister enemy whose treacherousness will demand more of them than what they have to give.

After forty kilometers, which take them an hour and twenty-five minutes, Kollmann is sure that Bud doesn't have to fear anything from the Ventoux. He has warmed up without expending energy. Right now the pack is stalking it as if there were some miraculous chance to outwit it. Only when the mountain is upon them will the pack break apart.

"Let's go ahead," he says to his driver. "If they go on dawdling like this, and I bet they will, you can go straight to Carpentras and pick up an hour on them. The real race will start afterward, and we can have a nice break in some bistro."

It's a wonderful feeling to speed along closed roads where there are no dangers lurking in the curves and the wind blows at you from the open sunroof. It takes away your breath, but also the heat and the sweat. Without having put in any effort, you sense something of the exhilaration that takes the biker on a downhill stretch.

Radio Tour is fading as they approach the town of Carpentras. After ten or fifteen kilometers the power of the short-wave radio gives out. But it is enough to let them know that the pack keeps dawdling along. In Carpentras the sun is already high and the shutters are closed as if a hostile army were marching in. But the whole population is out in the streets. It's a privilege to see the Tour come through twice. No other town on the Tour has it. A street festival with an encore, because once they have crossed town, they climb the Ventoux; its barren and intimidating shape is visible from everywhere, and no unified pack will return from it, but a succession of men, broken into many groups and totally worn out. The people of Carpentras know their mountain as well as the people of Sainte-Marie-de-Campan know the Tourmalet. But they are not mountain farmers, and Mont Ventoux is very different. The dirty white on the summit is not snow but sun-bleached volcanic rock. Around it are the flatlands of the Provence, because this mountain is a creation from hell. A brutally barren cone, almost six thousand feet high.

The people of Carpentras also know its diabolic atmospheric conditions on hot days like this one. As if its glowing flanks repel all oxygen and render it more inaccessible to the panting lungs of those conquering the summit. Even cars begin to stutter and stall, their radiators steaming. Could it be that the human engine is stronger? It remains to be seen, and the fat innkeeper at the entrance of Carpentras swears by it. Planning ahead, he has stocked crates and crates of beer in his basement, but the take-out sales beat all records; the road is black with people. When Kollmann and his driver arrive to take a little break, only lukewarm lemonade is to be had. They wash down sandwiches, thin and long like a child's arm, and even find room at the counter because most people are expecting the riders outside, under the burning sun.

According to the program they ought to be here by now. But this program was thought up many months ago in some cool Paris editorial office, without taking into account the stifling heat of this July day. So the riders tarry before the dread of the Ventoux, and after the lemonade and the sandwich, Kollmann still has time to light a cigarette and watch the beer bellies that couldn't face even three hundred feet of the Ventoux before ending in a ditch by the roadside.

His forehead exudes pearls of perspiration; the blue column before a red background on some aperitif poster has reached its limit: 105 degrees. Sluggish bluebottles crawl across sticky smudges on the counter.

Kollmann wipes the sweat, and not only his own. Every time the fat fellow in the net undershirt pounds his fist on the counter to make his point that bikers are immune to the heat, Kollman gets sprayed with drops of salty sweat oozing from rolls of fat. It makes leaving easier. They drive through town slowly, where not only people on their two legs are out to await the Tour. There is a frail grandpa in his wheelchair. They have tied a wet kerchief over his Basque beret to forestall heatstroke, and driving past them, Kollmann has to think of the large cabbage leaves bikers used to put under their caps; they looked like elephant ears.

He drank his lemonade too quickly and lets out a big burp, smelling of artificial lemon. But he hardly notices it because the whole car reeks of a mix between market stand and kitchen. Most lunches are eaten on the road, and lot of garbage ends up under the seats. It's about time we dug out the rotting peaches, he thinks.

Slowly they are driving through the shady pine forests outside Carpentras. When they thin out and no longer offer shade from the

sun, the riders come closer, still a solid pack. They have pedaled
through the town where they'll sleep tonight, where everything is
being prepared for their well-being. Only the Ventoux, boys, and
you've got it made. In the hotel kitchens fresh fish is lying on
blocks of ice, mountains of juicy steak and the finest vegetables.
And to drink: anything you could wish for. But first the Ventoux. It
has slowed them down until Carpentras, and within the peloton
they felt something like the comfort of home. But that's over now.

Many have been unsuccessful in controlling their thirst. How
can you turn down all the bottles handed to you from the rows of
people when your parched tongue only tastes salty sweat and the
sizzling air deludes you with mirages? The careful ones take just a
sip and then pour the cold mineral water over their head and neck,
but many have downed the bottles without quenching their thirst.
It wobbles in their stomachs and not everybody is strong enough to
avoid a cramp. As a result not everybody is strong enough to take
on the mountain, which they have had in front of their eyes for
many kilometers, like a nightmarish vision. As they come out of the
forest the mountain confronts them with all its cruel barrenness,
and they dare not lift their eyes to the dirty white summit.

The heat attacks them head-on as much as the rising road, not
yet bleached by the sun, and they suffer from lack of oxygen in
their panting lungs. The legs cranking them into a moonscape turn
to lead. No bush can survive here; even the smallest thistle withers.
But instead of going quailing, the riders enter into battle. Mont
Ventoux splits the field apart as if it were wielding a hatchet. There
are men who break away, as if it were a mountain like any other.
They even stay in their saddles, a baffling and unreal spectacle. Do
they have rocket fuel in their veins, because they manage to pull so
light-footedly ahead of those who are sweating blood and tears?

The road eating its way into the sides of the mountain with wide
serpentine loops is so narrow that no car can attempt a pass. Like
many others, Kollmann has gone ahead to take advantage of the
views the Ventoux grants to the observer. The ascending peloton

can be seen in its entirety from some favorable spots. It has torn apart by several kilometers, and with a mixture of satisfaction and nervousness Kollmann sees the yellow jersey gleam in the group out front.

He counts sixteen riders, among them Antonelli and Merlin and the Spanish mountain fleas who are thinking only of the points toward the mountain prize. In choppy spurts they try to break away, but the others immediately take a butt break. No gap is opening in the group, and Kollmann hopes that Bud will remember his advice. Whoever depletes his reserves too early on the Ventoux is hopelessly lost.

Fortunately the mountain fleas use the small ammunition of a low gear. Their fierce strokes don't surpass Bud's steady progress in a bigger gear; but does he have the strength to maintain his rhythm in this heat and on the steep gradient? They are still in the lower third of the moonscape, not yet at the infamous pockets where the burning air doesn't seem to contain any oxygen.

Sport? It's the devil's kitchen; an anteroom to hell, and all who led the riders into it should be locked up. That's what Kollmann thinks, and he watches from his lookout point as the breakaway group gets smaller. Only a dozen, and behind them smaller or larger groups absorbing one after the other single rider. And in a switchback on a lower level he sees the remaining riders, who can begin to measure their deficit in kilometers.

Halfway up the mountain now there are only six, and their sag wagons put themselves directly behind them. None of them will have to drop out because of a breakdown, but what good is the protection trailing behind them when what should be a road turns into a heap of fiery coal?

Bud has been careful with his intake of liquids. Maybe too careful, he thinks. A sweating body needs water and nourishment, and a spell of weakness could lie in ambush after every bend. On a mountain like this one, eating is impossible. Fourfold is your hold on the bike, which has to be heaved uphill: twice on the handlebars, twice on the pedals. He doesn't feel the injured thigh, but the elbow hurts under the pressure from his arms and hands.

Food is out. On the plain he ate, without much appetite, rice cakes and some fruit; now there is just the brew he had concocted with Doctor Lindner that morning. "A concentrate of everything you'll need," the doctor had said. "But wait till you get to the Ventoux."

He had even waited till the last third of the mountain. Now, every few hundred feet, he sips from his bottle. Not more than a spoonful; it takes no time at all, and he can maintain his rhythm. He has shifted down. Not as low as the two Spaniards, who are spinning wildly, but he is aware that on the first half of the mountain he rode in too high a gear. Now the heavy legs have resumed their rhythm; four kilometers below the summit, that's a good sign.

Others show signs of exhaustion. A kilometer farther up, where the rows of spectators thicken, there are only three out front, Perez, the Spaniard, Antonelli, and Bud. Merlin, who has climbed much more impressively than in the Pyrénées, has paid for his rescue efforts on behalf of Bud the day before. Another two kilometers to the peak. They can already see the observatory and its large dome, when Antonelli caves in, beaten by the heat and the spurts of the Spaniard.

Bud straightens up, and from behind he hears Mercier shout: "*Vas-y, Bud! Il est cuit! C'est dans la poche!*—Go for it, Bud, he's finished! You've made it!"

He turns around. A hundred yards behind, the Italian is zigzagging across the narrow corridor the spectators have left open; his are desperate and unrhythmic motions that don't lie. Mercier is right, the man is finished. Bud hesitates only for a moment. Should he throw all his strength into the last two kilometers? What strength? Whatever the devil's mountain has left him. He reaches for the bottle, takes a sip, and lets the Spaniard break away by thirty feet. Perez thinks he has shaken off the last rival and puts in one of those special shows that have always depressed the competition and consolidated the fame of the kings of the mountains. It earns him ninety yards' lead. But it is not an unbridgeable gap, because Bud takes on the challenge: He feels that he still has the energy for roughly two kilometers up the mountain. When Perez turns around, proud as the torrero after the final stab, he realizes he has only placed the banderillas—they don't kill, they just provoke.

He comes not quickly but steadily. He even sits in the saddle as if this were not the final sprint for the Ventoux but a lap on a velodrome. Even if every stroke on the pedals tears the shoulders wearing the yellow jersey from one side of the road to the other, he does not swerve. It is the unmistakable sign of the strong man on the mountain. In the next curve they are again side by side and behind them a gaping void.

Bud is satisfied. When fifteen hundred feet below the summit the Spaniard begins to sprint for the mountain points, Bud does not resist. The slate board on the motorbike indicates that in two kilometers he has gained a minute and forty seconds. He takes the last sip from his bottle and it tastes like the champagne of victory. The summit of the Ventoux. The corridor is narrow and they pat him on the shoulders from both sides; they make room for him only when the legs are allowed to rest and the mountain offers thanks with a dizzying downhill race.

Bud accepts the thanks as he has never done before. The rest is child's play: From the galley he has moved to a litter, and he lets himself be carried down to Carpentras, where he will win this stage. Of course he will. The Spaniard is not nearly as good a downhill racer as he is a climber; Bud left him behind after two curves, and even if the man approached one more time, he'd beat him in a final sprint.

Once again he comes in first, as on the Peyresourde, only this time he is not being hunted and no hail pelts him from the clear sky of the Provence. He gulps down the wind, his mouth open; at this height it cools him off, and the big dark patches of perspiration disappear from the yellow jersey. Once more it gleams before he enters the forest and the road becomes wider.

Elated by the triumph, he forgot to put the newspaper between the jersey and his chest. So what? The Ventoux is high but the environment is not that of the snowy mountains, and only the ascent is treacherous. Now the mountain rewards all pains with ever more gentle curves through which you can dance without applying more than a slight pressure on the brakes, as long as your eye is clear and your equilibrium intact.

After the pine forests comes the plain. A few more kilometers, and their slight descent makes them child's play, just right for the largest gear. Whoever hasn't been worn out by the Ventoux can crank out a tempo of sixty kilometers an hour. Bud can. He prolongs the exhilaration of the downhill and pushes into that of the plain. The sweat, blown away earlier, returns, but he doesn't feel it, because he can draw on energy he didn't know he had on the summit. He also doesn't know what damage he has done behind him when he lets go of the handlebars, throwing up his arms and crossing the finish line in Carpentras.

Could there be any doubts about this being the big divide? In addition to his delay of a minute and forty seconds on the mountain Antonelli, visibly stressed by the trial, lost another minute and fifty seconds during the descent. For Bud this meant a lead of four minutes and fifteen seconds, and wearing the yellow jersey unchallenged. Third place was behind by almost seven minutes, and Merlin, who made up lost time during a breakneck descent, was now in fifth, eight minutes and forty seconds behind. Things looked good for the Valetta team, and Mercier's bulldog face beamed like the lights of a country fair.

The pressroom with its heavy vaults looked like the basement of a fortress, although it was the refectory of a former monastery. Max Kollmann had to work overtime and had to cancel dinner with Doctor Lindner. The editors reserved an entire page for him, because the yellow fever in Germany was rising to new heights.

He'd pounded out twelve pages already, but there was still something to be said about the man who on the previous day seemed lost and by now was almost guaranteed to win the Tour de France. Kollmann sweated, though the spot behind the thick monastery walls was the coolest in all of Carpentras.

He had exchanged only a few words with Bud at the finish line. But it was enough. He could elaborate and embellish the interview, because he had been witness to the vigorous yet controlled battle on the devil's mountain as much as to the explosive satisfaction at the finish line. But Kollmann was an old hand. "*Qui rit vendredi, dimanche pleurera*," said a French proverb he remembered. "He who laughs on Friday will cry on Sunday." He heard his colleagues scream in all languages into the telephone shells that the Tour has been decided, because Budzinski had defeated his most dangerous rival on the Ventoux, regardless of his handicap the previous day.

The language of the men who had to interpret high drama with a zest comparable to the tempo of the biker racing downhill was flowery and emotional, so much so that it made the breakfast coffee taste salty. It went down well even though perhaps you should not judge the style by literary standards. The reporters sprinted toward going to press like bikers toward the finish line. And down-to-earth roughness was part of it.

Hoarsely, Kollmann explained to his colleagues on the night shift that they wouldn't get another line out of him and, furthermore, they could kiss his ass. He slammed down the receiver in legitimate anticipation of a late meal. He was one of the last to leave the pressroom, which reeked of cold tobacco and beer. A brewery had donated it by the case. And he waded through red, blue, and white photocopies of briefings that all said the same thing: Budzinski was sure to win the race. "*Qui rit vendredi, dimanche pleurera.*" Kollmann remembered the proverb again, although there was no good reason for it. Antonelli, in his quest for the yellow jersey, had been shaken off, done in more by the heat than by the mountain, and to all appearances he had been definitely defeated. There weren't any other powerful rivals, keeping in mind Bud's superiority on the mountain and his unquestioned skill in time trials. Nobody could beat him in the race against the clock during the final stage, if he remained well and healthy.

There were still the Alps, to be sure. But those two stages were not threats since the organizers, moved perhaps by some humane impulse after the considerable effort of the Ventoux, did not want to push the race onto the highest snowpeaks. And Bud had proven that even at critical elevations above fifty-four hundred feet he retained his rhythm and his punch. Everything spoke in favor of the man who had defended the yellow jersey on the Ventoux with impressive daring. Nevertheless, Kollmann could not bring himself to join the euphoria that had taken over the Valetta team.

Hunger drove away these thoughts, but then it was Lindner who drove away the hunger. He ran into the doctor under the large archway of the monastery.

"I'm glad I found you, Max. I was afraid I'd have to look for you in every restaurant."

"Something wrong with Bud?"

"A lot actually. He has a fever over 101."

Kollmann looked at him, not understanding. "You're out of your mind, Martin. Say that again."

"Over 101. I'm not joking."

"Shall we go see him?"

"No. He's asleep. I've done everything that can be done. With luck, he can start tomorrow. But nobody must get wind of it, otherwise they'll attack from all sides and finish him off."

"Of course," said Kollmann, "not a word. Tell me more. I really wanted to go eat something, but my appetite is gone. There are too many ears in a restaurant. Let's walk around for a while."

They walked through the dark alleys of Carpentras; there was light from the occasional bistro, where the great stage that had probably decided the outcome of the Tour was being discussed. Experts as well as the man on the street, who understands a lot about the riders on the road, were in total agreement.

"Why does he have a fever?" asked Kollmann, "overexertion?"

"Foolishness. Unforgivable stupidity. On the summit of the Ventoux he enjoyed the wind instead of protecting himself against it. He raced down like a champion, but also like a beginner."

"What do you mean? He demolished Antonelli."

"That's true. But he forgot his newspaper in his pocket, the idiot. That's like jumping into cold water when you're in a sweat. Putting the paper between his jersey and chest would've protected him, and since this jersey is yellow there are all kinds of reasons to defend it with more than just pedaling legs. Bud hasn't yet learned all the lessons of a champion, and if he's caught pneumonia, it's the end."

"What an ass," said Kollmann.

Lindner nodded. "If he could stay in bed for a few days, it would be very simple. But tomorrow he has to be on his bike again, and nobody must know what's up."

"And what did you give him?"

"I already told you, Max. Everything that's possible. And if you want to know the whole truth: more than what's permitted."

Kollmann stopped. It was on a street corner next to a bistro from where accordion music and the laughter of girls reached them. The sleepy little town of Carpentras was still celebrating the Tour and the big winner of the day.

"You've given him more than what's allowed? What was it?"

The physician took his arm and pulled him along. "Listen to me carefully and keep it to yourself. Yes, I've doped him if you go by the senseless list of 250 medications the masterminds of sports have put together. But when a physician makes a diagnosis, he does not have to go by that list but by the effectiveness of the medicine. His professionalism requires this, and no sports organization can change that."

"There's also nobody in the world who would buy that theory."

"So be it. You know as well as I do that tricky cases exist, where doping isn't doping but a medical necessity. All of a sudden a rider has taken sick and it isn't some water carrier but the number one of the Tour. The yellow jersey, everybody's target. He's chosen a difficult profession and he belongs to the few who are worth the effort. Winning the Tour will earn him half a million; maybe even more, if you consider the top fees of the winter season. At the moment, all of this is hanging by a very thin thread. All will have been for nothing if he has a fever when he gets on his bike tomorrow, and the competition smells the rat."

"You don't have to lecture me on the mentality of bikers," growled Kollmann. "I could teach you a thing or two about them."

"I know, I know, Max. So you know that I can't cure him with herbal tea and homemade compresses. We have one night, that's all. Do you think I came to stand by as they rip the yellow jersey off his shoulders?"

""Well, then, stop beating around the bush."

"I would've finished long ago," said Lindner, "if you didn't interrupt me all the time. What I've done is not only logical but also legitimate; for example, I would've ordered the same thing for you because you too are stressed out. Ever heard of ephedrine?"

"I wasn't born yesterday," mumbled Kollmann. "It's pretty high on the doping list."

"Exactly. And do you know why? Because the trainers who know as much about medicine as you and I know of nuclear physics carry it around in their little cases by the pound. And they don't have to buy it on the black market either. A child can buy it without prescription in any pharmacy. It should follow that every able-bodied adult under the sun ought to be free to take it."

Kollmann nodded. "Seems that way."

"Here's the catch. Those shady characters with their little suitcases have no idea about the dosage, nor do they know the specific constitution of the biker in their care. Ideally, every biker should travel with his personal physician who knows him inside out. But that's not possible, and you know yourself how overworked the four Tour physicians are."

"You were talking about ephedrine."

"At the correct dosage, which is a question of milligrams, it's without a doubt conducive to high performance. But I didn't give it to Bud for that reason, and nothing could be worse than a constant diet of stimulants. Burnout would be unavoidable in the case of permanent achievers like Bud. I gave him ephedrine because there's no better medication against this kind of cold; you also have to keep in mind that he doesn't spend his eight-hour workday in an office but on a racing bike. I'm hoping for a multiple effect, if you know what I mean."

"I'm not stupid. But I can read between the lines; you're not talking about a guarantee."

"Aren't you expecting too much at this point? I can't turn the pedals for him any more than you can. But since I know his physiology better than you do, I'm convinced of the legitimacy of my medical treatment. Instead of committing a crime I've done something extremely reasonable."

"Sounds good. And you think it'll be enough?"

"Not quite, Max. Bud's clean, as far as medications are concerned. In special cases like his, you can do more for him than for Antonelli, who's been in the business for a longer time and perhaps broke down on the Ventoux because he's taken too much."

"Still, I haven't written him off. Experience, too, is a weapon, and I'll eat my hat if he doesn't smell a problem with Bud tomorrow."

"Well, eat your hat. Bud's eaten something else that he'll digest more easily."

"More doping?"

"Stop using that stupid word. We have to get the fever down without weakening him. I also gave him Testoviron."

What's that?"

"An androgen. They stimulate the metabolism of the heart muscle. They encourage the flow of blood and therefore increase heart efficiency. They generally tone the entire circulation and are an excellent counteragent for a general depressive condition. And you'll agree that tomorrow Bud will need a boost."

"But that stuff is also on the doping list, isn't it?"

"Why don't you worry about your supper instead?" said Lindner. "Goddamn it, I've taken it upon myself to take medical care of somebody who couldn't be cured with Grandma's home remedies, because he can't stay in bed tomorrow. That's not doping, only professional medical care. If Bud, at this moment, had to rely on Mercier or his masseur, he might as well give up."

Kollmann stopped. "Everything you say sounds reasonable, Martin, and I also know that nobody knows Bud's physique as well as you do. But aren't you making a guinea pig out of him? Isn't there a good deal of medical curiosity in everything you're doing?"

"You shouldn't have said that," Lindner flared up and his eyes flashed anger. "You understand your job, but I also understand mine. Do you think I got into a fight with my wife and came here just to stand by to see the kid get into something from which nobody could rescue him? What good is it to him if tomorrow night you pull all the emotional strings in describing to the readers how at kilometer 112 he dropped off his bike totally exhausted, with a high fever? I didn't give him stimulants, I medicated him."

"Good heavens, Martin, I'm the last one to question your abilities, but we mustn't forget that he can't risk a positive doping test after everything that's happened."

"And why should he? Everything is at stake, and the risk is so small that we have to take it."

"Of course he won't be among the first three places and therefore be marked for an automatic doping test. He won't ride this stage as the man in yellow but as a gray mouse. Today he won, but tomorrow they'll say: 'Also ran: Budzinski.' It's enough that he will be part of the large pack, and I guarantee you that there will be no battles tomorrow that might effect the overall standings. They are all trying to get over the Ventoux; you don't digest that one like a minor peak. But you can count on this truce only if no one notices what's ailing Bud."

"I can't give you a guarantee that nobody will catch wind, but I can guarantee that everything has been done to camouflage Bud's handicap. And I have the best conscience in the world, because I know what's happening elsewhere and because I've done nothing else but medicate him."

Kollmann made a face. "I'm not hearing this for the first time. *'Je me soigne'*, say the aces. I medicate myself, because I'm an ace. And if a little guy does it, it's called doping. It's that simple."

"Not bad, Max. There you have it in a nutshell. You could also talk about stabilizing the achievement factor and about stimulants. I have an interesting example. Ever heard of Coramin?"

Kollmann nodded. "Troussellier explained it to me once. It stimulates the metabolism and respiration and is supposed to be rather harmless, right?"

"Right. That's the reason you can buy it over the counter."

"Then why's it on the doping list?"

"Once it was canceled, and then put on again. In 1974, I think, and I can also tell you why. Orderlies injected the stuff by the canteenful and then were nonplussed if the poor devils, full of the stuff, didn't sit on their bikes like titans but got muscle spasms in their arms and legs."

Kollmann nodded thoughtfully. "I've seen such Saint Vitus' dances."

"There you go." Lindner raised his shoulders and with outstretched hands indicated helplessness. "It's quite a difference between a champion under medical supervision who's taking a carefully calibrated dose and a mediocre rider who swallows uncontrollably or shoots up. Injections are more and more common. Just look at the guys in the shower. The stings you see are not from mosquitoes, and their calculations are hair-raising."

"What kind of calculations?"

"Stupid ones. They do it by the rule of thumb. If champion X takes so much, I'll double it and will beat him. And if that's not enough, I'll triple the dose. They want victory through chemistry, get it? That's what leads to those Saint Vitus' dances."

"Wrecks, I'd say."

"That too. You'd be surprised at the numbers of addicts who skid from one overdose into the next and convince themselves that they can't get into the saddle without a shot. And the masseurs are careful to put a smokescreen before medical explanations. Thousands of medications will be invented, but never the shot that will provide talent and class."

"You're beginning to convince me," replied Kollmann. "And I have a hunch that I'll need either a shot from you or something to eat."

Lindner grinned. "Better eat. You don't have to win the Tour."

"The guy who intends to win it has cost me many a meal—this isn't the first time."

They found a restaurant that still served cold dishes, and Lindner kept Kollmann company until a grouchy innkeeper, with a demonstrative yawn, brought the bill. Outside, they looked up to the Ventoux and its black outline rising like a cone into a starry sky.

"It'll be hot again," said Kollmann.

12

EVEN IF THE STRETCH BETWEEN PROVENCE AND THE FOOT OF THE Alps didn't present major obstacles and there weren't any attacks, it would be a difficult day for Bud. They all had the Ventoux in their limbs. This year the Tour made a relatively small sortie into the Alps, but between Gap and Briançon they would have to face the dreaded Col de l'Izoard, at seven thousand feet the highest elevation of the Tour. Allos and Vars, the two six-thousand-foot mountains, were canceled from the route of this smaller stage in the high mountains. It was to be a difficult day for Bud because in every little rise he felt that wretched weakness in the back of his knees caused by the fever. And he could not retreat into the long drawn-out field, but had to control any breakaway attempt from the front. Those are the unavoidable duties of the man in yellow; it was his good luck that he had all the blue bodyguards of the Valetta team around him, and that nobody had the urge to break away in this stifling oven of Provence. The water carriers didn't miss a single fountain, and from the street cafés they swiped bottles by the dozen, paying nothing more than a friendly smile. They had no difficulties catching up with the field after such raids, the only ones tolerated by the owners of the cafés.

It was a small miracle that nobody noticed how much of an effort even this tempo, which a strong country mailman could have sustained for a while, caused the man in yellow, but there were plausible reasons. The Valetta team shielded him in their midst and allowed no investigative approach to his rear wheel. They swarmed around him like hornets to disguise the shifting of gears that was an unmistakable sign of weakness in a man who was known to take on the most vicious gradients in high gear. The man in yellow also owed this lack of attention from the competition to his brilliant performance on the Ventoux. What do you hope to gain on a flat stretch from someone who had stormed the devil's mountain under searing heat as if he had grown wings?

Therefore Bud, screened by his team, smuggled himself through the stage between Carpentras and Gap, and his weakness would have gone unnoticed completely if the dawdling hadn't come to a sudden end twenty kilometers before Gap. The distance was insignificant; the success of the operation amazing. During the twenty-kilometer chase, not even initiated by Antonelli, Bud lost fifty seconds.

Antonelli was fuming. Of course he had tagged along and, without sprinting for the stage victory, had made up almost a minute in his total point count. In twenty kilometers. What couldn't he have gained if they had been more aggressive? He cursed his two gregarios, his personal attendants, whom he had ordered to watch every move of the man in yellow.

"You slept, you assholes. If you had been alert, we would've known after a few kilometers that he's spent, and I'd be wearing the yellow jersey now. He would've arrived in the mop-up wagon, you idiots."

At dinner he was still raging and throwing against the wall the plates from which his maligned servants hoped to eat their dinner. Finally his team manager succeeded in calming him with an extremely convincing argument. Tomorrow they were riding into Briançon, and the Tour would see a significant and unexpected turn of events. Briançon, that was almost home. Thousands of fans would pour across the border to cheer Antonelli's big victory, maybe even the yellow jersey. At the place where Gino Bartali and Fausto Coppi had celebrated their greatest victories.

The thought of tomorrow and the two old *campionissimi* improved Antonelli's mood. It even made him euphoric, after he had his massage. Coppi had been the last *campionissimo*. There had been Baldini, Nencini, Gimondi, and also Moser, the man from the Tirol, but in the hearts of the masses, none of them had occupied a place as the likes of Bartali and Coppi. But he, Mario Antonelli, would find it, when he would conquer the yellow jersey tomorrow in Briançon.

Because the *campionissimo* had to be a man of the mountains. That was also the reason why the Giro d'Italia always ended in the Dolomites. Twice he had won it, and every time he had launched his big attack at the Stilfser Pass. But the Tour de France outshone the Giro, and tomorrow was the day he could win it. Only tomorrow counted. Forget the Ventoux and everything else. Mario Antonelli, who at the beginning of this Tour had tried to eliminate Ernst Budzinski with a spiked water bottle, kissed the golden amulet he was wearing around his neck and crossed himself.

At the same time Mercier, Kollmann, and Lindner were sitting in Bud's hotel room. The doctor had free access, and since Pau the team manager tolerated Kollmann—without, however, hiding his dislike for reporters. Especially if they had come from Germany. And ever since Bud won the yellow jersey, they were descending like locusts. The German press had discovered the Tour de France, sending yellow flames across the Rhine, inflaming the patriots as if they'd won the World Cup. No Altig, no Thurau had achieved that much; each day new reporters arrived, posing unsolvable problems for Lafitte, chief of the Tour press corps.

But also for the three men sitting at Bud's bedside. "Those guys are full of arrogant ignorance," scolded Mercier. "They're only after a story at the end of a stage. The race doesn't interest them, only Bud, and if they catch as much as three words from him, they have a page-long interview. If I don't ask for police protection, he won't catch a moment's sleep, and I wouldn't be surprised if one of them were hiding under the bed or in the closet."

He actually knelt down by the bed where Bud was resting with new bandages on his thigh and elbow. For the first time since he had struggled for twenty kilometers to arrive at the little town of Gap, a smile lit up Bud's face when his team manager got up, groaning.

"Aren't you exaggerating a little, Monsieur Mercier? Is everybody in a panic because I lost fifty seconds? Don't forget, it could have been five minutes. Nobody noticed that I was empty as a squeezed lemon; without the help of Doctor Lindner I would've ended up in the mop-up wagon."

The bulldog face didn't return the smile. "And don't forget that you acted like a total beginner. The summit of the Ventoux for you was the top of the world, at your command. Like some grandiose halfwit you rode into the wind instead of putting the paper in your jersey like every amateur does. And I hadn't noticed because at ninety kilometers an hour, I can't act as your nanny."

Before Bud could reply, Doctor Lindner stepped in. "Don't you think we should deal with the present facts instead of mistakes? It's Bud's first Tour, he's wearing the yellow jersey, and nothing has been lost. I'm confident that he will bring it to Paris."

"Tell these fairy tales to your grandmother," demurred Mercier. "At the end of tomorrow's stage, there's the Izoard, but that doesn't mean any more to you than to Bud, because it's also your first Tour. In his current condition he'll lose fifteen minutes on the Izoard, if he gets to see it at all."

"He'll not only see it, he'll conquer it. I gave him a thorough exam before you so graciously interrupted his recovery with your wise observations. It yielded better results than you'd imagine."

"Yielded results," Mercier huffed. "I'm not interested in your results. I know what Bud was worth today, and tomorrow you'll read in every paper that he wasn't able to even climb a molehill."

"We're probably also going to read about doping," Kollmann interjected.

"Doping? He didn't get checked."

"I mean conjectures. We no longer have the same Tour journalism as twenty years ago. Mercier is right. There are would-be detectives out there who have no idea that there's air in a tire but see in every rider a robot stuffed full with drugs. And don't forget that we kept Bud's cold a top secret. Nobody had even as much as an inkling, and now there are two camps in the press center: One thinks that he was just indisposed because he had overdone it the day before. The other swears that only with the help of doping did he win the Ventoux stage with such a lead. There are rumors that Antonelli has requested an extraordinary doping check."

"He of all people," hissed Bud and sat up.

Lindner pushed him down again by the shoulders. "Stay calm, kid. There are no extraordinary doping checks. That'll be the day, when any rider could make another one take an official piss as he pleased."

"I don't think Antonelli is that stupid," said Kollmann. "That doesn't come from him but from his entourage. Could also be reporter gossip. What's important is that tomorrow Bud gives the right answer to all this speculation. The whole camp is electrically charged."

"And I'm telling you that Bud will defend the yellow jersey on the Izoard," said Lindner.

"Even though the slightest knoll tested his strength today? Can't you even imagine how Antonelli could have taken advantage of the situation?"

"Forget today, Mercier. He was lucky. He paid with fifty seconds when it could have cost him a lot more. We all know that. But the illness is gone. Bud recovers more quickly than anybody else, even if you don't want to hear about my test results."

"All right, all right, doctor." Mercier got up and crushed his cigarette in the ashtray. "You know how stressful such a stage is for the team manager. I'll continue my housecalls now; see you at dinner, Bud."

Bud nodded. It took some time before Kollmann took up the conversation again. "Are you really sure Bud's over it, Martin?"

Lindner nodded. "I've risked strong medication, and if it hadn't been for that stupid chase outside Gap, nobody would've noticed. Temperature, pulse, circulatory system—all is completely back to normal."

"That's what you say. But tomorrow he'll be a target. On the Izoard, of all places. The only advantage I can think of is that they've eliminated the Allos and the Vars. If you have two six-thousand-foot mountains in your legs before the Izoard, it's a hellish place."

"It comes last?"

"Yes. Whoever has the lead on the Izoard will win the stage in Briançon. All you have ahead of you is the descent. You also have to reckon with the support that's expecting Antonelli. From Briançon it's a stone throw to Italy. The town will be swarming with Italians, and if you know Antonelli, you know he can push himself for a spectacular coup."

"Do you also know," said Bud, putting a suitcase under his feet to raise them higher than his heart, "that I have the means to blow him apart?"

"Well," mumbled Kollmann, "I know what you mean. But I don't like it, and it would be useless."

Bud sat up abruptly. "Do you want to forget the dirty mess he concocted against me with Benotti?"

"Of course not, Bud. But I'd like to explain to you why all of a sudden you're remembering the dirty trick, and why I don't consider it appropriate to fight him with other weapons. Look, in the Pyrénées I had to spur you on with the Antonelli business, to keep you in the saddle. You won the yellow jersey that day and afterward saw no reason why you should take action against him. With the exception of legitimate battle, of course. But now, just because you fear this fight, you want to resort to other means by which he could be eliminated."

"And you don't consider those legitimate?"

Kollmann looked after the smoke of his cigarette. "In your place I'd stick with the duel on the road. Do you seriously think that Antonelli would be disqualified if you, several days after the event, come out with a shocking accusation? 'A burned-out rider seeks revenge, or justification,' if you like; that's what they're going to think. And don't think for a minute that the race management will do something about it. First the witness Benotti has to be brought in from Italy, and in the meantime the Tour has arrived in Paris. It has to keep rolling and can't tolerate protests of this sort. Besides, what guarantee do you have that Benotti wouldn't cave in when confronted with the winner of the Tour, Antonelli? I have no witnesses for my extortionist conversation with Benotti, and Antonelli is a rich man and able to pay. Will you please forget the entire mess and try to beat him according to the rules?"

It worked. Bud avoided Kollmann's glance, but the defiant look was gone from his eyes. He stared at the ceiling and his silence meant agreement.

Lindner saved him the reply. "In this case, there isn't much more to be said. From a medical point of view you're taken care of; none of the medications are on the doping list, but despite the Izoard you'll reach the finish in better shape than today. It's almost your dinnertime, and I'm off. Are you still staying around, Max?"

Kollmann nodded. "I'll try to take over from his old Basque farmer and explain the Izoard to him."

Bud slept better than in Carpentras, and he got up refreshed. His limbs no longer felt leaden, and when Doctor Lindner knocked on his door very early he was already in the shower.

"You're up early, Bud. What time is breakfast?"

"Seven-thirty, doc. You know mountain stages get on the road early."

"Well, they don't exaggerate; nine-thirty isn't the middle of the night. Do you feel better than yesterday?"

"No comparison, doctor." Bud stepped out of the shower and wrapped himself in a large towel. "But I can't help thinking of those miserable last twenty kilometers yesterday."

"Forget them, Bud. You can't just brush off a fever like yours. You should have stayed in bed instead of racing a bike. Today everything will go better, and I'll give you a big vitamin shot as well."

He opened his bag to prepare the injection. "It's not a miracle drug, but it's going to be helpful. You know that I've always been honest with you. If I were one of those shady doping characters, I'd give you cortisone instead. Yesterday I had to take emergency measures, and I don't want to fill you up with chemicals. You're ready for the Izoard on your own. But you must preserve your energy for it."

"Kollmann and Mercier told me that much already. The stage is tricky. Not one of the usual mountain stages where you have time to warm up before the mountains. The distance is fairly short; you ride along at an elevation of about three thousand feet until all of a sudden, at the very end, the Izoard. Antonelli will try everything to finish me off before the mountain."

"Nevertheless, be glad you don't also have Allos and Vars. Three mountains at six thousand feet would be too much for you today— but one you can manage, even if it's the Izoard."

"Others will manage it too. The question is, in what time?"

"After yesterday's fifty seconds, you're still ahead of Antonelli by three minutes and twenty-five seconds. That's a big advantage, Bud."

"Not a big one if you just got rid of a fever, and never rode a mountain that high."

"I thought you were feeling well?"

"I said that I feel a lot better than yesterday. A shade of a difference, doc. How I'm going to feel on the Izoard is anybody's guess; and now that all of you have stuffed my head with this damn mountain, you can kiss my ass."

Doctor Lindner didn't follow this invitation, but administered a shot into the very same and left the room mumbling good wishes, because he was familiar with such irritability in bikers in such circumstances. It might even be a good sign.

13

ALL OF GAP IS AROUND FOR THE START. IT REMINDS BUD OF PAU, because the people know the mountains and aren't just spectators as in the other towns on the stage. Everybody knows Allos, Vars, and Izoard, and everybody notices that not all the men signing their control slips at the starting line and taking their goodie bags give the impression of being vigorous conquerors of peaks. The Tour has left its mark and not only with band-aids and bandages, as Bud and many others have to show for their falls. After three thousand kilometers their young faces are hollow cheeked and older, and the people familiar with their mountains know what they will look like a few hours later in Briançon.

Antonelli takes off like a tiger that has been grazed by a shot and is now trying to catch its hunter. A tempo of fifty kilometers an hour, as if there were no Izoard, which will take terrible revenge for such a waste of energy. Around him the strongest of his team, but also other teams, have joined the hunt against the man with the yellow jersey. The battle has flared up on the large road by the lake of Savines, but Valetta is there as well and pulls Bud along. As was to be expected, neither he nor any other of the blue jerseys go into the lead. Rather, they're trying to break the rhythm, which is difficult to accomplish in this speeding pack, after Saint-Clément turning to the right toward Guillestre, where the mountain road toward the Col d'Izoard begins.

Antonelli's lightning and persistent assault hasn't yielded any noticeable results at the provision checkpoint in Guillestre, apart from the fact that they are ahead of two-thirds of the pack. The yellow jersey, surrounded by four blue teammates, is still there, and the man who wants to wear yellow in Briançon, by all appearances, must consider his plan a failure. But it's something he has taken into account. Bud probably has recovered somewhat from his weakness and taken it easy drafting the rear wheels, but such weaknesses you don't blow away in one night, and at the Izoard he will expose them.

And then the mountain in all its majestic fierceness towers above them. In the switchbacks after Arvieux, called the First Hammer of the Izoard in the local jargon of the peloton, the front group has shrunk to a dozen riders. Antonelli's men, who on the plain set the tempo, have fallen behind, as had been planned. At this point nobody can help the *maestro* who wants to become a *campionissimo* today. With short, irregular strokes he shakes up the group as if he wants to increase the impact of the hammer with his own force.

Merlin is still at Bud's side. The rest of the blues fell behind at the timberline; as the rocks looking like ugly grimaces of gnomes begin to pile up right and left, every switchback swallows another man from the breakaway group. And it's getting colder on the Izoard. Low drifting gray clouds cover the sun; and the wind, blowing from the summit, tears them into shreds. And when they brave it head-on after a curve, it charges the men as if it wanted to push them over the edge into the abyss.

And then the Casse Deserte. The grotesque rock formations pile up to terrifying heights, and although the Casse Deserte is a kind of saddle fooling the bikers with a level stretch, it is the Second Hammer of the Izoard. *Faux plat,* say the French, false plain. After the abrupt pitches you think you can catch your breath, but not only does the wind, which attacks you head-on, take it away, but so does the road, which is flat only in appearance. It is still climbing, and if you shift to a higher gear to take advantage of the seemingly favorable conditions, you pay a high price.

Bud has to pay it, and he's not the only one. Even the Spaniard Perez, who long ago has secured the mountain prize for himself, is losing his rhythm. The Casse Deserte breaks the harmony of the group that up to now believed in a combined conquest of the peak. Only Antonelli races through it as if the closeness of his home country lends him wings. And he unleashes energy that demoralizes his pursuers and perplexes the men in the accompanying cars.

And then the climb from the saddle to the summit. The Third Hammer of the Izoard. On this short stretch leading into eternal snow, piling up to the right and the left of the road on the summit, Antonelli takes away almost two minutes from the man wearing the yellow jersey. In comparison, the Casse Deserte was a trifling matter of seconds, but if you add it all up—and if he risks everything during the downhill race—he can take the yellow jersey. But how does someone who has struggled for rather than stormed the seventy-four-hundred-foot summit recuperate the reflexes needed for a victorious downhill race?

People are wearing windbreakers, even hoods, and the gusts have torn the publicity banner announcing the Big Mountain Prize from its poles. Six hundred feet farther down, where the gradient drops steeply, Kollmann, in order to take Bud's time, has found a parking spot between leftover patches of snow. Bud passes the spot two minutes and forty seconds after Antonelli, recognizes Kollmann, and, for a split second, presses his right hand on his chest.

Is he saying that the yellow jersey is still his? Or that he has placed a newspaper in front of his chest? Or did he reach for the gentian from the Tourmalet, which he preserves carefully every day together with the letter of the old Basque? Tomorrow he'll have to put it into a blue jersey.

Kollmann saw how recklessly Antonelli sped through the same curve. Not even a finger on a brake. It was the daring final sprint of a downhill racer. Bud races giant slalom, brakes in the curves, and doesn't have the slightest chance to make up his loss.

Nevertheless, at this moment the yellow jersey is still his. But forty-five seconds are no longer capital against an Antonelli flitting downhill. He comes out of every curve with an advantage, and farther down, where the road evens out, he cranks into the highest gear; in Briançon he will have torn the jersey off Bud's shoulders, Kollmann is sure of it. He cannot help but admire the man who wants to be a *campionissimo* today; he has raced a spectacular stage.

And Bud knows it too. As far as the Casse Deserte he hoped to be able to check the Italian's infernal determination. But then he literally remained in place, on this false plain between the bizarre towering rocks, and on the last pitch after the saddle he almost blacked out. The storm and the cold hardened his muscles and left his fingers without feeling. But below the timberline the sun returns and the wind softens. He bends down low over his handlebars and once again feels the blood circulating through numb legs.

He brakes more softly in the curves, and as he comes out of them, he puts it in the large gear. It is going better and better as the long valley leading to the fortified town of Briançon approaches.

Antonelli must have finished already. Never before did an opponent leave him behind like this, but he will not yield the yellow jersey without a fight. And he feels that the Izoard's evil voraciousness has not devoured all of his strength. Past the next curve a long straight. Almost an avenue, because deciduous trees have taken over from the dwarf pines of the Izoard. And far out front a blue jersey. That must be Merlin, who had passed him on the Casse Deserte.

The downhill race has cleared his head, and simple trains of thought begin to circulate, just like blood. Merlin has had either a spill or a breakdown; or quite simply, he, Bud, has been faster. And yet Merlin is a good downhill racer.

Can he still save the jersey? The thought is like a whip on his legs, which on the mountain were empty and now speed up on the softly inclining road, moving closer to the blue point. And where the road in a wide loop rises once more toward the mountain fortress Briançon, he catches up with a surprised Merlin, who has had neither a fall nor a breakdown.

It is the last kilometer; he's pumping up energy that should have been consumed by the Izoard. He doesn't hear the people scream and applaud along the road, and he no longer sees anything as he crosses the finish line. Only a mechanical pull on the brakes prevents a collision with Mercier, who grabs his handlebars like the horns of a bull. Two others support him and loosen his cage straps, so he won't fall off the bike.

At the finish the situation is chaotic. The walls of the old fortified city become a giant cauldron where disbelief, enthusiasm, and deep Italian disappointment are simmering. A stew that makes the reporters racing to the press center groan, because in this stage, they have to deal with more emotions than in ten others, and because the takeover of the yellow jersey by Antonelli has been written already on hundreds of pages.

Budzinski has defended it by exactly eight seconds. More precisely, he has reconquered it on the last part of the descent, because it was already Antonelli's at that point.

A mind-boggling result that dwarfs everything that has happened up to this point. Thousands of *tifosi,* who had come across the Italian border and who were already celebrating the changeover of the yellow jersey with bursts of temperament that made the old walls of Briançon quiver, forget Antonelli's impressive ride over the Izoard. All they see is the yellow jersey on Bud's shoulders. And with the jealous love of mothers for their firstborn, they remember the great *campionissimi* who in Briançon have, in times long past, sported the yellow outfit. The man who had intended to become the next *campionissimo* in Briançon senses it with vivid intensity, and it makes him bitter.

All hell had been let loose in the press center. It was always like this when the Tour came through, because the French town with the highest elevation had only a modest communications system. Normally it was sufficient, but when more than one hundred international calls are placed, not to speak of the national ones, the system collapses. Fortunately it was only 4 P.M., when those who had arrived there first got put through.

But soon silence descended upon the elementary school building of Briançon, the only one that could accommodate a horde of reporters. Since there were fewer pupils than Tour reporters, many had to sit on the floor; but it didn't bother men who were used to writing, eating, and occasionally sleeping in cars, like Kollmann.

It didn't bother him that after two hours squatting on the floor, writing on his knees, his call hadn't come up. He had a lot to say about this stage in general and about Bud in particular. He knew his fellow Germans; they were not so much concerned with the yellow jersey hanging from the thinnest of threads as with its defense, which made for salty coffee also on the east bank of the Rhine.

However, what were eight seconds after more than three thousand kilometers? In eight seconds nobody could light up a pipe or walk a hundred feet.

But what mattered was yellow. And television. Naturally the Izoard had been broadcast live, and the camera had remained with Antonelli after Bud's cave-in on the mountain. He must have looked like a corpse, Kollmann thought. Of course he was considered a phenomenon now. Hadn't Antonelli raced downhill as if it hadn't been him at the handlebars but Saint Anthony of Padua?

And then the German TV screens had remained yellow. Koeppke, Kollmann quietly grinned to himself, will present himself with a yellow tie and tomorrow *Der Spiegel*'s top reporter will turn up to show the other sportswriters how to explain the phenomenon Budzinski to the German intelligentsia who, unlike the French, have little feeling or understanding for this sweaty, down-to-earth male world.

For the moment the phenomenon was little more than a sore, worn-out bundle being kneaded by the large hands of a masseur.

The old yellow jersey, covered with the dirt of the mountain, was lying on the floor, and the new one was hanging over the chair.

When the masseur left Doctor Lindner arrived, and he took a lot of time to examine the man who had come from very far away to reconquer a jersey that they'd practically already taken off his back. And he was quite satisfied when he went to fetch the necessaries from his big bag. Then he walked through the picturesque fortress of Briançon surrounded by precipitous mountains, before he went to the schoolhouse to inform Kollmann about Bud's condition and everything that he had said to him.

This was smooth teamwork, and even the telephone connections collaborated. Kollmann had barely finished his notes when his call went through. He was ahead even of many Italians shouting into their phones as if they wanted to be heard in nearby Turin; but they did nothing but voice their despair to helpless operators on the other end. After Kollmann had finished his long talk and withdrawn his head from the soundproof shell, dripping with perspiration, Lindner asked him if he could place a call to Germany for him with his privileged press ID card.

"It's useless," said Kollmann. "See for yourself. There are about sixty reporters waiting, and the Italians are already hoarse from complaining. In Briançon it's always like this. I was just lucky. Who do you want to call anyhow?"

The doctor scratched his chin. "I promised my wife that I'd stay with the Tour for a week and return after the Alps. But it's impossible. I can't abandon Bud right now. She'll raise a terrific stink, but over the phone it's tolerable, and she'll get a consolation prize: She can come to Paris for the finish of the Tour."

Kollmann wiped his forehead, dirty and sticky from the Izoard. "I didn't realize what a henpecked husband you are."

"I'm not part of the itinerants like you, Max. If I'd done the Tour a dozen times like you, it would be different."

"Listen, you middle-class husband." Kollmann pulled a green reservation slip out of his wallet. "Tonight we have reservations in a mountain village about fifty kilometers from here. Briançon can accommodate only a small part of the whole caravan. What's more, this jerk Lafitte has given us a double room, and I don't even know if you snore. Tell you what we'll do: We'll forget about the long drive and the accommodations and spend the night in Italy. The border is only a few kilometers away. Many of my Italian colleagues will go as well, but there are plenty of hotels, and you can use the telephone there."

"Not a bad idea," said Lindner. "Shall we eat over there as well?"

"Of course. Most of the local restaurants are full anyhow, and you'll have to wait for your food longer than for a phone call. I'm ready to leave. Unless you have to go back to Bud."

"No need, Max. I've given him everything he needs and he wants to go to bed right after dinner."

"I thought so. He's suffered more than on the Peyresourde. I thought he had lost not only the yellow jersey but also the entire Tour. But his final sprint was sensational. I think he still has a chance."

"What's your estimate?"

"Fifty-fifty," said Kollmann.

"And as his physician I'm telling you that he's going to win, Max."

"The Tour so far has always been decided on the road," growled Kollmann, "and it has many turns."

14

THEY HEADED TOWARD THE ITALIAN BOARDER; LAUGHING CUSTOMS officials raised the barrier without further formalities when they saw the blue, white, and red Tour de France sticker on Kollmann's car.

"By the way, where's your driver going to spend the night?" Lindner wanted to know.

"Don't worry about him. He's a *débrouillard,* if you know what I mean."

"You mean someone who finds a bed anywhere, either in a farmhouse or with a waitress."

"Or vice versa," Kollmann grinned. "In any case, tomorrow morning at ten I'll find him at the starting line, well rested or not. And if you like, you can ride along on our jump seat instead of the crowded heap Troussellier has assigned you to."

"We'll see, Max."

"Okay, Martin. Tonight we'll take a break from the Tour. We need it. When I close my eyes, all I see is bikers. Not a word about the Tour. Not even about Bud. Agreed?"

"Agreed." They took the road toward Sestrière, gaining once more in altitude. After fifteen minutes they found a village with wooden chalets and hotels and the appearance of a winter resort. It was still daylight, although a red setting sun was casting long shadows.

"Let's stay here," said Kollmann. "A nice place and a short trip back. To go on doesn't make sense. The question is: will they have room for us?"

He stopped in front of a small hotel at the edge of the village, and the young desk clerk, who had recognized the Tour de France sticker, made a deep bow that put them into high spirits. He leafed through a large book, somewhat out of proportion for the small hotel, and took some time pondering the situation; a little too long for their high spirits.

"*Je suis desolé, messieurs*—I'm terribly sorry—I have only a double with bath." His French was almost without accent.

"We're Germans," Kollmann said, as if it could change "double" into "single."

"*Tiens, des Allemands.* Bud's a great rider. He's ruined a glorious day for Antonelli."

Kollmann was happy that he didn't say Budzinski, but he wasn't happy about the double room.

"Isn't there anything else?" He reached ostensibly for his wallet, a gesture no self-respecting Italian desk clerk can ignore. The young man opened the big book again, wetting his right index finger. But whether his mouth watered for the tip or not, no two single rooms were to be had.

"In God's name, let's take the double," said Lindner. "I don't snore and I think we should enjoy this time off rather than spend half the evening looking for suitable quarters."

"Right you are, Martin." And to the desk clerk: "Okay, we'll take the double."

"For one night only, right?" His gaze went from their faces, covered with grime and sweat of the Izoard, to the convertible outside, which could also have used a good wash. "Yes," replied Kollmann. "Although we would have nothing against a rest day right here."

The young man laughed pleasantly. "You wouldn't regret it either, messieurs. But perhaps you'll like it enough to come back someday, who knows."

"First of all we'll have to wash off the dirt of the Izoard. We don't want to walk around your handsome hotel like bandits. You said double with bath, right?"

"Of course, monsieur. All our rooms have bath or a shower."

"Unlike many French hotels."

"*Merci*, monsieur. We're honored to offer you our hospitality."

While the young man pulled two registration slips from a drawer, Lindner nudged Kollmann with his elbow. "Stop it now. If you go on like this, I'd guess you're gay."

"I'd like to convince you of the contrary, but unfortunately the Tour isn't the place for such things, as you may have noticed. In the editorial office at home they imagine me every night in bed with an enchanting beauty who's waited only for me. Instead, I'm happy if around midnight some sulky waiter will bring me something to eat. That's how distorted things look from a distance. But you saw for yourself and besides, we didn't want to talk about the Tour."

They completed their registration forms and the clerk asked if they wanted to have dinner.

"But of course, monsieur, and a sumptuous one as well."

"In that case you should be in the dining room by nine-thirty."

"We'll make an effort, just like a certain Budzinski, who also made it just in time."

"But Antonelli will win the Tour."

"Does this mean champagne is on the house?"

"Not yet," said the clerk and laughed. "Maybe you can return for it later."

"No fool, that young man," said Kollmann as they entered their room. "Who's first in the bathroom?"

Only then did he see the bed. A large French bed.

"I'm supposed to get under the same blanket with you. Some nerve, these Mediterraneans."

Lindner shrugged. "Right now, I'm more concerned with my empty stomach. Perhaps we can have a couch put in; maybe you can arrange it while I take a bath."

Without bending down or using his hands, Kollmann kicked off his shoes, mumbling something like "go take a leap," and threw himself down on the blue bedcover. Through the open window he saw the snowy peak of the Izoard glitter in the last rays of the setting sun, and he got up once more to close the window because the wind coming from the mountains was becoming cold.

Half an hour later they went downstairs, dressed in clean shirts and jackets, somewhat rumpled from the suitcases. It was nearly ten but to their surprise, they found the dining room full of people, and to their second surprise, a gray-haired waiter with the noble head of a Roman led the way to a table offering a splendid panorama of mountains in the sunset, and—two women sitting there.

Both men bowed slightly. The impression that they had been expected became conviction as the two heads, one fair, the other a brunette, responded with a friendly nod. They were drinking their coffee, and from crumbs and spots on the tablecloth it could be assumed that they had already eaten. They were not unattractive. No beauty queens, but certainly not of a kind to be ignored by gentlemen traveling alone.

The menu was as impressive as the headwaiter. When they had ordered they made an effort to start a conversation with the two women, who were showing signs of getting up from table and asked for their bill. Kollmann stayed with French, and unnecessarily asked if they understood.

"*Oui, monsieur, français et anglais.* We are teachers."

"And from where, if I may ask?"

"From Milan. And you're the two Germans from the Tour de France? They're already talking about you in the hotel."

Kollmann laughed. "I'm sure they're talking more about Antonelli and Bud."

"Certainly. We all trembled at the TV and were hoping the yellow jersey would have a different bearer."

"And we dreaded it. But don't you think that this is cause for a toast, because one has won and the other hasn't lost?"

Blonde and brunette exchanged a glance that wasn't as questioning as it was supposed to be. And Kollmann stepped on Lindner's foot because he considered the opening move promising, and justly so. He ordered four glasses with the wine, but before it was poured, Lindner remembered his wife.

He got up and excused himself. "I'll have to place a call to Germany."

"You're both journalists?" the blond one asked.

"Only I," said Kollmann. "He's a doctor. Bud's doctor."

"How exciting. But shouldn't he be with him right now?"

"He's been with him already, madame. Bud's asleep at the moment. But we really didn't want to talk about the Tour tonight; we wanted to take a vacation from it instead. That's why we're in Italy."

"And we've met you."

That had a nice sound, Kollmann thought, and was quick to rejoin that this was his first evening of the entire Tour in really delightful company .

"You're a charmer. You could be Italian," the brunette laughed and her dark eyes sparkled, provoking Kollmann to a somewhat daring but nevertheless fitting reply, from which the flirt might be spun on. But Lindner ruined it.

"An hour wait here as well. I'll have to wake her up and that's when things get unpleasant."

Since he was saying this in German and with some preoccupation, the women, not understanding, imagined it was a difficult case. He was a doctor, after all.

"Problems, monsieur?"

"It depends," Lindner growled and emptied his glass of wine with one swig. "Italian communications aren't any faster than the French ones."

"We're high up in the mountains, not in a city," the blond one replied with a smile. Then the gentlemen's first course arrived, and they had to order more wine.

Before the main course arrived they knew that the blonde was called Isabella and the brunette Sandra, and undoubtedly it boded well for the evening that they all went by first names. Max and Martin ate heartily and nurtured hopeful projections, until the doctor was called to the telephone.

He returned fifteen minutes later with a face as if he had bitten into Italy's most sour lemon. There was no need to ask any questions.

"She's really sore."

"Not even the lure of Paris worked?"

"On the contrary. She wished me a good time with my friends Budzinski and Kollmann. And that she would stay at Tegernsee where she's found nice company."

"She knows how to get at you. Alludes to some holiday flirt."

"She just wants to get back at me, Max. You know her."

"All the better. Let's get back at her as well. I think our chances here are pretty good if we take the initiative. There's a stage win in this, I can smell it."

He enjoyed speaking so openly and brashly in front of the women, who didn't understand any German, but Lindner picked dejectedly in his cold meal.

"*Martin a des ennuis*—Martin is worried about something?" Isabella asked, mixing curiosity with concern.

Kollmann suppressed a grin and nodded. "He is indeed. Someone in Germany who isn't well at all. He'd prefer to have the patient right here." It wasn't even a lie, unless you took into account that the patient was doing pretty well where she was. More or less like Kollmann himself, who ordered more wine and continued the offensive.

"What a pity that we have only one evening. Such delightful encounters are some of the nicest things in life, don't you agree? If we were in Germany I'd propose a drink to a more intimate friendship, but that isn't done in Italy, or is it?"

The women giggled, but it didn't sound like a rejection.

"You think you're such a charmer and you sweet talk like a traveling salesman," growled Lindner. "I'd prefer going to sleep."

Kollmann stepped on his foot. "You're out of your mind. Drink something." And to the women: "He's too conscientious a doctor. We'll have to cheer him up. Let's drink to friendship, friends! Extraordinary circumstances require extraordinary measures, and we'll never be this young again." He raised his glass and all joined in, even without the German custom of linking arms, and without the kiss.

Nevertheless, things were getting cozier; under the tablecloth, Kollmann's hand had reached Sandra's knee and not encountered any reticence. By midnight the stage victory had moved within range. Isabella and Sandra almost maternally sympathized with the awkward arrangement for Max and Martin to get into the same bed and under the same cover. Fraternally, as they had drunk to it, they would divide the two rooms. No tossing of coins, because the die had been cast a while ago: Max with Sandra and Lindner with Isabella. It would have been too optimistic to assume that these auspices had soothed Lindner's dejection altogether, but his mood was beginning to brighten. Since Kollmann recognized his threshold of reluctance and didn't want it to interfere with imminent success, he suggested ordering champagne for the room.

"Now you are really out of your mind."

"Noble and with style, Martin. I'm disappointed: You are not a man of the world after all."

"I think you watch too many movies. I presume you have a silk dressing gown in your suitcase for such occasions? Absolutely required in the film at this point."

"Lay off this minute and don't ruin the final sprint. We'll go to our rooms now, separately, of course, and order two bottles of champagne. We'll all toast and then you take Isabella and one bottle and do a disappearing act. This is going to be the best night of the Tour, even if we have to sleep a little on the road tomorrow. But there's justice in this world."

"What do you mean?"

"I mean that the ruined rest day in Pau is paying off tonight. '*Un bienfait n'est jamais perdu*'—a good deed is never lost, the French say."

"You're taking this for the good deed you've done for Bud?"

"Exactly. And I don't mind in the least that you get to share it. But we're being rude to the women. Let's speak French."

And so they did until the bill had been paid, after which they went, without saying good-bye but in a cheerfully conspiratory mood, to their respective rooms. Rendezvous at the gentlemen's in fifteen minutes.

The champagne arrived within five minutes on a cart and a silver ice bucket. The waiter proceeded to open one of the two Veuve Cliquot bottles.

"Don't bother," Kollmann said. "We'll take care of it. Bring us two more glasses."

"*Bien sûr,* monsieur."

The young man withdrew and Lindner observed that he could have saved himself the grin.

"Don't be so uptight," said Kollmann, rummaging in his toiletry bag for eau de cologne. "*Un certain sourire,* a certain smile, should not disturb the lucky guy."

Even Lindner was snickering now. "Don't forget the manicure, Don Giovanni. By the way, your perfume reeks like an entire whorehouse. The little waiter will faint when he brings the glasses."

But Kollmann didn't even listen and whistled '*O sole mio*', carefully parting his hair in front of the mirror. The waiter brought the two glasses and, bowing politely, wished them a pleasant night.

"Say what you want: These Italians really have style."

They lit up cigarettes and Lindner asked if he could put on his slippers.

"Not yet. Don't you realize how stupid that would look?"

"Well, at least let's have something to drink."

"A gentleman waits for the ladies, Martin. You can wait another five minutes, can't you?"

The fifteen minutes became thirty, there was no sign of life. "They're making themselves pretty," said Kollmann. "One has to grant them some time."

After three quarters of an hour even Kollmann became restless. "I'll go and see what's up."

The silence in the hotel at this late hour irritated him, and he knocked very softly at their door at the end of the corridor.

No answer. He put his ear to the door, gently at first, then pressing his ear to the wood. Nothing. No sign of life. All of a sudden he had the feeling that inside they were holding their breath. He turned the doorknob very gently.

Locked. Should he go on knocking and make a fool of himself? He chose the retreat instead and found the doctor about to open a bottle of champagne.

"Yes, Martin—I think we'll need it."

"Gone sour, right?"

"And how. Not a sound from the room, but I bet they're not asleep."

Lindner poured and both emptied their glass in one draft.

"Impressive idea, your champagne, isn't it?"

"And the bill will be even more impressive," growled Kollmann. "We'll pack one bottle for a better occasion."

"As you like. Let's drink up and go to bed."

"What a treat. With a fellow like you. And for half an hour I had my hand on Sandra's knee and even higher. A plowed field, that, I'm telling you. Can you figure out women?"

Lindner hung his pants over the back of the chair and shrugged. "Maybe they thought we were in for group sex when you ordered the champagne."

"Do you think so?" Kollmann mussed his hair, kicking off his shoes at the same time. "It's quite possible that they got discouraged, because with two bottles and four glasses, the hotel staff was in on it."

"Also keep in mind that they're staying for a few more days, not just overnight like we are."

"Nevertheless, I'll call them," said Kollmann. "I want to know what's going on. Room twenty-eight, right?"

He had the night porter make the connection, and the phone rang six times before a voice answered, and it didn't sound the least bit sleepy. He recognized Sandra immediately. "It was a pleasant evening, Max, but we have gone to bed already."

"But you agreed to come over." Kollmann thought he heard a giggle in the background and raised his voice: "Is this your idea of a deal? We have champagne waiting for you."

"I wouldn't shout like that, Max. You'll wake the whole hotel."

"So what? Do you expect me to remain calm after having been stood up?"

"Look at it this way, Max." Sandra's voice became soothing as if she had a disappointed child on the other end of the line. "You're shouting and couldn't care less, because the two of you are going to leave in a few hours. We're staying instead, and our boyfriends are coming for the weekend. What do you think they would say if we had joined you?"

"And why would you have to tell them?"

An indulgent laugh pealed through the wire.

"Max, please. All your preparations. Without the champagne and all your talking, it might have been possible. But we have to consider the circumstances. Italian men are very jealous, in case you don't know."

"And why didn't you say so right away?"

"Because we liked the idea, believe it or not. But then we talked about it, and that cooled us off. You two are far from being diplomatic Don Giovannis. Think of it next time."

Kollmann gave up, wished her a good night, and hung up. And he didn't have to give any explanations to his companion, who was already under the covers. "Move over to the right," he growled while he undressed.

During the short night the two heroes, hard hit in their masculine pride, now and then bumped into each other in the center where they had hoped to encounter a gentler presence. They had breakfast in their room to avoid curiosity, and arrived at the start on time, where they were greeted by Zander, a little tired but giving off the air of a man who has spent a most agreeable night.

15

THE ONLY OBSTACLE IN THE STAGE FROM BRIANÇON TO GRENOBLE, and early on, was the Col du Lautaret, which the bikers took without an effort and Kollmann in his sleep. Next they left the dreaded Galibier and L'Alpe d'Huez to their right to reach Grenoble through the valley of Romanche. It was the farewell from the high mountains, whose powerful presence had brought about a climax but no decision. Bud's thin lead of eight seconds held at the group finish in Grenoble and during the next stages.

Not that Antonelli didn't try to cut it. He strained at the bit, was looking for a surprise attack again and again, but finally realized that it was a waste of energy. On the plain the Valetta team protected the yellow jersey with perfect discipline and watchfulness. The Tour's history is full of such futile skirmishes for seconds, over hundreds of kilometers, when the road is level and the hunted one has the strong support of his team and no breakdown. Both held true for Bud. He had overcome his weakness, and the six Valetta riders still remaining in the race had the same strength as the half-dozen rallying around Antonelli.

The race became a chess game between the two teams. The offensive moves of the Italians were countered by the defenders of the yellow jersey with discouraging precision. Daily they lay in wait for each other out in front of a field that was marked by the stress of the Tour, and whenever the Italians made an attempt at breaking away, the blue jerseys, a yellow one in their midst, caught up to their rear wheels with disheartening swiftness. And the blues were conserving energy because they never took the offensive.

"Stay on the alert like a lynx," Mercier implored his men every night. "Our task is not to attack but to control. Every single move of Antonelli is checked, and Bud lies low as long as possible on your rear wheels. Only if the macaronis really manage to open up a gap should he engage himself."

Two days before Versailles Antonelli stopped the energy-consuming tactics of aggression. That meant a truce before the last stage, which had turned into a clear duel between him and Budzinski. At this point all strategy and teamwork would cease. Racing against the clock, individually. Over large roads and narrow streets, winding around Paris for more than fifty-eight kilometers, until entering the Avenue de la Grande Armée. Then twice around the big loop from the Arc de Triomphe across the Rond Point and the Tuileries. It was to be expected that a final showdown under these circumstances would bring more than a million people into the streets.

The organizers were rubbing their hands. Bud's yellow jersey, ever since Briançon, was still hanging by the thin thread of his eight-second advantage. The drama of the conclusion presented an exceptional case in the lively history of the world's oldest stage race, and imaginations flared up like brushfires. Paris, the prima donna, forgot her haughtiness and vanity, and from Germany charter flights were pouring in. For the Italians the days of Bartali and Coppi had returned; the Germans were thinking of Max Schmeling, the boxing champion, Fritz Walter, Uwe Seeler, and Franz Beckenbauer, the stars of soccer, all at once.

Newspapers brought out their fattest headlines, wrote about the new Sun King who on this Sunday was riding from Versailles to Paris for his coronation. The language of the Tour is flowery, and on this Sunday it outgrew all applicable and existing limits. They pulled all registers, and whoever hit a wrong note certainly would not receive any ridicule. Everything the printing presses spat out was eaten up, because people, grown up in a push-button culture, needed heroes.

Antonelli or Budzinski? Eight seconds had to be either reduced or maintained over fifty-eight kilometers, after a distance of four thousand kilometers.

And the man on the street knew what the giants of the roads, as he called them, had gone through. The discussions at the bistro counters were as animated as they were endless, because conjectures at the moment of truth are always unnerving and without any certainty. In principle Bud did better time trials. But after four thousand kilometers and everything else that had befallen him, such principles weighed as much as swan feathers on a lake surface. Bud could afford to lose seven seconds and still win the Tour with the smallest possible edge. *Autant en emporte le vent.* It could be gone with the wind.

"Has there ever been a similar situation?" Bud asked Kollmann.

He shook his head. "It's never been this close. But about ten years ago, the Dutchman Jan Jannsen took the yellow jersey from the Belgian van Springel during the time trial of the last stage. By half a minute or so. The finish was at the Piste Municipale at Vincennes, because the princes' park was under reconstruction. In those days nobody had the bright idea of letting the Tour de France come to an end under the eyes of the president of the Republic. You see, Giscard has a more folksy sense of grandeur than did de Gaulle."

"If I lose, I'll never get on another bike."

"Others before you have uttered such nonsense. Don't get tense, kid. If you avoid that, you'll win."

Early on Sunday morning Mercier, Felix, and Bud drove the entire course. It had been closed to general traffic. They carried Bud's bike, and in some parts Bud got into the saddle for two or three kilometers without Felix having to slow down the car. The

course had its hills and tricky stretches but to a strong athlete it permitted high gears; Bud tried to memorize every important detail.
They turned around in the Avenue de la Grande Armée. Bud knew
the Champs-Elysées.

He had lots of time left. Even time for a second breakfast, which
Doctor Lindner prepared in his room. At this point they didn't
even trust the hotel kitchen and wanted to exclude any kind of
interference and intrigues. Bud had time, because time trials are
started in the reverse order of the overall standings. Every two minutes someone starts, first the bearer of the red lantern, last the
wearer of the yellow jersey.

It was Bud's turn around three o'clock in the afternoon—two
minutes after Antonelli, to whom the Italian press had promised
the title of Super Campionissimo. He was nine seconds away from
it. The start of a fifty-eight-kilometer time trial in itself does not
allow important conclusions, but Bud was impressed by the force
and the determination of the Italian. It was as if he had been cata-
pulted from the wooden ramp that sets off the electronic clock, and
he pulled ahead like a sprinter who has the last lap before him
when he hears the bell of the racetrack. To be sure, he couldn't sustain sixty kilometers at this speed. Was he trying to impress people
because he felt Bud's eyes in his back?

Mercier was already standing in the car—which had a sign,
BUDZINSKI, mounted on the hood—and he waved to him soothingly: "Don't let him bluff you. He's going to calm down."

Felix wasn't in the driver's seat yet. He was holding Bud's bike
on the ramp while he adjusted the rat-trap cage. "Antonelli wants to
provoke you into a lightning start that you'll regret," he whispered.
"Don't start like a rocket. Just find your rhythm as usual."

But Bud isn't listening any longer. He is all nerves. Because it's
not all as usual. It is the moment of truth. Not only of the Tour de
France, but also of his career. An obsessive thought that gnawed at
him all night. He turned down Doctor Lindner's sleeping pill. It

remains to be seen if he will have to pay for it or for the restless night.

His start is quick but less hectic than Antonelli's. Possibly he'll lose a couple of seconds on the first kilometer. But there are fifty-eight of them, and he has experience and a successful record in time trials. Does it amount to an advantage? Indirectly perhaps. Antonelli, with five more years of experience as a pro in his head and legs, has also won great time trials. The Nations, for example, in which Bud has never participated. But in Lugano he won against the top world specialists, and during that stage in Bordeaux he took almost a minute away from Antonelli.

Bud was also in top shape then. Antonelli came in third, which sufficed for keeping the yellow jersey. Perhaps he held back energy that Bud exhausted completely?

It'll become clear very soon. At the moment he knows only that the race against the clock is the most difficult of all. You're completely alone; you cannot estimate your lead from the way the race develops, because there's no pack, and nothing happens from which you can profit strategically. Only the clock is your adversary. You can't deceive it. It registers every stroke on the pedals and there's no catching your breath behind the rear wheels of your opponents. If you want to win, you have to find your own rhythm after the start, and the optimal position for offering the least wind resistance. Only then will you economize your strength against the wind. Early on, Bud learned to round his back and keep his nose close to the handlebars; his hands grip low on the drops.

Bud has the course in his head like the slalom racer his run of flags. The ease with which he can crank in the highest gear after five kilometers tells him that he can initiate the second phase of the race. This second phase, and he knows this from his body, has a lot in common with the strategy of a successful trotter—with the difference that the bike racer is driver and horse in one. Drivers who push the horse into an exaggerated speed at the start and try to sustain it consistently don't come in first. The strategy of the master consists in holding back his horse after a lightning start to let it catch its breath for the big final sprint. But Bud has no means for comparison. He sees no rivals, only the empty stretch of the road winding itself through two thick human hedges that have waited for the yellow jersey and cheer him on.

He hears the shouts without noticing them. More important is the sense of his strength and the equilibrium of his body, feeling the road through the thinnest of tires, pumped up so hard that even the tiniest jagged pebble could provoke a blowout. But every gram of material saved counts during time trials, and if you're lucky you escape a breakdown. Not that it would be irreparable. But it costs a minimum of twenty seconds, provided the people in the accompanying vehicle are fast and can make a flying exchange of bikes. And you have to regain your rhythm in the high gear.

Bud feels the air pressure in the tires; they are so hard that they don't cushion even the smallest bump but travel from the racing saddle into his arms and provide a paradoxical feeling of security. Nothing must soften. Especially not his stroke. It has to be round, decisive. That is athletic strength and harmony that has nothing to do with the bike, although man and bike have to be one.

He stays in the center of the road, where it is rounded and clean. Never, during time trials, has he cut curves in order to gain a few centimeters. To be sure, in the total count they add up to a few meters, but if you cut the edge of the road with screeching tires you also cut the little stones with the thinnest of tires, because no road is as clean at the edge as in the center.

And you have to be wary of the spectators. Where they are standing packed together, they pay no attention to the edge of the pavement—the pavement that belongs to the rider, not to them. In their excitement they move in on you, narrowing the corridor you need. Bud knows all of this, remains in the middle, and is undecided if he should back off from the effort that makes his lungs burn. Not a sign from Mercier's car.

He knows that he is fast, the chronometer at his left wrist tells him so; it's his only ally. All in all he feels he is faster than Antonelli. It's the instinct of the rider that unleashes his strength and senses the upcoming barrier, where caution is essential. There is the road lined with poplars that block the wind coming from the side. It was his intention to change his tempo here, after the strenuous effort of the starting phase. After all he has done, his timing should put him ahead of Antonelli, and he is surprised that still no sign is forthcoming from Mercier's car.

Slowing the tempo is not the same as braking, which you can't permit yourself during a time trial. It is enough to turn your head. The car with the white sign BUDZINSKI is only a few yards behind him, as if it could push him. Felix reacts instantaneously. To the old fox of the Tour, Bud's glance over his shoulder means something. It can't be a mistake. Felix's watchful eyes have bike and rider under complete control. He sees the chain jump during gear shifts. From the jumping of the wheels, he knows that the tire pressure is all right, and the almost immobile torso and the whirring even rhythm of the legs tell him that all is well with the energy that propels the wheels.

He also senses Bud's predicament. The man who must consider himself the loneliest one on the planet wants to know where he stands. Without as much as giving a glance to Mercier, who is standing next to him, he comes up to Bud's side. Fat Mercier has only a sunroof, and he fills the opening like a commander the hatch of his tank. He is hanging on to the frame right and left, and now and then he reaches for the walkie-talkie with its long antenna, which informs him of the positions of the other riders.

Only in an emergency should Felix drive at the same level as Bud. Especially in the case of a problem. The car could offer illicit assistance in the pacing, or at least screen him from the side wind.

But he drives up to him because the lonely man who is about to either win or lose the Tour de France has given him a sign. To his surprise, Mercier, leaning out of the sunroof, shouts: "Everything okay, Bud? Any problems?"

Felix looks to the right and has anticipated Bud's reaction: Why the useless gibberish? If anybody is in need of an answer, it is Bud, and his inquiring look is a furious one.

"How much, damn it."

Again Felix marvels at Mercier who, making a megaphone of his hands, shouts: "*Cinq d'avance*—five seconds gained." In doing so he is losing his balance because Felix has to brake before a curve, and he bumps his head on the three replacement bikes on the roof rack.

Why is he lying? Felix thinks. He'd heard very clearly that Bud had gained seventeen seconds on Antonelli, and he is already beyond the tenth kilometer. Why does old fatso say only five? Why does he cheat him out of twelve seconds? After reducing the tempo and putting himself once again behind Bud, in order not to risk a protest on the part of the race commissioners for assisting a rider, he asks Mercier, who grins.

"I want to spur him on a little, Felix."

"But he had a fantastic start. Seventeen seconds ahead after ten kilometers. I hadn't reckoned on this much."

"Nor did I. But I know him better than you do. He now wants to pause, as he says. It's necessary, let him. But I'd prefer that he push himself just a little more. That's going to demoralize Antonelli, see?"

"But what if he overdoes it? Bud's very good at controlling his energy during time trials, but I think it's very dangerous to double-cross him."

"That's my business," growls Mercier. "Who's team manager— you or me?"

And he leans out of the sunroof once again, like a field marshal, showing the forces who's in command.

"He's riding like a clock," he says after a while, and his tone is somewhat more conciliatory. "Nineteen seconds at this point."

Bud is irritated. He has put all his effort into the start and sustained it for longer than planned. Only five seconds against Antonelli? Is the Italian that strong? No use racking your brain over it. Just don't tense up now. He will go into his phase where he will catch his breath, even if Mercier is going to rage. It is not braking. A few grams less force on the pedals, and the lungs will get some oxygen in exchange. It's like letting go of the gas pedal in fourth gear by just a few millimeters.

No spectator is able to notice it. But Mercier the former rider, does, of course. He has the eyes of an eagle for that. His rhythm is becoming too harmonious, his stroke too rounded. The ultimate push, which makes the shoulders tremble, is missing.

"He's slowing down," he growls from his field marshal position and reaches for the walkie-talkie. "Let's hope he doesn't grab the handlebar on top."

Bud wouldn't even think of it. He doesn't reflect how much money it would cost him to lose the yellow jersey on the last day, but he is determined to pit all his strength and willpower against such cruelty. All this torment should not have been in vain.

Sport? People may think it is. Now that he is throttling the tempo in order not to destroy the cold calculations of the battle after twenty-one days, he is noticing the people in the crowd again. He sees a priest in his long habit shouting, "*Allez, Bud!*" and waving his round hat; he sees a fat woman at a small picnic table by the roadside and a girl, waving, with long blond hair and a yellow T-shirt that looks like the jersey under which his sweat is boiling. Beautiful girl, he thinks, and it occurs to him how long he hasn't had one. Maybe a month, but it seems like a year. It is also possible that he has aged years during this struggle.

The Tour is more difficult than he had thought. Everybody who warned him and told him that you can't win it just like that was right. And Antonelli is experienced. To hell with your experience. And to hell with the rising gradient. He'll take it in high gear. It pulls somewhat in the legs, but there is the top, and a few meters behind him the speedometer in Mercier's car trembles around sixty.

"He's accelerating again," says Felix.

"It's high time," Mercier snaps. "At the last tracking he was down to ten seconds."

"You know as well as I do that he's saving strength for the final sprint."

But the field marshal has no desire to talk to an argumentative mechanic. He reaches for his walkie-talkie and holds his cold cigar into the wind.

It is blowing head-on, and Bud feels that it is reddening his eyes. But they remain clear, even if his head stops thinking and if the increasing crowds once more become a fuzzy black hedge. He must accelerate without tapping his reserves. But he doesn't understand what Mercier is shouting. At the halfway mark he is supposed to be neck-and-neck with Antonelli. And his watch indicates that he has cranked an average of forty-five kilometers an hour, or more. The Italian must be strong as a bear, if he's able to keep this up. What Bud doesn't know is that Mercier has lied to him again. His lead has increased to twenty seconds, and together with the small amount that saved him the yellow jersey in Briançon, this means almost half a minute.

After forty kilometers, at Paris Faubourgs, Mercier signals him fifteen seconds' advantage. "Go for it, Bud! Don't hold back!" Should he? Does he have these reserves? Eighteen kilometers can be miserably long if you're fading. Bud shakes his head. Only when he sights the Arc de Triomphe will he go into the final phase of his race, when he will tear the bike apart with all the strength that he has left.

Danger is lurking everywhere. It is over only after the finish line. What if someone throws a stone? If a dog runs into his bike? If the fork breaks? If Antonelli is faster?

Avenue de la Grande Armée. Imposing and large, the Arc de Triomphe looms on the horizon. And Bud accelerates, as if it were pulling him toward it like a giant magnet.

The applause is soaring, drowning out the loudspeaker that is specifying the positions. His aching back is bending still lower over the frame; still more fierce the whirring rhythm of his legs.

Bud understands the loudspeaker only when he is racing down the Champs-Elysées toward the Rond Point, where it makes its famous bend. At the elegant Fouquet's they wave to him with bottles of champagne and what the loudspeaker is saying almost throws him off the bike that is carrying him toward his victory: He is a minute and ten seconds ahead of Antonelli. All of Mercier's figures were false.

But there is no time for reflection in a head that feels wild triumph rise, and at the same time fears a fall on the world's most famous elegant avenue. There is no other enemy left. Idling, he rounds the curve at the Rond Point, then at the Tuileries, and his spread-out hands lightly touch the hoods, ready to tighten their grip at the slightest sign of danger.

But there is none. Even the Place de la Concorde is his in all its spaciousness, and only a tiny rise in the road toward the finish line in the Champs-Elysées is ahead of him when he returns from the Tuileries Gardens across the Concorde. He could straighten up now and wave to the crowd, which is showering him with a unified chant of "Bud! Bud! Bud!"

But what if he has misunderstood? If Mercier is right instead of the voice on the loudspeaker? If the "Bud! Bud!" shouts are not just enthusiasm but imploring shouts of encouragement, because it is a question of seconds? His ears register the ecstasy like the sounding of horns. Therefore he decides to finish his first Tour de France at full speed, with his back bent over the handlebars. And he flits across the finish line as if a rabid pack of dogs is at his heels. The people along the road and those who lift him off the bike, misunderstand: They see the great champion who, up to the last minute, is giving his utmost to his admirers, what the French call "panache."

He doesn't realize what this last sprint has done for his popularity, and all of a sudden he is out of it altogether. He doesn't remember who pulled his feet out of the pedals and how he came to be in this blue tent, the provisional shelter at the finish. He does notice, however, that he is neither in the saddle nor standing up, and that the head bent over him is that of Doctor Troussellier, chief of the Tour's medical corps. And he also knows that he has won the Tour de France.

But why is he lying on a stretcher? Does he have to go to hospital?

"What's the matter, doctor? Are you taking me away?"

The physician puts his hand on his shoulder. "Certainly not into the mop-up wagon, Bud. To the victory celebration, if you feel like it. Nobody wants to put you away. You passed out. A minute or so. It happens, but you could have come in a little more calmly, considering your lead."

"How much?"

"One minute and twenty seconds ahead of Antonelli, Bud. In the total count you won by a minute and twenty-eight seconds. That's fantastic! But tell me: Why'd you pedal like a madman after you had the victory in your pocket? You could have ordered a glass of champagne and drunk it down in peace without losing the Tour."

Bud throws off the blanket and sits up. "You can blame Mercier for that. I didn't ride against Antonelli, but against a lie. I'll make him pay for it."

There is commotion outside the tent. The bullish team manager fights his way through the policemen stationed at the entrance. "What's going on here? Do I get my man for the presentation ceremony or not?"

Before Doctor Troussellier can step in, Bud stands up. "I'll get on the podium, Mercier, but not with you."

For the first time he has addressed him without calling him Monsieur. The Tour is finished, and he is finished with Mercier.

"Do you realize that you hounded me to death with your fake numbers? A few more yards and I would've dropped off the bike. I wouldn't even have reached the Arc of Triomphe, you imbecile."

For the first time in his career Mercier is at a loss for words. And he doesn't know what to do with the bottle of champagne in his hands.

"But he has to . . ." he stammered finally, "he has to see the president of the Republic."

On stiff and wobbly legs that must get used to solid ground again, Bud stalks past him.

"I can do so by myself. I don't need you." He adds: "I'd like a glass of champagne. But not from this one," and he points to the bottle in Mercier's hand.

Doctor Troussellier grins. "I have yet another glass for you, Bud. Not to drink from, but to pee into. As stage winner you know your duty."

But at this, the bulldog once again becomes the combative team manager, forgetting the "imbecile" thrown into his face by the winner of the Tour de France. "He'll return to your damn urinal, but first he'll go to the winner's ceremony. The president and all of Paris are waiting for him." As a gesture that he wants to forget what bikers occasionally utter after the finish line, he offers Bud the open champagne bottle. But Bud has taken some mineral water from the doctor's folding table and waves him off. "It's not that simple, Mercier. The two of us are through."

"*On verra*," the bulldog hisses, baring his teeth, "We'll see, Monsieur Bud. A contract is a contract, and now we're going to the victory ceremony. You don't win the Tour de France every day, and I've waited a lifetime for this moment."

"Okay," says Bud and he goes outside with Mercier, but not arm in arm, to plunge into the crowd thronging by the thousands around the red-carpeted victory stand.

A kiss by the maid of honor, a handshake with the president of the Republic; TV cameras and microphones pointed at him by the dozen. From the crowds of people uninterrupted cheers, drowning out everything he is saying.

Only now do fierce pride and satisfaction begin to surge in him, and they stifle the rage against Mercier. He throws up his arms and once again feels his legs strong, which had faltered when he ascended the stand. Then he has to lower his hands to shake many others, but he also finds time to feel for the letter of the old Basque in the breast pocket of the yellow jersey. It is rumpled from many stages, and the writing has yellowed from his sweat, but the dried gentian flower from the Tourmalet has remained intact.

16

A LONG WAY FROM THE CHAMPS-ELYSÉES, IN A SMALL RESTAURANT on Rue de la Gaité in Montparnasse, three people were celebrating the Tour de France victory of Ernst Budzinski in their way. The noisy commotion of the final day had not reached this far, because Paris, unlike the towns in the provinces, was able to absorb an event like the Tour without batting an eye. Up here, on Montparnasse, it was a Sunday evening like many others. Even on the Champs-Elysées, where the stands had been dismantled and the trash swept up, life had returned to normal, with long lines of cars moving sluggishly between the Arc de Triomphe and the Place de la Concorde. Only in the editorial offices of the newspapers was the great race still in its final spurt.

Max Kollmann had finished and had accepted Martin Lindner's invitation to Montparnasse. He was wearing the only proper suit he packed for the Tour, never to pull it out of the suitcase, and he felt like someone reentering civilization from the bush. All the more since the woman with them was none other than the very pretty and elegant Kaj Lindner. She was wearing a white summer suit with blue pinstripes, and to someone emerging from the wagon trek of the Tour she smelled of the breeze of summer and vacations. Kollmann, torn away from the company of shirtsleeved, sweaty men, felt somewhat awkward, his tie knotted too tightly, his fingernails groomed with his teeth more than with a file.

Of course she had come. What woman of her class would turn down Paris? It wouldn't be a cheap trip for Martin. He had had his way, but there was a price for it, and she had come to claim it. Paris was just the right place for it.

Kollmann sipped his drink and grinned to himself. Tomorrow morning, when he was going to sleep in—really sleep in for the first time since making the giant loop through France in the wake of the riders—the doctor would be summoned to one of those days on the town that, while reestablishing matrimonial peace, ended with an empty wallet.

But Lindner had wanted it this way. To each his own. Had she continued to sulk at Tegernsee, he and Martin would have stormed the Montparnasse, and the question remained if it wouldn't have been more manly and less expensive.

Again, Kollmann had to grin, and this time Kaj Lindner noticed.

"What's so funny, Max?"

They had been on familiar terms for years and were good friends, although Kollmann, without a doubt, was the man who had infected Lindner with this incomprehensible passion for French country roads when the summer was at its height and when normal people took a vacation together. But Kollmann liked her question, because there was a twinkle in her eyes and obviously she was far from being the witch who had almost ruined Bud's victory.

Indeed, ruined. Without Martin, Bud would not have made it. Without a shadow of a doubt. But that was beside the point. He had been spoken to, and he had to give an answer. He chose the simplest.

"I'm really happy for Bud, Kaj, and also that you permitted Martin to help him. Without him, Bud wouldn't have made it. I'm talking about a huge achievement; but I don't know if you can appreciate the full importance of it."

"Perhaps you're wrong," Kaj said with a charming smile. "I felt your yellow fever before leaving Munich, and the experience on the Champs-Elysées impressed me more than you might think.

He's quite a guy, your Bud, and the Germans couldn't have fêted him more than the French."

Martin laughed. "Lo and behold, you're beginning to understand that it was more than just spleen that brought me here. Did you also notice how the women are after him?"

"And how! They almost tore the jersey off his back! But didn't he want to join us? I would've liked to get a closer look at your hero."

"I hope so," said Kollmann, "but we can't be sure. He's at the Valetta banquet on the first floor of the Eiffel Tower, and all the big bosses are present. He has to wait at least until the speeches are over. You know how it is: whose bread I eat . . ."

"Does he get his money right away? Is this also the big payday?"

"He's really the one who pays. All his winnings go to the team."

"And he gets nothing?"

"Of course he does. Apart from the fat Valetta premium, he has to bring it in on his bike over the next weeks. He probably signed about forty contracts, and that means he's riding his bike somewhere every day. Tomorrow night he starts in Roubaix."

Kaj looked at him in disbelief. "He doesn't get a break at all?"

Kollmann nodded. "He has to bring in the harvest. But it sounds worse than it is. They are relatively short races on racetracks or round circuit races, and Martin will be better able to explain to you why they don't present a major difficulty for men fresh from the Tour de France. They are in full swing like a warmed-up engine. The only stress is the traveling."

"How much does he earn?"

"Quite a bit, my dear, because he's also a good accountant and does not sell himself cheaply. He'll make about ten thousand marks per start."

"But that would be four hundred thousand marks."

"Just about. By the fall he'll have that much. And during the winter, he'll fetch another four hundred thousand, during the six-day-six-night races, although I don't like it one bit."

"Are you jealous?"

"Nonsense. But alas, I know him too well. He'll be cashing in all winter long and forget that a new spring and another Tour de France lie ahead."

Lindner shook his head. "I won't stand by idly, Max. Do you want such a talent to go down in the bad air of the winter race tracks?"

"Of course not. But you know how hardheaded he is. You have no idea how much talking I had to do to convince him to go to the Valetta banquet at the Eiffel Tower. He was determined not to exchange another word with Mercier. Can you imagine the scandal if the winner of the Tour had not turned up in the presence of the Valetta bosses? But he promised to take a cab and join us as soon as the official stuff is over."

"But we won't wait for the meal, right?" asked Kaj.

Lindner signaled the waiter. "Of course not. If he comes, he's eaten already. We'll order something special for your well-being and drink a toast to his; it's not every day that my wife discovers the Tour and that it's won by Bud."

Bud arrived shortly after eleven, and not all the people in the restaurant recognized him instantly, even if for three weeks no one in France had appeared as often as he in the papers and on the TV screens. The young man in khaki pants and blue blazer could have come from any tennis court or golf course; people only knew him in a jersey and racing pants, and they had to take a second look before recognizing the person who, a few hours ago, had won the hardest road race in the world. Even Kollmann was surprised by his civilized appearance after the three-week-long chain gang of the road. "The ship's stoker has ascended to the bridge." Kaj, too, who knew him only from photographs and on the Champs-Elysées had seen little more than the yellow jersey, was surprised. She didn't have the trained eye of the two men who, at a second glance, noticed how much he had tightened his belt, and how loosely his jacket fit.

"You lost about ten pounds on the road," Lindner said. "I hope dinner was all right."

Bud smiled, but it was a forced smile. "Mercier has ruined my appetite. I left half of it."

"Then you'll eat with us?"

"Why not? I've been craving oysters and lobster. You'd forbidden both on the Tour, doctor."

"With good reason, kid. But today you can order what you want. A dozen oysters? The Belonnes here are particularly good."

"Two dozen," said Bud, "and the biggest lobster they have. I have to feel human again."

Kollmann grinned. "Your appetite is making a comeback. You're beginning to feel the effort you've made."

"Maybe, Max. I'm glad to be here with you. It was an awful day." He turned to Lindner: "Why aren't you drinking champagne? Don't you want to celebrate with me?"

"Of course we do, but we waited for you."

"This is my treat. I owe a lot to the two of you. And nothing to Mercier, and I told him so."

"At the banquet?"

"Why not? In front of all the spruced-up guys from Valetta. Am I a person or a racehorse? What he did to me today stinks to high heaven. He lied to me during the entire time trial and hounded me up shit creek, where I could have croaked."

"Easy, Bud," Kollmann muttered. "We have a lady at the table with us."

Bud indicated an apologetic bow toward Kaj Lindner. "I'm sorry. Your manners get a little rough in the pack. And you know women only from their waving by the roadside."

Something flashed in her brown eyes that excused and at the same time irritated him. But Kollmann interrupted. This wasn't only a chat between friends but also about business. He needed material for the follow-up report his newspaper expected from him the following day.

"Did you have a confrontation with Mercier in front of everybody?"

"And how," muttered Bud. "None of you could be aware of the dirty trick because you had to wait at the finish line. Mercier consistently gave me the wrong times and completely upset my economy of energy and time. Out of some harebrained ambition he wanted to whip me into a grand stage victory. Agreed, I took a minute and twenty seconds away from Antonelli, and tomorrow perhaps the papers will compare me to Coppi or Merckx. But nobody knows what a senseless torture that meant for me. He forced me to spin the fifty-six-twelve until I almost blacked out and felt worse than on the Peyresourde."

"What is the fifty-six-twelve?" asked Kaj.

Kollmann answered for Bud. "You have to imagine the fifty-six times twelve like the fifth gear on a car. Fifty-six times twelve—that's the language of the sprockets. Fifty-six cogs in front where you're cranking, twelve on the small rear sprocket that drives the rear wheel."

"Sorry, Max—this is Chinese and algebra at the same time."

"If you didn't interrupt me, we'd be getting there," Kollmann said indulgently. "Listen. Fifty-six times twelve is the maximum that the legs of a biker can manage to move. If the road is even or descends, someone like Bud can turn such a large gear over a long distance. But beware if the road should have the slightest rise, which in the car you'd notice only from your tachometer. The legs turn heavy all of a sudden, because they have to put more pressure on the pedals."

"Now I understand."

"Not yet all of it; you're beginning."

"He has to shift down to a lower gear, right?"

"Right. But Mercier prevented this by giving him the wrong times. He completely upset Bud's strategies. After a quick start he wanted to have a rest phase to catch his breath, if you like. That's the most reasonable tactic during a time trial, and it's also a tactic that Bud masters superbly. Everything depends on the correct dosage of force. Today he lost all control over it, because he was given the wrong times."

"Deliberately so," muttered Bud.

"Has Mercier admitted to it?"

"He squirmed like an eel and tried to get out of it, but he had to admit it. And do you want to know what he's telling me now? That my market value has gone up because of the lousy minute-and-twenty-eight-second lead over Antonelli. Ten seconds would've been plenty and while he insists on the public and the ovations, I can counter that a closer race would've been more exciting."

"Nevertheless," said Lindner, "the issue of the market value isn't altogether off the mark."

"Manager talk, doc. All contracts are made a few days before Paris, and I wouldn't have cashed in one more penny if I had left Antonelli behind by fifteen minutes. Instead, this fifty-six-twelve has given me legs like lead."

"Agreed, you cranked it too long. But after a good massage, you're going to climb the Eiffel Tower."

"I'd prefer to climb into bed. Fortunately I can sleep in. If I leave for Roubaix at three in the afternoon, I'll be in time."

The two dozen oysters were served on ice on a huge silver platter, and Bud washed them down with champagne at racing speed that made Kaj Lindner's surprised eyes even larger.

"Is it true that they increase your energy?" she asked with suggestive mockery.

"Kollmann says so," grinned Bud. "Every time he has something planned during a stage, he slurps oysters. But I don't think they'll make my legs less heavy. I'll need a cane when I get up."

Kollmann ignored the allusion and, like Lindner, thought of the Italian adventure at Briançon, without success and without oysters. Bud, cheered up by the champagne, stuck to his legs.

"Never before did I have muscles like rock; here, can you feel it?" He took her hand and placed it on his upper thigh.

"Well, it doesn't feel like stone at all," Kaj laughed, but before she withdrew her hand he felt a slight pressure that electrified and reminded him that nobody, except for the masseur, had touched him there over the past three weeks.

Kollmann changed the subject. "You mustn't put all the blame on Mercier, Bud. During many stages I've watched you push the fifty-six-twelve too often and too long, and it was a complete waste of energy."

"He who wins is also right," muttered Bud and proceeded to attack a majestic two-pound lobster. He ordered more champagne for the others, who had arrived at the dessert.

"To better understand what fifty-six times twelve means," Kollmann turned to Kaj, "you have to realize that with this gear combination you cover 8.7 meters with one stroke. That's every long-jumper's dream, ever since Bob Beamon at the Olympics in Mexico jumped 8.9 meters. You can imagine how much energy is consumed by such a high gear. Bud's too careless with his energy, even if today, admittedly, his team manager deceived him and forced him to make unnecessary efforts."

"At least you're admitting that," said Bud, chewing on his lobster. "I'm done with him and with the entire Valetta team."

"You're changing teams?"

"It hasn't been finalized yet, but I have every intention of doing so."

"Sleep on it. After this Tour victory they'll increase your annual salary quite substantially."

"You think others are offering me peanuts? Let me tell you something, Max. Mercier remains in any case, because he's announcing everywhere that it was he who brought me to victory, and everybody believes him. But I'll never forget what he did to me today."

"He's a bulldog, but not a bad man," Lindner observed.

But it was only more grist for Bud's mill. "You may understand something about pills, doctor, and a lot more. But you have no idea about the strange world of the pros. Do you know what I am for a man like Mercier?"

"A rider in his care, I think."

"Care? Ninety percent of people like him only care for their own reputation; that much I've understood by now. Most of them have been in the saddle themselves. Then they borrow someone else's legs and put their head on them, if you follow me."

"I think I do. You're saying that they're doing the thinking for those who are cranking. It could be useful, couldn't it, provided these people have some experience?"

Bud waved a white-toothed lobster claw as if he wanted to attack the doctor. "Obviously you need team managers, but don't you understand that Mercier today didn't guide me but deceived me? For the first time in my life I collapsed. Blacked out. And now the idiot is proclaiming to the whole world that his instructions have brought about the victory. The Valetta bosses at the Eiffel Tower believed it, and tomorrow all of France will believe it."

"All of Europe," said Kollmann, blowing smoke across the table. And then, wrinkling his brow, he asked a question that interested him more than the emotions of a champion, which he had witnessed, taken in, and written about a thousand times before: "Did you say all this in front of the TV cameras?"

He saw immediately that his concern was unfounded. He was dealing with a real champion.

Bud took a generous gulp of champagne and played with the long stem of his glass without putting it down. "You ought to know me better, Max. What I'm telling you here, because I want to let off steam, I'm not shouting from the rooftops to millions of spectators. Officially, all is well between Mercier, the Valetta team, and myself. But I should be able to unburden myself with my friends."

"Your health," Kollmann and Lindner said, almost simultaneously, and raised their glasses. And as Kaj joined them, Bud felt another spark, this time from her large brown eyes, but he felt it with the same intensity with which he had felt her hand.

Some time ago, he thought, she despised me. Was it the victory? Was it true that all women adore success and that the winner can take it all? The champagne, which wasn't his first this evening— Valetta had let it flow generously at the Eiffel Tower—made his head and voice heavy; it was also past midnight. "I'll have to race in Roubaix tomorrow night, and I can't afford to come in last. Let me go to bed, friends."

Lindner and Kollmann nodded at the same time, and the physician spoke for both of them. "We have to apologize, Bud. It was selfish of us to make you come here. If anybody's in need of sleep, it's you."

"You don't have to apologize for anything. I had to speak my mind and also wanted to celebrate, okay?"

"Clear as champagne, Bud. I'll call a taxi for you. We'll stay a little longer, because we don't have to race in Roubaix. And we all have something else to do."

"What would that be?"

"Celebrate your victory, to which we have contributed a little. Or do you want us to give up now? Just think how much beer is flowing on your behalf in Dortmund tonight."

Bud gave some autographs to people who had been waiting discreetly, and had the taxi take him from Montparnasse to his hotel on the Place Vendôme. The driver had to wake him when they got there, and he didn't have to make change for the big bill either.

17

THOSE WITHOUT NAMES IN THE TOUR WENT HOME, AND THERE were many among them who, during these three weeks, could have made more money as unskilled construction workers. The hard core of the aces, however, pedaled through France to bring in the harvest, and also took some excursions into Belgium and Italy. Only a dozen riders or so, the first in the total point count, the mountain kings and the sprint specialists with several stage victories in their record. The organizers padded the field with local champs and, if they had a mind to, occasionally with some of the losers, because the public has a soft heart for them. They got a tenth of what Bud made; five times a week, sometimes only four.

He deposited money almost every day. Checks, but also a lot of bills from the cash boxes of small-time promoters, who lost it all if it rained. When he saw their disconsolate faces, he didn't insist on every last penny he'd been promised, and let a thousand bill go now and then. He was earning well, and living out of a suitcase was more strenuous than the races themselves, where nobody got humiliated. It was the spectacle that counted. People wanted to see the heroes of the Tour and sympathized if they didn't do their very best evening after evening. The autograph was a hotter item than the final sprint, although, like exuberant kids, the riders now and then went for it, to the jubilant cheers of the spectators.

Naturally, German organizers wanted to have Bud as well, but Daniel Dousset, king of French managers, held them back. The first weeks belonged to the traditional tour; Belgium was occasionally included as the bicycling circus moved through the north of France. Only later, to please Bud (and to increase the total revenue), would they enter the areas of the Ruhr and the Rhine.

The first races already demonstrated to Bud that he had reached the height of his popularity. People wanted to see him, and he commanded the highest appearance fees. There was no sense of envy among the other riders, but rather a more practical than warm camaraderie, because life is not bad in the wake of the crowd-puller.

Even his relationship with Antonelli improved. One evening in Reims the Italian ordered champagne in honor of Bud and embraced him in front of the press photographers, an event which the next day covered half a page in most papers. The lions no longer clawed each other but dealt gentle strokes.

Bud got along best with Merlin. He saw to it that his teammate—who, after all, had come in fifth—received contracts for the same races as himself, and he brought up Merlin's asking figures as well. He received at least a quarter of Bud's earnings, a respectable sum after forty races. Even the very best is lost in this profession if he only thinks of himself, and Bud had not forgotten Merlin's rescue operation between Béziers and Marseilles. Without it, Antonelli would have won the Tour that day.

Many rode for a tenth of Bud's wages and were happy with it. Many had been sent home, like migrant farmhands after the harvest has been brought in. They were only the window dressing; nevertheless they would be back next year to slave away for a pittance. As he cashed in his big earnings, Bud often asked himself why they would return. The Tour demands the same of everybody, and only to a very few is any real reward given.

He also talked to Merlin about it, because he often rode in his car from one town to the next. Valetta had put a car and driver at his disposal but he preferred riding with Merlin, unless they had to cover greater distances by plane. Merlin observed philosophically that the pleasure the small fry experienced in their suffering was in inverse proportion to their chances of winning. "Their reward is honor, believe me. I know someone in my town who rode the Tour five times and never made it beyond sixtieth place. But he's still dining out on it."

Bud replied that he would rather go back to working in a factory than slave on the road for the sake of honor only. At age fifteen the racing bike had been a thing of wonder, and he would take it apart five times a day and put it back together again. But two years later he had considered it only a means by which he was spared the factory. "I told myself: If I don't earn ten times that much on the bike, I'll throw it away."

"In the meantime it's become somewhat more than that," observed Merlin. "Just open a newspaper. Since Merckx, nobody has been more popular than you."

Bud felt that he was saying it without envy, and they became friends because of it.

In the second week of August they were racing in Liège. They had arrived from Cannes by plane and were grumbling about the big jump from the vacationers' paradise on the Riviera to the muggy and smelly air of the Belgian industrial city. And about the organizers who, ignoring all considerations of distance, decided on the schedule according to the wishes of the local promoters. There seemed to be no coordination, because a few days later they had to return to Marseilles. Apart from the money, they now began to count the days of the tour.

Bud felt listless, burned out, and down at the heels; when he closed his eyes and thought of the Liège racetrack, his stomach turned.

"What a shitty job," he said to Merlin. "We should have relaxed for a few days on the Riviera."

"But the contracts . . ." Merlin shook his head. "If I skip Liège, it wouldn't make waves. But you're the ace. It won't go on without you."

"I could be sick for a few days, couldn't I?"

"You're as fit as a fiddle, pal. A little out of sorts, but it'll pass. Do you think I wouldn't have enjoyed another night in Nizza? Did you get a look at the woman I had with me?"

Bud nodded. "Did you sleep with her?"

"And how. Three shags, if you want to know the truth. That's exactly what you need."

"You may be right."

"Of course I am. Isn't it enough that we slave for weeks? Do we also have to be monks? Honestly, I've been wondering about you. Women are after you because yellow makes them wild. It's always been like that during the Tour, but you act like a greenhorn."

"You should see my mail. Unequivocal offers with photos, and not the passport kind. I could ride a second Tour de France just to get laid."

"Too strenuous. Just do it now and then. It loosens you up more than the best massage and you get it out of your mind."

"You talk like I was a bull."

Merlin lit a cigarette, which he considered equally harmless to competitive athletics. "Let me tell you something, Bud. Every day we eat just as much as during the Tour. But we don't burn it up during these sham races, where we take in so much money. So we need a valve to let off steam, right?"

"My doctor would like your philosophy," said Bud. "He'd laugh his head off."

"I don't care. Did he supply you well for this part of the Tour?"

"He did. But if you're thinking of doping, you're on the wrong track."

"Ah, stop using that stupid word. I trust he gave you cortisone, just in case?"

"He did. But only for emergencies."

"Go ahead and take it. The stuff drives away melancholy and

fatigue and you look as if you have a lot to get rid of." When Bud didn't reply, he asked: "Do you have a girlfriend? I mean, a steady one?"

Bud nodded. "At home, in Dortmund. But I've kept my distance. She's no longer on my mind, if you know what I mean. She wanted to come to Paris for the last stage, but I made excuses and got out of it. I think first I'll have to digest my new situation."

"Do you find it difficult to be famous and to earn a lot?"

"Let me have a cigarette," Bud said. The black tobacco made him cough and he had to pause before going on: "Don't think the Tour victory has gone to my head. I wanted it and I knew that I could win. I came to win. But it was much harder than I had expected."

Merlin blew smoke through pinched lips. "Tell that to the reporters. I know what's up. You know that I was your rival even though I'm on the same team. I also joined in order to win, but you were stronger; so was Antonelli. Today I know that I have to give up any thoughts of a Tour victory."

"Luck is part of it."

"Save yourself the trouble. Don't remind me now about Béziers–Marseilles, because I pulled you along. I did so in my own interest, understand? And now it's paying off. Without you I wouldn't have landed all these contracts."

"You have more experience than I do, Didier."

"But you're the greater biker. I don't need a newspaper to tell me that. I've studied you often enough on the road, not only on the Tourmalet. I've always made good money in this shitty profession, and I still do, but I'm lacking that certain something you have."

"Who says so?"

"Call it my experience. And you have to gather your own. Only then can you win the Tour as often as Merckx and Anquetil."

"And why should I take cortisone?"

"Do you really think they only breathed in air? I've experienced the phase you're going through right now four times. Not as a winner, of course, but this miserable nomadic life and its dutiful turns on the racetracks is bound to wear down the strongest. After all, we're not going to the office and at night, we put on racing shoes instead of slippers. A guy needs something different now and then, if he doesn't want to go off his rocker. Take cortisone or a girl."

"Why not both?"

"Now you're talking. I've tried it. Three shags in a row."

"And at the next race you fall off the bike like a tired fly."

Didier Merlin laughed as if he had never heard a better joke. "Take a good look at me and then look into the mirror. I had a lot of fun last night, and so did the girl. Pity we had to leave Nice; she'd confirm what I'm saying. Don't I look like a man in top shape?"

Bud saw a suntanned face that the trials of the Tour had not managed to devastate, and he looked into lively and sparkling eyes.

"And don't I spin my daily workload every night, just like you? But you don't just look tired, you look fed up."

"Only during these last few days."

"Who cares? People want to see a radiant Tour winner and not a sourpuss. And it really pisses them off when they realize that you're in it only for the money."

"Am I supposed to throw kisses to the crowds?"

"Of course not. But you really should have a good roll in the hay. Then this whole circus will be more fun and more human. If I can be of help, let me know. Discretion guaranteed, especially with the press. Besides, I'm not a manager taking a percentage."

"*Sacré,* Didier." Bud slapped his shoulder and his laugh spread from the corners of his mouth to his eyes. "I've won the Tour and I'm capable of looking after myself."

When he arrived at the hotel in Liège, Bud got a cortisone tablet from his medical kit, which Doctor Lindner had given him for this grand tour.

On the racetrack that evening, he felt better than he had felt in a long time. Sitting in the saddle felt good. His weight, increased by four pounds since the end of the Tour because of reduced efforts and rich food, shifted from his legs into the saddle. His muscles were loosening up because of the easier circulation in his veins, which were opening up, and it felt as if his legs once again were in harmony with his body. He had lost that harmony when Mercier had driven him to extraordinary efforts during the final stage.

Belgium is a country where cycling is a religion and where more races are run than anywhere else in the world. And where the fans have a fine intuition for the harmony between a man and his bike—for the man who seems to be playing on his pedals and yet spins them more forcefully than those who, swaying their shoulders and gritting their teeth, appear to be engaged in hard labor. Bud also felt no pressure in his lungs. Breathing came as easy as pedaling, and the enthusiasm of the crowd, swelling from an admiring murmur to a stormy applause, flattered him like a soft tailwind.

Without any effort, playfully, he increased his tempo, forgetting all the tacit agreements that are part of such a parade of stars. Within seconds the yellow jersey had outdistanced the many-colored pack, where the head shakes became more violent than the cranking.

Antonelli rode up to him. "What's gotten into you? Are you mad? We were agreed that Vissers should win because he's from Liège."

Bud didn't respond. He shrugged and curved up the ramp where the track is most difficult and where your elbows touch the spectators leaning over the partition. His eyes, clear and shining in the draft, actually saw individual faces. No longer an anonymous crowd, but faces of men, women, and children, and he felt emanating from them a charge of enthusiasm that spurred him on. Everything was easy. He felt the pressure of his hands on the handlebar down into the tips of his toes, and invariably his rear wheel pushed ahead more forcefully whenever he increased this pressure. Gone was the feeling of claustrophobia inside the whirring field, where you have to watch for jostling elbows and minimal distances between buzzing tires. In the curve he shot down and noticed how he could wiggle through them everywhere and play with them as much as he liked.

The monotony of the continuous rotations inside the drum became pleasure instead of drudgery. Again he rode up to the balustrade where the straightaway runs into the steep face of the track. A girl was standing there and he could ride up to her so closely that her long black hair fluttered in his draft wind. He saw her large dark eyes and raised his hand to greet her. And again. And the others caught up because the man in yellow was climbing up to his girl, forgetting the race.

"That's better," said Antonelli when he was rolling next to him. "It doesn't pay to be unreasonable and in fifteen minutes we're done."

Bud again didn't answer, because he hadn't even listened. He rode up to the balustrade a few more times, but when the Belgian Vissers pulled ahead and the man with the board indicated the last five laps, he sped up. And it seemed as if the track didn't present itself to be conquered but came flying straight at him.

After three laps he caught up with the Belgian; his sprint was so irresistible that the local hero seemed to pedal in place, and people forgot that they had wished for his victory. There were discussions, as the bikers loosened their straps, and there were flowers for Bud. Long-stemmed red roses wrapped in clear plastic. During the victory lap he rode up to the balustrade and stopped. With one hand he held on to the railing, with the other he offered the flowers to the girl, and his lips kissed a cheek that not only didn't resist but pressed against him. At the same time he whispered his hotel and room number.

The hotel was close by and Bud could reach it faster on his bike than in a car. He rode in the blue sweat suit of the Valetta team and decided to shower in his room. That way he escaped the fans very easily and he did something he hadn't done in a long time: As he opened the door to his room, he whistled so loudly that it could be heard on three floors. But when he entered and closed his door, it took away all whistles and words. The girl was already lying in his bed, her back turned to him and the blanket pulled up. The lightning speed of timing was puzzling, but before he could consider it, he was in for a second surprise.

The hair protruding between blanket and pillow was blond. And when he pulled away the blanket, it was Kaj Lindner who, bursting with laughter, lay there, naked. She turned on her back, and it wasn't just the sight of her tanned body that took away his breath.

He swallowed twice before he could get out: "How did you . . . Mrs. Lindner . . . get into my bed?" Only to realize at the same moment how stupid the "Mrs. Lindner" sounded under the circumstances.

She was still laughing, crossing her arms behind her long hair, which reached down to her breasts.

"You're reacting exactly the way I thought you would, big bear. I'm here, isn't that enough? It's a skip and a jump from Cologne to Liège, and you're worth it."

Bud, still in his blue Valetta sweats, felt terribly dressed and, at the same time, terribly helpless. The laughing face, the blond hair, and the large brown eyes melted into those at the balustrade at the racetrack, and his pulse raced like on the Tourmalet. Never before had he pulled at a zipper so vehemently or thrown his pants into a corner, and all the rest.

"Stay as you are," he heard a voice from the bed, as he turned to get into the shower. "I'd like to smell you as you are, coming from work."

He had the presence of mind to turn the key in the door. And then there was just animal groping and the violent gyrations of two bodies. It was over before it had begun.

When Bud lay beside her, out of breath but still clinging to her as if he wanted to make sure that he hadn't been dreaming, not

Doctor Lindner but the brunette from the balustrade came to his mind. Kaj wasn't aware of it; her thoughts were elsewhere.

"Did you have a woman during or after the Tour, Bud?"

He shook his head while she lit a cigarette; he noticed that there were already four stubs in the ashtray on the bedside table.

"How did you get into my room, Kaj?"

She was blowing smoke through her stub nose, which gave her that young look.

"Look at the smoke, Bud. It passes even through keyholes."

"What do you mean?'

"It means that I have the room next to you and that there's a connecting door. It cost me a tip to the desk clerk. Besides, I told him that I was your fiancée. I don't think he believed me, but, as you must know by now, money talks."

"Give me a cigarette," Bud said.

When she had given him a cigarette and a light, he realized that it didn't solve his problem. He sat up in the rumpled bed and she realized with satisfaction that things between them weren't over.

"I have to talk to my manager, so we won't be disturbed."

"Okay. I have time. The whole night if you like."

"And Martin?"

"I'm beginning to think that you're feeling guilty, silly. As for myself, I'm not in the least, if you want to know the truth. And in case you should have bourgeois second thoughts, don't worry: He's at a physician's congress in Berlin."

Bud heaved half a sigh of relief, with one lung only, so to speak. "I still have to talk to my manager, Kaj. He's capable of breaking down a locked door."

"Okay, Bud. But hurry up, before you shrivel into an average citizen; everything about you is larger than in other men."

He treasured that remark as he slipped into his sweats. He said that he would be back in five minutes and raced down the corridor to Merlin's room. Didier's surprise was genuine. He was blow-drying his hair and didn't see any reason to interrupt his activity.

"You have to go down to the lobby right away, Didier, or there will be a disaster otherwise."

"You look as if the police were after you."

"Worse, Didier. Did you see the tall brunette at the balustrade, just before the curve?"

"I'm not blind. You kept riding up there, and then gave her your flowers. For her you ruined Visser's victory, right?"

"Right now that doesn't matter. But she might be turning up any minute."

"Congratulations. I didn't think you'd follow my advice that quickly."

"But she mustn't come, because there's another one lying in my bed."

"You must be kidding, Bud."

Merlin stared at him, incredulous, and then he burst out laughing. Bud stamped his foot, furious.

"Stop it this minute and help me before it's too late. I'll explain later."

Merlin, still laughing, slipped into his blue sweats. "I give you a friendly advice and you get yourself a whole harem. And now you need a eunuch to help you out."

"Nonsense. Take her for yourself if you like her."

Merlin grinned. "That sounds a lot better. I'll be downstairs in a minute. But what am I going to say to her?"

"What do I know? Tell her that my fiancée has arrived unexpectedly, or something like that. But get going, I have to get back. My door is unlocked."

"All's quiet at this point," said Merlin and put on yellow sport shoes. "When two women run into each other in a situation like this, you'd hear it."

"Get going," snapped Bud. "There's time for everything but not for this."

He had a good overall view of the lobby because there were few people around. But he had not come too early. Before he could light a cigarette, more out of nervousness than desire, the black-haired girl entered through the revolving door and headed toward the elevators. You could tell that she was intimidated by neither the scrutiny of desk clerks nor the elegance of the lobby. But before she could reach the elevator, Merlin stepped in front of her.

"May I speak to you for a moment, mademoiselle?"

Frowning, she looked at the man in the blue sweat suit; he found her even more attractive than at the racetrack and was annoyed that she obviously didn't recognize him.

"I'm Didier Merlin, mademoiselle."

"That's right, you also rode. Please excuse me. I'm expected."

"That's why I'm here. I'm a friend of Bud's."

"And what does that mean?" she asked and frowned again.

"Can we sit down for a moment? It's important, mademoiselle."

She hesitated, looking toward the elevator, then said: "Okay, if you like. But I don't have much time."

He directed her toward an empty group of armchairs, far enough from the reception desk in order not to be overheard.

"Cigarette?"

She declined. "Come to the point. I'm expected, and you seem to know it."

"Yes," said Merlin and he thought that he was sounding pretty naive. "But something unexpected came up."

"Something came up?"

"Something disagreeable, quite unexpected. Bud's fiancée came from Cologne. As you know, it's not far from here. She wanted to surprise him."

Again, the frown and a look from narrowed green eyes, under whose scrutiny he felt quite stupid. Nobody's fool, this girl, he thought, and tried to look at her a little more perkily.

"He's really sorry and quite angry."

"And what do I get out of this?"

Now or never, Merlin thought and looked into the green eyes. You have to gamble high in order to win. Put the trump card on the table.

"Well," he said searching the green eyes, "for example, you could have me."

With the speed of a snake's tongue, her hand flashed from the table and slapped his cheek. It resounded through the lobby and heads craned at the reception. Then she walked back to the revolving door, with dignity, on high heels and shapely legs. On this low note ended the day for Didier Merlin. All he had wanted to do was to give some friendly advice to Bud.

Bud was in the shower when Merlin called. His voice sounded curt but the news was good. "Forget about the brunette. She took off. But you owe me a bottle of champagne, and the very best."

"Any problems?"

"She certainly isn't in my bed, I've got a burning cheek instead. A slap in the face in front of everybody in the lobby, if you want to know the truth. Are those problems or not?"

"I'll show my gratitude, Didier."

"I certainly hope so."

"Everything else okay?"

"Of course. But I've learned something. Some women only go for yellow. Like the one in your bed right now."

Bud had no intention to elaborate this topic with Didier right now. Relieved, he put down the receiver, standing in a puddle of water. He dried himself off and got back into bed with Kaj Lindner.

"Was it your manager?"

"No, a colleague."

"I thought so. Am I creating problems for you?"

"Not in the least," he said. He had a hard time not laughing out loud, because he had given the problems to the one person who had recommended what he was doing right now. It was exactly like during the Tour: There are some stages when everything is going smoothly and others where you stumble from one mishap to the next.

He couldn't get enough. For a third time he proved to Kaj the power of the shining superstar.

Late that evening they went out to eat. She would have preferred to go to sleep, but she also understood the appetite of the man who had more behind him than a race.

And she marveled at his appetite. She felt like a sparrow next to a gorilla. At the end of the dinner when he put away a fully mature Normandy Camembert of respectable dimensions, while she picked at her vanilla sherbet, she wanted to know if all of this was good for him.

"Ask your husband," he laughed. "I'm a good carburetor. During the Tour, the food is lighter, more balanced, if you like. But I still have to regain six pounds."

"I wasn't aware of it."

Bud grinned and ordered champagne. "Do you still remember your ironic remarks in Paris, when I ordered oysters?"

"Every word. And I knew already that I'd sleep with you."

"And that it would come about so quickly?"

"Not quite. But I want to tell you another thing: when the time came, I didn't want to beat around the bush. No appointment, no prim preparations. That's why you found me naked in your bed."

"*Pour une surprise, c'était une surprise*—for a surprise it was a real one, the French would say."

"Your French is amazing."

"Well, I knew about ten words when I joined Valetta. I was a much better biker. But cranking alone isn't enough. If you don't understand people and can't communicate with them, you're lost. Kollmann taught me the beginnings. All in all, I owe him a lot. Even you, I owe him."

"You're exaggerating."

"Why? He introduced your husband to bicycle racing and made him my doctor. Would we ever have met without him?"

Kaj raised her glass of sparkling champagne. "Let's drink to Max Kollmann. Isn't he following this tour?"

"He's been home for a while. Gone on vacation, I guess. What we're doing now is just a circus, but it brings in the dough big time, especially for me."

There was pride in his voice and she couldn't help noticing.

"Look, it's the Tour winner who brings in the money for the promoters. Especially if it was an exciting Tour. And this one was. So he gets the lion's share, and the others divide the rest. He who wins, cashes in. You can compare it to any business."

"So you'd be the chairman of the board."

"You can call it that. But only until next year. That's the difference between those elected and those who have to win that position all over again. There are no guarantees and no privileges."

"You want to win again next year?"

"Of course."

"In that case, the big yellow Zampano ought to get some sleep now."

He fell asleep like a tired child and it wasn't the sun that woke them both, but the telephone. "What's up?" asked Merlin. "Are you coming with me to Namur, or are you going with your fiancée?"

The irony in his voice woke Bud completely. He's still sore, he thought. Yawning, he asked what time it was.

"Nine-thirty," said Merlin. "Time for breakfast. But perhaps you'll be having *le café des pauvres?*"

Bud didn't get it. *Café des pauvres* means "the coffee of the poor."

"What's all this nonsense, Didier?"

"You may be rich now, Bud, but you still don't know enough French." His laughter sounded like the bleating of a goat. And Bud was annoyed because it was a jealous bleating.

"Will you tell me what it's all about?"

"Okay, listen. You know that people who can afford it take a liqueur and a coffee after a meal. At least a coffee."

"I know that much."

"And what do poor people do?"

"How should I know?"

"You have a long fuse, Bud. They make love. It doesn't cost anything and is *le café des pauvres*. Do you get it finally?"

"Of course. But did you have to wake me up to tell me such a dumb joke?"

"No, only to find out if I should take you to Namur. A friend has brought my car."

Bud didn't have a free hand to scratch his chin: with his left he held the receiver, and the right was busy with Kaj.

"Let me think, Didier. What time is the race in Namur?"

"At 7 P.M."

"In that case don't worry about me. I'll find a way, even if it has to be the train."

"Okay, Bud. See you tonight. Have fun with your fiancée."

Bud hung up and slid his arm under Kaj's back. His feet kicked off the sheet and blanket. Half sitting, half lying, he looked at her body in the filtered light; the sun was already high.

"How tanned you are, Kaj."

"And you. Where the sun reaches you, you're almost black. But the white parts are much larger because you're wearing such funny clothes. Why are racing pants so long? Look at it. Above the knee you're white as chalk."

"Racing pants have to be tight and long."

Brusquely she swung her right leg over his left one. He was aroused instantly.

"You have hair on your chest and arms. Why not on your legs?"

"Because we shave them. The legs of bikers have to be shiny like well-greased pistons."

Her fingertips touched the veins that felt like cords, and where the thighs turned white, they took on a bluish hue.

"You're tickling me and making me wild."

"Let me play, big bear. Cool down and turn on your belly."

He turned over and felt her fingertips glide higher.

"You have defined muscles everywhere—where others have soft, tired flesh."

"You sound as if you had experience."

"Some, Bud. Do you know that I'm ten years older than you?"

"Impossible." He lifted his face from the pillow without moving his back. "You have the body of a young girl."

"Maybe I'm well preserved, but I'm thirty-three years old. Too old for you."

He pushed his head back into the pillow. "Don't talk nonsense and keep going. I like to feel your hands."

With gyrating soft movements she moved higher, and laughed suddenly. "That's not a baby's bottom."

"It's the saddle, Kaj."

"I think the behind wasn't made for the saddle."

"Mine has been made for it. Do you know what your husband says?"

"About your behind?"

"About everything. I mean, when he talks about stuff like morphology and physiology. It has to do with proportions and leverage. He says, if there weren't a racing bike, it would have to be invented for me. He's taken thousands of measurements. Not only heart, lung, and those things. He's measured me with a tape as well and compared it to the measurements of previous champions."

"Yes, I know. He spent so much time on you that it often made me furious. He considers you an ideal combination of two great bike racers, but I forgot their names."

"Merckx and Anquetil?"

"Maybe so," Kaj laughed. "But I really don't care. I measure you in my way."

Bud grinned from his pillow. "At times it becomes an obsession with him, and he would be quite put out if he saw us lying here."

"What's that supposed to mean?"

"Don't you know that he wanted to mate me with the daughter of an old biker because he had fallen in love with his proportions? He was really convinced that with her I could have produced an unbeatable biker."

"And what did you have to say to this?"

"I told him that she was bowlegged and that I wasn't a breeding bull."

She laughed and pressed herself against him. "Do you like me better?"

His reply was passionate and asked for no response but Kaj.

Around noon she drove back to Cologne in her little sports car, and that night Bud rode the race in Namur, which he finished far back, and which went to his legs.

18

FIVE DAYS LATER THEY WERE RACING IN PAU. BUD PLACED SECOND after Merlin, a native of that region; his victory was greatly celebrated. Immediately after the race, which finished at dusk, Bud took the Valetta car and headed for Eaux-Bonnes. He had not been home yet after the end of the Tour, only telephoned his parents a few times; he would see them in a week. But this drive to Eaux-Bonnes seemed like a homecoming to him. He drove past harvested fields, felt the end of the summer that had brought him fame, and the harvest he was bringing in every day. The wind, blowing from the mountains, mussed his hair. It was cooler than during July.

It was dark when he turned into the little road leading to the Iribars' village; only now it occurred to him that he might be arriving at a closed door. He had never written. The reaping of fame didn't leave him any time. But from far off he saw light in the old Basque farmhouse, and before he had turned off the engine the heavy oak door opened and out burst little André.

"Bud! Bud! Grandfather was right. He said that you'd come."

Bud got out, lifted up the boy, and kissed him on both cheeks.

"Grandpa said that?"

"Yes, he was absolutely sure."

A white tablecloth was spread across the large table, making the kitchen look festive, and from the hearth came the pungent smell of roast lamb. The old man embraced him in the entranceway.

Then the young woman and her husband kissed him, and never since his Tour victory, making the rounds through the French countryside, had he felt such natural spontaneity. It was a home-coming.

"I'm beginning to think you waited with dinner for me."

"Of course, Bud," the old man laughed and pushed him down on the chair where he had sat twice before. He welcomed him like a son. "I knew that you'd come, but they didn't believe me."

"I simply had to come, you've guessed it. And I'm just as hungry as the time when I came begging."

"With a tiny difference," replied the old man. "Then you were a little worm who was about to give up, and now you're the greatest. But hadn't I told you so?"

Bud, dressed as then in his blue Valetta sweats, put his hands on the wooden table under the white tablecloth. "At this table I won the Tour. What I'm doing is a pilgrimage, if you'll allow me such a big word."

"We're honored," said the old man. "Whenever Pau was the goal of a stage, Bartali drove to Lourdes to put flowers into the grotto of Sainte Bernadette."

"One moment," Bud got up. "I have to fetch something from the car."

He returned after two minutes with a plastic bag, which he handed to the old man. "If André hadn't jumped at me like a puppy, I would've brought it in right away."

The watery eyes became large when a jersey came out, miserably dirty, but also undoubtedly yellow.

"It was my first, and it is for you. For all of you. It's the yellow jersey from the Tourmalet."

He took an envelope from his pocket, and the pressed gentian flower fell out.

"This I'll keep. It brought me good luck."

"Thanks, Bud." The large hand of the old farmer stroked the jersey and he announced: "It'll hang in my room, as it is, unwashed."

"Unwashed?" Dirty laundry, the eyes of the young woman said, had to be washed.

With a gesture that silenced all arguments he said: "You don't understand. It's going to hang as is, *basta!*" And to Bud: "Maybe a clean jersey is more appealing, but in this one, there'll be always you. I've seen almost all the yellow jerseys of the Tour but never held one in my hand."

"It's yours, because I owe it to you," said Bud, "and that's why I'm here, and the jersey stands for the flowers Bartali brought to Lourdes."

"You know, he won the Tour only twice," said the old man, "because of the war. But he made a record that will never be broken. In 1938 he won his first Tour, 1948 his second. Can you imagine, ten years apart?"

Bud grinned. "I don't want to wait that long."

"And I don't want to wait for dinner any longer," laughed the old man. "Can we eat now?"

When the woman cleared the table it was going on midnight and more wine had been poured than before the stage on the Tourmalet. But Bud asked the old man for a personal talk. The old man remained seated like a young one, let some of the wind blowing from the mountains come through the window and looked at him, expectantly.

Bud didn't know how to begin. He lit a cigarette and only after a few draws did he begin.

"What I'm about to say I wouldn't even tell my father."

"Don't keep me in suspense, kid. You still don't know old Iribar and the Basque way. Nothing will leave these four walls, even if you had committed a crime."

"I've fallen in love."

"So what? Is that all?"

"It's the wife of my doctor."

"Mmm, that's not exactly the rule, but in itself not a crime. Is she in love with you as well?"

"I don't really know. Last week, in Liège, we slept together. She was lying in my bed when I returned from the race."

"Just like that?"

"Just like that."

"Mmm, I want to tell you something Bud. It's been a long time since I was known in these mountains as a dashing fellow, but I haven't forgotten a thing. If I were a senile old man, I couldn't have told you about the Tour either, right?"

Bud nodded.

"Listen to me. When a woman is lying in your hotel bed, she obviously doesn't want to say rosaries but wants you to take action. That's what you did, and I wouldn't have acted differently. Provided she's not a witch with green teeth."

"She's beautiful," said Bud.

"And how old?"

"Thirty-three."

"O là là! A good age, but not for you. Does she have children?"

"No. And why should she be too old for me?"

Old Iribar reached for his shaggy white hair under the cap. "Look, Bud, your life has just begun and you're already famous. Let's not even talk about the money. And your little doctor-wife hasn't thought about it either, although you're taking in a lot more than her husband—who at your age was probably in his third semester at medical school."

Bud got angry. "If you want to hold it against me that I'm making too much money without having learned a decent profession, I should have kept my mouth shut. I had to talk to someone, and I trust you."

Soothingly, the old man put his large hand on Bud's fist, which was bunching up the napkin. "Let me finish, Bud. That you're earning a lot of money at an age where others are still in some professional training and have to be supported is one thing. How you deal with it, yet another."

"I know that tune. Successful pros are brainless musclemen, to whom everything comes easy. That's what you want to say, don't you?"

Old Iribar shrugged, irritating Bud with his ironic wisdom.

"I apologize, but I'm nervous. Damn it, it's all because I fell in love, and it's not my fault if that doesn't enter your stubborn Basque head."

"Are you thinking of marrying her?"

"Why not?"

"I thought so. One doesn't get so worked up over a casual flirt. And how do you know that it wasn't casual for her? That's the first problem. But there are others. First, she would have to get divorced, and she's also the wife of a man to whom, in my estimate, you owe a lot."

"That's right."

"Pretty shabby, don't you think?"

"Situations like this have always existed, and they always will."

Old Iribar drew down the corners of his mouth. "That's just big talk, Bud, and you want to soothe your bad conscience with it. But you've asked my advice, and there it is. Meet again, sleep with her, if that's what you want. I don't even think she would want a repeat."

"And why not?"

"Look, Bud, you may take me for a senile old peasant who only knows sheep, pastures, and mountains. But I know women, and I want you to remember one thing: They're drawn to power and success like the moth to the light."

"In my case you can't exactly talk about power," Bud interjected.

"Very well, leave that to the politicians and royalty. But you're not only successful, you're also a hero, because you've won the Tour. And do you realize that in these dull times there are hardly any heroes to be found? That's why you have to go looking for them. You have no idea how often we sat in front of the TV, trembling, rejoicing for you. My son bought a portable for the stable, so at milking time he wouldn't miss anything."

"You're getting away from the topic."

"Not at all, kid. I'm in the middle of it. What's happening here happened in millions of families. Imagine how many women would rather have gone to bed with you every night than with their chicken-breasted, thin-legged husbands."

"Maybe so. I got plenty of mail suggesting that. But only one is on my mind."

"And she didn't react any differently from all the others. Only she skipped the letter and just arrived. You didn't take her—she took you. Wanted to have a biker for breakfast. You don't seriously believe that she's in love with you? Did she say anything to that effect?"

"Something like this you just feel," Bud replied stubbornly. "Or don't you trust my intuition?"

"If you want to hear the truth, I trust you much more with a successful race across the Tourmalet. Admiration is one thing, love quite another. What do you want to do with her if you should live together?"

"That's my business."

"Nothing of the kind, Bud. For the time being, let's say for the next ten years, you can't live together with a woman. You modern bicycle racers don't ever get out of the saddle. You haven't even seen your parents since the Tour victory. And during the winter you're going to tear from one six-day race to another. Do you really think a woman like that wants a husband for four weeks out of every year? And when you will have time for her she'll be over forty. Have you thought about this?"

The old man tried to catch Bud's eyes but he kept them lowered, as if there was nothing more interesting in the world than his fingers, lying on the table like those of a scolded schoolboy.

"You have nothing to say to this, am I right? I'd be very surprised if things weren't the way I see them. And I want to tell you something else, because a certain Fausto Coppi comes to my mind. He also pinched the wife of a physician. Does the 'White Lady' mean anything to you?"

"Not much."

"From that moment on it went downhill with him. There was a highly publicized divorce, and he thought he could give her everything, with all the money he had earned cranking a bike. Then she was residing in her elegant villa and he continued racing. He raced and raced and raced, even when he was forty years old. And do you know why? Because he hadn't learned to do anything else, and because he felt superfluous at the big parties she was giving. He literally fled with his bike and tried to prolong his career, like an old actor. And then he caught a deadly disease during a race in Africa. That's the sad story of Fausto Angelo Coppi."

Bud had had enough. "In a minute you'll tell me that there are still bears on the Tourmalet that will devour me if I don't listen to you." He looked at his watch. "I apologize, it's one o'clock and I'm going to race in Bordeaux tonight."

"Why don't you sleep here? You can save time and pick up your suitcase tomorrow in Pau."

"May I?"

"Certainly. If you have another five minutes, I wanted to satisfy my curiosity. An old man like myself needs very little sleep."

"Okay," said Bud but he pulled away the glass that the old man wanted to fill again.

"I read that you want to change over to an Italian stable. Pellegrini, is it?"

"Right. It's almost a deal. I wanted to get away from Valetta, and the incident with Mercier during the final stage broke the camel's back."

"But Antonelli is number one at Pellegrini."

"He used to be. He's changing as well. They want me as their new captain, and you know that the Italians pay better than the French. Much better."

"How much did they offer you?"

"More than a million fixed per year. Without the bonuses, of course."

"Franks?"

"German marks."

"You're a rich man, Bud."

"Let's say I've forged ahead because of the Tour victory, and the money will keep coming in from the fall into the winter months."

"Six-day races?"

"Of course. You know that in Germany there's hardly any road racing, but more winter racetracks than anywhere else in the world. And the promoters are after me. Fifteen thousand marks a day; for every six-day race, that's ninety thousand. Nobody before me has earned that much."

"And you want to race all of them?"

"Most of them. You have to make hay while the sun shines. When I get home next week, I'll sign the contracts."

Old Iribar wrinkled his weathered brow. "I don't like it, Bud. If you move from one smoke-filled hall to the next, you'll lose your punch. Do you really have to pick up every mark when you have a contract for a million in your pocket? Your body has to recuperate after what's behind you. The really great ones of the roads never forgot that. Remember Bobet, Anquetil, and Merckx. They rode a six-day race now and then, because it's part of the show, but they never let go of a real winter rest."

"In Germany it's different. Our racing takes place in the halls, and I'm needed there, just as Altig, Wolfshohl, and Junkermann were needed. Besides, I'll have time left to relax."

"That's what you think." Old Iribar shook his head under the greasy beret. "You'll have to gear up for the spring classics, and your new Italian employers will demand a full program. They don't let go of an Antonelli to buy a tired pig in a poke."

"Naturally, I'll have to race the Giro," Bud conceded.

"Of course. And how are you going to prepare for it? Do you know that in the past, when the snow was melting, bikers came to Sainte-Marie-de-Campan or to Eaux-Bonnes in droves to train on the Tourmalet? They didn't hurry from one race to the next, they took their time to prepare for a big event like the Tour. I don't have to tell you that there are only a few weeks between the Giro and the Tour."

"There have been bikers who rode both tours."

"I know that," growled the old man. "But they paused during the winter and didn't dig their own grave."

"I'll talk it over with my doctor," said Bud, but bit his tongue immediately.

Old Iribar chuckled. "That's a good idea—a better one than taking away his wife. Let's go to bed. You'll have to do your circus number in Bordeaux tonight."

19

FROM BORDEAUX THE CARAVAN OF PUBLICLY CANONIZED AND popular heroes of the Tour de France wound its way eastward, over Tours, Nancy, and Metz, and it began to split up. A small group went with Bud to Dortmund for the first appearance of the Tour winner on German soil. It was a greater event than the German soccer championship of Schalke 04. A quarter million people lined the round course of eighty kilometers, and although many didn't buy a ticket, Bud's top wages still were a minimal expense for the promoters. He won after two hours with a large lead over the next riders, and the fans trying to tear the yellow jersey off his back were more of a danger than the competition.

Later they besieged his home. Again and again he had to show himself on the balcony, and into the night friends and acquaintances showed up who couldn't be turned back. He barely had time for his parents, but strangely enough, they enjoyed the storm. They were basking in it.

Not Bud. Ever since he had gotten off his bike as winner of the Tour, he had seen too much of it. When photographers and journalists stormed the house the next morning, he decided to run away, although he had one day off from racing, which would have meant two nights in his own bed.

Therefore he arrived a day earlier than planned in Cologne, where he was to start next. Early in the morning he called Doctor

Lindner from the hotel, but he dialed the private number, hoping to find Kaj.

He was in luck and her voice sounded cheerful. "When will you come to see us, Bud?"

"I'd like to talk to you alone, Kaj."

She hesitated for a few moments. "Is that necessary, Bud?"

"I'm asking you a favor."

"All right. Where and when?"

"Right away, if you can manage." He told her the hotel and the room number.

Max Kollmann was driving on the Autobahn toward Dortmund. The race of the previous evening had been of no interest to him. From an athletic point of view these moneymaking races of the stars were unimportant, and the commotion caused by Bud's first appearance at home, as the Tour winner, could be left to the yellow press. They had their heyday of euphoria and hyperboles. But Kollmann wanted to talk to the kid in peace and quiet, and he had good reasons for it.

He drove fast in order to get there around noon. His right foot pressed down the gas pedal. He was always driving in the left lane, as if the Autobahn were a road closed to the public for the Tour de France; hands on the steering wheel like the hands of a clock indicating ten minutes to two o'clock, and every twenty minutes a new cigarette in his mouth. He had some testy thoughts, but also some doubtful ones. This wasn't exactly his job. What he intended to do could be called an interview, a report; but if the Budzinskis didn't want to understand, he was little more than an idiot who, as a self-appointed professional counselor was inhaling exhaust fumes instead of enjoying a few more vacation days.

I have to do something, Max Kollmann thought. Just like that: interfere with someone's life. And he thought of the many interferences that were and were not being committed. Also of the diabolic thirst for glory on the part of parents who cripple their ten-year-old daughters' spines and instead of Olympic medalists make invalids out of them. And he thought of others who throw the girls into the water six hours every day so that in butterfly or freestyle, they would swim from one success to the next, but would never be able to have children. He thought of mothers of ice skaters who didn't realize that they were depriving their children of their youth, and who would gladly administer rat poison to the judges if nobody took notice. And he thought of athletes whose burgeoning muscles tore apart tendons because they didn't grow sufficiently in those anabolic powerhouses that were their bodies. He thought of sad supermen dancing only one summer, and of the thoughtlessness with which the troubadours of the media celebrated them and then cast them aside.

This Bud, this Ernst Budzinski, who had emerged into the international limelight from a drab miner's cottage, had changed. He was no longer the person who, earlier this summer, had started the Tour de France. Kollmann searched his memory for names of promising talents who had burned themselves out in a single season. Tinder. No wood to keep a fire going. Many came to mind. But also people like Anquetil and Merckx. Like Bud, they had come from nothing and at age nineteen, had taken the lead over the strongest pros. And at age twenty-three they still hadn't gone wrong. Was Bud—whose talent wasn't any less astounding—was Bud about to go wrong?

At the Dortmund exit Kollmann put the brakes on his imagination and on his car. He had to concentrate on slow-moving traffic and ask for the house Bud had built for himself and for his parent the previous year. Bikers only build houses after the first successes. It was a pretty house with a small front yard and flowers, and a polished brass plate that said BUDZINSKI. The man by that name opened the door himself, but it wasn't Bud and he looked more distinguished than Kollmann remembered him. Father Budzinski wore a suede jacket, and the matching pants were not from the department store but tailor-made. His beer belly pushed them way down to his hips, but in contrast to earlier days, the retired miner had shaved.

Kollmann sensed that he not only read his mind but found what he was reading flattering.

"Nice to see you, Mister Kollmann. As you can see, things have changed around here."

"Yes, I see," Kollmann said, entering into a room that was a combination of middle class, nouveau riche style, and a trophy museum. A display case housing more or less ugly trophies dominated the room. It was standing on a new Oriental rug. He sat down on the flowered couch in front of a color TV set while Father Budzinski opened the hatch of a remarkably well-stocked bar. He did so with an inviting gesture.

"You have a choice, as you can see. The times of beer and schnapps are gone in my house."

He says "in my house," Kollmann thought.

"Champagne? Or whiskey on the rocks?"

"As you prefer," said Kollmann.

"Let's have champagne. It's more festive, and we have every reason to celebrate, don't we?"

"Of course," said Kollmann. He watched the bloated face still showing the signs of the victory celebration from the night before.

And once again Budzinski seemed to read his thoughts. "It got late last night, as you can imagine. You don't celebrate a Tour winner every day."

"And Bud?" asked Kollmann. "Still asleep?"

"He left for Cologne an hour ago."

"But the race isn't until tomorrow, isn't it?"

Budzinski—who was not only retired at age forty-three but also looked like a retiree—scratched his chin. "He wants to get a thorough physical from his doctor."

"Mmm," mumbled Kollmann, "it still puzzles me. It wasn't that urgent, was it? I mean, when he's been away from home for so long. Doesn't he have a girl in this town?"

"Well," said Budzinski, still scratching his chin, "actually she was here last night and probably had intended to stay, as in the past, since we have all that room in the house, and we aren't that strict either. We were young once, weren't we? But what does he do? Says he's tired and sends her home. My wife was quite sad and cried. You know how women are. She probably thought already about marriage."

"She's not here?"

"Still out shopping, and that can take some time. Since all that commotion about Ernst, they won't let her leave the store. But that's not so bad: We can down a bottle in peace without her making a face."

He let the cork pop to the ceiling and was happy. "Those are the best shots, aren't they?"

"Not bad at all," said Kollmann, "I'd like to talk to you about Bud."

Budzinski, although not at his most alert, did not miss the undertone. Kollmann had not come to carouse. And he didn't beat around the bush either.

"Is it true that he wants to do ten six-day races?"

"You've hit it on the head." Budzinski nodded and raised his glass with the pride of a profiteer, which infuriated Kollmann. He ignored his glass and his flat hand hit the brand-new marble coffee table.

"Have you all gone out of your mind? That's almost everything running in all European indoor tracks between October and February."

"Not quite," said Budzinski and got up. "We have gone through it very carefully. There are enough intervals in between. Wait, I'll get the schedule from the office. We also have an office now. With a son like this, we need it."

He returned with a file of contracts. "Let's see. In October Madrid, Berlin, Dortmund, and Frankfurt. In November Munich, Ghent, and Zurich. I admit, it's a lot, but in December there's only

Cologne and Maastricht. And then January with Bremen, Antwerp, and Milan."

"Let me take a look at it."

He handed him the file.

It didn't take Kollmann long to total it up. "This is even worse. I count twelve, and if he really wants to reel off this program, he's done for. Every third-rate biker will thumb his nose at him during the next road season."

"First of all," and Budzinski raised his glass without toasting Kollmann, "not all contracts have been signed yet, and second, it's none of your damn business how many six-day races we're riding."

"What do you mean: 'we'? Are you his partner on the track? You're a thoughtless profiteer, if you want to know the truth, and you're going to ruin your son's career before it really gets started."

Budzinski burped and there was a nasty glint in his eyes, obfuscated by alcohol.

"If you've come to lecture us, you could have saved yourself the trouble. We don't need your advice."

"There was a time, and not too long ago, when Bud accepted it quite willingly. I'll leave you with your champagne, Mr. Budzinski. I thought I could talk rationally with you."

Budzinski, almost in a gesture of protest, poured himself another glass and drank it down with one swig. "Until now"—his tongue was getting heavy—"I've gotten along very well with the press. You can't accuse me of that. Go ask Ernst."

"I'm not the press, Mr. Budzinski. Most of those fellows breaking down your door these days and buttering you up don't have the faintest idea about your son's profession—which at times, in case you don't know, is a dirty profession. You can ask your Ernst that as well."

"But don't you see, Mister Kollmann, the boy also must have his reward. Should he ignore a million?"

"What you forget is that less than half will be left once he's paid taxes and his masseur."

Budzinski narrowed his little pig eyes to a conspiratorial smirk. "There are also some tricks, and in this I'm smarter than you think. Of course he can't do without a manager, and that's where I come in; no need to grin."

Kollmann laughed because the situation was so ridiculous. Now he really needed a glass of champagne and fished for a cigarette. The fatso who was sitting there in front of him in his tailored sport shirt bursting at the seams was about to slaughter the talent he had produced.

"Nevertheless I have to talk to Bud," he said. Budzinski filled his glass and said with rebellious proprietary pride: "With Ernst or with me, it's all the same. I've talked it over with him. Think of it— ninety thousand each six-day race. For that sum I worked three years in the mines."

Kollmann would have liked to call him a hopeless simpleton, but he bit his tongue and instead blew smoke into the arrogant, puffy face.

"Even if we assume, Mr. Budzinski, that you're right and Bud's a phenomenon who can ride tirelessly for months on end, there's still the risk of a fall. You know that Bud has a lot of enemies who can provoke a spill on those very narrow indoor tracks with masterful precision. And a fracture of the clavicle or a rib would be the least of it."

Budzinski made a dismissing gesture. "You know as well as I do that in the past Ernst rode a lot on the indoor tracks. He knows what's up."

"Agreed. But now his place is the road. The great tours are important for him, and the halls will take away his punch. I don't know if you understand this. If he would only do half of the six-day races, it would pay off two and three times on the road."

"You'll have to leave that decision to me," Budzinski said pointedly.

Kollmann was tempted to break the champagne bottle on this stubborn blockhead, but he used it instead to pour again and shot back: "And how was it, when he had his first wins as amateur on the track? Didn't he win in order not to have to go to the factory where you wanted to send him, and wasn't it me who convinced you that he could earn a lot of money on the roads?"

"So what?" Budzinski's calm was provoking; he went to the house bar to get another bottle. "I made the transition to pro possible for him, because I was of the same opinion as you. And now I get the damn feeling that you're not just playing the great discoverer and promoter but also the manager. Next you'll be demanding percentages."

That was enough, even from one who had gone to bed with the bottle and woken up with it. Kollmann was quite willing to make allowances for that but not for such an insult. He left the house without a good-bye, and even when he was on the Autobahn to Cologne, he cursed the man whose head had been fogged up with narrow-mindedness, greed, and alcohol.

Why was it, he thought, that so many fathers of stars suffered from victory syndromes to which they were not entitled and which did them no good?

20

When Kaj Lindner stepped into Bud's hotel room, he found her more desirable than ever. But she held out her hand—it seemed unintentionally quite far out—so that the planned embrace couldn't take place. Before he could say something she sat down in the armchair and took cigarettes and a lighter from her purse.

"So what's so important, Bud? Why did I have to leave everything and come here? I thought we could get together tonight at our house for a relaxed chat."

"And your husband?"

"He's here, of course, and wants to give you a physical. That's important, isn't it? Martin thinks that you've been overdoing it since the Tour."

He was irritated by her businesslike tone. And wasn't there a trace of irony in it?

"Can I have a cigarette?"

She handed him the pack and the lighter, and he sat down on the edge of the bed, not at the little table.

After a few draws he said: "Last time you were different."

He realized how aloof and silly this sounded and bit his tongue. But she came to his rescue and when he looked up, he didn't see any mockery in the large brown eyes.

"Don't be a child, Bud. It was beautiful in Liège. For me as well. But we didn't talk about a continuation, because there can't be one."

"And why not?"

"Bud, I'm ten years older than you and married to a man who's very fond of you. I don't say happily married, because I don't like big words. But you didn't think seriously of starting an affair with me that would be public in two weeks' time, or even that I would get a divorce?"

Bud did not reply and looked after the blue smoke rings of his cigarette. Old Iribar was right after all. The yellow jersey, sweat, and laurels of the winner, all that stuff he had talked about. Once a Tour winner for breakfast and then good-bye.

"Why don't you say something?"

"Because for me it was different than it was for you."

"It was beautiful, Bud, but I didn't lose my head."

"And I broke up with a girl yesterday in Dortmund because of you. That's the reason I'm here a day early. Does that tell you something?"

Kaj smiled, got up and sat down next to him on the bed. "It tells me that you are a silly boy, Bud. I'm a woman, and though not immune to foolishness, I keep my head on my shoulders. I like you and I hope we will remain friends."

"Friends! When a woman says 'friends' there is no love left."

"Was it love?"

"For me it was. It still is."

She put her arm around his shoulder, and her large brown eyes turned serious. "You're a big child. You have fame, money, and a whole life ahead of you. I'm at midway, and in a few years' time I'll be an old woman for you. Did you ever think about that?"

"You're the first woman I really loved, Kaj."

He pulled her toward him so violently that no resistance was possible. A button burst off the yellow blouse that was the color of her hair. He kissed her for a long time and then bent her back onto the bed with hands that seemed like a vise.

But the next moment he jumped up because someone was knocking at the door. And he hadn't even locked it. For a split second he was tempted to lunge for it and turn the key. But he stood there, rigid and helpless, while she got up, smoothing over her hair and blouse.

There was another knock. "May I come in, Bud?" It was the voice of Max Kollmann.

"Just a minute," said Bud. He looked at Kaj and pointed to the armchair. When she was seated he went to open the door.

Kollmann's surprise was complete and he had difficulty hiding it.

Apart from the missing button on her blouse, their embarrassment would have been enough to explain the situation even to a blind man. He slumped down in the second armchair and reached for his cigarettes. He busied himself with lighting one, and it granted them all some time, although none of them knew what to do with it. Bud sat down on the edge of the bed, like that time in Pau, when Kollmann had woken him in the middle of the night.

Kaj reacted with feminine logic and both men were relieved when she started to speak.

"You're sitting there as if the roof had caved in. Maybe you'd have a reason for it, if instead of Max, Martin would've turned up, and even then the two of you would be off the hook, and I'd be in the hot seat, right?"

She's right, both thought, and there was the slightest smile around the corners of Kollmann's mouth, while Bud's face returned to its normal color. Kollmann was a pal and would keep his mouth shut, even if it would have been better if he had found any other woman but Kaj Lindner in the room. Bud got up to get the champagne, which he had put on ice.

The bottle was already swimming among the watery ice cubes. He dried it off and Kaj had enough time to whisper to Kollmann: "I'm going in a minute. Come at five in the afternoon. I'll explain everything."

Bud put two water glasses from the bathroom on the table and loosened the cork.

"Shall I get another glass?"

Kollmann shook his head. "What for? One for Kaj and one for the two of us." And he held back a laughing fit that wanted to bubble up like champagne. It had to do with the stage in Briançon and two outrageously expensive bottles of champagne. He wasn't able to repress the entire laugh, which wasn't such a bad thing. It helped diffuse the tension. They toasted to each other.

"I'm only having this sip," said Kaj and looked at her watch. "I still have to do errands and you, Bud, are expected in Martin's office at five o'clock. He wants to do a full inspection, he said, and when you're ready, you'll come over for dinner. You'll come as well, won't you, Max, or do you have another engagement?"

"There's nothing I'd rather do," said Kollmann, and after a moment, there were only the two men and Kaj's perfume left in the room.

There was a trace of helplessness in Bud's gaze, and Kollmann avoided looking into his eyes. "Look, Bud, you don't owe me an explanation." He emptied his glass and fished for a new cigarette. "A date is no crime; but I have to admit I would have expected anybody else but her."

"So you want an explanation after all."

"Why?"

"Because you implied that much just now. Want to laugh? You'll get it, too. I've fallen in love with Kaj."

"Fallen in love? Am I hearing right?"

"You are indeed. And do you know why? Because she's different from all those girls who are after me. But the crazy thing is that she was after me as well."

"Her?" Kollmann let the burning match drop from his hand. "Kaj was after you?"

Bud nodded. "Or what would you call it if you returned to your hotel from a race, without the slightest suspicion, and found a naked woman in your bed?"

"Not Kaj Lindner. That's impossible, Bud."

"You'd be surprised: That's exactly how it happened in Liège.

'Distinguished Lady Jumps Unsuspecting Biker Before He Can Get Into His Well-Earned Shower.' *Playboy* would pay you quite a bit for this story, don't you think?"

Kollmann didn't reply and drew on his cigarette, shaking his head.

"I know, I'm committing an indiscretion in her regard, but I also know that you can keep your mouth shut. There's only one other person who knows about it."

Kollmann took the cigarette out of his mouth; there was an expression of surprise and anger in his eyes.

"Are you out of your mind? Do you realize what could come from all of this? At this moment, stupid as it may sound, you're one of the most prominent names in Germany, and if the tabloids get wind of it, they'll have the scandal of their dreams."

For the first time since Kollmann had entered the room, Bud's smile was genuine. "The only one who knows anything is the old Basque farmer from Eaux-Bonnes. The one from the Tourmalet, remember?"

Kollmann heaved a sigh of relief. "Okay, he won't do any damage. He seems to have become your father confessor."

"If you like. I went to him from Pau like the other time, before the Tourmalet. He's brought me luck."

"But in this matter, he won't bring you any luck, Bud. There's no future in this and the best you can do is to forget her as soon as possible. "He poured himself the last drop and searched for Bud's eyes. "You haven't mentioned what your old Basque had to say to all of this."

Bud did not avoid his glance. "He said the same thing as you, but I don't take orders from him, or from you."

"Of course you don't, kid. But your old farmer is nobody's fool. I'm beginning to like him—much better than your father, by the way."

The change of topic surprised and irritated Bud. "What has my father got to do with it?"

Kollmann lit a new cigarette. "First of all, I don't need to know any more to understand what it's all about. Kaj keeled over because all of a sudden she was like any other woman who adores a hero and wants to have a fling. Those are primordial instincts, Bud; notice that I put the emphasis on 'fling.' You may have noticed that today already."

"Noticed what?"

"Don't be so stubborn, Bud. Kaj hasn't lost her head because of you, and I bet she told you so."

"Maybe that was her intention," Bud said angrily. "But you came too early. Do you think I like it when people come bursting into my room?"

"This discussion won't get us anywhere." Kollmann looked at his watch. "I have an appointment at five o'clock and you have to go for your physical, right?"

Bud nodded.

"Fine, we have some time left and I want to tell you why I came. I have no doubt that Kaj will straighten out your head, but I'm afraid that fame and money have caused your father to lose his completely."

"You saw him at home?"

"This morning. I hoped to find you, which was logical; you've been away from home for a long time."

"Did you see my mother?"

"No, all I know is that she had cried. Understandable, when the son runs off and father struts around like a rooster, thinking only in figures."

"You're meddling a little too much in my private affairs," growled Bud.

"Let me tell you something, Bud." Kollmann's voice remained calm but his fingers began to drum on the table. "In a minute you'll tell me that I also meddled with your private affairs when I saved you in Pau from being disqualified. And let's not talk about the Peyresourde and other things. But if I remember correctly, you had no objections to those meddlings. Or did you?"

Bud lowered his eyes but remained stubborn. "I did the cranking by myself."

"In Pau you weren't about to go on cranking if I hadn't sacrificed a night and a rest day on your behalf. And where do you think would you have been without Martin Lindner?"

"I thought you wanted to talk about my father."

"At your pleasure. If you want to know my opinion, he would like nothing better than to stuff his belly into a yellow jersey and hold court with the industrial barons of the Ruhr, as Tour baron. He's lost the ground under his feet, and if you go on like this, you'll lose it too."

"Are you talking about Kaj again?"

"No. I'm talking about his greed. If he has his say, you won't let go of a single dollar the winter tracks are going to offer, and you're already doing too much as it is. Since the end of the Tour you haven't been out of the saddle."

"That's what every Tour winner does. I'd be crazy to turn down big money for petty earnings."

"Okay, let's not argue—but forty contracts are too many. Given your stamina you could get away with it, if it weren't for the six-day merry-go-round. Your father said at least ten, correct?"

"Just about. Maybe only eight. I'll think about it. You have to remember that in Germany I earn top fees, money they've never paid anyone before."

"I'm thinking of very different things," Kollmann growled. "Of four weeks of complete rest in December or in January, if you will. All the great names of the road have observed this rule because they knew that all the money lost on the winter racetracks, and more, could be picked up easily from the road races. What you're planning to do is going to ruin your health, believe me."

"So far I haven't noticed it, and if I should feel my energy going down, I can still get out of one or the other race."

"And break your contract. Do you realize what it would cost you?"

"Not a single mark, with a good certificate from Doctor Lindner," Bud smiled coldly.

Kollmann got up abruptly. "If this is your new attitude, I'm wasting my time. Besides, get Kaj out of your head fast, unless you want to look around for a new doctor."

"I still want to have a talk with her," said Bud and it sounded like a timid attempt at making peace.

"I couldn't agree more, and you'll see that I'm right. I have to go, it's half past four."

"Me too. We'll see each other at the Lindners' tonight."

He was on his way to the doctor's office, and Kollmann was on his way to the doctor's house.

Kaj Lindner greeted Kollmann in an ochre pantsuit that emphasized her long legs. She received him with smiling ease and he thought that it wasn't surprising that the kid had lost his head. But he had to know what was going on, and she was reasonable enough not to leave him in suspense.

"I'm glad you're here, Max. We're all alone. Let's go into the living room. What will you drink?"

"A small whiskey with a lot of soda and ice. It's hot and Bud's made me thirsty."

"He told you everything."

"Pretty much. I hope there isn't more to it and that your head is clearer than his."

"You can bet on it." She poured two whiskeys and put a bowl of ice and some water on the side.

"He told you about Liège?"

"He did."

"Good. That was all."

"But since then he's head over heels in love with you. He's taking it very seriously and I know what that means for him. I know him better than you do."

"I know, Max. You didn't expect this from me, did you?"

He nodded and lit a cigarette. "Right, Kaj. But I thought about it. Am I right in presuming that all of a sudden he interested you because the papers were full of him and he was on the TV screens every day? The woman in you woke up and got the better of you?"

"That's pretty much it," she said and raised her glass. "Somewhere I read that he was going to race in Liège and I got into the car. Martin was in Berlin."

"And everything happened the way you had planned?"

"Not really. It just happened. I felt like a crazy young girl on holiday, if you understand me."

Kollmann grinned. "I sure do. And when it was over, it was over. For you. You had wanted your hero and you had him. The dilemma is, that the hero has gone crazy."

"He'll calm down."

"You have to have a talk with him. You've kindled the fire, and you have to put it out without Martin smelling the smoke. You can depend on me, but you're on your own; I can't do it for you. And don't forget: he's very sensitive."

"I'm not a psychiatrist, Max. And besides, ever since I've been looking for him in the sports section, I find nothing but bullish language: toughness, courage, high class, willpower, all that stuff men would like to have to distinguish themselves from wimps. Isn't that true? And all of a sudden I have to hear about the sensitive superman, crumbling because of a little adventure."

Kollmann suppressed a smile and blinked into the low rays of the evening sun.

"The media sell their heroes packaged according to people's desires. But believe me, a little bit of everything you've mentioned is needed to win the Tour de France. Nothing else compares to the stress involved. And the masochism is reciprocal, so to speak."

"I don't understand."

"What I mean is that the heroes of the Tour are suffering. Out of their own free will. And that their admirers want to see them suffer. During any given Tour, sweat and blood are flowing in abundance.

Rationally this may be the most useless consideration, but emotionally it turns into a Mount Everest. Believe me, I've been with the Tour often enough. The Tour stimulates imagination in every conceivable way, and in one way it captured you as well."

She poured more whiskey and water, and her large brown eyes were without irony.

"Maybe you're right, Max. I hadn't looked at it that way. What tempted me was the out-of-the-ordinary experience; also the out-of-the-ordinary man, if you like. It was euphoria, but when it was over, it was over."

"Regrets?"

"None whatsoever. But since I've learned that it meant more for Bud, I'm a bit uneasy about seeing him arrive later on with Martin. I'm glad you're here."

"Bud will pull himself together. But the boy is in a very critical state. He's fêted everywhere like a king; and the one woman he wants, to put it mildly, turns him down. That must irritate him and it compromises his equilibrium."

"But is it my fault that he has the wrong expectations? Am I his property just because I went to bed with him?"

Kollman mussed his hair. "Look, he's beginning to deal with theoretical standards that practically don't apply to him."

"What's that supposed to mean?"

"It means, Kaj, that he's created for himself a ground on which he's not able to stand. Or rather, not yet. Without realizing it, he's living in an unreal world. He earned his first million already before the Tour. At the moment he's about to earn his second, and the third isn't far behind, because for that sum he'll sign the contract with Pellegrini. That's something he has to cope with. It's different with sons from upper-class homes who have grown up with wealth and who, at his age, are attending a university somewhere, uselessly and in the fast lane. You have to know his background. Old Budzinski, who isn't all that old, is on the lookout for money like a hawk. He was pensioned off early. The mines have ruined him. He considers money the best medicine and doesn't realize how bad it is for him. You should see him strutting around the house Bud built for him. But all of this is less important. I'm concerned for Bud."

"You think he can't deal with all that wealth?"

Kollmann shrugged. "He works hard for it and doesn't waste a penny. But he also doesn't want to lose out on anything. He's taking on too much and he probably overestimates the power of money. Perhaps he even thought to impress you with it, so you'd run away with him."

"You may be right, Max. He was showing off quite a bit when he took me out in Liège. It seems to me that the feeling of being able to buy everything has gained the upper hand over the understanding for things that can't be bought."

"Don't forget, my dear, that you've contributed your share to clouding his judgment. And society is doing the rest. Do you know the real problem with Bud and his kind?"

Her brown eyes questioned him and she wrinkled her forehead: "Something else?"

"Not really. Only society and stars like Bud don't notice it."

"What's that?"

"They don't really notice that those juvenile stars earning big money live in a void. Under a glass bell, if you will. Precocious nouveaux riches without a base."

"They've always existed."

"Of course. But these modern gladiators coming into money are quite different from smart exploiters who cheat others or make them slave for them. And Bud's a very special case. Even among bikers, who can't be compared to the pros of soccer—nor even to the boxing champs, although they are just as lonely in the ring as the man on his racing bike."

"That's too philosophical for me. I think of pros as people who earn their money in sports. More with their muscles than with their head, to be sure."

"To explain the difference, we'd need an entire night." Kollmann said it with an indulging smile that froze all of a sudden: "Do you take Bud for a brainless muscleman?"

"I didn't say that. What I mean is that he would give me more physically than spiritually."

"That sounds pretty conceited, my dear. If he came from a different background, he would have had a higher education and a university degree without the least difficulty. Then you could have talked about Goethe with him, but, as you said yourself, you had a pretty good time with him in Liège."

"Now you're overdoing it," she said, her eyes narrowing.

But Kollmann was not impressed. "I just wanted to tell you that I don't appreciate your elitist attitude. Bud's not only physically strong but also naturally very intelligent, and he's sensitive. Women of your class could give him complexes."

"And what's the recommendation of the teacher?"

Kollmann accepted the provocation: "He recommends making Bud understand, as tactfully as possible, that Liège was wonderful for you, but that for many reasons there can't be a repeat. And there couldn't be, in any case. Even if you had fallen in love with him, you could never be the wife of a bicycle racer, regardless of Martin and the whole scandal. For Bud there will be other women; that's what you should help me in getting him to understand, instead of sticking up your pretty little nose after all the mess you've created."

He wanted to reach for a new cigarette, but she took his hand. "I apologize, Max. I know you're right. I gave in to a whim and to tell you the truth, it hasn't been the first time either. Martin leaves me alone quite often, but you know I'm devoted to him. These flings never amount to anything."

"So was it necessary to have one with Bud, of all people?"

She took a cigarette herself and watched the smoke a while before she answered. "When I think about it, I must confess, there was something like revenge in it. The wretched Tour ruined our entire summer. I was stuck at Tegernsee on my own, and you know what happened? Because of this Bud and his yellow jersey I couldn't have an interesting conversation with anybody. And finally it got hold of me as well, and I took things in hand, in my own way."

Kollmann had to think of Briançon and grinned. Obviously she had been more successful.

He couldn't reply because Lindner arrived together with Bud. At least he hasn't said anything to Martin, Kollmann thought, and he felt Kaj's relief as well.

"So early?" she asked and got up. "I'll have to get busy in the kitchen."

She walked out with that jaunty step of her long legs that made her look so young.

"Don't keep us waiting for too long," Martin called after her. "We're famished and Bud will eat more than the three of us together. He'll surprise you."

He couldn't see her smile in the kitchen any more than he could know how she'd already discovered Bud's appetites in Liège.

He turned to Kollmann: "It went quicker than anticipated. Bud's body is phenomenal. Optimal results. If he had to, he could ride another Tour tomorrow. But we have to boost him morally. All this traveling, the races, life out of a suitcase . . ."

"Yes," said Kollmann with a poignant glance at Bud, "this gypsy life takes its toll."

Bud nodded. "At times it really does." Later, at dinner, he was less monosyllabic, and when the champagne stood on the table, it still became a lively evening.

Kaj drove Bud to his hotel but there was no chance for the talk he had expected to take place in his room. "Another time, Bud," she said. "It would look funny if I stayed out too long."

And her kiss barely brushed his cheek.

Later Bud lay in his bed like a biker unable to go to sleep because he has pumped himself full with stimulants.

21

THE CARAVAN OF THE TOUR HEROES WOUND ITS WAY BACK TO France and into the fall. Temporarily their itinerant circus was disrupted by the world championship of road racing in Varese. Bud, wearing the national jersey of the Association of German Bicyclists, could not place himself among the top finishers; He had three breakdowns and none of the team support he had been accustomed to. He missed the breakaway attempt of the almost unknown Belgian Dewaele; but since Antonelli was also among the defeated, he consoled himself quickly. The expert press carried commentaries critical of the organization of this particular championship. And since the rainbow jersey of the world champion could not have raised Bud's market value any higher, he had no regrets.

Almost without a pause he entered the big business of the winter racetracks, starting in October in Madrid. He had half a dozen six-day races behind him when he returned to Cologne. As usual, the six-day race in Cologne took place at the end of December. They were riding from December 27 to January 2, a peculiar date but perfect for both the public and the organizers.

For people it provided an outlet. Full of holiday dinners and home-sweet-home atmosphere they fled into the smoky hall, this noisy and droning anteroom of the carnival, beckoning also with New Year's Eve.

The Lindners had made a date with Max Kollmann for Kaj's first six-day race. It was the day before New Year's and they had obtained a box in the inner circle where, instead of beer, as in the upper seats, champagne was flowing. Between the whistles of the Sports Palace waltz cascading noisily from the upper levels, you could hear the whir of the hubs and spokes on the wooden planks. And during the final sprint laps, the panting of the riders.

The hall was approaching the feverish midnight climax, and the backs of the men in their garish jerseys bent down low over the handlebars. One, who was wearing large white stars on his shoulders and bending his elbows out too far, fell in the tight pack at the curve. He broke his clavicle under the white star, and his thigh looked like a raspberry tart. He slid down to the balustrade at the boxes like a sack, but nobody paid attention as he was carried on a stretcher down to the basement, because the bell had rung for the sprint lap. How they whizzed. From their arched backs energy seemed to flow into legs spinning faster and faster, and the banked curves seemed to burst under the strain of the centrifugal force.

Twice the curve, twice the straight. But it is like a drum. Constant turning to the left, a constant rush in the small, tightly sealed oval. They would pedal the same distance as from Berlin to Moscow in these six days. The man in the yellow-black jersey who detached himself from the pack in the first curve after the bell, and who as quick as lightning shot down to the green line, pulled ahead with such force that the field appeared to be pedaling in place. The man was Ernst Budzinski and for the third time in a row that evening he won the sprint lap.

"Why is he racing like mad?" asked Lindner.

Kollmann shrugged. "Bud's crazy. He doesn't play the game."

"Which game?"

"Antonelli's. He wants to show off like a cock of the walk and infuriate the Italian."

"Maybe he just wants to impress some woman, who knows?" said Lindner.

If you only knew, thought Kollmann. Aloud he said: "I think it's about the brunette back there."

His words were drowned out by the loudspeaker: "Attention! Attention, please! The lady who has identified herself as an admirer of Mario Antonelli has increased the premium for the next sprint lap after ten laps to two thousand marks!"

The upper rows stamped raucously, and in the boxes the champagne glasses were put down. The elegant brunette in the low-cut dress had gotten up defiantly, and what she displayed made some of the show-offs at the nearby tables hold their breath, for different reasons than the bikers who were rolling out before the next chase.

She had started with five hundred marks and doubled that every time. And every time Bud, now rolling in the back of the field, had won the sprint easily, like child's play, as if he were pushing the others ahead of him.

"There will be revenge," said Kollmann. "The omnivore won't be allowed to devour every single tidbit."

Lindner nodded. "Unless he gives up the two thousand now."

Bud didn't. Before the bell had finished announcing the two-thousand-mark sprint, he darted off, an arrow among snails.

The elegant lady no longer watched, and it looked as if the stamping of the bleachers had pushed her down in her chair. She rummaged furiously in her small crocodile leather bag, seemingly undecided whether to write another check for the speaker, who looked at her expectantly.

But a limit had been reached, presumably not of the money but of furious disappointment. She slammed down her bag, and when Antonelli, hands on the upper part of the handlebar and gasping for air after the unsuccessful sprint, was searching for her eyes, she turned her back on him.

Lindner grinned, but Kollmann frowned. "What do you want to bet that Bud isn't even sprinting for the money?"

"What else?"

"The woman, naturally. He wants her because she's after Antonelli."

"Nonsense," said Lindner. As the waltz of the Sports Palace started booming again, accompanied by the whistling in the bleachers, he didn't hear what Kollmann was whispering to Kaj.

"Bud's doing this for your benefit. He knows we're here." Aloud he said: "In order to mollify this lady, Antonelli would have to throw Bud off his bike or, better yet, pull the Sicilian knife. If it were up to the women, there would be war in this hall every night. But the bikers have different tactics. Antonelli will think of something, I'm sure. If Bud goes on like this, they'll finish him off before the end of winter. They won't have to make much of an effort, because he's doing the job by himself."

Kaj who, up to this point had listened with big eyes, joined in: "What do you mean, he'll finish himself off?"

"Because in the stale air of this merry-go-round, he's riding past his career. Smell it. Up in the dome you could smoke a ham. I think we should move our legs a little and catch some fresh air."

Down a staircase they entered into one of those foyers where you walk on paper cups and mustard and where cold air fights against the warm smell of hot dogs.

"You'll have a beer with us?" Lindner asked his wife and helped her into her coat. "There's a nasty draft and this bad air makes you susceptible to bugs."

"But it's a lot of fun," Kaj said. "I didn't think it would be this exciting, really."

Kollmann laughed and handed her a beer cup. With his left hand he wiped off foam on his sleeve because he had held the other two cups together with thumb and index finger. "I ask your forgiveness, but to drink more elegantly, we should have stayed in the box."

"Alcohol is a disinfectant." Lindner grinned and drained his cup in two gulps. Dimly they heard the announcement of a new sprint. People around them threw down their cups and rushed back to the arena.

Applause roared but they were unable to make out whether Bud once again bagged them all.

"Basically, I couldn't care less," muttered Kollmann. "But I do care if the kid is burned up in these infernal halls."

Lindner nudged him with his elbow. "Come on, Max, you're exaggerating. At his last exam he had excellent results."

"Don't forget that was before the six-days began. You ought to examine him now."

"I will, you can be sure if it." And to Kaj: "Bud is his jewel, and he wants to wrap him in cotton wool."

"Don't talk like that." Kollmann made a grimace as if he had tasted sour beer. "You know as well as I do that everything about Bud is perfection. Too much so. He's good looking and everything he does, he does with an ease that defies all laws. Did you see the sprint earlier on? It looked as if he didn't crank the pedals but just caressed them and flew off."

"You see, we're of the same mind."

"Only I've been around this environment a little longer than you, Martin. I was always convinced that Bud could become another Merckx, but now he looks more like Koblet."

"Could you explain that a little more clearly?"

"Okay. The harmony of Koblet on a bike was of the same amazing perfection. It fascinates and makes you tremble at the same time. Too extraordinary, understand?"

"Not quite, to tell you the truth."

"But you do understand that this profession is too demanding to allow someone to play with his geniality? It has to break sometime. What Bud showed off tonight was nothing but vanity."

Anger flashed in Kaj's brown eyes, mixed with lack of comprehension. "If my eyes don't fail me here, he's the best of them. He proves it and makes good money because of it. Fifteen thousand per day, without the premiums, he told me."

"You're seeing it right and wrong at the same time," said Kollmann. "Do you know any great artist who does house painting?"

"What's this supposed to mean?"

"Well, there are rich people who would let him paint some

flourishes and pay him well for it. But does he need it? He's not a house painter. But enough of them are cycling right here. These six-day races are outdated, only the Germans haven't done away with them. In France there's only one during the entire winter and only because Grenoble was able to build a track into its Olympic stadium. Between the two world wars the six-days were the thrill of the large cities, and the biggest reporters from New York and Berlin were basking in their ambience. And as you've noticed, some of the thrill that worked up Grandpa has remained. But if you've stuck your nose into them as I have, you smell more than massage oil and perfume. You smell the combinations."

"What's that?"

"The agreements. A few riders decide; the others have to do as they say. Someone like me smells it, just as I smell winter revenues for clever managers and little pros. They have to make a living, because in the summer, on the roads, they don't get a chance. Most of them rest up during the summer, if the winter was profitable. But the time of the great ones is the summer, and that's why Bud's doing too much right now."

"But people come because of him, right?"

"Correct. But does he have to enter every single race? Of course the billboards need some big names, but the others are harder to get. Take Antonelli, for example. All of Italy expects him to win the Giro and the Tour next year. Whether he'll accomplish this is another question, but he knows that he has to recuperate in the winter. He's only racing two six-days, and he came to Cologne only because the organizers offered him more than he could get any-where else. They offered him almost as much as Bud. But he isn't pushing himself. Earns his wages like a seasoned pro and doesn't run like the greyhounds after a fake rabbit."

"Is Bud doing that?" Kaj asked provocatively.

"Maybe," Kollmann responded, smiling vaguely. "Did you get a good look at the brunette with the Sophia Loren cleavage?"

"But she was wild about Antonelli."

"Wait and see," said Kollmann. "They're almost done for tonight. Let's go back to the box before they're closing down."

They returned to their seats and drank another glass of champagne while the bell signaled the end of the race. One of the riders blew a trumpet to amuse people, and then the oval was empty like a crater.

"In the past they had to race through the night. Now they start up again tomorrow afternoon, when the schoolchildren will be coming."

He had to laugh at Kaj's incredulous brown eyes.

"They rode day and night, without any sleep?"

"One out of each team would catch a few hours here and there, but the other had to be on the track. Nowadays the race is suspended after midnight."

"And where do they sleep?"

"Downstairs, in the basement. Worse than jail. Each has a mattress and a locker, and nobody is allowed to leave."

"But we have to leave," said Lindner and asked for the bill from one of the waiters flitting back and forth between the spectators getting ready to go.

Kollmann shook hands with both of them. "Without me. I still have to talk to Bud. It's the best time. Did you enjoy yourself, Kaj?"

She nodded.

"There was a lot I didn't enjoy and I'm afraid we haven't seen the last of it."

Kollmann walked through the labyrinth and he didn't have to show his press ID to the ushers. Most of them knew him and greeted him. Cleaning women with buckets and brooms came out of a room that had a musty smell.

He went down yet another staircase and entered a dark corridor, long as a day without bread, his steps reverberating on the stone floor. Somewhere nearby had to be the heating system. It was warmer down here than up in the arena, and the maze of pipes, bent and straight along the ceiling and the walls, reminded him of the old Paris Vélodrome d'Hiver, the winter racetrack. The Vél' d'Hiv'. As a young journalist, he had been there often, and no winter track, not even the old Berlin Sportpalast, had fascinated him the same way.

But neither the Vél d'Hiv' nor the Sportpalast existed any longer. The Moloch of the big city had swallowed the old edifices with their irresistible flair. They brought in too little for modern times; the cost of maintenance was too high when the price per square foot in the center of the cities had risen to dizzying heights. Office buildings were more profitable, and bicycle racing in the halls had died. What continued every year, for a few days, in the halls of fairgrounds on tiny and dangerous tracks that could be dismantled was nothing but a bicycling circus.

He thought of the gala evenings at the Vél' d'Hiv', which began with the first autumn fogs and ended only when old women at the Metro station La Motte Picquet Grenelle adjacent to the belly of the Vél' d'Hiv' began selling their little bunches of lilies-of-the-valley in the early spring.

A spectacle for the common man as well as for the bigwig. More than in the Berlin Sportpalast, people were attracted by the atmosphere of this arena—all of Paris, in their dinner jackets and long gowns as well as the working class in their visor caps and Basque berets, there, under the floodlights hanging low from a tangle of supporting beams. Maurice Chevalier, Jean Gabin, and Marlene Dietrich were regulars in the boxes of the inner circle, just as were the large crowds that, together with baguettes and red wine bottles, lugged their expertise into the upper circles. The six-day races in themselves never meant much to them. They came because they were customers. The only thing that impressed them was the performance. Preferably the short races of the sprinters, who lay in ambush for each other like big cats before they darted down from the curve into a furious finish. The sprint was the purest and the most natural form of competition, and the people in the circles had made a science of it. As Kollmann walked down the long corridor he thought of Gérardin, Scherens, and van Vliet, the sprinter kings of his childhood. They had managed to get a summer sport through the winter in style. And in a natural way. But now it was getting through the winter with slapstick. To be sure even Berretrot, the king of announcers, whom they had called Monsieur Ten Percent, had provided some circus atmosphere, but what counted was the sport on the track, because the public didn't let itself be duped like nowadays. It wants to be duped, Kollmann thought and knocked at the door behind which he expected to find Bud.

It was the right door. The masseur, whose hairy gorilla arms swelled out from a tight and not overly clean T-shirt, looked up indignantly. It smelled of sweat, oil, and something undefinable and more pungent; the ventilation was bad. Bud was lying on his belly, his hands crossed under his forehead. He was completely naked. The white of his back and behind contrasted sharply with the dark tan of arms and legs. A human being is being kneaded and bent into shape so that he will ride in a circle. Does this rotary motion empty the head belonging to this body glistening with yellow oil? No, that worked normally. Bud had to turn his head only slightly because the massage table stood transversely from the door in the tiny room.

"You, Max? and so late? I didn't think you were still interested in six-day races."

"I'm not. But why are you playacting? You saw me with Kaj and Martin."

"That's right," said Bud and put his head straight down. "So what's new?"

"Nothing in particular. Certainly not an interview, in case you're wondering. Something between the two of us."

"And what might that be?"

"Listen, Bud, I'll leave this very minute and regret every second I ever spent on you if you play the stuck-up star."

Bud turned on his back and sat up. He put an olive green towel across his hips. "I'm sorry. Maybe I'm a little nervous."

"No wonder. You're going from one six-day race to the next, and you show it, too, if I take a good look at you."

"I get fifteen grand a day, and earlier tonight I pocketed another thirty-five hundred in sprints. Not a bad monthly income for a few hours, wouldn't you say? Others would kill their grandmother for that."

"And you kill yourself."

"Rubbish. Look, the amount of air I have in my lungs would be enough for you to last half an evening." He inhaled deeply and let the air escape in small intervals, like a little boy playing the steam locomotive. And without gasping for new air: "Here, check my pulse. If you count more than sixty, you can have the dough I made with my three sprints."

"Fuck off with your bragging," Kollmann hissed. "Don't you have anything but money on your mind?"

"Oh, yes, I do." Bud's grin was cold and defiant. "The brunette, for example, who was so generous and who worshiped Antonelli." When Kollmann didn't answer but laboriously lit a cigarette, Bud turned to the masseur: "That's enough for today, Pitt, leave us alone." The tone was peremptory, and new. He wouldn't have dared treat old Felix from Valetta like that.

When the masseur had disappeared, Bud jumped down from the table and slipped into a sweat suit. "I really don't need him any longer, Max. Tomorrow I stop racing."

Kollmann gaped at him as if he hadn't heard right. "You're getting out one day before the end?"

"Why not? I have to relax, and we can't win, Merlin and I. He has difficulty with the track. And I took him as partner for Cologne for friendship's sake. Let the fellow earn something as well. But the next time around I'll choose a track specialist who does more of the work."

"So you want to break your contract?"

"Tut, tut," Bud smiled indulgently. "Lindner will write me an excuse. Intestinal trouble or something of the sort. It happens often enough in this shitty job, as you know."

"And why are you getting out?"

Bud combed his hair in front of a dim mirror. "I didn't get just cash from the generous brunette, but also a note. I thought I might. She had bet on Antonelli but she goes to bed with me. A little bit of revenge feels good, right?"

"If I understand correctly, it's supposed to be revenge on Kaj."

"You've got it, and I don't mind you telling her either. Other mothers also have pretty daughters. Must be the wife of some well-to-do industrialist. She has a country house between Cologne and Aachen, and we'll spend New Year's there, just the two of us. Everything has been arranged. Her old man is cruising with his secretary on the Mediterranean. She takes revenge, I take revenge. Very normal, you see."

"You've gone crazy, Bud."

"Leave that to me. But perhaps I really have a case of the giddies. I'll get rid of it getting laid. Karin is her name, by the way."

"And when is the next six-day race?"

"On January 3, in Bremen. I get more than one day's rest."

"You call that rest?"

"Yes, that's what I call it," Bud said with defiant irony. "Why don't you come with me and have a look at the swanky hole where I'll sleep tonight? Three men are snoring there already, and if you want to take off your jacket, you have to open the door. I'm paid like a king and housed like a tramp. I need a real bed for a change, and if someone is lying in it, I have no objections."

"All you have to do is sign fewer contracts."

"The same old story. I have to bring in cash and if someone like the brunette turns up and coughs up big premiums as well, all the better. You see, I don't give a damn about Kaj Lindner."

Kollmann stepped on his cigarette stub. "You're carrying on like an idiot, Bud. And you're also taking dope."

"Lo and behold. And how would the great expert know this?"

"All I have to do is look at you."

"There are no doping checks at the six-days."

"I know that much myself. Otherwise the whole lot would be disqualified after two days. You're taking cortisone."

"How do you know?"

"Your eyes are shining and your face has filled out. And your Belgian masseur smells like a pharmacy to me, if you want to know the truth."

Bud avoided his glance and stepped into his leather travel slippers. "If you want to preach, go to the Salvation Army, Max. I have to catch some sleep now. But I want to tell you one thing: Do you really think you could stand all of this with egg yolk and sugar? They're all taking stuff, and I take less than most."

"Even that's too much."

"Tell that to your grandmother. Or your readers, what do I care. It fits my story nicely, doesn't it?"

"You've become an exceedingly conceited and stupid asshole," Kollmann growled and left without a word. On the stairs he met the fat manager Heydenreich.

"Did an interview with our star?" he asked condescendingly, sticking a Brazilian cigar between his golden teeth.

"Correct," replied Kollmann, "but not for the papers." And he left the fatso standing there, taking two steps at a time to get out of the stale air. Outside he breathed in deeply and shivered under wet snowflakes, too heavy to be dancing, making the black pavement glisten. Bud has climbed a mountain, he thought, and I helped him do it. But it's the devil's mountain.

22

THE BICYCLE RACER ERNST BUDZINSKI RESIGNED FROM THE Cologne six-day race two days before the end because of a medically certified intestinal colic, but he started on January 3 in Bremen and won, together with the German track specialist Haferkamp, under the shouting and cheering of the crowd. After the six-day races in Antwerp and Milan he was the last to arrive at the training camp of his new team, Pellegrini, on the Italian Riviera. It was almost over, but the optimism he brought with him carried over to his new team manager and his new bosses. They were agreed that he should cut some of the spring classics from his program, because Pellegrini's main goals were the Giro d'Italia and the Tour de France.

The target was Antonelli, who was riding for the competition Biancheri and who, for a starter, had won Milan–San Remo impressively. Followed by Paris–Nice, the first stage race of the season. Bud won two level stages, one in a sprint and the other with a half-minute lead, but in the mountains he fell back. It wasn't a total collapse, and he was able to conceal the fact from the public and the press by explaining that he was warming up and had too few road kilometers of training in his legs. Which was true enough. But it was also true that he had too many smoke-filled halls behind him. How much the mountains taxed him, only he knew. But he didn't talk about it and hoped that his form would return. In the overall standings he was eleventh.

Shortly before Easter he could have won Paris–Roubaix, the most difficult and most prestigious of all spring classics, through the hell of cobblestone roads in the north, and that was a good sign. Twenty kilometers before the finish line he was in a breakaway group of four and doing most of the leading work when a flat on the dreadful cobblestones from the last century threw him back. He had to wait more than a minute for a new wheel because Pellegrini was stuck in the crowd of sag wagons. He stood helplessly in icy wind, at the edge of a road that didn't really merit that label, and he cursed the rain pouring down from Flemish leaden gray clouds like buckets of the blackest pitch.

By way of compensation, a few days later he won the Walloon Arrow, and the papers wrote about a great comeback. It flattered him and reconciled the Pellegrini staff. They remained confident, even when no other victory in the spring races was forthcoming. You have to give him time, they said. The Giro isn't far away, and the kid knows what he wants and what he's capable of.

Indeed, Bud knew both. But he also suspected that he didn't have the energy of the previous year. It was the mountains. In Belgium he had gotten off his bike at the infamous Wall of Grammont. Others did so as well, because the paved road has such a steep gradient that in earlier times horses went on strike here, and even today cars with heavy loads got stuck.

Bud had gotten off where, in the previous year, he had cranked his bike uphill. Straight as an arrow he had pedaled where others used the whole breadth of the road or put their feet on the pavement. Experts who caught sight of him among the panting ranks of foot-folk rubbed their eyes. "A passing weakness," wrote some, but others predicted difficulties in the mountains. Compared to the real mountains, the Wall of Grammont was a molehill.

He knew so himself and tried to suppress the fear of the approaching Giro d'Italia. And he talked himself into believing that there was enough time left to warm up before the Dolomites, and what's more that the Giro wasn't raced as mercilessly as the Tour de

France. Everybody had said so. Even Kollmann. He would have liked to talk to him now and reestablish the rapport, but Kollmann had shown his face only briefly during Paris–Roubaix, and after a short interview of marked coldness he had disappeared.

Doctor Lindner as well seemed more distant when he went to see him in Cologne a few days before the start of the Giro d'Italia. Had Kaj told him about Liège? Or Kollmann? But since the doctor didn't drop the slightest hint, Bud discarded the thought. During the exam, which lasted longer than previously, Lindner took more notes than usual, and Bud was about to think that he was being dismissed like a national health plan patient when Lindner sat down behind his large white desk and offered him a seat.

"I can't tell you everything yet, Bud. You have to come back tomorrow when I'll have the results from blood and urine tests, but I'm telling you one thing right now: Not only did you overexert yourself, you also doped. A lot."

Bud avoided his eyes, and the doctor saw that little was left of the defiance of early on that winter.

"I know I've made mistakes, doctor."

"You know that—well, well." The sarcasm of his nod was also in his voice. "And I, my friend, also know what you want from me now. You want a few miracle pills that, in one sweep, clean out the entire mess you've made for yourself and rebuild the man who entered the Tour de France last summer. If you think that, you've come to the wrong man. For that you'd have to go back to your masseurs from the winter tracks. They don't have the right pill either, but they act as if they did, and if you believe them nobody will even talk about you next year. I'll tell you what's the matter with you, Bud. Fame and money came over you too quickly. There were people who thought you could handle both. Kollmann and I, for example. But you laughed at us and shoveled money like an idiot. You thought you had a machine for a body; all it needs is the right fuel to keep it running without interruption and in high gear. Your natural resources are unusual, but with chemical additives you tried to make them inexhaustible. When you needed rest to regain your strength, you whipped yourself into performing. As if you had to triple the million Pellegrini offered you right away. Someone who could reign ten summers on the road ruins everything in one winter, out of greed."

Bud felt he was sitting in the defendant's chair rather than in the doctor's office, and he pulled himself up. "That's not true, doctor. I won the Walloon Arrow, and without the breakdown, I would've won Paris–Roubaix."

"Possibly," said Lindner. "Those are one-day races and your class still shows. In those you're intact and can cover up your missing reserves. Besides, you've taken stuff and probably went beyond your limits without noticing. I wasn't there to check you out. After all, I'm not your hired personal physician. For that you'd have to spring loose one of your millions. Have you ever noticed how much fun it was for me to look after you, and that I never asked an inappropriate sum from you?"

Bud felt uncomfortable in his chair.

"Can you imagine what bills I would've written if I had been as greedy as you?"

"I know." Bud's voice sounded dejected and he let his shoulders drop without avoiding Lindner's gaze. "But what should I do now? After tomorrow I have to be at the Giro start in Milan."

"When all is said and done," Lindner tapped his pen on the glass top of his desk, "you should really go to the mountains and relax or, for that matter, to the seaside."

"But I have to ride the Giro. It's part of the contract."

"I imagine so. And the Tour on top of it."

"Can I manage both?"

"Honestly, Bud, I don't know." Doctor Lindner drew circles on the glass top as if he were searching for some inspiration. "One thing is certain: You won't be able to win both."

"And nobody can order me to do so."

"Of course not. But do you really think that Pellegrini is spending a fortune on you to see you trot along? As if it were only a question of proving that you're able to ride the Giro and the Tour. Others before you have done that. But there were people who have won both, and they're counting you among those."

"I'm afraid, doctor."

"And you have every reason to be afraid, Bud. You're now paying the bill for the winter in which you earned more than a million. The most reasonable thing to do now would be to take the summer off, but the contracts are there, and the expectations. Just read the papers."

"I know. Only Kollmann is hardly writing anything. He isn't even coming to the Giro."

"He never did before, Bud. He isn't your personal attendant either."

"It would be great," Bud said haltingly, and it sounded like a child begging, "it would be great if both of you could be there."

"Am I hearing right? The great champion—who, during the winter, knew everything better—now needs assistance?"

"I'll be very much alone."

"Now, listen to me, Bud. I can't speak for Kollmann's time, but he will know why one tour per year is enough. As far as I'm concerned, I have to take time off from work and vacation to follow only half the Tour. Not to speak of my wife. She made enough trouble last year, and she will do so again. She has a head of her own, I'm telling you."

He knows nothing about Liège, Bud thought. Aloud he said: "But you're coming to the Tour?"

"If you should enter it at all."

"What do you mean?"

Lindner played again with his pen on the glass top. "I think I have to be more brutal with you for you to understand. You're no longer the same man. You're not the man who started in the Tour de France last year."

"If I had won Paris–Roubaix, you wouldn't talk that way, and I only lost because of bad luck."

"But I'm talking about two long stage races, Bud. Nothing has changed in the volume of your heart and lungs, and you have even more muscles than last year. But you won't recuperate as fast between the stages as last year. And I can't even begin to imagine how much you rode, and what you swallowed, this past winter."

"I really haven't taken that much, doctor, honest."

"This isn't an investigation, Bud," Lindner shrugged, "but you ought to know that you have to pay for what you swallow."

"And if I let go of the Giro?"

"That's a breach of contract."

"You could give me a medical certificate."

"I'll do nothing of the kind." Lindner hit his knuckles on the glass plate. "This isn't a six-day circus. The Pellegrini people will take you to a medical examiner, and what does that make out of me? There's nothing wrong with you except that you're not in top shape, and nobody knows better than you what you've done with it. You've made your bed, now you must lie in it."

And he said good-bye to Bud without inviting him home for dinner. That's Kaj's doing, Bud thought. She doesn't want to see me.

23

ALL OF ITALY WANTED TO SEE THE MAN WHO HAD DEFEATED Antonelli, and Bud was surprised at the warmth he encountered during the first stages in the north. He knew this would change, because Antonelli's fans were concentrated in the south. Nevertheless, basking in the crowds felt good and gave him a strength that the winter seemed to have eroded. He wanted to win a stage early on, to put his reputation in the right light, and then, saving energy, roll with the pack toward the south.

The big coup came in Florence. Bud won the sprint of a small breakaway group with an advantage of twenty seconds over the large pack, and since the differences in the total point count were minimal to that point, he advanced to fifth place. It wasn't a big time victory, but his reputation remained intact, and the experts judged him as biding his time.

On the whole the race developed as a mutual lying in wait of the two strongest teams. Pellegrini and Biancheri dominated the scene, and the domestiques feverishly competed with each other in the service of the two aces, Budzinski and Antonelli. Bud was still fifth in Naples and Antonelli eighth in the overall standings, but their time difference remained below one minute and out front were just *rouleurs,* whom the mountains would devour.

The Dolomites came last. For the time being Bud continued to benefit from the two teams blocking each other. There were days when he rolled so easily that he forgot the fear of the mountains. He no longer attempted to win a stage—unlike Antonelli who, down south, in the tip of the boot, won twice and pulled on the pink jersey of the leader in the total point count.

When they reached the north again Bud was fourth, a minute and forty seconds behind Antonelli, and many experts were confident that he would take the jersey from Antonelli in the fifty-kilometer time trial in Verona. Even Bud believed in this and when, on the eve of the trial, Kollmann arrived in Verona, his confidence became certainty.

Kollmann had not announced his arrival. It had been a spontaneous decision, determined more by personal considerations than journalistic ambition or necessity. In the international press reports about Bud's form oscillated from one extreme to the other, which he found irritating. This evening he sat for a long time in Bud's hotel room and despite all his initial skepticism, he was taken in by Bud's optimism. He really gave the impression of a man in good shape. There had been evenings during the Tour last year when he had looked more hollow cheeked and exhausted.

"The course is hilly, but not particularly difficult," said Bud. "Eighty percent in the large gear. And fifty kilometers is just right for me. Exactly the right distance to take the minute and forty seconds away from Antonelli."

Kollmann frowned. "It's the Stage of Truth, Bud, and you all have almost three thousand kilometers in your legs. With last year's condition, you'd make it, but you don't have that. I have no illusions."

"Do you think I got fourth in the total point count just walking down the lane?"

"No, Bud. But I also know that the Giro does not have the hectic pace of the Tour, and that you've benefited from the blockade between the two strongest teams. Up to now, let's admit, the race has been frozen. Strangely enough, the Italians go along with this, just as they support defensive soccer, which really doesn't fit their temperament."

"You're probably right," said Bud and got up to close the window where cool wind was blowing in from the mountains. "Your way of looking at things has always impressed me and helped me."

Kollmann lit a cigarette and blew rings that remained stationary in the suddenly still air of the room.

"This past winter"—the irony in his voice could not be ignored—"you talked differently. Do you remember the Cologne six-day? You were deaf then when I tried to get to the bottom of things."

Bud nodded. "I know you were right. But the money was flowing, and I couldn't get myself away from it. A few weeks' rest would've been better, but I can't change things now and I have to deal with this damn Giro. Do you think I can win the time trial?"

Kollmann swallowed a sharp reply because he heard the undertone of insecurity; the athlete needed encouragement before an important test of strength.

He paused, then said reflectively as if weighing every word: "This is the first time I've seen you in the Giro, Bud. How should I know what your chances and your condition are? Unless I'm mistaken, you haven't done much; you've stuck to rear wheels. It may have been smart tactics but also a cover-up game. If you win the time trial, it was clever tactics; if you lose, everybody will know that up to this point you managed to hide a weak condition."

"Mmm." Bud's expression showed that he had expected more encouragement.

Kollmann came to the rescue. "You probably had some difficult passages, but the last stages went pretty well, didn't they?"

"They did, Max. I attacked twice, to test myself. Five or six kilometers each time, and Antonelli's group got into a sweat. Then I dropped back into the field and saved energy at the rear wheels for the time trial."

"So did others. Everybody dragged their feet before Verona."

"I grant you that. They're all afraid of racing against the clock, and then the mountains."

"Fifty kilometers is long. Don't start too quickly, don't stroke too large a gear, and remember that Antonelli has the advantage of starting last. He can adapt to your times."

"Of course he's at an advantage, but if I ride with force, it won't do him any good. I want to win."

"By a minute and forty seconds?"

"Why not? A week ago I felt so empty that I wanted to give up, but now I sense my reserves."

Kollmann put his hand on his arm before he reached for another cigarette. "That sounds good, Bud. Too bad I can't be there and have to wait for you at the finish line, because they only permit sag wagons and race officials on the course."

"They have enough problems as it is," said Bud. "The spectators are not as disciplined as during the Tour, and at times the corridor they leave you becomes so narrow that you brush them."

"I know. And in the mountains everything Italian gets pushed along. The fellows are handed on like bricks in building construction. But let's not think about that. If tomorrow you land a big coup, even the Stilfser Pass will seem lower."

Bud is the fourth-to-the-last man to start the Stage of Truth. Two minutes before him the Italian Berbenni went. Two minutes after him there will be the Belgian Dewaele. Another four minutes will pass before Antonelli, wearer of the pink jersey, will hit the undulating course. Eighty-two bikers have started before him and most of them had better conditions than the men at the top of the overall standings, those who will decide the Giro victory. The wind has turned gusty, has changed direction, and the sun has disappeared behind a wall of black clouds hovering over the city. It happens quite often that the equality of chances during time trials is influenced by atmospheric conditions.

Bud launches his oily legs into the whirl of a lightning start. Just now he saw nervousness written on the face of Antonelli standing close by, and he wants to impress him. After a few hundred meters the large gear gets into full swing, but he still feels the tenseness of the start and still has to find the optimal aerodynamic position on the bike. Ahead of him the gray emptiness of the country road lined by black spectator hedges, behind him the sag wagon with Andreolo, the Pelligrini team manager.

A television motorbike comes up alongside him and in a curve Bud feels the camera at his upper arm; he curses the celluloid vultures, eager for the kill, and the spectators pushing into the road, leaving a passage of barely six feet in breadth. He's afraid of this human hedge, which cheers him on but also barks at him as if he were about to rob Antonelli.

Antonelli, this fink in pink. He wanted to poison me, Bud thinks, but I beat him by the rules of the game. Why not again today? And he feels that now he has the best position and that the tenseness of the start has dissolved. The TV motorbike disappears behind the next bend. He ends the furious speed at the spot he had selected this morning, together with Andreolo. He still has more than thirty-five kilometers ahead of him, but he would not be able to cover them in the forced speed of the start. He turns his head and sees Andreolo who is standing, his hair fluttering, in the open car, his arms outspread like a conductor allowing for a pause.

"*Benissimo,* Bud." And then he shouts in a mixture of French and Italian, making his hands into a megaphone: "Fifteen seconds under Bellini's best time."

Bud, who has straightened up for a moment, nods, signaling that he's understood, and then it seems as if he wants to drive his nose into the handlebar. He reaches for the bottle in his back pocket, prepared together with Andreolo. He has earned a swig.

And then the road again. It slips away under the thin tires like a gray conveyor belt and he takes it on in the middle, where it is curved. The spectators push him there, and even if he wanted to he wouldn't be able to cut a curve. And then, as he shoots out of a bend, he sees, about nine hundred feet ahead of him, the Italian Berbenni who had started two minutes ahead of him. Bud is now in the second, the "quiet" phase of his race, where he should economize energy, but his legs want this target. Everybody knows Berbenni is a flea who does much better in the mountains than in a time trial. He's too light for the large gear, and Bud sees how it hurts him. Yard by yard he draws closer, and when he pushes past him, the Italian doesn't even try to attach himself to his rear wheel. In a time trial he isn't allowed to anyhow, but in the Giro a lot is overlooked.

At the midpoint of the course Bud still has the best time, but Antonelli, who started a while ago, is also doing well. At kilometer thirty Bud knows that he might beat him but not take away the the pink jersey. Of course, he can push himself. He wants to start accelerating twelve kilometers before the finish. Or should he begin earlier? Not wait until the little village with the poplars along the road, which he chose? Andreolo seems to think the same. Sounding his horn imperiously, pushing people back to the side of the road, he comes up alongside Bud.

"Put in everything you've got, Bud! *Fortissimo!*"

"How many kilometers?"

"Sixteen. You'll win the stage. Drink something and go for it!"

Bud drinks, and he thinks of the computer that calculated for a newspaper that he wouldn't win this stage. Computers. Soon these fucking gadgets would speak, make poetry, and compose music. Only crying and suffering nobody could program into them. That's all they'll leave to us.

On a gradient he gets out of the saddle to maintain the high gear. After the hump his legs whirl as if he had the finish in sight and not fifteen kilometers ahead of him. "*Forza!*" shouts Andreolo behind him. Again the plain. The course is winding back to Verona, and as the lines of people thicken, the corridor they leave him is still narrower.

"Only ten more," Andreolo is shouting, "but Antonelli is catching up."

Is it possible? Does he lie like Mercier in Paris? Don't these pigs have any conscience?

He tries to bend his back even lower over the frame, but it's as if his lungs are going to burst, because they no longer get enough oxygen for this torture. A sickening weakness rises from his calves into his knees. Now he knows that he entered the third phase of the race too early. His stroke loses its harmony and turns heavy, his torso tenses up, and his sweat is a cold one.

If they only made room. Automatically his hand reaches for his back pocket, but the water bottle is empty. He finds rice cakes, but is unable to chew them and spits them out. Only sugar cubes remain in his mouth, stuck to his dry tongue. Still seven kilometers. He started sprinting too early and has no reserves left. And the reflexes diminish with the reserves. All of a sudden, Andreolo's shouting comes from far away, and he is like the jockey whose whip no longer produces tempo, only a foaming horse's mouth.

Bud is tense. For a second he straightens up and then again gropes for the right position, as if it were enough to sit right on the bike. The energy is gone, and nobody can bring it back. He no longer hears time checks and, after the ears, his eyes are also giving out. Only his legs continue to work, as if they had nothing to do with his body or his senses.

But the bike needs to be driven, and when a negligible little descent allows him once again to reach a tempo of forty, the small corridor the spectators have left him is not enough. His elbow collides with bodies and he is not able to head off the impact. Under the terrified screams from hundreds of throats, the man who had wanted to win this stage falls, and the velocity makes him slide for several yards on the pavement. It's a miracle that Andreolo's mechanic is able to stop the car. He has fallen on his left side and doesn't move. And he hears them say that he is unconscious and hears them shout for a doctor.

Consequently he can't be unconscious. But he keeps his eyes shut and feels piercing pain in his arm and his hip.

Then Andreolo's hand, gently turning his head.

"Do you hear me, Bud?"

He nods.

"Where does it hurt?"

His right hand indicates his left side and he sees how the mechanic is taking a new bike from the roof rack. Ride on? No way. Stop, the end, he can't go on. Nobody will force him into the saddle. He closes his eyes again but is feeling strong hands under his shoulders and in his back. Without his assistance they pull him up, put him on his legs—which, to his surprise, support him.

"Bend your knee."

He puts his right arm around Andreolo's shoulder, lifts his left leg, and stands there like a stork.

"Okay. Bend your left arm."

He bends it.

The torn flesh burns like hell, but once again Andreolo says that it is okay. Next to him is the mechanic with the new bike and a bottle.

"Drink this."

Bud empties the bottle. It's forbidden sustenance, but nobody cares at this moment. A motorbike announces another rider with a piercing whistle and the crowd is opening up the corridor that hadn't been large enough for Bud.

Andreolo takes the bottle out of his hand and puts the handlebars of the new bike into his hand. "Get going, Bud, only four kilometers."

His right hand grips the tape of the handlebars while his left waves him off. "Stop, finished, *finito*. I can't go on."

Andreolo grabs him by the shoulder and shakes him so that he totters because the aching leg loses its balance. "You want to give up four kilometers before the finish? Are you mad?"

"I said I can't go on."

"And I said that you'll go on. Nobody gives up four kilometers before the finish!"

"I'm injured."

"But you haven't broken anything. Are you a biker or a weakling? Every second standing around here counts against you."

"So what? If I give up, the count won't matter. I'm finished and have had it with your Giro. Look at this damn crowd that doesn't even make room."

But Andreolo has already heaved him into the saddle, and the mechanic tightens the straps of the pedals. He no longer resists.

"Make room, people, damn it all! Don't you see he needs room?"

When they push him, the first heavy raindrops are falling, and he rides into the thunderstorm, the lightning, and the purplish black sky over Verona. After another hundred yards another rider is passing him, and now he knows he has only Antonelli behind him, who started last.

Antonelli. He's the one who keeps Bud in the saddle. His legs turn and he doesn't know where the strength is coming from. He doesn't feel the rain whipping his face as that time on the Peyresourde. The road opens up because people are seeking shelter. But he didn't know how long four kilometers could be. He does know, however, how miserably slow he is cranking because he can't get the high gear going, even if the glistening black asphalt provides an ideal condition.

On the last kilometer Antonelli catches up with him and zooms past him like an arrow. That means he is six minutes faster than Bud, not to speak of the seconds beyond this. But Bud does arrive at the finish. They put him on a stretcher and for the first time, he is taken to the hotel in an ambulance.

He took a bath and after his routine work, the masseur treated the abrasions. Then came Andreolo with the Pellegrini physician, who made his diagnosis. It's a positive one. Nothing broken, no tendon has been hurt. Other things don't interest him. The man can be sent on his way to the Dolomites.

Why don't they talk French so I can understand them? Bud is thinking. In the semidarkness of his room—he had lowered the shades because his head hurt—he blinked at the two men at his bedside. And he saw them double because he couldn't focus his eyes any better than his thoughts. The pictures weren't clear, just like during the ridiculous little descent, when his eyes stared but no longer took in the dimension of the road.

"You can start tomorrow," Andreolo said in French.

Bud shook his head without raising it from the pillow, but he didn't say anything while the doctor packed his things.

And when they were alone he said to Andreolo: "Was this supposed to be a medical exam? He didn't do much more than feel my pulse. My doctor is more thorough."

"You can depend on him."

"Mmm." Bud sat up. "I want to tell you something, Andreolo. Do you know who you can depend on in this fucking job? Only yourself. And I know there's nothing left. I'm empty, finished. I might not have fallen if the spectators had left me enough room, but all of a sudden, my strength was gone. I would've lost a lot of time anyhow."

"A fit of weakness. Tomorrow it will be forgotten."

"And after tomorrow we'll be in the Dolomites. Do you expect me to prolong this farce one more day?"

"You're going on."

"No he isn't," a voice boomed from the door. "He's not going on."

Both turned their heads in surprise, because in the semidarkness they hadn't noticed Kollmann enter the room.

"At last," said Bud. He sounded relieved, and he pointed to the armchair the doctor had vacated.

"Who's this?" Suspiciously Andreolo eyed the man, who was taking off his sunglasses but kept the cigarette in his mouth and sat down without hesitation.

"Max Kollmann, a friend of mine. Signor Andreolo, my team manager," Bud indicated with a gesture of his hand, but they didn't shake hands.

"You haven't broken anything?" Kollmann asked in German.

"No, I didn't. But I was only half conscious when I fell. You're right, Max. It's over. I'll never make it across the mountains."

"Speak French, so I can understand you," muttered Andreolo.

"Pardon. Je ne passerai pas la montagne." The irony in his voice was cold and cutting.

"Is this guy trying to convince you of that?"

Kollmann blew smoke into the angry eyes of the Roman face framed by gray curls. "I don't intend to convince anybody, Signor Andreolo. I only see what's going on, and know the man involved better than you do."

"Are you team manager or am I?"

"I've heard that somewhere before," grinned Kollmann. But he turned serious again. "If you're a good team manager, you have to take him out of the race. You couldn't find a better opportunity."

"What's that supposed to mean?"

"It means that a biker who's had a serious fall can withdraw with good grace from something that has become hopeless. At the moment hardly anybody but him knows this. If he gives up now, his reputation as champion remains intact, and the whole world will talk about bad luck. If he should give up at the first mountain because of total exhaustion—and it's inevitable if he continues— he'll be called a failure. You have to grab your chance to play the upper hand. If you don't withdraw your trump card from the race right now, you are, to put it bluntly, the ultimate idiot of a team manager."

"I object to this tone," hissed Andreolo. "You're not talking to an idiot."

"That's not what I said. I only pointed out how you could become one. You see, the Pellegrini firm expects another success from you like last year. Then it was Antonelli. But he preferred to change teams. You're under pressure to succeed. The Pellegrini folks have given you Budzinski, and if you don't get a trick with this trump card, you'll be considered a dead loss yourself, am I right or not?"

Andreolo shifted uneasily on his chair. In his eyes there was a mixture of stubborn contradiction and humiliation.

They're all alike, Kollmann thought. He went on: "This pressure to succeed makes you blind, although you were a good racer yourself and really ought to know that this one here has nothing more to gain in the Giro, but everything to lose."

"I resent this insolent defeatism, sir. Agreed, Bud lost seven minutes today to the best in time trials, because he fell, and fell back to fourteenth position in the overall standings. But damn it all, I've seen worse situations in my career."

"Unfortunately," Kollmann said with a thin smile, "your career as team manager with Pellegrini most likely will come to an end if you force him to go on. If I were in your shoes I wouldn't consider the situation a disaster, but take advantage of it."

"Take advantage of it?"

"Of course. Just consider this: It was a harebrained idea anyhow to let Bud enter the Giro as well as the Tour. You're all thinking commercially, and I admit that the kid thought the same way all winter long. It wouldn't have been such a bad idea, by the way, if Pellegrini, in full executive power of the new employer, had canceled a few six-day races. But what did you do? You looked on stupidly and didn't want to understand. And for reasons of publicity, you wanted to have him at the six-day race in Milan as well, instead of ordering him to training camp. He went from the halls to the road and has to pay the consequences. And you have to share them. And now you don't even want to realize that this is a one-time chance to save what there is to save."

"What would be saved if he gave up?"

"At this moment just about everything. He leaves the Giro scot free and enters the Tour in as good a shape as possible; and the Tour is your main objective. Have a talk with the physician now, and tonight you give a bulletin to the press. His injuries necessitate his withdrawal from the Giro, *basta.*"

Andreolo shook his head slowly but he no longer looked defiant. Indeed, it would be worse to see Bud fail in the Dolomites than to pull him out of the race with good reasons. And the argument of the Tour was solid. It was the main objective.

"Maybe you're right," he said slowly. "We have to make the best of a tricky situation. But the Pellegrini bosses will have a hard time swallowing this, since Antonelli will win the Giro with flying colors."

"He'll win in any case, but at least you save yourself a trump card for the Tour."

"If I could only be sure," sighed Andreolo and buried his head in both hands, showing only his gray locks.

"There are no guarantees," Kollmann said roughly. "But there isn't any other choice either. I can take Bud tomorrow morning in my car to Germany. We'll go directly to his doctor in Cologne."

"Okay, I'll go along. But I demand to be informed about every move he makes in Germany."

"I'll vouch for it," said Kollmann.

24

ERNST BUDZINSKI LEFT THE GIRO D'ITALIA ON FOUR WHEELS rolling north, while the Giro was approaching the Dolomites. He thought of it as a miraculous rescue from the worst of tortures, and from disgrace. Once again Kollmann had shown up just in time. Last year, at the Tour, he had achieved his staying in the Tour, and now, at the Giro, he had prevented his going on. Apart from some malicious comments, the reaction in the press had been one of comprehension. He had a seventeen-day grace period, and already on the drive to Cologne, he began to believe in a new miracle.

Kollmann drove straight through. He was reserved and mono-syllabic, and whenever he opened his mouth, it was not to pay compliments. Bud had his profitable winter slapped around his ears like a schoolboy his poor schoolwork.

His replies were meeker than during the Cologne six-day race, but Kollmann was fair enough not to kindle endless discussions. "Turn down the backrest and catch up on your sleep. There's nothing else to do, and you need it."

And despite all the curves, Bud slept until the Swiss border. To doze, to stretch out his legs, was a gift he owed to the man at the wheel, sitting straight, smoking one cigarette after the other, covering kilometer after kilometer. In his half-awake state he caught himself wanting to embrace Kollmann. Somewhere in Switzerland, Kollmann stopped to call Lindner in Cologne and announce his freight. It could be as late as midnight, he told him. Then he did some shopping. Milk, cookies, fruit, and two bottles of beer. The German border guards didn't ask for the passport of Budzinski, who was asleep. They knew him and they also knew what had happened in the Giro. I'm driving home with a corpse, Kollmann thought.

It was ten minutes to midnight when he parked the car in front of Lindner's house. Even Kaj was still up; she had a big dinner in the oven.

"Not for him," mumbled Kollmann, pointing to Bud, who was rubbing his eyes. He only knew where he was when he stumbled through the front yard. They took him to the guest room, and he fell asleep while undressing.

Although during dinner Kollmann had to fight against a leaden fatigue, he told the Lindners everything that could not be found in the papers. They learned about the diplomatic injury and also that a severe attack of weakness had brought about the fall. "Even without the fall, he would have lost a lot of time during the last kilometers."

"And you think that he would've broken down in the mountains?" asked Lindner.

"Absolutely. He was empty, Martin, and he wouldn't have gotten this far if the Giro were ridden at the speed of the Tour."

"Do you think he took dope? Or better: Could he have been given things he didn't know about?"

"Hard to say. The Pellegrini people must have known that after last year's story, they couldn't take a risk. He passed two doping checks, but I'll eat my hat if the bottle they gave him after the spill was clean. You see, he didn't want to go on and without stimulants, he might not have arrived at the finish line."

Lindner nodded. "And the risk of being found out was minimal, because he wouldn't have placed among the top three."

"Exactly. You should give him a urine test tomorrow morning."

"As best as I can. I don't want to give away anything."

"Naturally. He also should be under lock and key if the reporters turn up. Kaj will see to that."

"Very well. But she'll also see to it that your guinea pig will sleep in. Listening to the two of you I get the idea that we're dealing not with a person but a chemical experiment."

"It's a question of hauling somebody out of the mess into which he got himself," mumbled Kollmann and got up.

He was allowed to sleep longer than Bud, who was needed for blood and urine tests on an empty stomach. After breakfast, Lindner again was busy with him, and at lunchtime, he offered a guardedly optimistic prognosis. "It doesn't look as bad as I thought. The quality of Bud's regenerating capability is extraordinary."

"And what do you prescribe?" asked Kollmann.

"First of all, a few days of complete rest. You could take him to Dortmund this afternoon. I would've kept him here, but he wants to go home, right, Bud?"

Bud nodded. "I've never yearned so much for my own bed."

What he really needed was his mother. Without being aware of it, he felt like a soldier between two battles, and he had never felt this way before. "Of course I'll give him a ride. What happens next?"

Lindner looked up from a full prescription pad. "I'll finish the prescriptions now, Max. He'll get this and some things I have in stock. A respectable little pharmacy, but it doesn't have to hide from the light of day, and he'll stick religiously to my orders. He has sixteen days left until the start of the Tour. Of these, six days are complete rest. Then he starts with easy training, increasing on the stationary bike and then on the road. For one week, and before leaving for France, he'll stop by here for a day. We'll travel together."

"You're going to do the whole Tour?" Kollmann was surprised. "What's Kaj say to that?"

"She's agreed, right, Kaj?"

"Yes, I have." and Kollmann didn't know how to interpret the laugh in the large brown eyes.

"In that case we can travel together. I'll take a larger car, and

Martin won't have to fight with Lesueur and Troussellier for a seat."

"And we'll take Bud to the start in Strassburg. What do you say, Bud?"

"I don't know what I'd rather do."

"In that case," Kollmann grinned, "all you have to do is to get back on your feet."

He adhered to doctor's orders with rigid discipline. In the first days it didn't require much of a sacrifice, because without ever going near the bike Bud slept twelve or fourteen hours every day. He could feel how the medications purified his body, which he had abused so much. He let his mother spoil him, and she also managed to keep his father at a distance, with his greedy talk about money and fame. At the end of the first week he resumed training and gained confidence daily, even if old Wittkamp behind the stationary bike made him sweat and groan at some of the more violent spurts. But he didn't cave in, and the man who had trained him already as an amateur was happy with the results on the plain. There were no mountains. Certainly none that deserved the term. Not to speak of the crucial elevations over fifty-four hundred feet. At the Giro he had canceled that rendezvous, and he knew that it would have become a sad performance.

But now he felt his strength and form return. When he woke up in the morning he felt fresh without deceiving himself, and he wished for the bed in the Basque farmhouse, from which he could jump on his bike and take on the Aubisque—and then, why not the Tourmalet? He imagined its steep ramps and once again felt like the man who had conquered them.

The winter and its smoky halls had taken away that feeling. They had made him rich, and debilitated him when hard asphalt took the place of wooden tracks. "Sympathy is for free, envy you have to earn," Kollmann had said. He was right. The racing cyclist needed envy, and he was ready to earn it.

He wrote a letter to old Iribar and asked him to come to the little church of Sainte-Marie-de-Campan, where the ascent starts to the Tourmalet. This time they would be coming from the other side and have the Alps behind them, because the Tour started in Strasbourg. They were riding clockwise, and the bell would toll for the winner in the Pyrénées.

Antonelli had won the Giro with a big lead, and not only his fans considered him the favorite. Many experts were on his side, because he had finished the Giro with his reserves intact. He had played with a listless competition, from which Bud had dropped out before his weakness would have become apparent.

But there were also times when fear assaulted Bud. Had he atoned for the nonstop abuse during the winter, or would every-thing that had come down on him during the Giro return? In those moments he had long telephone conversations with Doctor Lindner. The optimism of the doctor strengthened him. Blood and urine tests were satisfactory, even if not as superior as last year. He spoke of a positive development.

Kollmann was equally convinced of this when he picked Bud up in Dortmund, two days before the start of the Tour. He arrived with a comfortable car and driver and insisted on leaving when Bud's father suggested toasting to the success of the new French campaign. "We have important things to do, Mister Budzinski. Doctor Lindner is expecting us."

They stopped in Cologne only for the duration of the physical for which everything had been set up. Lindner was satisfied. He talked about a new improvement and opened a bottle of cham-pagne. "I think we can drink a glass to Bud with some confidence."

This time Kollmann did not refuse, and he marveled at the nat-ural serenity with which Kaj sent off the expedition into the French adventure. A year ago, he thought, she would have made a major scene.

25

THE EVENING BEFORE THE START IN STRASBOURG, WHERE Germany ends and France isn't beginning yet, became a huge fair with fireworks, Riesling wine, and dancing in all the squares; and the cyclists were long asleep in their beds while the huge train of hangers-on were still shaking hands with each other and drinking another glass. But everything about the Tour smelled fresh the next morning. It smelled like new paint and shone like new automobiles without a speck of dust on them, and the sun was there as well, flooding the Alsace from a limpid sky. At the big presentation ceremony it made the spokes and handlebars sparkle, and when the iridescent dragon, coming from the Kleber Square, slowly wound its way through the streets, Bud couldn't help but notice how many of his fellow Germans had turned up. It felt like leaving a German town.

Belfort was the goal of the first stage, and although the stage was relatively short, it turned out to be a treacherous hors d'oeuvre. After the Rhine plain, which under the midday sun became an oven, the road twisted into the Vosges and up its highest elevation, the 3750-foot-high Ballon d'Alsace. Bud would have preferred a quieter start, because the Alsatian mountain had the powerful gradient of a major mountain pass. Such a demanding test was not without risks for him, but it was also better suited than any other condition to make him evaluate his capabilities.

He could not afford to let Antonelli out of his sight. If Antonelli attacked, he had to follow suit. When the road started to climb in the coolness of dense pine forests, they watched each other like hawks, out in front of a long drawn-out field. But Antonelli didn't attack. When halfway up the mountain two Spaniards and two Frenchmen broke away from the front group, Bud met his inquiring look, and he knew there was still a truce between them. He stayed in the saddle, and Antonelli stayed by his side.

Bud was relieved not to have to break his rhythm. The tempo was energetic but not frenzied, and when the forest became more sparse and the large naked summit built itself up before their eyes, he was satisfied with the test, because he felt air in his lungs without having to pant, and power in his legs. Whether or not he could have checked an attack by the Italian, he was not able to judge. They caught up with the breakaway group on the descent to Belfort and pulled the whole field with them. The group finish didn't bring any differences in time and the Belgian sprinter Dewaele took over the yellow jersey. He wore it for three days and everybody knew that he wouldn't bring it across the Alps.

The race was as if sealed. It looked as if nobody wanted to tear it open before the Alps, and this general lying in wait reminded Bud of the Giro. But he was in better shape, and in the Jura mountains he had sunshine in his spokes. Only by the breadth of a tire did he lose the final sprint for the stage victory in Aix-les-Bains, and that night Doctor Lindner assured him that he had nothing to fear from the Galibier.

The Galibier was the roof of this Tour. Bud was not familiar with it. Would his power reserves be sufficient for the 7668-foot mountain, the highest he'd ever had to take on? Kollmann said it would be easier than the Tourmalet. Even if the ascent was twice as long, the road was a boulevard and the inclines gentler.

"The danger will come less from the mountain than from yourself," said Kollmann. "Do not be tempted to crank too large a gear. Besides, there isn't only the Galibier. Croix de Fer and Télegraphe are hefty chunks as well."

Shortly after the start in Grenoble the field tore apart, to spread out even more at the Col de la Croix de Fer. But most of the late-comers were able on the thirty-kilometer-long descent to catch up with the mountain specialists. They had barely arrived when the ascent to the Col du Télégraphe started and threw them back again. Bud, who had done well on the Croix de Fer, was struggling with shortness of breath on the upper half of the Télégraphe, but he could maintain his position in the fifteen-man front group. Was it the barrier of 5400 feet? But Antonelli panted as well, and his stroke on the pedals seemed heavier than Bud's.

Below, in Saint-Michel-de-Maurienne, he spied a signpost that made him calculate: ELEVATION 2136 FT, COL DU GALIBIER 33 KM. To climb in thirty-three kilometers from 2136 feet to 7668 feet. To establish the rhythm, you had to find the right balance between gears and energy reserves. The Galibier winds its last switchbacks up on the Plan Lachat, and just under the summit they slip into a dark, cold, and humid tunnel. Bud did not reach it in the break-away group, made up of Antonelli and a few mountain specialists, but he wasn't afraid. He was barely thirty seconds down, and his strength would have been sufficient to stay at Antonelli's side. But he preferred to keep to his own rhythm.

It was cold on the Galibier and dirty snow lined the roads. He caught up with the breakaway group on the descent and together with them he climbed the Col du Lautaret, the last obstacle of the day. In Briançon, which this time they reached from the north, the time differences were considerable. The king stage of the Alps had completely reversed the total point count. Antonelli and Bud were out front, and the Italian took the yellow jersey with forty seconds' advantage over Bud. Perez, the Spanish mountain flea was third, almost three minutes down.

In Briançon the Italian *tifosi* from across the border demanded settlers' rights. Antonelli put on the yellow jersey at the same spot where, in the previous year, he had failed. However, Bud was breathing down his neck, and in the defiant mountain fortress, the repeat of last year's duel made for a seething atmosphere, Neapolitan style. The organizers rubbed their hands, although Didier Merlin, the best of the Frenchmen, occupied the fifth place in the overall standings and had rather modest chances.

It didn't matter that Bud did not join when Antonelli and Perez sprinted for the stage victory. He was satisfied with himself and secure as a proud champion who had shaken off a big weight and found the way back to himself. The last hundred yards before Briançon he had just freewheeled, and his boyish laugh was shining through the patina of sweat and dirt of the mountains.

Later, when he had taken a bath and had had his massage, Lindner and Kollmann came by. They weren't planning a side trip to Italy this year. They brought a bottle of champagne and let the cork pop like boisterous boys.

"Let's drink to a great day," Kollmann said. "If we could sing, we'd serenade you, Bud."

The bottle went around without glasses and Bud took deep gulps that made his Adam's apple jump.

"This tastes better than last year in Italy." Lindner wiped foam from his mouth and laughed. "I didn't think you'd be capable of this ride across the Galibier and the other peaks."

"The ascent to the Galibier isn't all that hard. Just miserably long, and Max was right. You shouldn't stroke too large a gear and not change the rhythm. I remembered it and lost hardly any time at all. Antonelli consumed more strength. For him it was a question of prestige to win in Briançon."

Kollmann held up the empty champagne bottle to the light. "Nice draft, Bud, but tell me, why didn't you sprint along? The stage victory was in your grasp as well, don't you think?"

"Possibly. I was just happy and cut back when I saw the finish."

"Is it also possible that you would've liked to win but wouldn't have appreciated the walk to the doping test?"

"Stop that nonsense, Max," hissed Lindner. "Why do you ask

him and not me? I did give him something for the Galibier, but no forbidden substances, *basta*."

Kollmann shrugged his shoulders. "What's the fuss, Martin? Am I not allowed to ask? All the dynamite that must have been swallowed today could have blown up the entire Tour."

"What do I care? But I know what I'm doing and I stand behind it, too. That's why I'm here."

"Calm down, Martin. Forget what I said. But tell me how he's weathered the stress."

"I'm not yet done with the exam, but I have a good feeling. Don't you, Bud?"

Bud nodded. "I felt weak only on the Télegraphe, but it passed quickly."

"What was it?"

"Shortness of breath. I thought of the fifty-four-hundred-foot barrier, but at seventy-six-hundred feet on the Galibier, I breathed more easily. I had energy reserves and wasn't afraid one bit when I didn't see Antonelli anymore. On the ascent I clung for a long time to his rear wheel and observed him. He was by no means stronger than me, and sometimes I felt tempted to attack him. But I didn't know the mountain."

"It's better this way," said Kollmann. Turning to Lindner, he remarked: "If he did save energy during this difficult stage, things look a lot better than at the start in Strasbourg. Do you have a way of checking on these reserves?"

"Mmm." Lindner shook his head slowly. "A little bit. But it's not like a gasoline gauge. What counts is the race itself. But I'll do my best. Leave us alone now, Max, we'll meet later. Fortunately tomorrow's stage is easier."

"Yes," Kollmann agreed. "They've left out the Izoard and the Vars. However, the Altos, close to the stage finish in Digne, is another six-thousand-foot chunk."

"Very difficult?"

"Not really. It depends if there's a sprint before it."

"The only thing that concerns me is what Antonelli will do," said Bud. "And I'm pretty sure that tomorrow he won't feel like sprinting."

What followed between the Alps and the Pyrénées, in scorching heat, were the traditional transit stages of the Mediterranean and the Auvergne. Gardeners opened their hoses to cool off the pack like a field of roses, and girls in tiny bikinis that wouldn't have covered a cyclist's nose stood by the roadside with buckets, making life a little easier for the water carriers and their daily shifts. Those were days when only crickets did their chirping work; no dog could be brought out of the shade. Nobody has found better words for this paralyzing heat than Alphonse Daudet.

From just rolling the Tour went into crawling, but people crawled out of the shade to see the unfathomable. Men moving forward only because of their muscle power, through the soft and smelly black sticky tar, which reduced their hourly average to that of the country mailman. It also took away the deceptive aspect of their unison. In fact, it seemed as if the stinging sun were spreading a layer of companionable complicity over the large pack. Gone were the days of suspicious lurking. They made a pact without talking about it, and if the yellow jersey stopped at a fountain, it was not a signal to attack. In the dozing field Mario Antonelli had changed from target to companion.

In the accompanying cars the journalists were dozing, catching up on lost sleep, or they went far ahead of the pack to cool off in some swimming pool or in the sea. Others preferred a lunch at a properly set table to the hasty snacks in the cars turned campers, because there was nothing to write about the sleepy field. They would still arrive in time for the mass sprint at the end of the stage.

Those were the few hundred yards when the sprinters woke up. Bud never participated in their crunch, this petty bargaining for tenths of a second of prestige, when hands were at work yanking at other jerseys or elbows pushing aside the adversary. It was a dangerous game, and Antonelli feared it as well. The only thing he had to defend was the forty-second lead over Bud, and given the way the more or less neutralized race was going, nothing was going to change.

Until the time trial at Perpignan. Bud could consider the flat course of forty-five kilometers as a jump start for the yellow jersey. Kollmann had warned him against using the big gear in this broiling heat, but when he heard his interim timings, he pulled ahead and won the stage. Antonelli had to content himself with third place after the Frenchman Mallet, but he kept the yellow jersey, since he was only thirty-two seconds slower than Bud. He had a lead of eight seconds overall, just as Bud had had last year in Briançon. The duel had a beautiful symmetry.

Eight seconds. Bud knew that he had lost them during the last few kilometers. Not that he had started sprinting too early, as in the Giro. But he had not managed to sustain it. His legs became heavy from cranking the big gear, and his lungs wanted to burst when he crossed the finish line. Ten kilometers earlier he'd had a lead of a minute. Was it a warning signal? He talked about it that night with Doctor Lindner, who put the blame on the heat. And it didn't worry him either that his pulse had not yet slowed to under sixty. "After this effort at over a hundred degrees in the shade, it's altogether normal. Be happy about your stage victory."

Bud slept badly and thought of the Pyrénées. He had seen stars when he had gotten off his bike after the time trial, but Lindner had not noticed it, as he hadn't noticed the shaky legs carrying him to the winner's podium. It was forgotten two days later in Luchon. There hadn't been any battles of note, and no changes in the top group. But now, on the Tourmalet stage, they would be inevitable.

The Tourmalet, this time from the other side. Since the Alps, Bud had known that he would attack here. Immediately after Sainte-Marie-de-Campan, where old Iribar was waving his beret. For days he had seen him in his mind's eye, seen the white hair fluttering in the breeze. And he saw sunshine in his spokes. He would wave to the old man and then storm the Tourmalet. Eight seconds to the yellow jersey. Why shouldn't he take ten times that much from Antonelli on the way to the summit?

He had a big disappointment waiting for him in Luchon. From the daily mountain of mail, getting larger by the day since the Alps, he fished a letter from old Iribar, and it wasn't good news. He had taken ill, and with a trembling hand he wrote that he would not be able to come to Sainte-Marie-de-Campan. But he would sit in his armchair in front of the TV to witness Bud's big day.

The Tour hadn't fallen into Luchon like a swarm of locusts. It almost seemed as if they wanted to make even the final sprint gentle, in order not to disturb the elderly clientele of a dusty old spa in the Pyrénées. Bud had to think of Eaux-Bonnes, where time seemed to have come to a stop. Last year he hadn't seen anything of Luchon. They had pulled the yellow jersey over his shoulders, and nobody who experiences that has eyes for anything else. Now he took in the little town with its old hotels. Their facades and their plush interiors had faded like the faces of the old people who have come to cure their lungs in the wind blowing from the snowy peaks of the mountains. He remembered having read about the famous therapeutic climate, and between cedars and old linden trees he felt the atmosphere of a sanatorium, and in a strange way it attracted him.

They lodged him in one of those hotels where old ladies play bridge and old men forget to lift their eyes at the frisky step of young girls. They had reserved one floor for the Tour, but it didn't fit in. A frail white-haired lady looked at Bud through her lorgnette, but she didn't want an autograph, and from the wrinkled mouth drawn down, you could read her thoughts: I'm at the end, and why would a young person want to ruin his health by the stupid cranking of bicycle pedals?

Nevertheless he would have enjoyed staying longer than one night in his hotel room. Just to sleep in and eat the breakfast of these people—in bed, of course, around eleven o'clock when the sun is already high above the mountains. Coffee with lots of milk and crisp croissants with salty butter. No jam. Maybe a soft-boiled egg, and then sleep again, maybe even until evening. Why not? But as he felt the masseur's hands on his back and thighs, he realized how little these people enjoyed things that to him seemed unattainable privileges. Suddenly he saw the Tourmalet as the most powerful of all challenges, and also old Iribar, as he was waving his beret. If I get the yellow jersey, he thought, I'll drive from Pau to Eaux-Bonnes at night to make him a present. Bartali drove to Lourdes, when he was in Pau. Me, I make my pilgrimage to wise old Iribar.

They started early in Luchon and the wind from the mountains was fresh. But the sky was cloudless and when the ascent to the Peyresourde began almost immediately after the start, the burning sun made the asphalt sticky where there was no shade from trees. Last year black clouds had been shredded by the flanks of the mountain and the road had been white with hailstones. As he pushed himself into the mountain between high fir trees, Bud saw the fog in front of him through which the red taillights of Kollmann had piloted him and taken him to the yellow jersey.

Now blinding sunlight is engulfing the Peyresourde, and from the southern side it seems easier to him. To be sure, the whole pack takes it on together and cautiously, as if they all want to protect each other. But everybody looks out for himself. Protecting others is not part of the mountain stages. And after the Peyresourde comes the Aspin, then the Tourmalet, and then the Aubisque. And soon the sun will burn even hotter. It's a day that won't forgive a single mistake.

When the road winds through the brown and green pastures of the summit, the field has stretched out but not torn apart. After the descent they pass through the small town of Arreau in a solid pack, but then the time of kindness to each other is over. The ascent to the Aspin begins to separate small groups from the large field, although the tempo in front does not increase noticeably. Even the mountain fleas don't really want to jump before the Tourmalet. Bud sees them weave around him in low gear like nervously flickering low flames, but he knows that he doesn't have to be concerned about them. They've lost too much time on the plain.

Only Antonelli counts. They don't let each other out of sight on the thirteen kilometers leading to the 4500-foot summit of the Aspin, always in the breakaway group, buzzed by the mountain specialists, who are fighting their own battle. Then the descent to Sainte-Marie-de-Campan, where the prelude comes to an end because the Tourmalet begins in all seriousness. At the church square, Bud looks around, although he knows that old Iribar won't be there. Freewheeling, he loses thirty or forty meters that have to be regained; the mountain is ahead of them and the battle is starting up.

Bud has studied the profile of the mountain, which he only knows from the descent. He knows that the first five of the seventeen kilometers are irregular and require a lot of shifting. Then comes a constant 8 percent gradient as far as Gripp, which is more of a shepherds' hamlet than a village. In Gripp the summit is very near, and he doesn't want to think beyond. He's riding behind two Spaniards and a Frenchman, lightweight fellows who are shaking up the front group with their short dry sprints, as if testing its readiness to be blown apart. But again and again, together with Antonelli, Bud closes the gap, and midway up the mountain half a dozen riders still cling to their rear wheels.

To beat Antonelli on the Tourmalet. Considered rationally, it doesn't make any sense, because there is still the Aubisque and the long flat stretch to Pau where he can catch up with the conqueror of the summit. Bud, however, has his mind set on defeating the Italian on the Tourmalet. Ever since the Alps. And he isn't just thinking of the few seconds needed to take the yellow jersey. He wants to beat him soundly. Humiliate him and shake him off his rear wheel like an undesirable parasite. It is not cold-blooded calculation, but seething revenge.

Antonelli smells it. He who will be *campionissimo* like Coppi and

Bartali if after the Giro he wins the Tour is ready to meet the challenge of this primitive form of combat. He also knows that the winner will wear the yellow jersey. He doesn't see the mountain fleas either; he has eyes only for the other. Yard by yard, like Siamese twins, they gnaw their way into the mountain; whenever one of them drinks, the other one reaches for the bottle as well.

Behind them are their sag wagons and a whole fleet of press cars. They all have eyes only for the big duel, and the television motorbikes make the road narrow because millions want to see it live in their homes. At Gripp there are only seven men left in the breakaway group, and when Bud lifts his head, searching for the summit, he sees it high above the road creeping under the cement avalanche guards toward La Mongie. They have long since left the timberline, and the panorama is one of overwhelming solemnity—but only for the men in the accompanying cars. This dimension is missing from the bicycle rider's field of vision. To the riders the mountain is only an energy-devouring, devious enemy. Much higher and harsher than Bud expected, the peak is towering behind La Mongie.

The two and a half kilometers before La Mongie are the most difficult. Bud knows this. The road is wide like a boulevard; it has no switchbacks, which can give you the illusion of stalking the mountain rather than taking it on in open combat. And there are no trees to shield you from the sun. The sun lets the air shimmer above the asphalt, softening it, as if the steep straight gradient weren't enough of a torture.

Nevertheless, Bud attacks. He doesn't know why, and he doesn't know where he gets his strength. From his subconscious rises the irrepressible will to take on Antonelli where the mountain is most difficult. Three times he accelerates, three times Antonelli forces himself to close up to his rear wheel. The fourth time, when they have reached La Mongie, he stays back, and the mountain fleas have been shaken off as well. Still four kilometers to the summit. The journalists pass the lonely man out front to measure the distances on the Tourmalet. For a few seconds Kollmann and Lindner are by his side. When they are gone, Bud's glance returns to the road. He doesn't want to see the peak he's approaching miserably slowly.

Did Kollmann shout "shift back"? Maybe. But would he have shaken off Antonelli in a lower gear? Out of the question. He who wants to win has to crank in a big gear and gamble big. Again the television camera is by his side. The cameraman wants to catch every stroke of the pedal, and the race official, on his slate board, indicates fifteen seconds' lead over Antonelli. Theoretically he's the new wearer of the yellow jersey. The final reckoning will not come until Pau, but such news lifts his morale and frees energy for which there is no rational explanation. And the cameras whir, and all of Europe sees him climb.

Bud does not shift back. He conquers two kilometers of elevation in a relatively large gear that eats strength and gains new seconds. This Tour will be decided on the Tourmalet, just as the last one was, Signor Antonelli. The last kilometer. The hedge of spectators thickens, because thousands have occupied the summit since early morning. They caught a beautiful day for sunbathing, and they are congratulating themselves. At this noon hour, with red wine and bread, they want to see the men who, thirsty and sweating, are coming from down below by virtue of their own muscle power.

Another eight hundred yards. In the small corridor they leave him Bud gets up from the saddle, has managed almost half of it when the road winds into the last switchback. It turns to the right and from the bend goes straight up to the summit. It is a brutal ramp.

Little more than four hundred yards. All of a sudden he seems to be pedaling on the spot. Instinctively he shifts back, before he zigzags like a drunk, needing more room than what's afforded to him. In this last gradient strength and rhythm break in the man who, right now, still looked like the triumphant winner of the

Tourmalet. They push him a bit, but the front wheel loses its way.

Almost standing up, the body tilts to the left. A moment ago he saw stars. Now it is dark before his eyes.

He feel arms around his body. The human hedge is too thick to fall down. They lay him on the dry grass at the edge of the road. A few minutes later Doctor Troussellier, the Tour physician, is kneeling by his side.

26

AT THE SUMMIT HOTEL THE TRANSISTORS WERE SCREAMING IT INTO the air, which was shimmering over dirty fields of snow, and like an echo the outcry came back to the spot where the man who minutes ago had looked like the conqueror of the Tourmalet was lying. It happened less than two hundred yards below the summit, and already Lindner and Kollmann were engulfed by the stream pushing downhill.

It was slow and halting in the crush of people because the road had to be kept open for the following riders. Two panting and furiously shouting Spaniards claimed it; they would have liked nothing better than to hack their way with a sword through the throng of people. Behind them came Antonelli. Kollmann, pressing Lindner's arm to him at the steep drop-off, saw a piece of yellow flit by before they had fought their way to the spot where Bud was lying.

Policemen had pushed back the crowds, and the Tour physician made room for Lindner. "Collapse," he said. "He's conscious, but I won't let him go on."

Kollmann looked at Bud. They had put a cushion under his head and covered him with a blanket. A young woman was soaking a towel in a child's yellow plastic bucket and put it on his forehead.

Lindner knelt down and immediately reached into his medical bag. Someone handed him a cup of warm lemonade, and he dissolved some tablets in it. While Bud sat up to drink, Kollmann looked at his watch, which he had stopped on the summit. Seven minutes had passed, and even if Bud could get back into the saddle right away, everything had been lost.

Or was there another chance? Lindner had taken Troussellier aside. Another minute passed before Bud got up and asked for his bike. Andreolo, parked with his sag wagon on the meadow, cast an inquiring glance at Lindner.

"Out of the question. If the finish were down at Argèles, I might let him go on. But there's still the Aubisque, and even if he could pull himself together—which we have no way of knowing—it wouldn't make sense. He'd lose half an hour to Antonelli. Besides," Doctor Troussellier went on pointedly, "I already said that he wouldn't go on, and I'm the Tour physician."

Bud shook his head. "I'm not getting into the mop-up wagon."

"As far as I'm concerned, you can rent a room on the Tourmalet. Ambulance and helicopter are needed for serious injuries, as you know. At the moment you may not be able to sit on a bike but certainly on a wooden bench."

Lindner and Kollmann were annoyed at Troussellier's cynical arrogance. "Fifteen minutes ago he still would have liked to caress him uphill, because he had looked like a smoothly running machine, and now he drops him like a hot potato."

"Bud could ride with us," said Lindner.

"Yes, why not? Do you want to, Bud?"

"How far ahead is Antonelli?"

"More than fifteen minutes."

"Things like this happen. Shall I give it a try?"

"No, Bud. In a minute the mop-up wagon will push the last stragglers up to the summit, but that isn't the point. Don't you realize that you broke down out of exhaustion? Like an idiot you went up the Tourmalet as if the finish line of the Tour was on this summit. The devil knows what got into you. Perhaps you thought it was all like last year, if only you could master the Tourmalet."

"Something like that," mumbled Bud.

Only now, as he stood there before him, did Kollmann realize how deep his eyes had sunk into their sockets.

"Can you walk up to the summit, Bud? It's only two hundred yards, but we have to hurry."

"Why?"

"Dear God! The last stragglers are coming by now, and in a few minutes the mop-up wagon will be here. According to regulations you have to get in. Hasn't it dawned on you yet that you've just dropped out of the race?"

Bud's nod showed resignation down into the tips of his fingers. "Let's walk up, Max."

In single file, between the hedges of onlookers, they went uphill. First Kollmann, then Bud and Lindner. Three or four riders worn out by the Tourmalet, with staring eyes that no longer took in anything, passed them. Bud stalked like a sleepwalker.

Above, Kollmann's driver was set with two wheels already on the pavement. Only when Bud sat with Lindner in the back of the car, his bare knees pressed against Kollmann's backrest, did they begin to understand the misery of their mission. And Kollmann, who had pulled out his notepad to begin his report, didn't have as much as ten lines by the time they arrived in Argèles-Gazost. They made good time on the closed road, passed small and larger groups of bikers on the plain, and were relieved to have left before the mop-up wagon. Behind it the road would be open again to traffic, in which they would have found themselves hopelessly stuck.

In a village at the foot of the Aubisque, they stopped. The doctor got some milk for Bud into which he mixed dextrose and some medications to stimulate the metabolism. When the farmer heard who the milk was for, he wouldn't take any money. Instead he added a bottle of homemade brandy. The bottle circulated. Bud drank little, but Kollmann and Lindner guzzled; when they reached the summit of the Aubisque, there was little left. Kollmann wrote more rapidly, although Radio Tour announced that on the Aubisque, Antonelli had shaken off the two Spaniards. Bud's defeat seemed to have given him wings. On the descent to Eaux-Bonnes Bud said that he wanted to see old Iribar, and Kollmann began to curse.

"I don't have time for such whims. I have to get to the press center in Pau as quickly as possible. That's my job. People at home want to know why there's no longer a Budzinski in this Tour. And don't think that I'll spare you. You could still be at Antonelli's side, if you hadn't lost your head. I can't believe it."

Lindner answered for Bud. "Let him go to his farmer, Max. It'll distract him. What's he supposed to do in Pau? He would have to run the gauntlet and have the reporters on his tail. I can get him later. It's not that far, is it?"

"Have it your own way. It's not far. They'll be looking for him again and we'll have trouble with the Tour management and the Pellegrini guys."

"Does it really matter at this point?"

"Not really, Martin. You're right. He's been demobilized, so to speak, and is no longer part of it. Never has anybody been eliminated in such a stupid way."

In his rage Kollmann lit one cigarette after the other, and after Eaux-Bonnes he let Bud show him the way into the village. Radio Tour announced that Antonelli was alone out front between Eaux-Bonnes and Pau. The clock on the small but massive church steeple struck four o'clock when they stopped in front of the white-washed old farmhouse with the steep roof. Kollmann remained in the car; Bud and Lindner got out.

So this is his stage finish, Kollmann thought. And he could have won the yellow jersey. Aloud he said: "Check if the old man is there, but hurry. I'd like to catch up with Antonelli."

The whole family was sitting in the semidarkness of the kitchen with its smoked-up beams and the tiny windows, and the TV was so loud that Lindner and Bud entered without being noticed. Above a white pillow in an armchair rose the Basque beret of the old man. A tartan wool blanket was spread over his knees, because the thick white walls kept out the heat. There was garlic, mutton and black tobacco in the air, and to Bud it seemed the smell of home, although in the Ruhr district the smells were very different.

Little André was the first to notice the man in his racing outfit. He looked at him as if he had seen a ghost before shouting: "Bud's here! Look, it's Bud!"

The surprise was a complete one. Shaking his head, old Iribar clutched Bud's arm with both hands. "*C'est pas vrai,* it's not possible. He has come!"

The young farmer turned down the TV, where Antonelli was pedaling toward his victory. His wife filled an earthenware jug with wine and got glasses from the cupboard.

"Not for me," said Lindner, to whom nobody paid any attention because old Iribar wouldn't let go of Bud's arm. "I have to go."

He needn't have said it, because Kollmann tore the door open and crashed through the entrance. "What's the matter, Martin? In twenty minutes Antonelli will be at the finish line, and damn it, I want to be there. Unless you come right away, I'll leave. The Tour continues, even without Budzinski."

He pointed to the TV screen that showed, from a helicopter, wobbly images of Antonelli pedaling toward victory. Behind him, a big void. They would never catch up with him.

"I'm coming," said Lindner. "I'll pick you up in two hours or so, Bud."

Bud didn't reply. Kollmann should not have said "Budzinski," he thought.

When they had left, he sat down at his customary place at the narrow side of the table and drank up his glass in one swig. The farmer pushed the armchair of the old man close to him.

He has become thin, Bud thought, and he saw the watery eyes sunken in their sockets. But he also saw them sparkle and heard the voice, which had sounded shaky, become stronger. And it wasn't flattering what he said.

"You raced like a real idiot, Bud. As if you'd never seen the

Tourmalet. You should have known how sparse the switchbacks are from that side, from Sainte-Marie. I sat here and watched how the long straight stretches ate your strength and your morale, because you didn't think of calibrating your race. You only thought of Antonelli. You wanted to finish him off on the Tourmalet, just like last year. But you finished off yourself." He pointed to the screen. Antonelli's yellow jersey stood out vividly before the green of the meadows. His stroke was smooth, as if he had just started and didn't have four mountains behind him.

"He's now putting to good use reserves he hadn't tapped earlier, when you frittered them away with your senseless fireworks. Your gear on the long straights was idiotically high. If you hadn't over-taxed yourself so stupidly, you'd be with him."

"That's right," said Bud, "I behaved like a beginner. I should have raced the way I did on the Galibier."

"You were smart then. You let him pull ahead without losing strength or your nerves. And in Briançon you were again by his side. Why'd you do everything wrong today?"

Bud reached for his glass, which the woman had filled again. "I really don't know. The Tourmalet must have made me crazy. I'd like to get drunk. Maybe I just lack experience."

"No more wine," the old man snapped at the young woman. "Take away the jug. It's enough that he's been defeated. We don't need a drunk victim."

Antonelli had reached the edge of Pau and could no longer be defeated. And the reporter made a plausible projection that reached as far as Paris. He was altogether invincible. Five stages before the end of the big loop he was in the lead by almost ten minutes over second place. It was his big day.

Old Iribar was still pondering Bud's last words: "What did you just say about experience?"

"That I don't have enough of it."

"*Mon Dieu*, Bud. Some people call that which they have done wrong all their life their life's experience. And now you're looking for an excuse for incredible foolishness. Experience. We call it that when we're at our wit's end. Do you want to know what we call it here?"

Bud turned his head from the screen where Antonelli was entering the main thoroughfare of Pau. He still had two kilometers to go.

"We say: Experience is a comb you get by the time you're bald."

"Does that mean I can pack my bags forever?"

Old Iribar pointed to the huge crowds cheering Antonelli. "This year you won't get any of this. You've ruined your entire season and no winter manager will make any efforts to get you."

"But I'll prepare myself for the next road season like never before."

"Don't set your expectations too high, Bud. Something inside you could have cracked."

"What do you mean?"

The old man scratched the shaggy hair at the back of his head, and on the screen Antonelli, arms raised high, crossed the finish line. "Do you remember your visit here?"

"Would I be here if I didn't?"

"And you admit that you've doped?"

Bud shrugged. "They all take something."

"I don't think so. Only those running from one race to the next."

"On this Tour I haven't taken anything illegal, that's for sure."

"Maybe so. But you were not the same person as last year. Then you were filled with the rage of a true champion on whom they had tried to pin a fraud. Since then you've cheated with illegal drugs—not others but yourself. You've come to cry on someone's shoulder, right?"

"You don't mince words when you slap me with the truth."

"I'm not done yet. You should thank your doctor on your knees that he hasn't given you anything illegal. Your collapse was a natural one. With doping, you would've postponed it, but in this heat it could've been fatal."

"Maybe you're right." Bud got up and switched off the television. "I've prepared the way for Antonelli like a beginner. Say what you like, it must have something to do with experience."

"It doesn't take any particular experience to recognize the imponderable elements of your profession. Breakdowns and falls can't be predicted any more than the day's weather, and basically you can't do anything else but prepare yourself thoroughly for the season on the road. Every great career has been built like that—and nobody who relied on talent alone ever had one. Bicycle racers are in permanent training, and in the long run cannot cheat anybody."

"Last year Antonelli cheated me," Bud said defiantly.

There was a glint of ironic consent in the watery little eyes of the old man. "Let's put it this way: He tried to cheat you. And what did you do? You didn't denounce him but gave him the response of a great champion. That was some response. And didn't we work it out right here, in this kitchen?"

"Yes, we did. I wish I could bring back that day. Do you remember, I was practically out of the race, just like now?"

"Only now there isn't a loophole to get back in."

"The doctor will be here in a while to get me. We're taking the train to Cologne. Does that take us through Paris?"

"I don't know," said old Iribar. "Never been there and never will." His voice sounded tired all of a sudden. "And," he added, "I will not see another Tour de France."

"Nonsense." Bud shook his head. "Next year, I'll bring you another yellow jersey."

"No, Bud, it'll be too late. My time is running out, but yours is going on, and I want you to become the same man who once found this house."

"But I am who I am."

"No, Bud." Groaning, old Iribar straightened up in his armchair and put his weathered face close to Bud's. "You weren't the same when you came to see us last summer after the Tour. Success and money made you forget the most fundamental principles of a profession. If you rise in a normal profession—let's say you become director of something—you may change your style of living. Your work then consists in delegating responsibilities. I hope I make myself clear."

"I think so."

"There you go. You can afford domestiques but they don't push you up the Tourmalet. The work always remains the same, and every stroke on the pedal you have to do yourself. You felt like a hero because you made big money but you forgot that a star's currency is his performance. You've fallen from high up to pretty low, and the Pellegrini people won't let you forget it."

"I know. I still have to face them in Pau. I wish I could stay here."

"Not this time, Bud. They'll be expecting you in Pau. You're not a nameless water carrier who can disappear without anybody noticing it. Not yet, Bud."

"You mean that's where I'm headed?"

"I don't know, Bud. Honestly. But I know how rapid and steep a career can fall that has begun as steep as yours. You wasted your capital and you'll notice very quickly that those who cheered you yesterday will have forgotten you today."

"You think I'm finished?"

The fatigue went out of the watery eyes and they didn't avoid Bud's glance. "I told you, I don't know, Bud."

"I didn't dare ask the doctor. Do you know what I was thinking when I lay there in the ditch below the Tourmalet?"

"Weren't you unconscious?"

"Not for long. Maybe half a minute, maybe only a few seconds. And the first thing that came to my mind was my insurance policy, and I was relieved to have taken out a good one. I felt like a sports casualty, a premature retiree, you know?"

"Oh, yes, Bud. You saw yourself as superfluous, someone like me who makes himself useful with some light work before the armchair claims him. A little early at twenty-three. At your age I was the most daring and fastest smuggler in the village. Three trips a night, if need be."

"You think I'm finished?"

"Will you stop it!" The thin fist with the thick blue veins came down on the table, but it no longer had the force to make the glasses jump. "I'm not inside your body."

He breathed deeply, and his fist opened before it reached for Bud's arm. "But I'd give anything to be in it. And you know what I'd do? I'd forget the cheap money of the winter tracks and in the spring, when the snow is melting, I'd come here and work out in the mountains. You have to get to know them better."

"May I come here?"

"Of course you may come here," said old Iribar. "But I can't give you a guarantee on the prescription, and I won't be here either."

Bud reached for the hand on his arm and he was startled how cold it was. "Of course you'll be here."

"It's much longer from one summer to the next than you young people think," the old man said, and his smile was tired.

27

AT DUSK ON THIS JULY DAY, DOCTOR LINDNER RETURNED TO THE village. The crickets were chirping in the meadows, and the wind blowing from the mountains had refreshed the air. They arrived in Pau as the first rockets of the fireworks in honor of the Tour de France whooshed into the purplish black sky. In the square in front of Henry IV's castle there was dancing, and outside Antonelli's hotel there was a black throng of people.

"*Tiens, voilà* Budzinski," a young man said to the girls in white skirts going to the dance. But they barely turned around to look at the man who got out of the car, still in the red jersey in which he had left the race on the Tourmalet. They're saying "Budzinski" again, he thought as he went through the empty hotel lobby. No sign of Pellegrini, and the desk clerk who handed him the room key, said that it was past dinnertime. Perhaps they could serve him something in the restaurant. But nothing warm.

For the men who, bustling and noisy, were crowding the long tables of the pressroom, it was one of those great stages that required overtime. There was the clatter of typewriters and the frenzy of the Italians shouting their vowels into the telephones, as if they had to reach their editorial offices without a wire by sheer vocal force. Antonelli *campionissimo*.

Only Kollmann had an almost empty page in front of him, and two empty bottles of seltzer water. In front of him, to the side, he saw Ferruccio hammer on his keyboard like a pianist in a *fortissimo*. Line by line, like garlands, a euphoric dance of fingers that required no thoughts. Antonelli *campionissimo*. And Ferruccio was the tenor who exalted him. Kollmann perceived him as through a veil and sensed how he maintained the direct dialogue with his readers. His behind moved along as well, as if he wanted to speed up his fingers even more, and now and then there appeared a smile on his lips, which were holding a cigarette.

Kollmann's ashtray filled up faster than his page. He tore it out of the typewriter to start all over again, but then his right hand reached for the cigarette, and the left lay idle on the keyboard. This was not writing. He scraped together some facts, cursing Bud, the Tour, and his job. Why had he believed in Bud? Indeed, why?

Already a few weeks ago during the Giro at Verona he should have known that the kid was burned out. Had burned himself out. Not an ace but a joker. Easy game for Antonelli and the other aces. Why didn't he dissuade him? Because he believed in the possibility of a miracle. He, Max Kollmann, who knew that the Tour was utterly unforgiving, more exacting than any other race. His eyes wide open, Bud had ridden into disgrace, which no champion can permit himself. Now it was hammered down on hundreds of typewriters around him.

A year ago all this had happened here in Pau as well. But that time they had written for the wastepaper baskets. In the wee hours Bud had been cleared of all suspicion of having doped, and the next morning, the Tourmalet had been his springboard for the Tour victory. This year, against all racing logic, his strength eroded by greed and doping, he had attacked again at the Tourmalet. But the Tourmalet had devoured him, like so many others before him.

When Kollmann had gotten this far with his thoughts, he remembered the Peyresourde. I shouldn't have helped him there, he thought. Then he wouldn't have won the stage, and probably not the Tour either, but he would have remained who he was. He would not have earned a million during the winter but saved his energy for this year's yellow jersey, which now Antonelli was wearing. Kollmann started writing again. But it flowed slowly and haltingly and when he looked up, Ferruccio's wiggling ass and his flying hands irritated him. Nothing against Ferruccio. But his foot was itching and he would have liked nothing better than to land a good kick into that rotating rear and kick the typewriter on which he wasn't writing anything off the table. He felt worn out and blocked, as if he himself had failed on the Tourmalet.

When his telephone call came through, he postponed it and went out into the street to collect his thoughts. He waded through newspaper pages that a few hours ago still were hot reading material and had been reduced to trash by the Tourmalet. A torn-up headline attracted his attention: *Tourmalet Juge de Paix*—"Tourmalet, Justice of the Peace." The Tourmalet as the adjudicator between Antonelli and Bud. His verdict had destroyed Bud and made the other the *campionissimo*.

But weren't the triumphant shouts pouring from the press center mostly due to Bud's enormous stupidity? Not only to that. Antonelli was also a great champion and a cunning fox who, in the battle on the roads, didn't employ just his legs. Perhaps last year one could have caught him as he bribed one of Bud's water carriers to exchange water bottles. But would he have been caught? The practices in the professional life of bicycle racers aren't any more honest and decent than in all others, it's only that their activity is called sport, which many people still mistake for authentic chivalry.

Often enough Kollmann had gotten a glimpse behind the scenes and seen the ruthless elbow jostling of ruse, deceit, and envy. He also knew that the big names had an easier time than the nameless crowd in slipping through the net of regulations. And besides, last year, Antonelli had been punished by Bud according to the rules. And according to the rules, he now was on his way to become *campionissimo*. Bud, powerless because of an accumulation of mistakes, had put him on an express train of victory that would carry him to Paris.

Kollmann went through the streets still thronging with arguing people. Shrill loudspeakers invited people to the big Tour party, but his ears took in the noise without registering it. The figure of a finished champion is a sad one. Kollmann caught himself sketching this image as he returned slowly to the press center. Underneath it all he sensed the cheap and shabby injustice toward the man who no longer had sunshine in his spokes. Couldn't they let him go down with the merits of a deserving fighter, a conqueror of peaks who was struck down by misfortune as his hand reached out triumphantly?

And this was the truth. Half the truth at least—and the stuff from which news stories are made that let the morning coffee get cold and salty. As Kollmann sat down again at his typewriter in the almost empty pressroom, he decided to make a gesture of friendship toward Bud, perhaps the last one. All of a sudden it flowed. He slipped into the role of Ferruccio, only he was celebrating not a radiant hero but a sad one. It became an entire page in print, reserved for him though it was finished long past the copy deadline. It was a story in which Bud looked better than he had looked at the Tourmalet. And among those many who read it the next morning and felt the tears well up was Kaj Lindner.

More sports literature from BREAKAWAY BOOKS

THE QUOTABLE CYCLIST: Great Moments of Bicycling Wisdom, Inspiration, and Humor. Edited by Bill Strickland.

THE YELLOW JERSEY, by Ralph Hurne.

THE LITERARY CYCLIST: Great Bicycling Scenes in Literature Edited by James E. Starrs.

METAL COWBOY: Tales from the Road Less Pedaled, by Joe Kurmaskie.

SPOKESONGS: Bicycle Advetures on Three Continents, by Willie Weir.

THE WHEELS OF CHANCE: A Bicycling Idyll, by H. G. Wells.

THE RUNNER'S LITERARY COMPANION: Great Stories and Poems about Running. Edited by Garth Battista

THE QUOTABLE RUNNER: Great Moments of Wisdom, Inspiration, Wrongheadedness and Humor. Edited by Mark Will-Weber.

THE ELEMENTS OF EFFORT: Reflections on the Art and Science of Running. By John Jerome.

FIRST MARATHONS: Personal Encounters with the 26.2-Mile Monster. Edited by Gail Kislevitz.

THE OTHER KINGDOM, by Victor Price.

BONE GAMES: Extreme Sports, Shamanism, Zen, and the Search for Transcendence, by Rob Schultheis.

THE QUOTABLE RUNNER TRAINING LOG. Mark Will-Weber

THE PENGUIN BRIGADE TRAINING LOG. John Bingham

THE WALKER'S LITERARY COMPANION, Edited by Roger Gilbert, Jeffrey Robinson, and Anne Wallace.

THE QUOTABLE WALKER, Edited by Roger Gilbert, Jeffrey Robinson, and Anne Wallace.

WIND, WAVES, AND SUNBURN: A Brief History of Marathon Swimming. By Conrad Wennerberg

THE SWEET SPOT IN TIME: The Search for Athletic Perfection. By John Jerome.

STAYING WITH IT: On Becoming an Athlete, by John Jerome

STAYING SUPPLE: The Bountiful Pleasures of Stretching, by John Jerome.

THE ATHLETIC CLASSICS OF JOHN JEROME: Deluxe boxed set.

IT'S NEVER TOO LATE: Personal Stories of Staying Young Through Sports, by Gail Kislevitz.

TOWARD THE SUN: The Collected Sports Stories of Kent Nelson.

LOW AND INSIDE: A Book of Baseball Anecdotes, by H. Allen Smith

THREE MEN ON THIRD: A Book of Baseball Anecdotes, by H. Allen Smith

CHANCE by Steve Shilstone. A baseball novel, a literary riddle.

THE PIGSKIN RABBI, by Willard Manus.

GOLF WITHOUT TEARS: Stories of Golfers and Lovers, by P. G. Wodehouse.

THE ENCHANTED GOLF CLUBS, by Robert Marshall.

TENNIS AND THE MEANING OF LIFE: A Literary Anthology of the Game. Edited by Jay Jennings.

FULL COURT: Stories & Poems for Hoop Fans. Edited by Dennis Trudell.

HOCKEY SUR GLACE Stories by Peter LaSalle.

CAVEMAN POLITICS, by Jay Atkinson.

EYE ON THE SEA: Reflections on the Boating Life, by Mary Jane Hayes.

PERFECT SILENCE, by Jeff Hutton. A novel of baseball and the Civil War.

BREAKAWAY BOOKS

IN BOOKSTORES EVERYWHERE
1-800-548-4348
Visit our website–**www.breakawaybooks.com**